More praise for *Hotspur*

"Colorful and exciting, and not without intrigue, greed, mystery, and drama . . . A quick, light read, perfect for an airplane trip or a winter afternoon wrapped in a blanket by the fire."
—*Port Folio Weekly* (Virginia Beach, VA)

"*Hotspur* is one mystery you will enjoy taking your time with. . . . The author has a writing style all her own and she makes a habit of giving readers their money's worth. The storyline is so complete that one can't help but take his or her time in getting to know the characters, enjoying the cast of animals, and concentrating on the mystery."
—*Mystery News*

"Fans of the Mrs. Murphy series are going to love *Hotspur*, an enchanting tale where the animals delight the reader with their ready wit, common sense, and love for their humans. Sister is a memorable heroine."
—Harriet Klausner

"A page-turner filled with wry observations of small-town southern life. Brown combines her strengths—exploring southern families, manners, and rituals as well as the human-animal bond—to bring in a winner."
—*Booklist*

HOTSPUR

RITA MAE BROWN

BALLANTINE BOOKS · NEW YORK

A Ballantine Book
Published by The Random House Publishing Group

Hotspur is a work of fiction. Names, places, and incidents are a product of the author's imagination or are used fictitiously.

This book contains an excerpt from the forthcoming hardcover edition of *Full Cry* by Rita Mae Brown. This excerpt has been set for this edition only and may not reflect the final content of the forthcoming edition.

www.ballantinebooks.com

ISBN 0-345-42823-4

Manufactured in the United States of America

First Hardcover Edition: December 2002
First Mass Market Edition: November 2003

OPM   10   9   8   7   6   5   4   3   2   1

Dedicated with admiration to
Mrs. Paul D. Summers, Jr., MFH.
Her hounds sing her praise.

CHAPTER 1

A wind devil swirled upward, sending tiny bits of stone dust glittering in the sunlight.

Even though it was the fourteenth of July, the morning proved breezy and quite pleasant at sixty-one degrees.

The staff and friends of the Jefferson Hunt were walking out hounds. Since it was seven-thirty in the morning, "dedicated friends" was perhaps a more accurate term, Sister thought to herself. The master, Jane Arnold, called Sister by all, walked behind her pack. The huntsman, Shaker Crown, a medium-build fellow, strode in front of the hounds.

Two whippers-in, Doug Kinser and Betty Franklin, flanked either side of the pack, and the dedicated friends, two this morning, tagged behind the master.

This two-mile walk down a crushed gravel road served to exercise hounds and to introduce the young entry, those hounds that would be hunting this fall for the first time, to the ways of the pack. As the summer progressed and the length of the walks became longer, fat melted off the human bodies. People looked healthier, more fit.

It amused Sister that millions of Americans, overweight and overfed, emptied their pockets on one fad diet after another. If they'd only make it a habit to walk out hounds they'd lose the pounds, save their money, and experience the most beautiful time of the day.

1

On any given morning, Sister saw bluebirds, indigo buntings, goldfinches, cardinals, robins, ravens, and hawks roaring over in search of breakfast—or maybe just a good time.

Rabbits, moles, shrews, even wild little sleek minks rustled in the meadows off the roadside.

Safe in the trees, cicadas, their Winston Churchill eyes surveying all, sang with deafening exuberance.

Clouds of black-and-yellow butterflies swirled up from the cow patties and horse patties dotting the verdant pastures of After All Farm, the glorious estate of Theodora and Edward Bancroft. Gleaming white fences, painted every two years, divided the pastures, and each fence line boasted a lovely coop or stone jump. Theodora, called Tedi, delighted in designing jumps and set them perfectly. Building the jumps seemed to give the wealthy but directionless woman something like a purpose in life.

As the small group walked briskly past the western pastures of After All, three old pensioners lifted their wise heads. Peppermint, the oldest at thirty-four, had taught two generations of Bancrofts to hunt.

From the other side of the pasture he nickered in acknowledgment of the humans and hounds he knew so well. Behind him Domino and Merry Andrew also stopped munching for a moment. In the background a pristine covered bridge crossed over Snake Creek. Tedi had built it in the heat of one of her architectural enthusiasms back in 1981.

"Hello, old man," Sister called, waving to the gray horse.

"Good to see you, too," Peppermint answered before turning to drink deeply from the creek.

"Good horse never forgets the pack or the master," Shaker called over his shoulder.

"Indeed," Betty Franklin agreed with a smile. She was the happiest she'd ever been in her life. She'd lost twenty-five pounds and felt like a teenager again.

Cora, the head bitch, gaily walked in front, and the young entry following tried to imitate their leader. The second-year hounds acted like the sophomores they were. Truly "wise idiots," they at least knew better than to float out of the pack.

As they walked, the hounds kicked up little puffs of gravel dust. Inquisitive grasshoppers flew tantalizingly close to their black moist noses, darting away in the nick of time.

Raleigh, Sister's devoted Doberman, flattened his ears to block out the din of the hounds. He considered himself hunt staff and if a youngster strayed from the group Raleigh pushed him back in before a human could react. Hounds, like humans, thought the better of getting into an argument with a Doberman.

Dr. Walter Lungrun, young, blond, and athletic, was walking next to Bobby Franklin, who was huffing and puffing.

"Goddamn that Betty," Bobby said, cursing his wife loudly. "Told me if I don't do hound walk and lose fifty pounds she's going to divorce me."

"She won't have to divorce you, you'll die first!" Sister called back to him.

"Probably why she wants you on these morning jaunts, Bobby. She'll inherit your enormous wealth," Walter added, knowing quite well that Bobby and Betty both worked like dogs at Franklin Printing and weren't amassing any great fortune for it.

"You notice I only drag my ass out when I know you're going to be here, Doc. If I grab my chest, you'll know what to do." Bobby winked.

Sister noticed a hound's head come up, drawn by an enticing aroma lifting off the meadows.

"Nellie, settle," Sister quietly said, and Nellie dispelled her brief notion of making a wild break for the rising fox scent.

They walked and chatted for another half mile, then returned home by the route they had come.

At the covered bridge, Shaker noticed Peppermint stretched out by the creekside. Eyes sharp, he turned to face his pack. "Hold up."

The hounds stopped.

"What's up?" Betty asked as she pushed a stray lock of blonde hair off her forehead.

"Walter, go over there and check on Peppermint, will you?" Shaker called back to the physician.

Walter, a former star halfback at Cornell, put one hand on the top rail of the fence and gracefully vaulted over it. He loped to the unmoving horse, who was being watched over by his two old friends.

Walter called to Peppermint. No response. When he reached the aged animal he knelt down and felt Peppermint's neck for a pulse.

"Oh, Pepper, what a good horse you were." He gently patted the dead animal's neck, then rose and recrossed the green meadow back to the waiting group.

He leaned over the fence and simply said, "Gone."

Sister lowered her head for several moments as the news sank in. She'd known this horse for more than three decades. As sad as she was, Tedi would be devastated.

"Shaker, Bobby, take the hounds back to the kennels," she instructed. "Betty and Walter, if you can spare the time, stay with me. We need to bury this fellow before Tedi comes out and finds him. She loved him so." Sister paused. "A last link with Nola."

"And it is July, he'll blow up fast," Shaker said under

his breath. Then he called to the hounds in a singsong voice, "Come along."

The hounds followed after him, though Cora couldn't help a glance over her shoulder at the horse she remembered well.

"Walter, do you mind finding one of Tedi's men? Just ask him to meet us at the bridge with the backhoe. Button his lip. I'll tell Tedi once we've properly buried Peppermint."

Walter jogged across the bridge as Betty and Sister went to the carcass at creek's edge.

Betty knelt down to touch the large shoulder. "What a great one he was. Godspeed, Peppermint. You had a wonderful life."

Sister, with Raleigh at her side, consoled Domino and Merry Andrew before sitting down beside Peppermint. "Jesus, Betty, I'm getting old. I remember Pepper when he was steel gray. He's pure white now." She referred to the fact that gray horses, born dark, lighten in color as they age.

"Remember the time Tedi hit every fence perfectly in the hunter trials? Tedi couldn't find her distance if you gave her measuring tape. But by God, she won the blue ribbon that year. I think it was one of the happiest moments of her life." Betty continued stroking the animal's beautiful gray head. "He did it for her. Pepper didn't much like showing. He liked hunting." Betty smiled, marveling at the capacity of animals to love humans, creatures who so often failed to reciprocate.

"God, I hope we can pull this off before Tedi finds out. I mean, I hope she's not up there in the barn or gardening or something. If she sees the backhoe rumble out of the equipment shed, she'll be curious." Sister plucked a blade of grass, sucking out the sweetness. "Peppermint was the last horse Nola hunted. Tedi is going to be upset."

"That's why you sent Walter—in case the news has to be broken now."

"Yes, I did, didn't I?" Sister grinned, an appealing, girlish grin for a seventy-one-year-old woman, thin as a blade and just as sharp.

"Poor Tedi, not that I wouldn't cry my eyes out if Outlaw died, mind you." Betty referred to her adored and sturdily built horse.

"We all would. Even that asshole Crawford Howard would cry if Czapaka died." Crawford was a rich, blowhard member of the Hunt, and his horse, Czapaka, endured him with only occasional moments of justified rebellion. Sister and Betty had known each other for all of Betty's forty-odd years, so Sister spoke with complete candor to her. Had it been anyone but an old friend she would never have openly criticized Crawford.

"Tedi's such a dear soul." Betty sighed.

"Strange life."

"I don't wish inherited wealth on anyone. It's a real curse," Betty declared. "It's one thing to earn a pile of money, it's another to never work for anything at all."

"I agree. I've known very few people who weren't scalded by it in one way or t'other." She pronounced "another" the old Virginia way.

"Tedi has surely had her share of suffering."

"That she has."

They halted their conversation, rising as a large backhoe chugged over the hill, down the farm road, then rattled through the covered bridge. Walter stood behind the driver, Jimmy Chirios, an industrious, cheerful young man only two years in the Bancrofts' employ.

Jimmy cut the motor and looked down at Peppermint. "Just like that?"

"A peaceful death." Sister had to shade her eyes to look up at him in the morning sun.

Walter hopped off the equipment. "Jimmy, we can't bury him here. The creek floods wicked bad every couple of years. Higher ground."

Domino and Merry Andrew, having moved away when the backhoe arrived, now returned to stand near their fallen friend.

"This side of the bridge is anchored on high ground. You wouldn't have to drag him but a hundred yards. Did you bring a chain?" Sister inquired.

"Yep." Jimmy handed the thick chain to Walter, who looped it around Peppermint's hind legs, then snapped the heavy hook around another loop of chain on the back of the big yellow machine.

"Slow," Walter ordered as the two women walked up to what they concluded would be the ideal spot above the abutment.

As Peppermint was dragged to his final resting place, Domino, his bay head bowed, and Merry Andrew, curious as always, followed behind, somewhat obscuring the mark Peppermint's body made. Walter unhitched the chain, then unwrapped it from Peppermint. Jimmy started digging.

The rise, just above the bridge abutment, was a good place. Rain had softened the earth two days earlier, and the clawed jaw of the backhoe easily bit into it. Jimmy rapidly dug out a seven-foot-deep trench, then squared the sides, forming a tidy rectangle. As they were all country people, they knew that animals could smell decay under the earth. A good six feet or more for a grave was mandatory or, sure enough, whatever was buried would be resurrected by scavengers. And much as one might have missed the deceased, one did not wish the return of a hoof or a leg.

"Looks good," Walter hollered through hands cupped to his mouth.

But Jimmy decided the side of the grave closest to the bridge needed more tidying.

He lowered the jaws into the earth. A crumble of rich alluvial deposit rolled down into the bottom as he swung the captured earth over the side of the grave.

"Stop!" Sister cried. She astonished them all by leaping into the grave.

"What the hell are you doing?" Betty said as Walter leaned over the grave. Then he, too, jumped right in.

At the bottom edge of the freshly dug hole, Walter and Sister stared at the whitened bones of what looked like an elbow.

"Human?" Sister asked.

"I think so." Walter carefully brushed away the earth until more bone was revealed. Unable to resist, Betty joined them. Jimmy clambered down from the cab of the backhoe and knelt down at the edge of the gaping hole.

"I can't believe this," Betty gasped.

Walter kept brushing. More arm bones. Then a hand. Definitely human.

The long rays of the morning sun crept into the tomb, causing the royal blue of a huge sapphire flanked by two diamonds to glitter in the light.

"The Hapsburg sapphire," Betty whispered.

"Sweet Jesus." Sister's hands shook as she reached to touch the sapphire, then pulled back.

CHAPTER 2

Creamy suds of disinfectant swirled down the large kennel drain as Shaker washed the feed room. The female hounds, called bitches or gyps, drowsy after their exercise and breakfast, lounged on the benches on their side of the kennels. The dog hounds on their side, separate from the girls, did likewise as well as being scattered throughout the runs like so many canine statues.

A few hound ears perked up, then dropped back as Sister Jane and Betty hurried into the kennels.

Shaker turned off the power washer. "Sad job putting old Pepper in the ground." He hung the washer nozzle on a wall hook, then glanced over at his boss and dear friend. "Janie, you look like you've seen a ghost."

Ashen-faced, still a little shaky, she replied, "I have."

The three repaired to Shaker's office next to the kennels. The open windows let in the breeze carrying the tang of hound scent.

"Here, you'd better sit down." He pulled out his desk chair for Sister. "You, too, Betty." He moved over the spartan extra chair for Betty Franklin, who dropped into it. Betty kept swallowing.

"We have seen a ghost. We have." Tears welled up in Betty's expressive eyes.

Shaker, always a bit awkward in emotional situations but a feeling man nonetheless, patted Betty on the back.

9

"On Hangman's Ridge?" They hadn't walked out that way, but it was the first thing that popped into his mind. The ridge was reputed to have been haunted since Lawrence Pollard had swung from the oak for having masterminded a land speculation deal that had impoverished all who had invested in it in 1702.

Sister shook her silver head. "Nola Bancroft."

He perched his spare frame on the edge of the desk, a flicker of disbelief on his sunburnt features. "What are you talking about?"

Sister closed her eyes, inhaled deeply. "After you took hounds back, Walter got Jimmy to bury Peppermint. We couldn't put him by Snake Creek, so Betty and I thought just above the abutment by the covered bridge would be high enough." She took a deep breath. "Well, Jimmy did a fine job, but I saw bones. I jumped in, Walter after me—"

"Me too," Betty chimed in. "It was an elbow."

"Walter brushed away the earth, and the arm bones appeared and then the hand. The Hapsburg sapphire was still on her finger. . . ."

Raleigh wedged himself tightly next to Sister's leg since he could tell she was upset.

"My God, I don't believe it! After all these years."

"Twenty-one years," Betty added. "Just a pile of whitened bones and that ring. The little metal belt buckle from her dress was there, too. Remember when Paul Ramy kept asking each of us what Nola was wearing the last time we saw her? Well, we'd all just seen her at Sorrel Buruss's party."

"She had on a blue flowered sundress," Sister recalled. "Everyone teased her that she bought the dress because the blue matched her eyes and she sassed back that she bought it because it showed off her cleavage." Sister smiled, remembering the impossibly beautiful younger daughter of Tedi and Edward Bancroft.

Nola had been twenty-four years old when she'd disappeared more than two decades earlier.

"Uh, is she still in the grave?" Shaker lowered his voice.

"I don't know." Betty shifted in her seat. "The sheriff showed up with Gaston Marshall, the coroner. Ben took statements from each of us and told us we could leave."

Ben Sidell was the sheriff. Betty, like many county residents, often called him by his first name.

"What did Gaston do?" Shaker asked.

"He made the sheriff's assistant take pictures and then he got down in the grave and they started cleaning off the dirt. They were very careful. We were excused before they'd finished the job. Maybe there will be clues left."

"What a pity old Sheriff Ramy isn't still alive for this," Betty said.

"I always thought Sheriff Ramy pretty much died the day his son Guy disappeared. His body just kept on for a while longer," Sister added.

Guy Ramy had been courting Nola. The Bancrofts did not consider the sheriff's son a suitable match for their daughter. They offered strong resistance, which only made Guy more attractive to the headstrong Nola. And he wasn't bad-looking to begin with. He disappeared when Nola did, so at first people naturally figured they'd run off to get married without parental blessing. But as days passed, then weeks, no one heard a peep. Even Sybil, Nola's older sister, didn't hear from Nola, and the two sisters were close. Sybil, married but a year to Ken Fawkes, plunged into a depression. In a sense, the whole family did as the weeks passed into months. As Sybil had married beneath her, to use Tedi's phrase, she felt guilty because she thought her marriage had put even more pressure on

Nola to marry a Randolph, a Valentine, a Venable, a De-Jarnette, names considered suitable in Virginia.

No one ever saw or heard from Nola Bancroft or Guy Ramy again after Saturday, September 5, 1981.

"Walter's still there. As a medical man, Ben asked him to stay. The worst was what to do about telling Tedi. We all agreed she couldn't find her daughter and Peppermint together. The sheriff allowed Jimmy to haul Peppermint up on the ridge and bury him there so Tedi won't have to see that. And he said he wouldn't fetch Tedi and Edward until Nola's body is completely free of its tomb. Well, I guess it isn't a tomb, but you know what I mean. Oh, it's just awful, Shaker."

The thought of Tedi Bancroft viewing the skeletal remains of her beloved daughter made Shaker grimace. "Can't someone else identify her?"

"Actually none of us can. Not even Tedi. We assume it's Nola because of the sapphire. The coroner will have to go by dental records."

"Assuming the skull is there." Betty furrowed her eyebrows.

"Betty," Sister said, looking at her sternly.

"Well, we don't know how she died. Killers do really strange things. I mean, some of them are fascinated with death. They keep coming back. And who knows but what they might find Guy right there with her. Maybe he killed her and then shot himself."

"He'd never kill Nola. He loved that girl," Shaker said with conviction.

"Furthermore, how could he bury himself?" Sister sensibly added.

"Well, I am shook up. I'm not being very logical. But I can't help it. The sight of that big ring on that bony finger will stay with me forever."

"Yes, me too." Sister sighed, dropping her hand to pet

Raleigh's sleek head. "Let's pray that Walter can talk Ben out of fetching Tedi. Edward can come down. Or Ken, or Sybil, or anyone but Tedi. Anyway, I think the only reason Ben would subject them to this is to see if he can jolt something out of them," Sister said shrewdly.

"None of them did it," Betty flatly stated.

"But people suppress things, Betty. Maybe the grisly sight will force out a memory that will help put the pieces of the puzzle together. I don't know about you, but I'm sure I've suppressed plenty in my own life."

"Haven't we all." Betty cracked her knuckles, a nervous gesture.

"You know what my memory of Nola is?" Shaker asked. "I see this beautiful girl just flying her fences on Peppermint. Like that great big old stone wall down there at Duelling Grounds." Shaker mentioned a farm where they hunted. "Everyone takes the low end, but she'd put him right to the four-foot section and sail over, hands forward, eyes up, big smile on her face."

"Girl could ride," Betty agreed as she smiled in remembrance.

In these parts, indeed in most of Virginia, the ability to ride was considered one of the social graces. It had nothing to do with money and a lot to do with talent. Or at least determination, should one lack talent. Nola had it all: talent, determination, and money.

Sybil, a very good rider herself, pitted herself against Nola or rode with her as her partner in hunter pairs at hunter trials and hunter paces, outdoor competitions. They were fun to watch.

Golliwog, a large calico, sauntered into the kennel. She'd been waiting up at the house for Sister to return and she was quite irritated about her delay. Not only was Sister overdue, but Golliwog had artfully arranged a large field mouse on the back porch for Sister's delectation. But the heat was rising, the mouse ripening with it. Golly did not like such unsavory things, although Raleigh did, of course. This was just one more reason that dogs were inferior to cats in Golly's mind.

"*I am sick and tired of waiting for everyone!*" she complained.

"Pipe down, Golly!" Sister ordered the cat, a useless order, of course.

"*We found Nola Bancroft's body,*" Raleigh informed the imperious creature.

Nola had disappeared long before Golly was born— the cat was now in the prime of life—but she had heard odd snippets over the years concerning the Bancroft girl who could have been a movie star. Not that she paid much attention, since she always preferred to be the topic of conversation herself.

"*What, she just popped up somewhere?*"

"*Peppermint died this morning and we found her when Jimmy Chirios dug the grave with the backhoe.*"

As the dog and cat considered the morning's events, Sister stood up. "Well, we've got to do something, but I don't know exactly what."

"Pay a call," Betty suggested.

"Yes, I know that. We've got to let the club members know. She was a member of Jefferson Hunt, after all."

"You're right. I'll get the telephone tree going," Betty said. Shaker pulled the club directory from his long middle desk drawer, handing it to Betty.

"I suggest you don't," he said.

"Why?" Both women stared at him.

"Wait until you talk again to the sheriff. He might not want the news out quite that fast."

"Shaker, this is Jefferson County. Gossip travels faster

than light," Sister truthfully stated. "Even now the phones are ringing throughout the county."

"But it shouldn't be on our heads. He's going to want to talk to anyone who remembers Nola, which is anyone in our club over twenty-five, and that's most everyone."

"He's right." Betty handed back the directory.

Sister, usually politically astute, considered the wisdom of Shaker's suggestion and realized she'd been more rattled by the discovery than she'd thought. "Right." She rubbed her temples a moment. "Do you know what keeps running through my mind? It's Peppermint. He loved her. He would do anything for Nola. He carried all the Bancrofts at one time or another, but he loved Nola best of all and now he's led us back to her."

"In death," Betty said, sounding a trifle morbid even to herself.

"Fate." Shaker reached for his old briarwood Dunhill pipe, his father's.

"Aren't death and fate the same thing?" Betty wondered.

"No, ma'am, not by a long shot." Shaker leaned against the desk. "Not by a long shot."

CHAPTER 3

As the last human left the grave site, a tremendous clap of thunder shook the earth.

Inky, a member of the gray fox clan who happened to be black, had been watching the activity at the grave site so intently that she jumped at the thunder. She looked toward the west. Roiling low clouds would be directly overhead in fifteen minutes or less.

Her curiosity, overcome by the weather, gave way to a mad dash for her den, a tidy place two miles west of After All Farm. Inky lived on Sister Jane's place, Roughneck Farm, at the edge of the cornfield, near a mighty old walnut, on high ground above a small tributary feeding into Broad Creek. She lived very well and at one and a half years of age she was a sleek, healthy creature with unusually bright eyes.

The first huge raindrops splattered around her just as she reached the border of Roughneck Farm. Another few minutes and she'd be home. The sky, dark now, seemed close enough to touch. Sister pulled out onto the farm road in her new red GMC truck. Her headlights caught Inky for a moment, but the fox did not stop to give the older woman the pleasure of her company. She raced for her den, shooting in as thunder rumbled overhead and lightning momentarily turned the sky lavender green.

Inky hated getting wet. She nestled in her sweet-smelling hay bed, which she'd carried home after the last cutting.

Like all foxes, reds and grays, Inky was a highly intelligent, adaptable creature. Part of this adaptability derived from being omnivorous like humans. Whenever that insufferable cat, Golliwog, would fuss at Inky for visiting the kennels where she liked to chat with Diana, a young gyp, Inky would remind her as she left that Golliwog was an obligate carnivore.

This would infuriate Golly, who in retaliation would stir up the hounds. Then Shaker would open the front door of his clapboard cottage and speak to the hounds to quiet them. Golly could be vengeful, but she was smart. Inky had to give her that.

As Inky dried herself she wondered who was in that grave. The human emotions had cast a strong scent that carried up to her. As soon as the storm was over she thought she'd go out again and visit her parents, who lived deeper in the woods near strong-running Broad Creek. Perhaps they would know something. And she wanted to tell her family that Peppermint had passed on. He had loved chatting with his former adversaries, as he'd dubbed the foxes. Peppermint had always had a quaint turn of phrase like the older gentleman he was.

Inky knew that when humans were feeling wretched the shock waves would vibrate over the countryside. Her curiosity was thus more than a mental exercise; it was key to survival.

"Hello, Inky," Sister said, noting the lovely animal racing beside the road.

"I worry that she's getting too tame." Shaker pressed two fingers around the knot of his tie.

Never comfortable in a coat and tie, he was a proper fellow. Given the circumstances, he would not cross the

Bancroft threshold unless respectfully dressed. Lean and wiry, Shaker exuded a toughness that belied his kindly nature.

Both Shaker and Sister had hurried to clean up after Betty had hopped into her car. She'd pick up Bobby, fill him in, clean up herself, and meet the master and huntsman at After All.

"The legend of the black fox."

"Bull. We've always had black foxes." He half snorted. "We just don't always see them."

"I know that." She turned the windshield wipers to a higher speed. She wasn't 100 percent familiar with her new truck yet, so she had to fiddle with the stick on the steering column.

"Be nice when you learn to drive this thing."

"Be nice when you learn to treat me with respect."

"Oh la." He half sang. "Janie, none of this bodes well, does it?"

"No, it doesn't. And I know I'm using Inky as an excuse, but you will recall a black fox gave us a hell of a run just before Ray died, and then again before Raymond died." Ray, her son, was killed in a freak harvesting accident in 1974. Her husband, Raymond, died of emphysema in 1991. "And Raymond's grandmother would always rattle on about how her mother swore that in 1860 all they hunted was black foxes."

"Hunted Yankees after that." Shaker, born and bred in Mount Sidney, Virginia, half smiled as he said it.

"Jesus, think we'll ever get over it?"

"The Jews built Pharaoh's pyramids five thousand years ago and they're still talking about it. The Irish still fuss about Elizabeth the First like she just left the throne. People have to have something to bitch and moan about." He caught his breath for a moment. "If you ask me, people can't do without their tragedies. Makes them feel important."

"You might be right. The Bancrofts aren't like that, thank God. Shaker, I can't exactly fathom it. Not to know where your child is for all those years and then to find out she's been buried on your own property all along. A ring on a bony hand."

"Horrible." Although he wasn't a father, he could sympathize as could most anybody with a heart.

"When I lost Ray, well, you were there. Yes, it was dreadful. Yes, I wanted to die with him. But at least I knew. I could say good-bye. I could grieve. All those years that Tedi and Edward hoped and prayed and then settled into a dull ache of a life. And now, to finally know where Nola is. Where she's been all along . . ."

"I think Tedi knew."

"In her heart—yes, I think she knew Nola was dead the night she went missing. But Edward could never give up."

"Alice Ramy broke bad."

"Wonder who's going to tell her?"

Alice Ramy, the mother of Guy Ramy, turned bitter and disruptive after her son's disappearance. Her only positive outlets seemed to be the prize chickens she bred and her gardens. But even these activities led to frustration. At least once a year her dahlias would be shredded when the prize chickens escaped into her gardens for a feast.

Shaker shifted nervously in his seat as they drove through the majestic wrought-iron gates, the serried spearpoints gilded, of After All Farm's main entrance. "Ben Sidell will tell Alice."

"There are plenty of people who still believe Guy killed her and then disappeared. Some ass would come back from a vacation in Paris and declare, 'Saw Guy

Ramy on the Left Bank. He's bald now.' You know perfectly well they never saw a goddamned thing." Sister's knuckles were white on the steering wheel. She, too, was nervous.

"Guy Ramy might have killed someone over Nola, but he would have never killed Nola," Shaker said.

They peered out their windows through the streaming rain. Half the hunt club members were already there. A tightly knit community, the Jefferson Hunt Club supported one another instantly through every crisis—but felt free to gossip about one another with equal alacrity.

A red Mercedes S500 was parked closest to the front walk, trailed by a silver Jaguar, a 1987 Ford pickup, a hunter green Explorer, and a Tahoe. The number of trucks suggested people had walked away from their farm chores to hasten to the Bancrofts'. A Toyota Land Cruiser announced that Ralph Assumptio was there. He was a cousin on his mother's side to Guy Ramy.

Sister had to park halfway down to the barns.

Shaker picked up the golf umbrella resting slantways across his feet. "You stay there. I'll come 'round to your side."

He opened the door and the rain slashed down.

When the arc of the red and yellow umbrella loomed outside, Sister opened her door and stepped down, ducking under cover.

She clutched Shaker's strong forearm. "Well, let's do what we can."

A huge hanging glass lantern, supported by four heavy chains, cast diffuse light into the rainy evening. The white columns glistened as did the slate roof of this magnificent Palladian triumph.

The fan window above the oversized black door was handblown glass, as were all the paned windows.

After All, one of the great mansions of the early eigh-

teenth century, had received many visitors in both joy
and sorrow.

As they reached the front door, Walter Lungrun opened
it before the harried butler could get to it. For a moment,
with the light framing his face, Sister felt an odd sense of
comfort—something akin to homecoming. She shook off
the unexpected feeling, deciding that all her nerve end-
ings were on red alert. Of course she was glad to see him.
She'd known Walter, at a distance, since his childhood.

"Sister, thank God you're here." Walter bent down to
kiss her cheek. "You, too, Shaker. Tedi and Edward are
in the living room. Ken and Sybil, too."

A servant hung their dripping raincoats in the coat
closet. They heard Betty and Bobby come through the
door as well as other people behind them.

Walter took Sister's hand and led her to the living
room, crowded with people. Shaker walked on her other
side. People parted for Sister. They usually did.

Tedi sat perched on the edge of her Sheraton sofa, the
cost of which alone could buy most Americans a lovely
home. When she looked up to see one of her oldest friends
and her master, she burst into tears again and stood up,
throwing her arms around Sister. "Janie."

Edward, whose eyes also were wet, stood up next to
his wife and embraced Sister when Tedi relinquished her.
Then Tedi hugged Shaker, and Edward shook his hand.

"Thank you for coming, Shaker."

"Mr. Bancroft, I'm terribly sorry for the circumstances."
Shaker, always correct as a hunt servant, addressed Edward, a member, by his surname.

"Yes, yes." Edward's lip began to quiver and Shaker
reached for his hand again, holding it in both of his.

"Janie, sit with us." Tedi pulled her down on the sofa.

A servant in livery—the Bancrofts, wonderful though
they were, had pretensions—offered refreshments on a

tray. Perhaps they weren't pretentious. It was the world into which both had been raised. This was part of life.

"You knew it was Nola." Tedi wiped her eyes.

"The ring." Sister draped her arm around Tedi's thin shoulders.

"Edward went to see. I couldn't go. I just couldn't." Tedi choked, then composed herself. "I don't know how Edward did it."

Sister looked up at the tall man, severely handsome with a full head of closely cropped white hair and a trim military mustache. He greeted guests and shepherded them away from Tedi so she could talk to Sister for a moment. "He's a strong man."

"Guess he had to be." Tedi leaned into Sister. "You can't run a business like his without people trying to tear you into little pieces."

"Tedi, I don't know if something like today's discovery can bring good. But—maybe it can bring peace."

Tedi shook her head. "I don't know. I don't know about peace, but I must find out what happened to my—baby."

A chill touched Sister at the base of her neck just as a blazing bolt of lightning hit close to the house. Sparks flew, pink sparks widened into a halo of fireworks, and then the room went dark.

Ken Fawkes, the Bancrofts' son-in-law, said, "Dad, it must have hit the transformer. I'll crank up the generator."

Ken had fallen into the habit of calling his father-in-law "Dad."

The servants glided into the room, lighting candles, carrying hurricane lamps. Being plunged into darkness was not an uncommon experience in the country.

Sister wondered whether she should tell Tedi what she felt, felt so strongly that it was as if she'd been hit by that bolt of lightning. "Tedi, you *will* find out."

Tedi turned to look directly into her friend's warm eyes. "Yes, I think I will. I don't think I'm going to like it."

Sister kissed her friend again. "So many people want to see you, Tedi. I'll come by tomorrow."

"No, no, let me come to you. I want out of this place."

"Good." Tedi embraced her one more time, holding her tightly, then released her.

Sister nodded to people, shaking hands as she made her way over to Sybil, Nola's older sister. Sybil, an attractive forty-six years old, was red-eyed from crying. The sisters had resembled each other, but in Nola, Sybil's features had found perfection. Sybil's jaw was a trifle too long, her eyes a light blue, whereas Nola's were electric blue just like Tedi's.

Scattered throughout the house were family photographs. If Nola had not been in those photographs your eye would have focused on Sybil, a pretty girl. But Nola was there and you couldn't take your eyes off her.

On a few occasions, Sybil's resentment of her sister would explode. Everyone understood, even Sybil's own peers when they were children. It was damned hard to be outshone by your bratty little sister, and yet Sybil did love her. The two of them could fall into transports of giggles, pulling pranks, riding first flight in the hunt field. Both were good students, both were good with people, and both clung to each other as the children of the very rich often do once they discover they are very rich.

"Sister—" Sybil didn't finish her sentence as the tears came.

Sister took her in her arms. "Be strong. Grab mane. Eyes up." She told her the same thing she used to tell her when Sybil faced a big fence as a small child. And Sybil had been good to Ray Junior. Sister loved her for that. Sybil was a few years older than her son, yet always paid attention to him and rode with him. Both of them could ride like banshees.

Nola, while always friendly to Ray Junior, was too busy conquering men even as a fourteen-year-old to pay much attention to the boy. Nola had discovered her powers early and was determined to use them.

"I will." Sybil sniffed.

Ken joined them. "Thank you for coming." He embraced Sister.

"I'm just so glad you and the children are here."

"We haven't told the children all of it. Only that their Aunt Nola was finally found. What do you tell a ten-year-old and a six-year-old in a situation like this?" Ken shrugged.

"The truth—as gently as you can, because if you don't, someone else will," Sister forthrightly replied. "They're strong."

"Mother wants us to move back into the big house, but we can't. We're staying at Hunter's Rest, but I'll be with Mother every day," Sybil said.

Hunter's Rest, a two-story frame house, was located at the southernmost border of the large estate. It once housed the farm manager.

"If you need to get the children away, drop them with me. The S litter"—Sister mentioned a robust litter of fox-hound puppies whelped in mid-May—"need walking out and handling. And you know they're always as welcome as you are."

"Thank you." Ken placed his large hand on her shoulder. Apart from a slight paunch, he was holding his own against middle age. A few strands of gray appeared in his sandy hair and eyebrows. A small bald spot like a tonsure bore testimony to the encroaching years, but one had to be taller than Ken to see it.

Later, as Sister and Shaker drove back through the

continuing rain, Shaker loosened his dark blue tie. "Had the damndest feeling."

"What?"

"Well"—he paused, then sheepishly looked over at Sister—"I think I've seen too many TV mysteries."

"What?" she persisted, knowing he'd have to work up to anything that couldn't be proven by logic.

"Well, I felt that somebody in that room knew—knew what had really happened to Nola."

CHAPTER 4

The windshield wipers on the Mercedes S500 flipped at their highest speed as Crawford Howard and his wife, Marty, drove back toward town. They had met and married at the University of Indiana, made a fortune in strip malls, moved to central Virginia, divorced, and remarried, all before age forty-seven. Surprisingly, neither of them appeared exhausted by this process.

"Honey, slow down." Marty involuntarily shrank back as the water from puddles splashed against her side window.

"This machine can handle everything."

"This machine must still obey the laws of physics," she wryly replied. But knowing how he loathed being corrected, she hastened to add, "Edward was glad to see you. I know you've had a long day, but thank you for making the effort."

He slowed to forty-five miles an hour. "That girl must have been something. Those photographs of her all over the house—really something."

The Howards had moved to Jefferson Hunt Country after Nola's disappearance.

"Don't you think people are jumping to conclusions?" Marty's voice rose.

"What? That she was murdered?"

"Right."

"Honey, people don't commit suicide and bury themselves. If they commit suicide, sooner or later the body is found. And she disappeared in September, so you know she would have been found quick enough."

"Betty Franklin said the last time anyone saw her alive was at a party Sorrel Buruss gave for the first day of cubbing. But you're right. It's still hot in September."

"A first-day-of-cubbing party. That's a good idea."

Foxhunting rarely opened with a home run, more like a base hit. Cubbing introduced young entry, those hounds hunting for their first year, to the young foxes, being hunted for the first time. The older hounds and hunt staff helped steady the youngsters, keeping them running between the bases instead of straying off into center field. The young foxes, with a bit of luck, learned the rules from the older foxes, but in case a youngster was caught unawares, many a huntsman would steer his pack away to save the fox. If the pack couldn't be deterred, if scent was just flaming, a whipper-in would do his or her best to warn the fox. If hounds were far enough away, the whipper-in would speak to the fox. The sound of a human voice usually set the fox to running. If hounds were close, the whipper-in would smack his or her boot with their crop. The sound alerted the fox. The whipper-in didn't want to use his or her voice, if possible, in those circumstances, for the hounds would know the human's voice.

No one wanted to kill a fox under any circumstances, whether in cubbing or later in formal hunting. American foxhunting was purely about the thrill of the chase—the joy of good hound work and hard riding. Unfortunately, most Americans formed their concept of foxhunting from the English traditions. This was a misunderstanding American foxhunters fretted over continually.

"Wonder why we don't have a party like that anymore?"

"Bad organization." Crawford rarely let slip the opportunity to criticize, implicitly suggesting he could do better.

Foxhunting clubs, like all volunteer organizations, rolled with the ebb and flow of individual enthusiasm. One member might host an annual breakfast or party for years, then grow weary of it. The master might suggest that someone else pick up the slack, but she or he couldn't exactly give orders. Orders usually attend paychecks.

"Well, darling, perhaps we should host one. Bring back a lovely tradition."

He braked sharply as a deer shot across the road. "Big rats, that's what they are." Then he returned his attentions to his recently remarried wife. "Wouldn't hurt. And let's do it properly. None of this platter of ham biscuits and a pile of doughnuts. Mumm de Cramant." He mentioned a champagne of which he was particularly fond.

"Cristal." She loved Louis Roederer.

"I'm not serving $270 bottles of champagne. As it is, the de Cramant is running about $70, although if I order a few cases from Sherry-Lehmann I can get the price down. Don't worry, sweetie, they'll be damned impressed when they taste it."

"I'm sure you're right." She noticed the sign to the entrance of the Franklins' small farm swinging wildly in the increasing wind. "Turning into a filthy night. Almost as if Nola's ghost has stirred up the winds."

"Now, Marty." He laughed.

"I believe in spirits. What about the ghosts at Hangman's Ridge? People have seen them, and people who aren't"—she weighed her next word—"flighty."

"Pure bunk. Anyway, this will all blow over, forgive the pun. If there's any evidence left on the body at all, I

guarantee you it will lead back to Guy Ramy. It just figures. So the real work is finally tracking him down. You
know someone around here knows where he is or helped
him get out of town. Boy's father was the sheriff. Man
might have been the sheriff, but I'll bet you he protected
his own."

"But honey, everyone who knew them said Guy
loved her."

"Men kill the women they say they love every day."

"Makes me wonder why the compliment isn't
reciprocated."

"Women are more moral."

"Do you really believe that?"

"I do. I know you're my moral superior. And I wished
when we were younger I'd asked you about things, deals,
people. But I didn't." He shifted in his seat. "Although I
still think you can't make an omelette without breaking
eggs. Not that I'm condoning smashing people to bits,
but competition is the lifeblood of trade, it's the lifeblood
of this country. Someone has to win and someone has
to lose."

"I guess Nola lost."

"Don't worry over it, Marty. This will get settled now
that the body has surfaced. Really. And there's nothing
we can do about it except do whatever the Bancrofts
need done." He slowed for the entrance to their farm,
Beasley Hall. It was named long before they bought it. It
was named for Tobias Beasley, the original holder of the
land grant from Charles II. "Wonder if Edward Bancroft
has more money than I do? If I'd inherited what he inherited I'd have turned it into four or five billion dollars by
now. You know, these people who inherit fortunes let
gentlemen investors manage their money. The invest-
ments return maybe three percent or four percent a year.

I can't understand anyone being that passive about their money."

"I don't know if Edward has as much as you do, honey, but he's not passive. He ran the Bancroft empire until a few years ago when he retired."

"Coffee."

"What, dear?"

"Their money started in coffee, of all the damn things. I'd never put my money in anything where Mother Nature was my partner. But I guess it was a different time. Early nineteenth century. That ancestor of his had to be pretty damned smart."

"Now they just seem damned, don't they?"

"The Bancrofts? No. Marty, don't let this Nola thing affect you. The Bancrofts made whatever adjustment they had to twenty years ago. Sybil married a decent enough fellow, they have two grandchildren, and sure, you never forget a child, but I don't think you can say they're damned." He pulled into the new garage attached to the original main house, an addition Crawford had commissioned.

The new wing was tastefully done and didn't resemble a garage. If anything, it was the tiniest bit overdone.

The garage doors rolled down behind the red Mercedes.

The first building on this site was a log cabin built in 1730 by Tobias Beasley's grandson. Over the years it had been replaced with a handsome brick structure boasting a huge center hall and four-over-four windows. Each generation that made money added to the main house. This meant about every thirty or forty years a ballroom would be built or more bedrooms with sleeping porches. Whatever excited the owners' fancy was added, which gave Beasley Hall true character.

Crawford opened the door into the mudroom and ushered his wife through.

"Thank you, dear."

"Nightcap?"

"How about a small brandy with a rind of orange on the rim."

He laughed at her but made her the drink and brought it upstairs to their huge bedroom, decorated by Colefax and Fowler. Crawford could have hired Parish Hadley out of New York, but no, he had to go to London. The woman who put the English country house look on the map, Nancy Lancaster, whose mother, Lizzie, had been born a Langhorne of Virginia, was influenced by Mirador, the Langhorne seat in Albemarle County. Crawford liked telling people he and Marty were simply bringing her talent back home. Nancy Lancaster, born in 1897, had been dead since 1994, but her decorating firm soldiered on.

The simple truth was that Crawford was a dreadful snob.

They slipped into their scarlet cashmere bathrobes from Woods and Falon, another English firm, and nestled into an overstuffed sofa suffocating with chintz-covered pillows.

Marty enjoyed unwinding on this sofa before retiring to bed. When she and Howard had separated and Crawford's lawyers had played the old starve-the-wife routine, she'd had ample time to consider the financial impact of divorce on middle-aged women. She realized she could not make a graceful transition into the ranks of the *nouveau pauvre*.

"When *is* the first day of cubbing this year?" Crawford put his arm around her.

"September seventh, I think."

"Time to leg up the horses."

"Time to leg up ourselves."

"Oh, honey, you look fantastic. In fact, you look better than when I married you."

"Liar."

"It's true."

"You can thank the business—and yourself."

One of her demands for returning to Crawford, who had been unfaithful to her, was that he buy her the landscaping firm where she had been working to make ends meet. She'd fallen in love with the business. When the owner, Fontaine Buruss, died an untimely death in the hunt field, Crawford made a handsome settlement upon Fontaine's widow. Marty had never been happier now that she was running her own business. She had a real purpose of her own.

He kissed her. "Funny how things work out."

"You look pretty fantastic yourself." She winked at him.

He'd lost his paunch, changed his diet, and worked with a personal trainer. He'd also endured liposuction, but he wasn't advertising that fact.

The rain slashed at the windowpanes, and Crawford's heart beat right along with it. When Marty winked it meant she wanted sex.

Crawford, like most people with business drive, also had a high sex drive. He adored making love on a rainy night, too.

He reached up and rubbed her neck. "Did I tell you how crazy I am about you?"

What he didn't tell her was that he had not given up his long-standing goal of becoming joint-master of the Jefferson Hunt and that that very day he had put his plan in motion. By God, he would be joint-master whether Jane Arnold wanted him or not.

CHAPTER 5

Large, overhead industrial fans set high in the ceiling swirled, their flat blades pushing the air downward, and window fans also sucked in air from the outside and sent it over the sleeping hounds. This arrangement kept flies out of the kennels as well.

It was late afternoon, the day after Nola had been discovered. The rains had been followed by the oppressive heat typical of the South.

The Jefferson Hunt Club Kennels, built in the 1950s, were simple and graceful. The building's exterior was brick, much too expensive to use now thanks to higher taxes and higher labor costs. The large square structure housed the office, the feed rooms, and an examination room where a hound could be isolated for worming or the administration of medicines. At the back of this was a 150-foot-square courtyard of poured concrete sloping down to a central drain. The roofline from the main building gracefully extended over one side of this courtyard by about eight feet. Lovely arches much like those underneath the walkways at Monticello supported the overhang.

Open archways bounded the courtyard, again like the ones at Monticello. The dog hounds lived on the right side and the gyps on the left. Each gender had its own runs and kennel houses with raised beds and little porches.

The puppies lived at the rear with their own courtyard and special house. A small, separate sick bay nestled under trees far to the right.

The design—simple, functional—was pleasing to the eye. Doorways into the sleeping quarters were covered with tin to discourage chewing. The center sections of the doors to the runs were cut out and covered with a swinging heavy rubber flat, like a large mud flap on a truck, so the hounds could come and go as they wished. Eventually someone would get the bright idea to chew the flap, but a large square of rubber was easier to replace than an entire door.

All sleeping quarters were washed down every morning and evening. Painted cinder-block walls discouraged insect infestation. The floors sloped to central drains.

Many hounds slept in their raised beds, the wash of refreshing air keeping them cool. Others were dreaming in the huge runs, a quarter of an acre each, filled with large deciduous and fir trees. Some hounds felt the only proper response to blistering weather was to dig a crater in the earth, curling up in it. Fans whirling over kennel beds was sissy stuff.

Two such tough characters, Diana and Cora, faced each other from their shallow earthen holes, now muddy, which pleased them.

"Hate summer," Cora grumbled.

"It's not so bad," the beautiful tricolor replied, her head resting on the edge of her crater.

"You're still young. Heat gets harder to handle as you get older," Cora said. She had recently turned six.

Six, while not old, gave Cora maturity. She was the strike hound, the hound who pushes forward. She sensed she was slowing just the tiniest bit and knew Dragon, Diana's littermate, would jostle for her position.

Cora hated Dragon as much as she loved his sister. Quite a few hounds loathed the talented, arrogant Dragon.

Being the strike hound didn't mean that Cora always found the scent first. But she worked a bit ahead of the rest—not much, perhaps only five yards in front, but she was first and she wanted to keep it that way.

If another hound, say a flanker, a hound on the sides of the pack, found scent before she did, Cora would slow, listening for the anchor hound, the quarterback, to speak. If the anchor said the scent was valid, then Cora would swing around to the new line, racing up front again. She had to be first.

If the anchor hound said nothing, then Cora would wait for a moment to listen for someone else whom she trusted. All she waited for was *"It is good."* If she didn't hear it soon, then she'd push on.

For years the anchor hound of the Jefferson Hunt had been Archie, a great American hound of substance, bone, deep voice, and reliable nose. Archie, a true leader, knew when to knock a smart-ass youngster silly, when to encourage, when to chide the whole pack, and when to urge them on. He died a fighting death against a bear, ensuring his glory among the pack as well as among the humans. They all missed him.

Diana, though young, possessed the brains to be an anchor hound. No one else exhibited that subtle combination of leadership, drive, nose, and identifiable cry. Cora knew Diana would become a wonderful anchor, but her youth would cause some problems this season. Like a young, talented quarterback, Diana would misread some signals and get blitzed. But the girl had it, she definitely had it.

In fact, the whole D litter, named for the first letter of their mother's name as is the custom among foxhunters, oozed talent. And in Dragon's case, overweening conceit.

Puppies taunted one another, their high-pitched voices carrying over the yards drenched in late-afternoon sunshine.

"Pipe down, you worthless rats," Cora yelled at them. They quieted.

"Too bad Archie can't see this litter. He was their grandfather. They're beauties." Diana watched one chubby puppy waddle to the chain-link fence between the yards, where he studied a mockingbird staring right back at him from the other side.

"Babblers." Cora laughed. *"They are beautiful. But the proof is in the pudding. We'll see what they can really do two seasons from now. And don't forget"*—she lowered her voice because gossip travels fast in close quarters—*"Sweetpea just isn't brilliant. Steady, God bless her, steady as a rock, but not an A student."*

Sweetpea was the mother of this litter.

"I wish it were the first day of cubbing." Diana sighed.

"Don't we all. I don't mind the walking out. Really. The exercise is good, and each week the walks get longer. You know next week we'll start with the horses again, which I enjoy, but still—not the same."

"Heard the boys in the pasture yesterday." Diana meant the horses. *"They're excited about starting back to work so long as Sister, Shaker, and Doug go out early, really early."* Diana sniffed the air. A familiar light odor announced the presence of Golly grandly picking her way through the freshly mowed grass toward the outdoor run.

Diana rose, shaking the dirt off.

Cora, too, smelled Golly. *"Insufferable shit."*

Diana laughed. *"Cora, you're crabby today."*

"It's the heat. But that doesn't change the fact that that cat is a holy horror." Cora curled farther into her cool mud crater. She wasn't going to talk to the calico.

Golly reached the chain-link fence. *"Good afternoon, Diana. Your nose is dirty."*

Diana sat down at the chain-link fence. *"Keeps the bugs off."*

"I wouldn't know. I don't get bugs."

"Liar," Cora called out.

"Tick hotel," Golly fired right back.

"Flea bait. You hallucinate. I've seen you chase the ghosts of fleas," Cora replied, giggling.

"I have never hallucinated in my life, Cora. And you can't get my goat, ha," she said, *"because you're a lower life-form and I'm not letting you needle me."*

"Oh, if you aren't hallucinating, then what are you doing when you, for no reason, leap straight into the air, twist around, race to a tree, climb up, drop down, and do it all over again? You're mental."

"Spoken like the unimaginative canine you are." Golly raised her chin, half closing her eyes. *"I'm being visited by The Muse on those occasions."*

"I'm going to throw up," Cora said, and made a gagging sound.

"Worms!" Golly triumphantly decreed.

Diana, thoroughly enjoying the hostilities, said, *"Just got wormed Monday."*

"Well, I walked down here in the heat of the day to give you girls some news, but since you're insulting me I think I'll go hiss at the puppies, teach them who's boss around here."

"You can tell me." Diana lowered her voice and her head, her dirt-encrusted nose touching the fence.

"You're a sensible girl," the cat replied.

In truth, Diana was sensible and also quite sweet. She loved everybody.

Cora, upright now, walked over. *"Well?"*

"*Who said I was talking to you?*" Golly opened her eyes wide.

"*Oh come on, Golliwog, you know we're dying to hear it,*" Cora coaxed, buttering her up.

The luxurious calico leaned forward, her nose on the chain-link fence now. "*It was Nola. The family dentist identified her not an hour ago.*"

Cora thought for a moment. "*This will stir up a hornet's nest.*"

"*If only we had known her . . . we hear and smell things.*" Diana frowned. "*We might have been able to help find out something useful.*"

"*The last hound that knew Nola Bancroft would have been Archie's grandmother. She lived to be eighteen, you know,*" Cora said. "*It was a long, long time ago.*"

"*You'd think if any of us had known about the murder, or if any of the horses over at After All Farm knew, they would have told. We'd know. We pass those things down,*" Diana said.

"*Undomesticated.*" Cora meant that undomesticated animals might have witnessed something at the time.

"*Who lives that long?*" Diana wondered.

"*Turtles. That snapping turtle at After All Farm, the huge one in the back pond, he's got to be forty years old, I swear it,*" Cora said.

"*Amphibians aren't terribly smart, you know. Their brain moves at about the same speed they do,*" Golly said with a laugh. Then she thought again. "*But they do remember everything.*"

"*How old is Athena?*" Diana asked, thinking of the great horned owl. "*They live a long time, don't they?*"

"*Don't know,*" the cat and hound said in unison.

Diana lay down, her head on her paws, her face now level with Golly's face, almost. "*Why does it matter? To us, I mean?*"

"Because it really will stir up a hornet's nest, Diana. People start buzzing. Old dirt will get turned over, and I promise you, ladies, I promise you, this will all come back to the Jefferson Hunt Club. Sooner or later, everything in this part of the world does," Cora said.

"Think Sister knows that?" Diana asked. She loved Sister.

"She knows. Sister has lived almost six hound lifetimes. Think of what she knows," Cora said, shaking her head in wonder.

"Well, exactly how do you think this will affect us? Will people not pay their dues or something like that?" Diana asked.

"No. People drop out when it's a bad season. No hunt club has control over the weather, but people act as though they do, the fair-weather hunters, I mean." Cora observed human behavior closely. *"Or when there's a club blowup, which happens about every seven years. Archie always said humans do things in seven-year cycles. They just don't recognize it."*

"Crawford Howard." Golly curled her upper lip as she said his name.

"Up to his old tricks?" Cora snapped at a low-flying dragonfly.

"Cat intuition." Golly smiled. *"I have an idea. Whatever happened to Nola in 1981 was well done, if you will. When you're hunting you all go places humans don't. Sometimes even Shaker can't keep up with you when territory's rough. You might find something or smell something out there that could help solve this mess. After all, the best noses in the world are"*—she paused for effect—*"bloodhounds, but you all are second."*

"Second to none!" Cora's voice rose, which caused a few sleepers to open one eye and grumble.

Humans ranked the noses of bloodhounds first, followed by bassets second and foxhounds third, with all other canines following. Foxhounds thought this an outrage. Of course they were best. Besides, who in the world could hunt behind a bloodhound? The poor horse would die of boredom. This was a pure article of foxhound faith.

"This has to do with hunting? Is that what you're really thinking, Golly?" Diana noticed a few of the boys in the kennel were quarreling over a stick. How they had the energy to even growl in this heat mystified her. One of the troublemakers, of course, was her brother, Dragon.

"Yes, think about it. Cubbing starts September seventh. It's the end of July. Stuff happens when you're hunting. Everything speeds up. People reveal themselves out there."

"We sure hear them scream for Jesus." Diana giggled as she recalled a few of the oaths elicited by a stiff fence.

"I have never figured that out. The horse jumps the fence, not them," Cora said, laughing.

"Oh, but that's just it, Cora. Sometimes the human takes the fence and the horse doesn't."

They all laughed at that.

"We'll keep our nose to the ground," Cora promised.

"I have the strangest feeling that Guy Ramy will be coming back." Golly lowered her voice again. *"More cat intuition."*

In a way, Golly was right.

CHAPTER 6

The Hapsburg sapphire glittered on the small glass-topped table. Outside, the long summer twilight cloaked the grand old trees surrounding Roughneck Farm, and scarlet tendrils of sunset seemed to ensnare the wisteria that climbed all over the back porch. The rose and gold light reflected off the windowpanes of the neat gardening shed, casting intricate designs across the emerald lawn.

Tedi and Sister sat on the screened-in back porch. The humidity was particularly oppressive this evening. Sister drank dark hot tea while Tedi nursed a martini as well as a glass of iced green tea. The mercury was dropping with evening's approach. The humidity seemed determined to hang on. Sister believed drinking a hot drink on a hot day kept you healthier. No one else could stand anything hot.

Raleigh and Golliwog were curled up together in Raleigh's Black Watch plaid dog bed. Rooster, Peter Wheeler's lovely harrier, was stretched out in his own bed, covered in the Wallace tartan, next to Raleigh. Peter, an ex-lover of Sister's, had bequeathed his handsome hound to her and his entire estate to the Jefferson Hunt to be administered solely by the master—not the Board of Directors. Peter's eight decades on this earth had taught him a benign dictatorship was infinitely preferable

41

to democracy. He died peacefully last year, a quiet end to a productive life.

Both Sister and Tedi now knew Nola had not died peacefully, a fact they were currently grappling with.

The animals listened intently, even Golly, who under normal circumstances would have told Raleigh how lucky he was to have her in his special porch bed.

"I knew. I always knew. So did you," Tedi said sadly.

Sister heard a squirrel clamber up the wisteria on her way to her nest in the attic. "We hoped. We always hoped."

"I'm done crying. I know, Janie, that I can be all over the map, as you say." She held up her hand to quell the protest. "I am a little different. I was never able to think the way you do. You think in sequences, you see patterns. Edward's like that. I don't. I gather it all up in one big basket, then dump it on the table and start sorting. But I eventually find what I'm looking for even if I drive everyone crazy doing it. It's just the way my mind works."

"You are an original," Sister said, smiling. "I'm lucky to know you."

"Do you realize we've known each other all our lives? But it seems like a split second. I don't understand it. We're seventy-one years old and I don't feel old, I don't act old, at least I don't think I do. I don't know where the years are. Are they hiding in my pocket? Are they wherever Nola is? What happened?"

Sister shrugged. "Wherever they are we sure packed a lot into them." She sipped her tea.

"Yes, we did." Tedi inhaled, her bright blue eyes flickering for a moment. "I'm not avoiding the subject."

"I didn't think you were."

"I know Nola was murdered. I didn't need the dental chart to prove those bones were Nola's any more than I needed Ben Sidell to tell me her skull had been crushed. A blunt instrument, he said, or a large rock. They aren't going to find the answers to this under a microscope, it's been too long. Too long."

"Well, he has to go by the book. Otherwise he won't stay sheriff for long."

"I know that. I just want to know who killed her. I still think it was Guy Ramy. Dog in a manger. I can't have her, so no one else can have her."

"But Nola was perfectly capable of running off with Guy and he was madly in love with her."

"They all were. And she wouldn't have run off with Guy. Headstrong as she was, Janie, Nola loved money. I think she might have allowed herself a flaming affair. And enjoy it all the more knowing I did not approve nor did her father. But marry Guy?" She shook her head. "No."

"I think she would."

"Why?"

"She knew in time you and Edward would forgive her. You'd have made a settlement on her with the appearance of the first grandchild. After all, you acquiesced to Ken in time."

A silence followed this.

"Maybe."

"No maybe about it. Nola could play her father like a harp, and eventually you'd have given in as well. So long as she was happy."

"He wouldn't have made her happy." Tedi's voice dropped a quarter of an octave.

"Tedi, there's ripe disagreement on that subject. People started talking about it in 1980, when Nola and Guy first fell in love. Opening Hunt. You could feel the electricity."

"Odd. They'd known each other all their lives."

"Not so odd. He went away to college, graduated, put in two years in the service. She hadn't seen him, hardly, for six years."

"I don't understand it."

"No one does. That's why love is love." Sister smiled. "Freshen your drink?"

"I'll do it." Tedi rose, walking to the small bar in the pantry just off the kitchen, the wide, uneven heart pine planks creaking underfoot.

A larger bar, more elaborate, still stood ready between the living room and the dining room. Raymond had loved to throw big parties. Sister had gotten out of the habit after his death in 1991; she figured hunting was her form of throwing a big party. Although she did always have the Opening Hunt from her farm, with a huge breakfast following at the house. Raymond and Ray both had gloried in these occasions. She rather more endured them and hoped she was a gracious hostess. The glitter on the table held her eye. Two diamonds of two karats each flanked the eleven-karat sapphire and picked up all available light, throwing it back on the large square-cut blue stone. Sapphires are usually too muddy or too pale. This one was a perfect royal blue—like a strip of startling water in the Caribbean.

Tedi called from the pantry, "You could pour me more tea, please."

Sister poured tea from a graceful cut-glass pitcher, ice cubes tinkling inside, into Tedi's frosted glass.

Tedi rejoined her. "Are you surprised I'm not crying? I'm not on the floor frothing at the mouth? It's not that I don't care. I do. I care passionately, but I don't have one tear left in my body. And I don't trust my emotions."

"What do you mean?"

"When Nola disappeared I went to pieces. There's really

no other way to put it. Fragments of Tedi Prescott"—she used her maiden name—"were scattered from here to Washington and back. I wore out the road driving up there to the FBI. I just knew Paul Ramy wasn't up to the task. Especially when Guy went missing. I was a total wreck. I regret that."

"Honey, any mother would have been torn to shreds inside."

"Yes, but I missed things. If I could have kept my wits about me, especially in those early days, I believe I might have picked up information, clues, nuances. I didn't. All I felt was pain. I believe we were very close to the killer, to finding out who the killer was, and he slipped through our fingers to land God knows where."

"We were all distraught."

"Which works to a killer's advantage."

"Can you go over it again? Will it upset you?"

"No. I mean, I have been over it. I last saw Nola at Sorrel Buruss's party. I think that's the last time any of us saw her alive. We'd patched things up in the stable before hunting that day. She apologized and so did I. Had a whopping fight the night before over Guy. Anyway, she was in high spirits, I was in neutral spirits. Edward was grumpy but putting a good face on it since we were at Sorrel's. Fontaine was an ass, as usual." She mentioned the handsome husband of Sorrel. "Since Nola wouldn't go to bed with him, he thought Sybil might be honored at his attentions. She slapped him square in the face. Sorrel, accustomed to his outrages, simply flipped him an ice cube to hold to his face. Nola laughed and laughed. Fontaine's face grew redder and redder. I was furious when I saw Fontaine pressure Sybil. She's a bit retiring and perhaps too anxious to please. I remember being very proud of her that she stopped that insufferable womanizer. Do you remember?"

"I do. And Peter Wheeler made a toast to Sybil. Let's see, 'Here's to Sybil, beloved of Apollo. Let her be an example to all women.' "

"Everyone was pretty well lubricated except you. I used to wish you'd drink with us, and now I'm glad you never did. You were smarter than all of us, and you look better for it, too. Ah well, then." Tedi sipped some martini, chased it with green tea. "Nola left without saying good-bye. The last time I saw her."

Sister raised her index finger. "I overheard Sybil saying that she and Ken would meet Nola at the C&O downstairs. Some band was playing they wanted to hear. But I was talking to everyone and I can't say I was paying particular attention to Nola."

The C&O was and remained a popular restaurant and nightspot over in Albemarle County.

"And I didn't know until the next morning that Nola never showed up. It wasn't that unusual for her to say she'd be somewhere and not show. Nola was always open to a better offer, her words." Tedi's memories, bittersweet, haunted her. "I didn't know until I saw Sybil at church. I was furious that Nola had stayed out all night but, well, it wasn't the first time. I didn't start to worry until Sunday supper."

Leaning back in her chair, Sister glanced outside at the sky, darkening from turquoise to cobalt, then back at Tedi. "Here's what I think, knowing what we now know. Nola was killed sometime between seven in the evening and early the next morning. You and Edward were building the covered bridge. The earth was still soft around it, remember? She had to have been killed in that time frame, because people don't go burying their victims in broad daylight. Whoever killed her had to have known about the bridge work. That was a drought summer. The earth was hard as rock. Thanks to the bulldozers, the embankment and the base for the bridge weren't packed tight yet. You were just putting the roof on the bridge. So whoever killed Nola knew that."

"That's right," Tedi whispered.

"And we'd hunted through there Saturday morning. I've checked my hunt records." Sister, like many masters, kept a detailed hunt diary. "We had forty-one people the first day of cubbing."

"Everyone in the county knew about the bridge work," Tedi said, a wave of hopelessness washing over her. She fought it off. "A lot of people knew, anyway." Tedi reached for the ring. "I should have never given this ring to Nola. For her it was the Hapless sapphire, just as it was for its first owner."

"Old sorrows," Sister said.

"It was made for the Empress of the Austro-Hungarian Empire, Elizabeth. She had dark hair, was a wonderful, wonderful horsewoman like Nola. Loved foxhunting. Rented hunting boxes in England and flew her fences. But hers was not a happy life. Her son committed suicide, and she was assassinated. I often wonder, if she'd lived, would Franz Josef have signed the Declaration of War of 1918?"

As a foxhunter, Sister had always found the empress's story irresistible. "As I recall, the Bancrofts bought this right after the First World War," she said. "Nolan couldn't have worried too much about the history of the stone if he gave it to his wife. She lived a long, happy life." Nolan was Edward's grandfather, who had lived through the terrifying action at Belleau Wood during the Great War.

Tedi held the ring up to the light; bits of rainbow struck off the diamonds, little dots splashing the walls. She slipped the ring on the middle finger of her left hand. "This was on my baby's finger when she died. Now I'm wearing it. Every time I look at it I'll remember her laughter. I'll remember how much I loved her. I've not spent one day that I haven't missed her, felt that ache. It's kind of like my tongue going back to the site of a missing tooth. I swore I would find out what happened to her but never did. Now—this. Sister, I will find Nola's killer even if it kills me."

"That makes two of us."

CHAPTER 7

"Jesus Christ, Doug, watch what you're doing." Shaker rubbed the back of his elbow where a heavy oak board had smacked him from behind.

"Sorry," the handsome young man apologized. "It's this heat. I can't think today."

Sticky, clammy humidity added to the discomfort this Monday, July twenty-second.

Shaker put down his hammer, tilting his head to direct Doug's attention across the road.

Doug followed Shaker's eyes. Wearing a torn tank top and equally torn jeans, an old red bandanna tied around her forehead, Sister toiled on the other side of the dirt farm road building a new coop, a jump resembling a chicken coop, with Walter Lungrun's help.

The old hunt club truck, Peter Wheeler's 1974 Chevy with the 454 engine, was parked off to the side of the road.

"Can't slow down," Doug pretended to whisper, "she'll cuss us."

"I heard that."

"I thought you were working, not eavesdropping," Shaker said.

"Women can do two or three things at the same time. Unlike men," Sister said, laughing.

"Doc, are you going to let her get away with that kind of abuse?" Shaker looked to the blond doctor for help.

"I suggest you call the state employment commission and register a complaint of sexism," Walter solemnly intoned.

"Oh, do make it a complaint of sexual assault. At my age, I'll be a heroine."

They all laughed at that and decided spontaneously to take a break and sit under a huge chestnut tree.

This particular tree was much studied by Virginia Tech students motoring up from Blacksburg, as it was one of the few original chestnuts to survive the horrible blight that almost entirely killed this most beautiful of species. The disease had started in New York State in 1904, spread west to Michigan, north to the border, and south to Alabama. Within a few decades most every native American chestnut, many over one hundred feet high, was dead.

This tree had survived because it was alone.

They were working at Foxglove Farm, a tidy farm north of Sister's farm. You could see the long, flat top of Hangman's Ridge to the south from high spots on Foxglove.

The staff and dedicated members of a hunt club worked harder during the summers than during hunt season. Puppies were whelped. Young entry had to be taught their lessons. Foxes would be carefully watched, wormed and other medicines put out for them to ensure their health. Seasoned hounds might need a few reminders of their tasks. The hunt horses would be turned out for vacation time. Young horses, called green, would be trained to see if they could become staff horses, a harder task than being a field hunter. Neighboring landowners would be visited, always a pleasure. Old jumps would be repaired or replaced, and new jumps would be built in new

territory to be opened if the club was lucky enough to secure new territory.

Foxglove had been part of the Jefferson Hunt territory
from the late nineteenth century, when a group of farmer
friends had merged their small packs of hounds together
into one communal pack. Many of these men had been
veterans of the War Between the States. Their sons and
grandsons were destined to be shipped overseas to the
horrors of the First World War.

Out of this raggle-taggle mess of hounds, a systematic
breeding program emerged under the visionary second
master, Major H. H. Joubert, called Double H by all. He
blended his tough local Bywaters hounds from northern
Virginia with a little Skinker blood from Orange County
Hunt. Then he folded in a lacing of English blood.
Whether by guess or by God, Double H's system worked.
He was a smart master, he bred for the territory, and he
studied other packs of hounds, ever eager to improve his
pack and his methods.

Hound men had been bragging about their animals
since the early seventeenth century and a few very wealthy
colonists imported hounds from England, products of a
line that could be traced to a single source.

In 1670, the Duke of Buckingham fell from favor at
Charles II's court. In his disgrace, he retired to North
Riding in Yorkshire and established a pack of hounds
solely devoted to hunt fox. If the vigorous, robust duke
offended His Majesty the King, he pleased subsequent
generations of foxhunters, all of whom owe him a debt.
Until Buckingham's time, packs hunted stag, otter, and
hare somewhat indiscriminately.

The Duke of Buckingham, a fashionable man as most
Buckinghams were and still are, prompted his contemporaries Lord Monmouth and Lord Grey to specialize in
foxhunting down in Sussex. These gentlemen began to

study their quarry and to consider, intelligently, the best type of hound to hunt such a wily foe.

Thomas, Sixth Lord Fairfax, born in 1693, drew inspiration from this older generation of Englishmen. He lived a long life, dying in 1781, and he kept good records concerning his hounds. Lord Fairfax also had the wit to repair to Virginia in 1748, where he had been granted an estate of 5 million acres—the Northern Neck. The entire Northern Neck between the Potomac and Rappahannock Rivers was his backyard. And he brought his passion for foxhounds with him. Young George Washington hunted with Fairfax, his cousin Col. William Fairfax, and the Colonel's son, George William Fairfax. When George William Fairfax married the enchanting Sally Fairfax, young Washington fell in love with her, an unrequited love. But foxhunting repaid his passion by giving Washington a lifetime of pleasure.

Then, as now, foxhunting imparted a certain social cachet, and men eager to rise found a good pack of hounds was one way to do so. Ripe arguments continually erupted about who had the best hounds. Some argued for the French Bleu hound; others said the large Kerry beagle was best for the New World. The black and tan had many admirers, and any white hound was always claimed to go back to the medieval kennels of King Louis of France.

Out of this mix came an American hound much like the American human: tough, quick, filled with remarkable drive to succeed. The American hound was of lighter weight than his English and French brothers. His clear voice could be heard in the virgin forests covering Virginia and Maryland even if he couldn't be seen, and this remains a prime virtue of the American hound.

The Revolutionary War slowed down the remarkable progress that had been made up to that point. After

1781, foxhunters returned to their passion—a passion undimmed even at the dawn of the twenty-first century.

When Sister took over as the fifth master in the hunt's history she was grateful that she inherited a great pack and she didn't have to start from scratch. She knew her hound history. She simply had to be reasonably intelligent so as not to screw up Double H's original plan.

The home fixtures—Roughneck Farm, Foxglove, Mill Ruins, After All, and Beveridge Hundred—nourished the diverse creatures who had been living there since before the white man settled in Virginia in 1607. Decent soil, a wealth of underground and overground water, and the protection of the Blue Ridge Mountains a few miles west conspired to make this a kind of heaven on earth.

Not even a hot, muggy, buggy day like today diminished the glory of the place. Each and every resident believed that she or he lived in God's country. To make it even sweeter, most of them liked one another. And those few who qualified as flaming assholes were appreciated for providing ripe comment and amusement for the others.

As Sister's mother used to say, "Nobody's worthless. They can always serve as a horrible example."

One such specimen was just puttering down the road.

Alice Ramy stopped her Isuzu truck with a lurch. The four workers sitting under the chestnut tree looked up, composing their features so as not to look discomfited at the lady's arrival.

Alice's unhappiness seeped through every pore, marring her pleasant features.

"Sister, if you or your hounds come near my chickens I am taking out a warrant!"

Alice delivered this message at least twice a year. It was usually the pretext for something else.

"Now Alice, my hounds have never so much as glanced at your fine chickens."

"No, but that damned dog of Peter Wheeler's killed three of them. Dog should have followed Peter to the grave."

Rooster, Peter's harrier, had chased Aunt Netty, an especially fast and sneaky fox, into and then out of Alice's chicken pen. But poor Rooster—the pen door slammed shut and he was stuck with the corpses of two Australorp chickens. Netty, a small fox, dragged off the other one. No easy task since the beautiful black chickens were quite plump.

"Hello, Mrs. Ramy." Shaker smiled.

"Mrs. Ramy." Doug touched his head with his forefinger in greeting.

Doug, skin color that of coffee with cream, was experimenting with long, thick sideburns.

"Alice, good to see you," Walter lied convincingly.

"Hmmph." Alice's reply sounded like a balloon deflating.

"You know, Alice, we're building coops here. We could build one for you." Sister's eyes brightened.

"Ha! Don't you dare set one foot on my land."

"How about a hoof?" Sister felt mischievous.

"Never."

"Well, Alice, I know you've lost more chickens and I know Peter's harrier hasn't been off my farm. Now just what or who do you think is dispatching your chickens?"

Alice generally ignored what she didn't wish to hear, and she did so now. Unbeknownst to her, Aunt Netty was sauntering through the hayfield at that very moment. When she heard Alice's strident voice she stopped to listen.

Aunt Netty thought Alice a pluperfect fool because

she shut her chicken yard gate but she never poured concrete along the edges of the pen. Digging under was a cinch. Netty considered the Ramy residence one big supermarket.

Strolling down the fence line from the opposite direction was Comet, a gray fox, Inky's brother. He, too, stopped when he caught a whiff of the nearby humans.

"You'll say anything to hunt!" Alice curled her lip, heavily impacted with hot pink lipstick.

"Of course, Alice, I'm a master." Sister laughed, but good-naturedly.

She'd known Alice most of her life and while she had never really liked the woman, she'd grown accustomed to her.

Alice put her hands on her rounded hips. "I know what you all are thinking. I know what everyone is thinking. You think Guy killed Nola. He didn't."

"I don't think that for a minute, Alice. Sit down here on the grass with us and have a Co-Cola." Sister reached into the cooler and handed an ice-cold can to Alice, who accepted the Coke but not the seat.

Aunt Netty's ears swept forward when she heard the pop of the can's pull tab. She liked sweets, considering Coke a sweet. She wondered if she could open the cooler when the humans returned to their coops. Might even be doughnuts or brownies in that cooler. Wouldn't hurt to look.

"Well, a lot of people did." Alice's voice softened. "But you didn't. I remember, you didn't."

A slight breeze rolled down over the mountainside, causing the leaves to sway. The old chestnut tree was so huge, Alice was sheltered in its shade even standing yards away from the workers.

Walter spoke in his most soothing baritone, which could be hypnotic. "Mrs. Ramy, finding Nola has shocked everyone. With the advancements of forensic science, we might learn more now."

"What good does it do?" Alice betrayed more anguish than she wanted.

"I don't know." Sister stood up and put her arm around Alice's shoulder, patting her. "Maybe it will bring peace to Tedi and Edward."

"Well, it won't bring peace to me. No one will believe me unless Guy is found. People think he's in"—she shook her head—"Berlin or Quito or"—her tone darkened—"in this county I hear everything. And I know plenty of people think Paul covered up for Guy. If Guy had killed her, Paul would have brought him in. His own son." Alice finally decided to sit down.

"I believe he would," Sister replied.

"Has Ben Sidell visited you?" Walter asked.

"Yes. Impertinent. Ohio." She uttered "Ohio" as if it were a communicable disease.

"Good farms there." Sister wished she could think of something to say to make Alice feel better and to go away.

"If they're so damned good, then let those people go back to them. He accused me of covering for my son. Oh, not in so many words, but that's what he meant. I should have knocked him down." She drank her Coke in five big gulps.

Comet crouched down, slinking through the hay, and nearly bumped right into Aunt Netty.

He giggled.

"*Hush.*" Aunt Netty glared at him.

Comet did stop giggling, but he still had a silly grin on his face. Reds thought they were superior to grays. Comet, a gray, couldn't have cared less but he did respect Aunt Netty. Her speed and tricks were legendary among foxes.

"He's been calling on all of us, even people who were children back in '81," Sister said.

"I don't know any more today than I did that September. I never saw Guy again after that Saturday. Never." She breathed in deeply. "Why can't the past stay in the past?"

"Never does," Sister simply said.

"You lost a son and a husband. We're both all alone." Alice blurted this out. "Nobody cares what happens to old women."

"Now, now, Mrs. Ramy, people do care. They do." Walter was gallant. "And raking up the past, well, it sets teeth on edge. Don't worry about what people say. They love to talk, don't they? And the sillier they are, the more they gossip. And furthermore, Mrs. Ramy, you don't look your age. Don't call yourself an old lady." His voice conveyed sympathy and warmth.

"Damn right!" Alice stood up, brushed off the back of her khaki Bermuda shorts. "You know, Jane Arnold, I could never for the life of me imagine why you'd want to be master of the hunt. Too much work and too much danger. But now I know why you do it." She walked away a step. "You're surrounded by such handsome men." With that she climbed over the fence and drove off.

Shaker ran his hand through his auburn curls. "Her elevator doesn't go all the way to the top."

"I'd better call on her in a day or two," Sister said.

"Why?" Doug asked, feeling that Sister had been kind enough.

"Because she's alone."

"She brought it on herself, poor thing," Walter quietly said, and without rancor.

"We all pretty much make the bed we lie in. Or is it lay in?" Sister held up her hand. "Isn't grammar a bitch? Anyway, she is a neighbor. This is awful for her, too. And who knows, maybe I'll get us the right to pass through her farm."

"Spoken like a true master," Walter said, laughing as he headed back to the coop.

The two coops faced each other from opposite sides of the dirt farm road. During a hunt it was great fun to jump one, canter across the road, and sail over the other. However, some horses would jump out of the hayfield, their hooves would touch the dirt road, and they'd suck back. If the rider didn't squeeze hard with his or her legs, the horse might refuse the next coop, which meant horses behind would stack up with dolorous results.

Some would fuss because they were ready to jump and the nervous humans messed up their rhythm. Others would think to themselves that this must be quite a scary situation if Old Paint up front had chickened out.

Sister, who also being field master led the field, could never resist slowing a bit to look over her shoulder to see who made it and who didn't. The results would provoke a stream of laughter back in the tack room or in the kennel as she, Shaker, and Doug finished up the chores of the day. Not that the master herself hadn't supplied laughter and comment over the years. That's part of the appeal of foxhunting. Sooner or later, you'll make a spectacle of yourself.

As the humans returned to their task, Aunt Netty and Comet crept over to the cooler. Netty used her nose to pop the lid right up. Both foxes peered into the ice-filled container.

"*No brownies,*" Aunt Netty mourned.

"*Pack of Nabs.*" Comet spied the little pack of orange crackers beloved by Southerners and loathed by everyone else.

"*What's wrong with people?*" Aunt Netty moaned.

"*This should be full of sandwiches, brownies, chocolate chip cookies!*"

"*Lazy. They're getting lazy as sin,*" the young gray concurred with her negative assessment.

"*I don't know what this world is coming to. Why, there used to be a time, young one, when those two-legged idiots would charge off on the hunt, we'd send someone to keep them busy, while the rest of us would raid their trailers. Hamper baskets full of ham biscuits, corn bread, cinnamon buns, fried chicken.*"

"*Aren't things still like that when they have tailgates?*" Comet inquired.

"*Sometimes. But, you see, women work now. In the old days more stayed home, so the food was better. That's my analysis of the situation. Actually it's my husband's, who as you know is inclined to theorize.*" She eyed the pack of Nabs. "*I'm not eating those things.*"

"*I will.*" Comet reached in and flipped out the cellophane-wrapped crackers.

Walter, nailing the last board in place, a top board over the peak of the coop, looked up. He whispered, "Tallyho."

Sister stopped and turned to look. "Aha. Aunt Netty. That gray with her is out of last year's litter on my farm."

"*They see us.*" Comet picked up the crackers.

"*Let them look all they want. Can't very well chase us. I'm telling you, a praying mantis can run faster than a human being. My God they are slow. Makes you wonder how they survived.*" She slapped the cracker pack out of Comet's mouth. "*Open that pack and eat it. Give them a show.*"

"*Okay.*" Comet tore open the crackers and gobbled them down.

"Aunt Netty, I know that's you." Sister shook her finger at the red fox.

"*So?*" Aunt Netty laughed.

"I'm going to chase you this fall," Sister promised.

Shaker and Doug stopped work to watch the two foxes.

"Reds and grays don't much fraternize, means the game's good. Plenty for them to eat, so they might as well be friends," Shaker noted.

"*You can chase me until the Second Coming. You will never catch me, Sister Jane,*" Netty taunted.

Comet swallowed the last of the Nabs. "*Jeez, these things are salty. And I can't open a can.*"

"*Me neither. Put an ice cube in your mouth and let it melt. That will help. Now you see what I mean—a cheap old pack of Nabs when it could have been fried chicken. Just terrible. Standards have fallen.*"

Comet did as he was told.

"*I'm going closer. Give them a thrill.*"

Comet couldn't talk because he had an ice cube in his mouth, but he watched as Aunt Netty sashayed to within twenty yards of Sister and Walter. She stared at them for a moment, then leapt straight up in the air as though catching a bird. When she landed she rolled over and scooted back into the hay. Comet, too, disappeared into the hay and headed back to his den above Broad Creek, which traversed many farms on its way to spilling into the Rockfish River.

"She's a pistol," Walter said, slapping his leg.

"Fastest damned fox. Not the prettiest. That pathetic brush of hers looks more like a bottlebrush," Sister said, laughing, too.

"When I first started hunting with you, I didn't really believe you could identify the foxes. But you can. They're all different from one another."

"And she's sassy. She's not happy unless she has people flying off horses like pinballs spinning out of a pinball machine. She likes to hear them hit the ground." Sister giggled.

Shaker was picking up the leftover wood bits. "Well, we recognize them as individuals and they recognize us. She came right on up to you to give you a show." He tossed the wood fragments in a five-gallon kelly green plastic bucket.

"That she did." Sister picked up the wood bits at her coop. "The gray looked healthy."

"Lot of people don't like running a gray," Doug said.

"I love getting on a gray. Love to start my puppies on a gray," Sister enthusiastically said, her voice rising a little. "They'll give you a good run—but in circles or figure eights. More contained. For the young ones, that's a help." She thought for a moment. "You know, cubbing is harder than formal hunting in the sense that you've got to give the youngsters, hounds, and foxes positive experiences. The leaves are on trees and shrubs. It's difficult to see. More to handle, I guess is what I'm trying to say. Kind of like the preseason in football."

"Still can't believe she came up here like that."

"Alice?" Doug spoke.

"No, Aunt Netty." Walter took the extra planks, unplaned oak, heavy, and slipped them on the back of the pickup.

"A lot more pleasant than Alice." Shaker dropped his hammer into his tool belt. "Alice never was strong on social skills and they're really rusty now."

A loud moo and the appearance of a large Holstein heifer, her calf in tow, captured their attention.

"That damned cow." Shaker took off his ball cap, wiping his brow with his forearm.

"I'll walk them back." Sister reached in the bed of the pickup, retrieving a small bucket of grain kept there for just such events.

"I'll walk with you," Walter eagerly volunteered.

"Best offer I've had in years." She smiled.

"When you two are done flirting, tell me, boss, how do you propose to get home?"

"You're going to pick us up at Cindy's barn in a half hour."

Shaker nodded in agreement as he and Doug climbed into the old Chevy pickup.

"Come on, Clytemnestra. Come on, Orestes," Sister called, shaking the bucket enticingly.

Clytemnestra followed and kept pushing Sister for the bucket. Once on the woody path, Walter broke off a thin branch and used it as a switch. Orestes stuck with his fat mother. Both were terribly spoiled and mischievous.

Out of the woods, they passed the lovely schoolhouse that Foxglove Farm's owner, Cindy Chandler, had restored.

"Can't keep this cow in. She opens gates, crashes fences. Bovine wanderlust." Sister slapped Clytemnestra's wet nose as the cow nudged her again.

"Picture of health."

"Raymond and I used to run cattle. Very cyclical business. Don't know if I'll ever go back to it."

They walked in silence for a while, punctuated only by Clytemnestra's mooish comments, the loud swish of her tail.

"Do you think Guy killed Nola?" Walter asked. He'd been in his teens at the time and remembered little of it.

"No."

"It's strange. On the one hand I'm glad Nola was found and on the other I'm not." Walter took the bucket from Sister, handing her the switch.

"I think we all feel that way. I try not to trouble myself with things out of my control," Sister said. "I can't do anything about the past, but maybe I'll be able to do something to help."

"Count me in." Walter growled at Clytemnestra, who balked at going back through her pasture gate.

"I do count on you, Walter. I do."

CHAPTER 8

Roger's Corner, a white frame convenience store, commanded the crossroads of Soldier Road, the road heading west from town, and White Cat Road, an old wagon road heading north and south. Far in the distance, a thin turquoise line rimmed the mountains. A first-quarter moon accompanied by a red star hovered above the last bright strip of twilight.

Roger, now in his middle forties, ate too much of his own pizza heated in a revolving infrared glass case. On the shelves, Snickers, Cheez-Its, Little Debbie cakes, and Entenmann's chocolate-covered doughnuts vied with bags of charcoal, ammunition, hunting knives. In the coolers, handmade sandwiches—including Roger's famous olive cream cheese on whole wheat—enticed folks to stop. If they hadn't tanked up in town, they pretty much had to stop at Roger's, because gas was hard to find in these parts. The next pump was over the Blue Ridge Mountains in Waynesboro.

The outside floodlights hummed in the night air accompanied by the flutter of saturniid moths and the buzz of many bugs, a few zapped by the lights themselves. A long sign, ROGER'S CORNER, white with well-proportioned red block letters, ran almost the entire length of the roof. Roger might never achieve his fifteen minutes of Warholian fame in the world at large, but his sign announced his presence emphatically in these parts.

Shaker Crown, his Orioles baseball cap pulled up off his forehead, worn out from the day's work and not much of a cook, leaned over the counter.

Henry Xavier, owner of the largest insurance company in town, had stopped by on his way home as had Ralph Assumptio, owner of the John Deere tractor dealership. Both men had farms on this west side of the county that were part of Jefferson Hunt territory and both men hunted with Sister. Most members didn't say they hunted with the Jefferson Hunt. They'd simply say, "I hunt with Sister Jane."

By so doing, they found out instantly if the person to whom they were talking knew anything about local society. If they were met with a blank they would graciously add, "the Jefferson Hunt." It was one of those little pride things like the way members of Green Springs Valley Hounds outside of Baltimore never discussed how big their jumps were. They shrugged and would say about their horse, "Oh, he got over nicely." Green Springs Valley Hounds, founded in 1892, boasted some stiff fences. It was not a hunt for the fainthearted, but such details were never explained, simply announced.

All groups cherish their ceremonies of togetherness, rituals that prove them set apart and special.

"Where's your chew?" Roger was ringing up Shaker's sandwich.

"Um . . ."

"Here it is. You left it on top of the Twinkies." Henry Xavier, known only as Xavier, picked up the neat round tin of Copenhagen Black and handed it to Shaker.

"Ah, thanks." Shaker tapped his head. "Vapor lock."

Ralph joined them, banging on the counter the gallon

of milk his wife had told him to pick up. "Day wasn't fit
for man nor beast."

"We built new coops over there at Foxglove. And it
was hateful."

"Thank God." Ralph lovingly stared at the round can
of chew in Shaker's hand. "Damn, I wish I hadn't promised Frances I'd give that up."

"Guess who showed up to bitch out Sister?" Shaker
asked as he pulled soggy bills out of his pocket, gently
peeling a fiver off the wad.

"Crawford," Xavier offered.

"On a mission," Roger simply said.

"Mission impossible." Xavier smiled as the others
laughed.

"That jumped-up jackass really believes we'll elect
him joint-master." Ralph put his milk back in the cooler
because he sensed this might be a ripening chat.

"Hey, if he dumps enough money into the club, who
knows?" Xavier's heavy brows, black with some gray,
shot upward. "Money papers over many sins."

"Sins I can handle. But he lacks the imagination to be a
sinner. He's just a Yankee jackass," Ralph said as he
walked back from the cooler.

"Aren't they all?" Shaker winked.

"I was born in Connecticut." Xavier smiled. He was a
genial man becoming portly. In this heat he favored seer-
sucker shirts, which somehow made him look fatter, not
thinner.

"Oh, Xavier, you were raised here. Don't turn P.C. on
us." Roger slapped at him over the counter.

"Well, do you guys want to know who rolled down
the road or not?"

"Shoot," Xavier said.

"Alice Ramy."

"What did she want?" Ralph couldn't stand it any

longer; he grabbed a tin of Skoal menthol chew, pulled the string around it, and with delight placed a pinch between his lip and his gum. He closed his teeth in contentment.

"Oh, the usual. Got up in Janie's face and said we couldn't hunt there and she'd loose the hounds of hell on us"—Shaker enjoyed his little reference to hounds—"and that Peter's harrier better stay out of her chicken coop, wait, make that her golden chicken coop."

"And Sister smiled through it all," Ralph said.

"And that's why Crawford Howard can't ever be a joint-master. His ego would be in the way. He'd fire back at the old battle-ax or buy up all the land around her and choke her out. Son of a bitch." Xavier knew a good deal about Crawford's local business dealings since he insured many of them. He hated Crawford, but business was business.

"True." Roger clasped his hands. "But you guys need a joint-master so Sister can train him to her ways. She can't live forever."

"She might come close," Shaker said with a laugh. "She was throwing around oak boards today like a thirty-year-old. Tough as nails, the old girl is."

"Don't make 'em like that anymore." Xavier admired Sister. After all, he'd hunted in the field with her when he was a boy. She'd been in her forties then.

"I kind of felt sorry for Alice," Shaker continued. "Guess Ben Sidell got her knickers in a knot. She felt he accused her of covering up for Guy, and you know, the whole ugly mess is flaring up all over again. Sister was real good about it. Said she'd call on her. I couldn't take it that far, but I do feel kind of bad for Alice."

"Alice doesn't make it any easier, and I should know," Ralph said, and shook his head. He was Alice's nephew; his mother was Alice's sister. "Everything has to be her way. If you take a can of beer out of her refrigerator, she opens the door behind you to make sure you didn't disturb the other cans lined up inside. You can't smoke a whole cigarette but what she whisks the ashtray and dumps the ashes. Jesus, Mary, and Joseph, she'll run you crazy. And now she's out of control. At least when Paul was alive he'd make fun of her and snap her out of it."

"Women dry up," Xavier simply stated.

"And men get sentimental," Roger, a sharp observer of folks, said. He reached for a brew. "Anyone? On me?"

"Thanks." Xavier accepted a cold can of Bud while Roger reached for an import, Sol.

"People dry up if they aren't tended to. I'm kind of worried about myself," Shaker joked.

"I don't want to hear, 'There are no women out there.'" Xavier punched him. "Clean up, get out, and start looking."

"Did Ben call on you?" Ralph asked Roger.

"Sure."

"Me too." Xavier sighed.

"Hasn't gotten to me yet," Shaker added. "I was hired on as a whipper-in that year. What a year."

"Give Ben credit. He's going over the file and questioning every name he finds in there. I talked to him." Roger liked the aftertaste the crisp Sol beer left in his mouth. He liked Mexican beers. "Guy stopped by here that last night. Bought something. I don't remember what. Dad was behind the counter. I was helping to unload the Coca-Cola truck."

"You had muscles then," Xavier teased him.

"Still do. They're protected by this layer of fat."

"You'll never have that problem," Xavier, also a bit heftier than in his running days, commented to Shaker.

"Most huntsmen stay pretty lean, takes a lean hound for a long race and a lean huntsman, too. Although I know one or two fat huntsmen. Pity the horse."

"Ever notice how a lot of fat people are really light on their feet?" Xavier thought about a copy of *Men's Health* magazine he'd seen on the rack at Barnes & Noble. A fellow in swim trunks was on the cover, his abs rippled like the proverbial six-packs. Xavier made a mental note to buy the magazine. He was standing around looking at his buddies, and except for Shaker they looked like overweight middle-aged men.

"I don't want to see it," Ralph blurted out.

"See what?" Xavier asked.

"The grave. The grave over at After All."

"Ralph, what made you think of that?" Shaker noticed how white Ralph's face had turned.

"First day of cubbing. We'll probably leave from the kennels, and if the fox heads east we could wind up over there, and I don't want to see that grave. Every time I think about Nola I get sick. I mean it."

A silence followed.

Roger broke it. "Me too."

"Ditto," Xavier sighed.

"I guess when the sheriff is done with the bones, he'll give them back to the Bancrofts," Shaker said.

"And that's another thing—all this bullshit about forensic science," Ralph exploded. "Nola's been in that dirt tomb for twenty-one years. They aren't going to find squat. You know why you hear so much about pathology and this miracle and that miracle? Because any law enforcement officer can tell you, murder is damned easy to pull off. So if you create this propaganda about how you can be convicted from one strand of hair, people believe it. I suppose it deters the weak-willed. I don't know much, but I can tell you those lab coat dudes aren't going to find much."

"They know her head was crushed," Xavier said. "Ben told me."

"Oh, come on. If we'd dug her up we'd know that, too," Ralph practically spit out. "Do you think he cares? The killer? People kill every day and never give it a second thought. They don't have a conscience. It would eat you or me up alive. But whoever killed Nola"—Ralph pointed his forefinger for emphasis—"walked away and thought he was right, or rid of her, or whatever he thought, but he didn't give a damn."

"I don't believe that," Shaker argued.

"Me neither. Killing a beautiful woman like that would haunt him for the rest of his days," Roger agreed with Shaker.

Xavier tapped his lips with his forefinger, a little stream of air escaping, then he said, "Maybe. Maybe not. If it was Guy, we will never know. Apologies to you, Ralph. I know he was your cousin, but let's just look at this from every angle. If it was Guy, it's done and he's gone. Maybe he'll return someday in old age, confess, repent. I don't know. Stranger things have happened, but if it wasn't Guy, I don't think the man who smashed in the side of her head cares that he killed her. He just cares that he doesn't get caught."

CHAPTER 9

The vents whooshed out cooling air. As Sister plumped up pillows behind her so she could read, she was grateful she'd installed central air-conditioning ten years ago and she wondered why she'd been so stubborn about having it before.

Raleigh slept stretched out on the floor and Rooster was curled up in a nearby doggie bed. Doggie beds liberally dotted the house. Golliwog thought she'd read with Sister, so she sat next to her as Sister opened a recently published history of the Hapsburg Empire. She didn't expect to find a mention of the sapphire, but she used the index to find the times Elizabeth's name appeared. As this was a scholarly work the tone was dry. She picked up the notebook she always kept beside her bed on the nightstand and wrote down to find a good biography of the last empress of the Austro-Hungarian Empire.

The phone rang at nine-fifteen, which meant it was an old friend. No one else dared call after nine in the evening since Sister retired early and rose before sunup.

It was Shaker, and he told her about Ralph's squeamishness about seeing Nola's grave while cubbing.

"Actually, Shaker, it probably isn't a good idea to go over there. I'm glad you called my attention to it. How was Ralph?"

"Seemed a little jumpy."

71

"He loved Nola."

"I remember that was how I figured out Ron Haslip was gay—he didn't have a crush on Nola." Shaker laughed, mentioning a hunt club member they all liked who, after years of pretending otherwise, finally came out.

"Guess you're right. A man would have to have been homosexual or dead not to have responded to her."

"Xavier warned me that Crawford's up to his tricks."

"I'll just bet he is." She pressed her lips together. "Hey, it's supposed to be bloody hot again tomorrow. Let's not walk out hounds with horses. Tell Doug. We can start up day after tomorrow—six, six-thirty in the morning. Let's try to beat the heat. Anyway, I could use tomorrow to catch up on my errands."

Doug, as professional whipper-in, was responsible for the staff horses, so he needed to know the schedule change.

"One more day won't hurt them." Shaker meant the horses. "Do you want to walk out on foot in the evening?"

"Tell you what, let's just give everyone a rest. I'll call Betty. We could all use a day off."

She hung up, then dialed Betty, who was madly clicking away on her channel surfer, furious that she and Bobby paid money for a satellite dish with 128 channels and there wasn't one damn thing worth watching. Betty, too, was glad for a day off.

Sister then picked up her book again, but the pages soon blurred. She hadn't realized how tired she was from working in the blistering heat all day. She turned out the light as Golly artfully arranged herself around Sister's head.

"Golly, will you settle down."

"Then stop hogging the pillow," the cat complained, but she did stop wiggling.

The memory of Aunt Netty cutting a shine made Sister giggle. Then she thought about Alice's distress and a pang of guilt shot through her for disliking Alice. She remembered that Guy's nickname was Hotspur. She thought of Henry Hotspur, Sir Henry Percy, the bold supporter of Henry IV of England.

She opened her eyes. "Damn."

"Now what's the matter?" Golly shifted.

"Golly, will you stop crabbing?" Raleigh rolled over onto his other side.

Rooster, snoring, missed the exchange.

"When something pops into my head like that, it's leading somewhere." She sat upright, which irritated Golly. "Am I trolling the depths of my subconscious? Do I even have one? I ask you animals, is there a subconscious or is it a human invention? And if I have one, you have one. We aren't that far apart."

"Glad you recognize that." Golly moved to the other pillow. She knew when Sister's brain clicked on she'd be up and down half the night writing notes in her book.

"Gang, I don't know about a subconscious, but I do know about memories. You either remember something or you don't. Repressed memories are something lawyers use to get criminals off scot-free. But there is imagination. Indeed. And Henry Hotspur is riding right at me, right out of Shakespeare's imagination and my own. I think he's got a message. I hope I can figure it out." She clicked on the light, making a few notes.

"Why do humans read?" Raleigh asked.

"To cure insomnia," Golly replied.

CHAPTER 10

As Sister settled in for the night, Athena started hunting. *Bubo virginianus,* great horned owl, her scientific and English name, cared little what she was called.

She was the queen of the night, and all other creatures need listen to her. If anyone challenged her supremacy she'd fly away as though in a huff, her wingspan seeming to cast a shadow even at night. Athena would then turn and silently strike the offender from behind; her balled-up talons could crack a skull. She feared no one. All feared her.

At two feet tall and nearly five pounds in weight, she could vanish in the blink of one of her golden eyes. How such a large creature could do this mystified other creatures. Like the goddess to whom she was sacred, Athena could appear and disappear at will.

Her cry, easily identified, was a deep, musical hoo, hoo-hoo, hoo-hoo. Sometimes she would vary the sequence and send out three low hoos. But her cry was distinctive and bore little resemblance to the barred owl's or the long-eared owl's, other hoo singers. Humans close to nature could tell the difference. Country people knew her song and her value to them. Athena rid them of raiders, rodents. Her worth was beyond rubies.

Other owls admired her and many wished they had her song. The short-eared owl emitted a little squeak.

The barn owl, thick in these parts and also a friend to farmers, hissed or snapped her bill.

The only owl not intimidated by Athena's sonorous voice was the screech owl, who would sing to her heart's content and the misery of all around her. Only ten inches high, this reddish or gray little thing could crank out a volume that was most impressive. And she hardly limited herself to a bloodcurdling screech that scared the urine right out of city folks visiting the country. No, she could purr, trill, pitch high, then run down the scale to a lower register. When feeling marvelous—"mahvalous," as she might say—she even provided tremolo.

Her sturdy ego meant that she, too, had no fear. In fact, a sly delight filled her when "visitors," meaning city folk, shivered at her concert. She'd then fly close to them, putting on a display of fierceness that usually made one of these two-legged twits cry, "Rabies."

As if she would ever get rabies. Puh-lease!

Already full from hunting, the screech owl sat in the old orchard by Roughneck Farm and hollered to her heart's content. The hounds couldn't shut her up.

Shaker and Doug, secure in air-conditioning in their separate quarters, could hear an occasional high note.

Bitsy, as she was known, rather hoped she could entice the hounds to sing with her. Sometimes one would lift his head and start a note, one or two others would follow or honor, the correct term, and within a minute the entire kennel would join her in ribald chorus.

They were really saying, *"Bitsy, shut up, for God's sake."* But the little brown owl thought she was the diva and they were her chorus in this great opera of life.

"Bitsy, do shut up."

Bitsy complied this time as this request came from Athena, who had landed on a branch opposite her. The

screech owl knew in her heart that Athena was jealous—
after all, the other owls never challenged her in song
contests—but Athena was Athena, so Bitsy shut up.
"Hello. I didn't hear you."

"Of course not, you idiot. You make such a racket."
Athena fluffed out her feathers, appearing even more
grand.

"It's such a beautiful night. And I have dined on deli-
cious mice this evening. Full of corn they were, raiding
the barns. So sweet and crunchy."

"Me too," Athena replied. She smoothed out her feathers. *"Come with me."*

Bitsy, thrilled to be asked to accompany the queen herself, spread her strong little wings and lifted off, flying
just to Athena's right.

Both birds noiselessly soared through the sky, passing
through the fragrant orchard where the apples hung
gathering sweetness for a fall harvest. Beneath them a
large pasture bisected by the dusty farm road appeared,
the grasses swaying in the light breeze. They climbed upward, heading north over copses hugging the creek beds
below. Within ten minutes of leisurely flying they passed
over the fearsome tree on Hangman's Ridge, then de-
scended to the low, narrow fertile valley that ran east to
west. A two-lane paved road, Soldier Road, ran through
this valley. Sister owned the land south of Soldier Road.
Foxglove Farm, the land north of Soldier Road, had been
in the Chandler family since 1803.

The animals knew where the human boundaries were,
but they looked at the land in geological terms. The long,
thin valley, cultivated fields, on which Soldier Road was
built, was the pinkie finger of a tiny glacier splinter that
had veered off from the main push so long ago, humans
weren't even around here to write about it.

Parked along the side of the road, facing west, not two

miles from Roger's Corner, Ralph Assumptio sat in his Toyota Land Cruiser. The motor was cut off.

Athena and Bitsy landed in a poplar by Broad Creek. Steep and fed by runoff from the Blue Ridge Mountains, the creek crossed the road below Hangman's Ridge at a diagonal. During hard, persistent rains, it often jumped its bed, spreading muddy waters over the low areas and in the worst of rains rising to drown the roadbed.

Ralph, his head in his hands, elbows on the steering wheel, was sobbing his heart out.

"It's never good when a man cries," Bitsy murmured.

"Mmm." Athena's gorgeous eyes opened wider, movement in the creek bed making her alert.

Inky, having eaten an early supper, was on her way to play at the kennels. Her den was by the walnut at cornfield's edge, a mile from the kennel if one could fly. Inky liked chatting with Diana and she liked sitting under the apple trees, too.

She noticed the Land Cruiser. SUVs reminded her of large hercules beetles. Curiosity aroused, she walked closer, then stopped when she saw the two owls in the poplar. She softly padded over to them instead. She could hear Ralph's sobs.

"Does he need help?" the glossy young fox asked.

"Not that we can supply," Athena said.

"Should we wait until he leaves, just to make sure?" Inky, a kindhearted animal, wondered.

"Let's examine the situation." Athena puffed out her chest. *"A man, alone, is pulled off to the side of the road, a road not heavily traveled except on the way to work and when they come home. He's not drunk and he's not sick. I can always smell sickness."* This was uttered with great authority.

"Wife left him," Bitsy said.

"*Could be, but he's reputed to have a good marriage,*" Athena said.

"*And it's not money. Ralph's smart that way,*" Inky said.

Indeed, Ralph was smart that way. He had graduated from Hamilton College in New York, then come back to Virginia to the university's Darden School of Business. He took a job at the local John Deere dealership and wound up buying it in his mid-thirties. Now in his forties, he owned dealerships throughout Virginia. He was rumored to have a silent partner, but no one knew who that might be. Some people thought the silent partner concept was jealousy, because Ralph came up on his own. A small percentage of people can't stand to be shown up by anyone. Ralph was a handy target for the stupid or lazy. He let them talk while he kept working— and making money.

"*Maybe he's received some kind of bad news, a friend is ill or someone that he loved died.*" Bitsy turned her head nearly upside down thinking about it.

"*Nola,*" Athena said.

"*Ah, all the men his age loved her, didn't they? That's what I hear.*" And Bitsy heard quite a lot sitting in trees or on a crossbeam in a hayloft.

Ralph coughed, snuffled loudly, coughed again, and wiped his eyes. He spit out the open car window. He wiped his eyes again, then reached into the glove compartment, pulling out a white aspirin bottle. He popped three into his mouth, swallowing them without water. He turned on the engine and drove off.

"*Been almost a week since she was found. Why is he crying now?*" Inky thought it strange.

"*Maybe it's just hitting him,*" Bitsy opined.

"*No,*" Athena crisply replied. "*It's worse than that.*"

They sat there for another fifteen minutes chatting, then the two owls flew toward the Chandler barn.

Inky crossed the road, trotted up Hangman's Ridge, and walked along the flat ridge toward the huge old tree, well over three hundred years old.

A whisper drew her eyes to the tree.

Inky thought she saw a ghost, a man in his mid-thirties dressed in fine clothes although his neck had been unnaturally stretched and his tongue hung out.

" 'For I do not do the good I want, but the evil I do not want is what I do.' Romans, chapter twelve, verse nine." His anguish was palpable.

Inky knew spirits existed. Just like Hamlet told Horatio, there were more things in heaven and earth than we knew, but that didn't mean she wanted any part of them.

She raced back toward her den, deciding not to visit Diana tonight. A whippoorwill disturbed by her passing let out its characteristic call.

She dashed into her den, snuggling in the fresh hay she'd lined there.

"How sad humans are," she thought to herself. *"They hurt others and they hurt themselves and their misery flows down through the centuries. Maybe there really is original sin for them."* She closed her eyes and prayed to God, who, for her, looked like a beautiful gray fox. *"Thank you, dear God, thank you for making me a fox."*

CHAPTER 11

"I've always loved this spot, but now . . ." Sybil's voice trailed off. Tears rolled down her cheek.

"Honey, try not to think about it." Ken Fawkes thought that idea comforting, but it was impossible for either of them not to stare at the newly packed earth and not think about where Nola had lain for two decades and one year.

"When we were little girls, we'd sit up there, where Peppermint is buried now, and we'd look back over the creek and the meadows. I loved this time of year because it was cooler here and the cornflowers bloomed. Nola's eyes were cornflower blue. She said I had iris eyes. Most times they're pale blue, so that was nice of her." Sybil sobbed harder.

Ken wrapped his arms around her, resting his chin on her head. "You have lavender eyes. The most beautiful eyes I've ever seen."

"Ken, what do we do now?"

He couldn't answer right off. "Well, we keep on keeping on."

"Did you notice Mother wearing the sapphire?"

"Yes."

"I asked her why. She said she'd made a promise. The sapphire would remind her to keep it."

A horsefly buzzed near Ken's head, then moved away

as he slapped at it, releasing his grasp on his wife. "Bad luck, that ring."

Sybil smoothed her glossy hair. "I wonder. Maybe we just invest objects with our emotions. They're neutral."

"Well, don't you wear that goddamned ring."

"Don't worry. I won't." She noticed color coming up on his cheeks.

Ken stuck his boot toe in the turf, scuffing at it like a petulant child. "Talked to this new sheriff guy who hardly inspires confidence. I'm starting to think if his brains were BBs they'd be rolling around a six-lane highway."

"Paul Ramy must have had one BB, then," Sybil ruefully replied.

"A good ol' boy in the good old days. Shit." Ken grimaced. "Things are supposed to be different. I don't know if this Sidell is able to investigate roadside kill, much less this. The questions he asked me were pointless."

"Twenty-one years. I guess from his standpoint it's not pressing. No one else is in danger. If they were, more blood would have been spilled back in 1981."

"You're right." Ken slapped at another fly. "Biting. Must be rain coming up." He smiled. "Tuesday's a good day for rain. Better now than the weekend."

Domino and Merry Andrew trotted up from the other side of the hill. After nuzzlings and pats on the neck, they left the two humans.

"Ken, I don't think we should let Mom or Dad collect Nola. What's left of her." A dark note of bitterness and loss crept into Sybil's well-modulated voice. "They've been through enough. You and I should go get her. I didn't ask Sidell when they'd release her remains to us."

"Shouldn't be much longer. They photographed the grave, her position in the earth. They'll measure the bones.

Scrape whatever they can scrape and send it to the lab. Guess it will tell them something. I'm not a scientist."

"She was healthy as a horse." Sybil scanned the western sky; a few gray cumulus tops were peeping over the mountains. "The horseflies watched the weather report."

"They always bite before rain." Ken checked his expensive watch, tapping the crystal, a habit. "Still time to call the sheriff today. I'll see if I can make arrangements to get her."

"I think you'd better call the funeral director first."

"Why?"

"I don't think family members can pick up corpses. I think the law is, a funeral director or employee has to do it. I'm pretty sure. You can't just carry her out in a bag."

"No." Ken's voice became a bit indignant. "I was going to get a proper coffin and put her in that. There's nothing but bones. It's not, well, you know . . ."

Sybil acknowledged with a nod that she did know. One doesn't grow up in the country without a good sense of the disintegration of dead things. She knew, intellectually, that buzzards, worms, and beetles had their work to do. Without them the whole earth would be piled miles high with corpses. But why couldn't the Lord have made it a tidier process? The stench alone was horrible. To think of her sister's body decaying in the earth . . . she couldn't. She just couldn't. She struggled to remember her sister's staccato laugh, to snatch at something lovely.

The backfire of an engine drew their attention to the farm lane leading to the covered bridge. Jimmy Chirios coasted over the small rise, the farm truck emitting small puffs of dark smoke.

"That truck burns too much oil." Sybil was glad to switch to another subject.

"Your father refuses to buy a new one."

Edward, despite his wealth, was no more sensible about personal expenditures than the rest of humanity. He would squander money on some things, yet he was tight as a tick about others.

The dark green Dodge rattled across the bridge.

Jimmy pulled up to the couple. "Storm's coming. Heard on the radio. Coming fast. Flash floods."

The minute they hopped into the cab the wind shifted gears. The willows by the creek swayed like geishas.

"You did a good job filling in that . . . the grave," Ken awkwardly thanked the young man.

"Oh." Jimmy couldn't muster a smile even though he was being complimented. The thought of that whole mess upset him deeply. "Why'd they make me wait a week? Nothing else there."

"Can't be too careful." Ken drummed on the edge of the door, his elbow on the armrest. "Cops, I mean."

"Yeah." Jimmy drove them back to the big house. No sooner had Sybil and Ken reached the front door than the first big raindrops splattered across the immaculate lawn.

Sybil called out, "Mom."

"In the den."

They walked into the richly paneled den, a glowing cherry wood, its patina enhanced by age. Moroccan leather-bound volumes—dark blue, red with gold, green, black, saddle-leather tan—filled the shelves. Photographs, some among the very first made in the nineteenth century, also dotted the shelves, each sepia-toned image encased in either its original filigree frame or a plain, sterling silver one. There was so much silver at After All, it could have filled one of the legendary Nevada mines.

Tedi was seated on the chintz sofa, an album spread out before her on the coffee table. Images of Nola in her

Christmas dress, her senior year at Madeira; images of Nola in ratcatcher, reins in hand, Peppermint, young and handsome, by her side; images of Nola at twenty-two, accepting her diploma from Mount Holyoke, where she distinguished herself on the show-jumping team but not in the classroom; images of Nola as maid of honor at Sybil's wedding, and even a photograph of Nola at Opening Hunt in 1980, Guy Ramy in the background staring at her with a big grin on his face. Maybe he did love her. Tedi smiled back from those photographs, too. She was in her twenties, then thirties, forties, fifties, sixties. She remained thin, well groomed, and youngish thanks to excellent plastic surgery.

"Oh, Momma, don't."

Tedi, with steely resolve, said, "I know I missed something. The pictures help. Sit down, both of you."

"I'm all sweaty. Would either of you girls like a drink?" Ken, fearful of a possible emotional outburst, inquired.

"Sweet iced tea and my martini."

Sybil, next to her mother, squeezed her hand. "I remember when I used to think you were so uncool drinking martinis. Now they're all the rage again."

"Cycles. By the time you're my age, you've seen them all."

Within minutes, Ken and Edward joined them, each man handing his wife a drink.

Sybil gratefully tasted her daiquiri, the perfect summer drink, as the rain ramped up to a true downpour. "Mercy. It's really coming down."

Edward, tall and patrician with an aquiline nose, seemed a forbidding presence, yet he was a kind man, a good man. He stared out the window, then back at his remaining daughter. He smiled, taking a sip of his scotch on the rocks. "Feast or famine. It's either drought or a gully washer."

"True," Ken agreed from where he still stood.

"Honey, will you sit down. It's not like there's never been a sweaty man in this room before," Sybil ordered.

He perched on the edge of one of the oversized chairs. "Dad, how about eighteen holes tomorrow? David Wheeler and Pat Butterfield need us to clean out their wallets."

A flicker lit in Edward's eyes. "The money in David's wallet has mold on it."

"You're right. That money needs to see the light of day. Capitalism depends on the circulation of cash. We can take them." Ken's voice was a bit too hearty. "Greens will be slow, too."

"We should. Will you call them?"

"Already did," Ken replied, happy that his father-in-law was evidencing some interest in the outside world.

Privilege and the Fawkes name were not accustomed to each other. Fawkes was the surname of many poor whites in these parts. A few over the centuries had risen, but the name clung to them like a digger bee, wouldn't let go.

Ken's people, hardworking, all attended the Baptist church. The Bancrofts had never and would never set foot in a Baptist church.

Ken had worked his way through North Carolina State, made the football team as a walk-on. He proved so ferocious as outside linebacker that he won a scholarship for his junior and senior years. He majored in business, making respectable grades. He didn't know what he would do exactly. He just wanted to find some type of work he liked and make a decent living. But then he met Sybil and his compass shifted. Making do wouldn't be good enough.

Jealous folks said, "That Ken Fawkes landed in the honey pot."

And he did, no doubt about it. But he was reasonably intelligent. Edward created a niche for him through the Bancroft real estate business in a small local company. Ken started learning the business. He studied the roads, bought near crossroads, and developed subdivisions. Of course, some people said the hardest way to make money was to marry it. Ken never said that.

He exuded an air of masculinity. Women found him very attractive indeed, even though he couldn't be described as classically handsome.

Sybil bent closer to the photo album. "Amazing."

"What, dear?" Tedi thought her tea could use another hit of sugar, although her martini was perfect. "Ken, be a darling and put another spoonful in there for me. I'm having my late-afternoon sinking spell."

"Of course." Ken stood up, took her glass, and left the room for a moment.

"Twenty-five years ago this picture, and Sister looks the same. Her hair's silver now, that's all."

"The outdoor life," Tedi said.

"And you look fabulous yourself, my love." Edward, unlike many men, learned very early in life that you can never compliment a woman—especially your wife—too many times.

"Thank you, dear." Tedi smiled. "But I feel old. I feel, well, let's just say I comprehend vulnerability."

Ken returned with her tea. "Here's your sugar buzz." He looked outside. "Black as the devil's eyebrows."

"Nothing like a summer thunderstorm to make you glad you're inside," Edward said, savoring the distinctive deep sweetness of the scotch.

"I've been thinking." Tedi leaned back on the sofa. "A

ceremony is in order, a commemoration and celebration of Nola's life. We never had one—"

Ken quickly said, "We always hoped."

"Yes." Tedi never liked being interrupted. "That's over now. A service is in order. I've spoken to Reverend Thigpin and I've considered where Nola should have her final resting place."

Edward cleared his throat, waiting. Would Tedi pick the Prescott plot on the Northern Neck near Warsaw, the seat of the first Prescotts, or would she choose the Bancroft private cemetery, here on After All?

"And what have you decided, dear?"

"Let's make a special place, let's build low stone walls around it, plant white lilacs there, too. Love. It must be a place filled with love. Nola loved Peppermint. More than any man, she loved Pepper. I like to think they're hunting now with Ikey Bell carrying the horn." Ikey Bell was a famous huntsman of the early twentieth century.

No one knew what to say.

Finally Sybil broached the subject. "Mom, it's awfully close to where she was found."

"I know. But she had no peace there. She couldn't. She'll have peace with Peppermint. He loved her in life, he'll be with her in death. It's fitting, you see."

Edward stared out at the rain. His hand touched his Adam's apple. "Whatever you want. You know better about these things."

"And let's do all the things that Nola loved. Yes. Let's plant huge blue hydrangeas, and the dwarf kind, too. I say fiddle to snotty gardeners and snotty gardens. Isn't that a nasty word?" She brightened as though a burden had been lifted from her. "Red poppies next to purple iris and mounds of something snowy white. Let's use all the colors Nola loved."

"Cornflower blue." Sybil had tears in her eyes.

"Yes. And you know what she loved more than anything in the world?" The family hung expectantly on Tedi's next word. "Foxhunting!"

CHAPTER 12

The creamy coral of Crawford's Paul Stuart polo shirt reflected warmth on his face. Crawford liked the best. Paul Stuart was an exclusive men's shop on Madison Avenue. If he wasn't shopping there or at Sulka up on Park, he thought nothing of picking up the phone and ordering a dozen shirts from Turnbull and Asser in London, shoes and boots from Lobb, luxurious cashmeres and silks from a dealer in Turin. To his credit, he always looked splendid.

The morning, hazy, promised a muggy day. This July 28, the anniversary of the day Elizabeth's bold men dispersed the Spanish Armada in 1588 and Arthur Wellesley knocked the stuffing out of the French at Talavera in 1809. A student of history and business, he remembered odd dates.

He and Marty had attended early service at Saint Luke's and now he puttered happily in the tack room of his sumptuous stable with its fittings of polished brass, PavSafe floors that cost a fortune, impeccable doors and stall fronts painted deep navy blue, all made by Lucas Equine in Cythiana, Kentucky. His stable colors were navy and red. Many in these parts painted their vehicles in stable colors, or painted a small symbol or name in those colors on the driver's door. Crawford's red Mercedes had BEASLEY HALL in one-inch script, navy blue, painted on the driver's door, plus the car was pin-striped in navy blue.

His cell phone, perched on custom-made tack trunks also in his colors, jingled.

"Crawford here."

"Haslip," came the terse, mocking reply.

Crawford missed that Ronnie Haslip was making fun of him. "How are you?"

"Fine. Two things." Ronnie knew that with Crawford you got the best result by being brief and direct, most emphatically not the Virginia Way. "The hunt club is sponsoring a class at the Fall Classic Horse Show, Thanksgiving weekend this year. We'd like a perpetual trophy—silver, I think. It will cost quite a bit."

"How much?"

"Seven thousand."

"My God, Ronnie, how big is this thing?"

"Well, it's huge. Sterling silver. The kind of stuff they used to do in the 1800s."

"Why is Sister being so grand? Not like her, really."

"It's a secret. She wants us to do it in honor of Nola. The Nola Bancroft Perpetual Trophy, Ladies Over Fences."

"Oh." Crawford thought a moment. "Put me down for three thousand five hundred. That ought to get the ball rolling."

"That is exceedingly generous, Crawford. Not only will Sister be grateful, the Bancrofts will be thrilled, once they know, of course."

"Awful thing."

"Yes. Oh, I just heard that Tedi intends to bury her August tenth at the farm. The club will be attending en masse."

"Naturally." He found this news depressing even though he never knew Nola. Funerals were not Crawford's preferred social activity, but one must play one's part. And he was not an unfeeling man, simply an over-reaching one. "Ronnie, you grew up with Nola. Was she what everyone says?"

"And more." Ronnie laughed. "There was a capriciousness about Nola that was divine, really, unless you were in love with her. Then she'd run you crazy or break your heart."

"Was she aware of what she was doing to people?"

"I always thought she was like those Indian warriors collecting scalps. She'd keep four, five, who knows how many, on a string."

"Sleeping with them?"

"Well . . ." Ronnie didn't want to cast aspersions on any lady, but how could he put this? "Let's just say that Nola was a high-spirited animal with prodigious energy."

"For Christ's sake, Ronnie!"

"She'd have lunch with one fellow, go to a party with another, and home with a third. She was heartless." Ronnie laughed.

"You weren't in love with her?" Crawford couldn't resist this little dig.

"I wasn't rich enough for Nola," came the even reply, as Ronnie refused to rise to the bait.

"Neither was Guy Ramy, from what I hear."

"But he was as beautiful as Nola was. Jet-black curly hair, ice blue eyes, shoulders as wide as Atlas himself. Fearless on a horse. Not the best rider, but fearless."

"That's how he got the nickname Hotspur?"

"Yes and no. I'm assuming you know the life of Sir Henry Percy."

"Of course I do, Ronnie." A note of indignation darkened Crawford's voice. "I graduated Phi Beta Kappa."

Bold, impetuous, strong, Henry Percy was the eldest son of the 1st Earl of Northumberland. Henry was born on May 20, 1364. He was taught to fight like all noble-born boys, displaying a true gift for it. In his early twenties he harried the Scots, who gave him the name Hotspur for his vigorous border patrols.

When Richard II began to show clear signs that he wasn't up to the demands of being king, unrest grew throughout England. Many giggled that Richard would make a better queen than king. Hotspur and his father helped put Henry Bolingbroke on the throne in 1399, who then called himself Henry IV.

Hotspur's daring brought him fame and admiration that perhaps incited a certain jealousy in the king. But Henry IV was no fool. He rewarded Hotspur with lands and offices in northern England and Wales, two places where a strong military leader was necessary.

The Percys demolished the Scots at Humbleton Hill in Durham on September 14, 1402. Henry IV, who was vainly trying to suppress the Welsh, paled by comparison. Henry's ego clouded his usually calculating judgment. He wouldn't allow Hotspur to ransom the Scottish nobles he had captured, a common policy that would have fattened Hotspur's pocketbook as well as the crown's.

To add insult to injury, Henry wouldn't pay the bill for Hotspur's border warfare. Not only was the king jealous, he was cheap.

Furious, Hotspur and his father raised a rebellion to depose the king in 1403. Henry, more clever than the Percys realized, intercepted Hotspur near Shrewsbury before he could join up with his father. Though outnumbered, Hotspur fought like the lion he was but in the end he was beaten, hanged, drawn, and quartered. His violent end came on July 21, at the age of thirty-nine.

"There was always a sense," Ronnie's bass voice intoned, "that Guy would draw his sword against the wrong man."

"Sword as in weapon or sword as in cock?"

"Both."

"So he ran around on Nola?"

"Oh no. No, he was totally in love with her. But while she might have been in love with him, that didn't prevent her from enjoying other men's attentions."

"But people say she would have married him." Crawford began to understand how complex this was and how reluctant people were to tell what they knew. Let sleeping dogs lie and all that. Except the dogs were now wide awake.

"Some people. I think that opinion reveals more about the romantic nature of the speaker than it does about Nola."

"Exactly what do you mean, Ronnie?" Crawford lacked the patience for linguistic subtlety as practiced in Virginia.

"Unearthly beauty, child of Midas, marries country boy. People love that sort of thing. She wouldn't have married him. She saw what Sybil endured when she married Ken Fawkes."

"He's done quite well. With the old man's help, of course."

"Yes," Ronnie inhaled, "but he'll never be one of them. He was set up, then propped up by Edward, so everyone wonders about Ken's abilities. And Sybil bears the Fawkes name, not Bancroft."

"So?"

"Crawford. This is Virginia. No one forgets a god-damned thing. No way in green hell would Nola be Nola Ramy."

"But Ken's no slouch. In time, Guy may have proved he possessed business acumen."

"At the time that Nola was flaming around with Guy, Ken was struggling not just to master the real estate business but to master the nuances of the life into which he had married. Scott Fitzgerald said the rich are different. And I know that you know they are. Old money, I mean. Really old money."

"Not like my money." Crawford's voice had an edge.

"I didn't say that." Ronnie didn't have to say it.

"You weren't in love with Nola but you did like her?" Crawford changed the subject.

A beat passed, then Ronnie honestly replied, "She was a vacuous, spoiled child who had no feelings for anyone but herself. But she was also fun, enormous fun."

Crawford knew that in this assessment Ronnie betrayed his own emotions. Perhaps he was once in love with Guy Ramy or one of the other men Nola had so easily vanquished. "Then maybe it's better that she always be young and beautiful in everyone's mind."

"She would have been an impossible middle-aged bitch. Women like Nola can't age. It kills them."

"In her case, someone else did the job."

Ronnie didn't respond; he waited a moment and then asked, "I also thought you might want to know given the discussion we had about hunt staff last week that David Headdon left Shenandoah Valley Hounds last night. Left them flat."

"Hmm." Crawford smiled. The huntsman David Headdon was known both for his brilliance and his temper. "Does Sister know?"

"Sister knows everything."

Crawford chuckled. "Almost, but she doesn't know who killed Nola Bancroft."

Ronnie respected Sister, even though many people might have interpreted his coziness with Crawford as a betrayal of her. He truly believed that Crawford needed to be joint-master of the Jefferson Hunt. Let him pour money into the club until a true hunting master could be found to succeed Sister should she step down or step up to heaven. At this point in the political development of looking for a joint-master, Ronnie kept his support of Crawford quiet.

"You know something, Crawford, if anyone can find out what really happened now that Nola has reappeared, it will be Jane Arnold."

"Ronnie, you've been most helpful."

"So have you. Thank you for the donation."

"If you didn't like Nola, why are you collecting for the trophy?"

Sometimes Ronnie couldn't believe that Crawford didn't get it. He'd lived here over a decade. "Because Sister gave me the job and because it's the proper thing to do."

Crawford snapped shut his tiny cell phone, hopped in his car, and drove west toward Roughneck Farm.

CHAPTER 13

"I'm going. You'd better put a check by my name," Dragon, his handsome head held high, yelled over the other dog hounds.

"Pipe down," Dasher, his brother, growled.

Asa, Archie's relative, same breeding but one year later, sat in silent splendor. If young entry were going to foxpen, then he'd be there to steady them.

Shaker, clipboard in hand, wrote down the names Sister called out.

Sister would gladly have given Shaker Sundays off, but Shaker, like most hound men, wanted to be with his hounds. Sister was the same way. Covered with mud, red clay caked onto their work boots, both humans breathed in the heady odor of hound, shavings, and a hint of Penn-o-Pine disinfectant.

Doug had taken the day off, as he'd promised the new girl he was dating they'd canoe down the James River.

"If we have Asa, Cora, Delia, and Nellie for made hounds, then we can just take young ones. Those four will keep the freshman class in line." She rubbed her chin, unaware that she had mud on her hands.

"Supposed to rain again this afternoon." Shaker slipped the pen behind his ear.

"We're not sugar, we won't melt."

"Moisture will be good for scent." Shaker smiled.

"Last time we went to foxpen it was dust over there, but that's good for the youngsters. Every day they hunt isn't going to be a good scenting day, and I was proud of them. They pushed and pushed until they finally picked up a line. Took them forty-five minutes. That shows a lot of patience for youngsters."

The sound of a deep motor made all heads turn.

Raleigh left Sister's side, stood on his hind legs, and peered out the kennel window. *"Crawford Howard."*

"If only I were out of here, I'd pee on his leg," Dragon promised as the others laughed.

Shaker walked over, his head just above Raleigh's. It would have made a funny photograph. "Your favorite."

She laughed. "I have so many."

"This is your true favorite, Crawford." Shaker slapped the clipboard against his side.

She didn't reply, but her lip curled slightly upward.

"He's going to the house, Mom," Raleigh announced.

Sister figured as much. She called over her shoulder as she opened the kennel door, "Five-thirty tomorrow."

"Yes'um."

She was looking forward to the morrow. Foxpen delighted her. A foxpen is a fenced-in area, often hundreds of acres. Foxes can't get out and deer can't get in. Man-made dens and natural dens cover the land. The purpose of a foxpen is to introduce young entry to fox scent, a lighter scent than deer.

A good hound wants to hunt, and on a miserable scenting day, deer scent becomes enticing. No foxhunter wants his or her hounds chasing deer, particularly since there are now so many of them. Introducing a youngster to fox scent in controlled conditions helped to guide them on the paths of righteousness.

Hounds can't harm the foxes at a foxpen since there are so many dens in which to escape, so everyone can rest easy, but most especially the foxes. Hounds hunt by scent not sight, and by the time they were cast, the foxes, being nocturnal hunters, were usually in their dens. If not, the foxes soon found one, the trail of scent leading to their secure den. All in all it was a perfect setup.

The foxes enjoyed good food, regular wormings, and regular exercise. The hounds enjoyed the run followed by praise and cookies.

Sister laughed to herself as she and Raleigh trudged up to the house. Crawford so desperately wanted to be joint-master, but she couldn't imagine him rousing himself to go to foxpen before dawn.

Then again, too many cooks spoil the broth. Crawford, if she could find no alternative, could swan about and be one of those fellows who is better at running his mouth than running the fox. Still, he could write checks better than anyone else. That's something.

"Crawford," she called out as he headed for the back porch door of the simple Federal house painted a soft yellow with white trim and Charleston green shutters.

"Good morning." He turned, smiling.

"Have you had your breakfast?"

"I have."

She opened the door. "Another cup of coffee and a bran muffin?"

"One of your bran muffins?" He wiped his feet on the rug just inside the porch door.

"Yes. I'm in my domestic goddess phase."

"All this time I thought you were the goddess of the hunt." He'd picked up a few Virginia ways, even though most folks didn't notice since they were too busy criticizing him. It never hurt to flatter a woman, a truth southern men imbibe with their mother's milk. Crawford still had to think about it, but he was practicing, which was a great step forward.

He sat down at the kitchen table while Sister made a pot of Jamaican coffee, the aroma filling the room. The bran muffins, under a mesh cover, were placed before him along with a plate, utensils, and country butter.

"Ever eat bran muffins with clotted cream? Sounds awful, but it's a step away from heaven." She poured his coffee into a mug bearing the symbol of the Jefferson Hunt, a fox mask.

"Too rich for me. I shouldn't even use this butter."

"You have lost weight. Look good." She sat next to him at the large old farmhouse table. "What can I do for you?"

"Mmm, this is wonderful." He took a sip of coffee. "You and I both like good coffee, too. Well, I guess you've heard about Shenandoah Valley Hounds. I suspect it was one of those 'You're fired.' 'I quit!' things." Crawford was fishing. He could have asked Sister directly. "The huntsman leaving, I mean."

"If a master is discharging a hunt servant or a hunt servant is leaving, notice must be given by January first. After that it's considered bad form. You leave either party hanging," Sister evenly replied.

"Shenandoah would have endured him for another year?"

"Of course. David is actually a good huntsman. He's an erratic person. That's the problem."

"Booze."

"With huntsmen it generally is booze or women. One often leads to the other." She laughed.

He drained his cup and she refilled it. Both drank their coffee black, which Sister called "barefoot."

"I'll get right to the point. Shaker will be our huntsman for many more years, barring injury. Am I correct?"

"You are."

"Doug's a young man, talented. He could carry the

horn for Shenandoah." He held up his hand, even though she'd made no sign of protest. "Now give me a minute. I've thought about this. Five years with Shenandoah and he'd be ready to move up to a fancier, richer hunt or come back here should Shaker retire or become injured.

"Now I know that being left without your first whipper-in this late in the day might cause a ripple of discontent, but it can't be as bad as being without a huntsman."

"You're right about that." She listened intently, knowing other cards were stuffed up his sleeve.

"Do you think Shenandoah would hire him?"

"In a heartbeat."

"Do you think he would go?"

"This has been his home for years, but it would be a good opportunity, a step up. I don't think he would leave without my blessing."

"And would you give him that blessing?"

"I would, as would Shaker."

"I would be happy to pay the salary of the next professional whipper-in."

Her eyebrows raised. "Crawford, that's very generous. You must be in a giving mood today, because Ronnie Haslip told me what you just pledged to the Nola Bancroft Trophy."

"Ah." He wondered if Ronnie was calling to make him, Crawford, look good or if Ronnie had called to make Ronnie look good, boasting about what he'd managed to pry out of him. He wasn't sure about Ronnie. No matter. He was sure about himself. "You know I like the Bancrofts. And while I never knew their younger daughter, I'm happy to do this. Mostly, I enjoy supporting the club."

"And we are all grateful to you." Her smile was genuine.

When she smiled like that, Crawford could see her as a young woman. Odd.

"I'm sure there's a pool of people who might qualify for the job," Crawford said.

"I'd ask the Masters of Foxhounds Association director, Lieutenant Colonel Dennis Foster, if he knows anyone who is suitable. There are always people out there who might have the skills you need for the job, but the chemistry is wrong where they are." She wondered if he had a candidate who would then be his mole. She respected Crawford's intelligence but wished he didn't continue to think a hunt club could be run as a business. It was something quite different, halfway between a church and a charity perhaps. She was never sure.

"I'd be happy to help in the search."

She breathed a sigh of inner relief. He wasn't going to foist someone on her. "Crawford, would you still consider making the salary contribution if for this year I utilized an honorary whipper-in? I think Shaker and I can handle the kennels."

"Yes, but I thought the first whipper-in was responsible for keeping the hunt horses fit."

"True. But the hunt club could use that money. Desperately. Our truck is on its last legs. It's twelve years old and has 180,000 miles on it. These one-ton Duallys are so expensive now. Forty thousand dollars."

"Who will take care of the horses?"

"If I had part-time help, Jennifer Franklin after school, perhaps, I think we could do it. You don't have to give me an answer now. Maybe this feels like a bait and switch."

"No, I held out the bait. The workload is overwhelming. Can you really do it with one less pair of hands?"

"Like I said, I think we can."

"What would you do with the cottage?"

"Rent it out as a hunting box or convert it into an office. We don't have an office. Papers are stuffed in Shaker's house and mine. I'm not sure yet. I'll have to think this through."

But the fact that she had ready answers for the whipper-in position told Crawford she'd already considered encouraging Doug to apply for the huntsman's job.

"Let me buy the truck. GM is making the best right now."

A pause followed; Raleigh put his head on Sister's knee. Her hand rested on his shiny black head.

Golliwog, sitting in the kitchen window over the sink, remarked, *"Rain coming. Be here in fifteen minutes. It's on top of the mountain."* As no one responded, she raised the decibel level. *"Isn't anyone listening to me?"*

"Golly, hush," Sister chided her.

"It must be raindrops, so many raindrops." The cat warbled the song she'd heard on the golden oldie radio station.

Sister didn't listen to oldies, but Shaker did.

As Golly's singing filled the room, Sister stood up and walked over to the window.

"You're just awful." Then she glanced out the window. "Crawford, rain's sliding down the mountain. Are your car windows closed?"

"They are. This has been a wet summer."

"Compared to last one. I love the weather. Let me amend that. I love observing the weather. For instance, you'd think when raindrops are hanging from a branch, you know, hanging not dropping, that scent would be fabulous. My experience is that you can't find a damn thing."

Not schooled in the refinements of hunting or country

life, Crawford was nonetheless interested. "Doesn't compute, does it?"

"No, but there it is." She sat back down as the cat preened in the window. "I am overwhelmed by your willingness to share your resources. And I'm not unmindful that you want to be my joint-master." She smiled. "I would hate for you to give us all this money and be disappointed down the road."

"If you told people you wanted me, I'd be joint-master," he bluntly replied, but in good humor.

"Don't feel that I don't value you. I do. But Crawford, you are not a hunting man. You're still new to it."

"Ten years." This came out in a puff of wind.

"For the first two or three years, you, like every other beginner, were just trying to hang on. It takes a long time to learn about foxhunting, and the truth is most people are out there to run and jump. Real hunting is an art, and I don't pretend to be Rembrandt, but I know it takes study, then more study, and the recognition that these animals are often far wiser than we are. I guess I'm saying it takes humility."

Crawford could not believe that any animal was superior to the human animal, but he did know her assessment of his early years was accurate. "I'm willing to learn."

"And I respect that. You must also realize, surely you know, that if you are elected joint-master there will be one whopping fight."

He looked up from his cup. "I know. I've stepped on toes."

"Let me throw this out to you. I don't expect you to be a hunting master, Crawford, but you can certainly learn what it takes to run a club. Money is a big part of it, but the medley of breeding, of seeing to the health of your foxes, of landowner relations, of relations with the

Board of Governors, of opening new territory and maintaining the old, it's a great deal of work. One must treat people with a light touch."

"I'm not good at that," he honestly admitted.

"And you know nothing about hounds."

"That's true, too. One hound looks pretty much like the next to me. But I have ideas. I have resources. And if I do say so, Marty would be invaluable to our social members." He meant Marty would throw a lot of parties, a real plus.

"Promise me this: that this hunt season you will pay attention. Try to keep your ego in check. It will make a difference."

"So, you are considering me?"

"I am. And what about Bobby Franklin? He punched you and bodily threw you out of his shop last year. He's our president."

A club president ran the various committees. It, too, was a big job. The master was responsible for hunt staff, hounds, territory, and actual hunting in a subscription club—which the Jefferson Hunt was.

"Unusual circumstances." Crawford cleared his throat.

"Can you bring yourself to apologize?"

"Yes." This was hard.

"You have no children. People are blind about their own children, and what you told him about Cody may have been one hundred percent on the money. But few fathers could hear it."

Cody, the Franklins' oldest daughter, was currently in jail. The beginning of this dismal reality was her infatuation with drugs.

"I understand." He paused. "Do you think you were blind to your son's faults?"

"I'd like to think I wasn't, but I'm sure I was. He was a beguiling boy." She smiled.

"Speaking of children, it's funny. I've asked people about Nola Bancroft and gotten some wildly different replies. Some men thought she was Venus, others thought she was a bitch."

"I expect there were more of the former than the latter."

"True."

"We're like chemicals. We react with one another differently."

"What did you think of her?"

"Oh, she was great fun. As a woman, I saw her differently than men did, obviously. She had a great sense of humor, loved practical jokes, had energy to burn. She had lots of girl friends, which is important. You need friends of your own sex. But I thought she was heading for a fall."

"Why?"

She folded her hands. "She was getting a little too wild. Enjoying her hold over men a little too much."

"And Tedi didn't see it?"

"No. Well, she was beginning to sense it, but as I said, parents are blind."

"Here it comes." The rain hit the windows and Golly moved off the sill.

"Back on track. Bobby Franklin will be our president for as long as he can stand the job. He's good at it and we're lucky to have him. If you want to be a joint-master, you must work with Bobby. And Betty, too." Sister returned to what Crawford needed to do.

"You've never had a joint-master. Think you could do it?"

"If you or whoever stays out of the kennel, I can. I won't have anyone messing with my hounds or my breeding program."

"Well, what happens if you drop dead?"

"Crawford, I do make allowances for the fact that you are from Indiana, but for God's sake could you be a little less direct? Of course, I will drop dead one day, as you so bluntly put it. Who knows when?"

"Well, who will continue your breeding program?"

"Shaker."

"What if he's gone?"

"I've written it down. But you do point out a vulnerability. If you are chosen as a joint-master, I will need to be training someone to take my place when that time comes. A true hunting master."

"I understand that."

"Good."

They talked a bit more, then Crawford rose.

She accompanied him to the back door. "Would you like an umbrella?"

"No. I'll make a dash for it." He pecked her on the cheek. He'd grown fond of her even though she frustrated him. "Are you worried about this Nola thing?"

"The truth?" She took a deep breath. "I'm worried sick."

CHAPTER 14

At six-thirty on the morning of Saturday, September 7, a light easterly wind carried a fresh tang in the air, a hint of changes to come.

A hardy band of twelve gathered at the kennels in these last moments before sunup. Sunrise was 6:38 on this day. The first day of cubbing excited the hard-core foxhunters, the ones who would follow hounds on horseback or on foot, in cars, in rickshaws if there was no other way. For this happy group, hunting with hounds was a passion right up there with the ecstasies of Saint Teresa of Avila.

Those hounds waiting in the draw run, a special pen to hold the hounds hunting that day, leapt up and down in excitement. Those not drawn wailed in abject misery.

Not to go out on the first day of cubbing was no disgrace to a hound. Only a foolish huntsman or master would stack the pack with young entry. Each day of cubbing, like each day of preseason football, different young hounds would be mixed with different mature hounds. By the end of cubbing, huntsman and master would have a solid sense of which youngsters had learned their lessons and which older hounds had become a step too slow.

The older, trusted hounds understood this training process, but that didn't mean they wanted to stay behind even if they knew perfectly well they'd be out next time. No good hound wants to sit in the kennel.

Atop her light bay with the blaze, Sybil Fawkes's quiet demeanor belied her inner nervousness. She had accepted the position of honorary first whipper-in, the honorary meaning no remuneration, with excitement and fear. She could ride hard, but she wasn't sure she could identify all the hounds even though she'd come to the kennel almost every day since the end of July. Doug had spent a lot of time with her before leaving to carry the horn at Shenandoah, but she was still nervous.

August had drained Sybil. It hadn't just been the heat. The ceremony at Nola's grave, although restrained, even beautiful, had hammered home her loss.

She found herself snapping at her boys. Ken, sensitive to her moods, kept the kids busy.

Sybil's restorative time proved to be with the hounds. Working with the animals, with Sister and Shaker, gave her some peace. Their focus on the pack was so intense, it crowded out her sadness over Nola.

When she worried that she wouldn't make a good whipper-in, Sister encouraged her, telling her she'd make mistakes but she'd learn from them.

"I've been hunting since I was six and I still make mistakes. Always will," Sister had said.

Betty Franklin, who had been second whipper-in for over a decade, could have filled the first's boots but she had to work for a living. There might be times when she couldn't show up. Also, Betty had limited resources and one daughter to get through college. She couldn't afford the horses. She owned two fabulous horses, Outlaw and Magellan, and Bobby owned a horse. They couldn't afford any more horses, which depressed Betty.

But she was anything but depressed this morning. Butterflies fluttered in her stomach just as the real things were awakening to soft light.

Sister, too, had butterflies. Opening Hunt would mean the beginning of the formal season, but this, this was the true beginning and she so wanted her young entry to do her proud.

As Crawford and others had predicted, nothing more was learned concerning Nola's death. The murder crept into conversations but not with the earlier frequency and intensity.

Tedi accepted the offer of a sip from Crawford's flask as she sat on Maid of Honor, her smallish chestnut mare, who possessed a fiery temper—but then, she was a redhead. Tedi's salt sack, an unbleached linen coat worn in hot weather, hung perfectly from her shoulders, a subtle nip in at the waist. Salt sacks usually hang like sacks, but Tedi, a fastidious woman, had hers hand-fitted.

Every stitch of clothing on her body had been tailored for her over forty years ago. Good hunting clothes pass from generation to generation. A few fads might appear— such as short hunting coats during the seventies and eighties—but hunters soon return to the tried and true. A longer skirt on a hunting jacket protects the thigh. Sensible. Everything must be sensible.

Cubbing granted the rider a greater latitude of personal expression in matters of dress. One could wear a tweed jacket with or without a waistcoat depending on the temperature. It was already sixty degrees, so everyone there, seasoned hunters, knew by the time hounds were lifted they'd be boiling in a vest. Their vests hung back in their trailers.

People wore white, yellow, pink, or oxford blue shirts with ties. Their britches were beige or canary, as no one wore white in the field on an informal day.

Betty wore a pair of twenty-year-old oxblood boots;

their patina glowed with the years. Her gloves were also oxblood and she wore a thin, thin navy jacket with a yellow shirt and a hunter green tie.

Bobby, after asking the master's permission, rode in a shirt only. It wasn't truly proper, but he was so overweight that the heat vexed him especially. He wore a lovely Egyptian cotton white shirt and a maroon tie with light blue rampant lions embroidered on it. He'd worn the same tie for the first day of cubbing for the last fourteen years. It brought luck.

Shaker wore a gray tweed so old, it was even thinner than Betty's navy coat. His brown field boots glistened. His well-worn brown hunting cap gave testimony to many a season. He carried the cap under his arm. Protocol decreed he could put on his cap only when the master said, "Hounds, please!"

While spanking-new clothes were beautiful, there was a quiet pride in the faded ones, proof of hard rides over the years.

Edward Bancroft, more reserved and preoccupied of late, roused himself to be convivial. Ken Fawkes, also wearing a salt sack, offered his flask to one and all. He beamed with pride at his wife and counseled her before they set off that morning that cubbing would be more difficult than the formal season because hounds weren't yet settled. If she could get through cubbing, why, the rest of the season would be a piece of cake.

Ronnie Haslip rivaled the impeccable Crawford in the splendor of his turnout. His gloves, butter-soft pale yellow, matched his breeches. He wore Newmarket boots, the height of fashion for warm days but rarely seen because they wear out much faster than all leather boots. The inside of the boot and the foot was either brown or oxblood leather, but the shank of the boot was made of a burlaplike fabric lined in microthin leather. A rolled rim of leather topped off these impressive boots. Ronnie even wore garters with his Newmarkets, something rarely seen now.

His shirt, a pale pink button-down, fit him just right as did the dark green hunting jacket he'd had made while visiting in Ireland. A deep violet tie secured by a narrow, unadorned gold bar was echoed by a woven belt the same color as his tie. His black velvet cap, tails up since he was neither a master nor a huntsman, had faded to a pleasing hue that declared he knew his business. He carried an expensive applewood knob end crop with a kangaroo thong.

All the riders carried crops. Usually they saved the staghorn crops for formal hunting, but in Betty's case that was all she had. It wasn't improper to carry the staghorn while cubbing, really, it was just that once formal hunting started, riders were locked into a more rigid sartorial system. Then you had to carry the staghorn crop or none at all. Though they were rarely used on the horses, they proved useful. One could lean out of the saddle and hook a gate or close it with the crop. The really dexterous might dangle the staghorn end over their horse's flank and pick up a dropped cap or glove. This was always met with approval.

Today, Sister carried a knob end crop, an old blackthorn, perfectly balanced with a whopping eight-foot, twelve-plaited thong topped off by a cracker she made herself out of plastic baling twine. When she popped her whip it sounded like a rifle shot.

Her cheeks were flushed, her eyes bright; she couldn't wait to get going. As the wind came out of the east, there was no point in fiddle-faddling, she'd cast right into it. Hit a line fast and go.

The youngsters had shone at their foxpen outings. She wasn't worried that they needed to head downwind for a bit to settle. Anyway, the temperature would climb quickly. Off to a good start, a bracing run, then lift and bring everyone back to the kennels on a high note.

Positive reinforcement worked much better than negative, in Sister's opinion. Let the youngsters feel they've done well and they'd do even better next time.

Her old salt sack with its holes carefully patched, her boots repaired that summer by Dehner, a boot maker in Omaha, her mustard breeches and light blue shirt all suited her. She wore a bridle leather belt, matching her boots, peanut brittle in color. She looked exactly right, but she wasn't showing off.

Jane Arnold was a stickler for being correct. One intrepid soul mentioned to her that another hunt was allowing members to cub in chaps.

"Oh, how interesting," she replied, and uttered not another word.

That was the end of that.

Being superstitious, she pinned Raymond's grandfather's pocket watch to the inside of her coat pocket as she always did. John "Hap" Arnold, a hunting man, had a pocket watch devised wherein the cover had a round glass center so he could see the arms where they attached to the center of the watch. The outside rim of the watch, gold, had the hours engraved on it. She could see enough of the slender blued hands to make out the time without popping open the top. This cover came in handy should Sister smack into a tree or take an involuntary dismount. And she never had to open the watch in rain. As Bobby had his good-luck tie, she had her good-luck watch.

On the right rear side of her saddle hung couple straps in case she had to bring back tuckered-out hounds early. However, on the High Holy Days—Opening Hunt, Thanksgiving, Christmas, and New Year's Hunts—she carried a ladies' sandwich case, instead of couple straps, with the rectangular glass flask inside the case. When visiting other hunts she also carried this case. A small silver flask filled with iced tea rested in her inside coat pocket.

It took years to conquer the minutiae of hunting attire, ever a fruitful source of discord. An elderly member might fume that few wore garters anymore. A younger member would respond that boots stayed up quite well by themselves when bespoke by Dehner, Vogel, Lobb, or Maxwell.

Someone else would be horrified if a lady wore a hunt cap rather than a derby, and no one really wanted to say what they thought of chin straps. No master could disallow them, but behind the users' backs they were always called "sissy straps."

Ladies had been known to tear one another's veils off during formal hunting when one disdained the concave of another lady's top hat. One of the worst arguments Nola ever got into the last year of her life occurred when she sniffed that Frances Gohanna, soon to be Frances Assumptio, had a dressage top hat perched on her head instead of a true hunting top hat. Exactly why these trifles inspired such emotion amused Sister, but then foxhunters were passionate by nature.

Even Golliwog, viewing the assembled from the vantage point of the open stable door, was excited and took note of how the people were turned out. Once hounds were loosed she would take the precaution of repairing to the hayloft to watch the hunt. Occasionally an errant hound youngster would wander into the stable, and Golly loathed all that whining and slobber.

Sister, on Lafayette, rode over to Shaker. "Wind's picking up. I know we didn't want to run into After All, but we have two miles until their border. Best to cast east now."

Shaker, too, had noticed the shift. Their original plan was to strike north and hunt toward Foxglove Farm.

Then he'd swing the pack around to the bottom of Hangman's Ridge and hunt through the woods on the west side of the old farm road right back to the kennels. Given their hound walks all summer this territory would be familiar to a youngster if he or she became separated from the pack. The last thing either of them wanted to do was have a young one lost and frantic first time out.

Three couple of young entry were in the pack. Six to watch. The veterans were pretty foolproof.

"East it is." His voice lowered.

Sister left him and rode to the small field. "Sun's up. What are we waiting for?" She beamed.

"Here's to a great season," Crawford called.

The others murmured their agreement.

"Hounds, please," Sister called to Shaker.

He slapped his cap on his head and Betty opened the gate. She then quickly swung herself onto Outlaw, as good a horse as was ever foaled if not the most beautiful.

"*YAHOO,*" the hounds cried.

Thirty couple of hounds bounded out of the kennel, spirits high, then waited for Shaker to blow a low wiggly note followed by a high short one that meant, "We're on our way." This was blown as much for the humans as for the hounds. Humans have a tendency to dawdle.

Hounds gaily trotted behind their huntsman, Sybil to their left and Betty to their right. Sister followed forty yards behind, leading the field as the rim of the sun, shocking scarlet, inched over the horizon.

Beyond the apple orchard they passed an old peach orchard, filled with delicious Alberta peaches. Tempting though it was to cast in there, both huntsman and master wanted to reach the sheep's meadow between the farm road and the woods. That pasture's rich soil held scent. On a good day, hounds might tease a line into the woods or back toward the orchards and the pace picked up accordingly. Not that hitting a scorching scent right off wasn't a dream, it was, but sometimes, especially with young ones, a teasing scent helped organize their minds. You never knew with scent.

A black three-board fence marked off the meadow, a coop squatted in the best place to jump. Shaker on Gunpowder, a rangy gray formerly off the racetrack, effortlessly sailed over. His whippers-in had preceded him into the field. Sister could always push up a straggling hound.

"Noses down, young ones!" Cora commanded.

"I got something. I got something!" Trident, a first-year entry, squealed.

Asa ambled over, sniffled, *"Yes, you do, son. That's a groundhog."*

The other hounds laughed as Trident, ears dropping for a moment, accepted his chastisement, then decided he'd follow Asa. He couldn't go wrong then.

A sweetish, heavy, lingering line greeted Diana's sensitive nose as she probed a mossy patch amidst the timothy swaying in the east wind. *"Pay dirt."*

Although only in her second year, Diana, tremendously gifted, had earned the respect of the older hounds.

Just to be certain, Asa touched his nose to the spot. *"We're off."*

Both Diana and Asa pushed forward, Cora already ahead of them. Her nose, while not as extraordinary as Diana's, was plenty good enough. Yes, this line was perhaps fifteen minutes old and, on the dew, the temperature in the low sixties, it would hold for perhaps another five or ten minutes in the hay. Then the rising sun plus the wind would scatter it forever.

Trident inhaled the light fragrance. *"This is it! This is it! I'm really hunting. It's not foxpen. This is the real deal."* He was so overcome, he tripped and rolled over.

Trudy, his littermate, laughed as she moved past him, her nose on the ground. *"Showtime!"*

Archie used to say *"Showtime!"* when hounds would find. It made everyone laugh, relaxing yet energizing them.

Hearing their former anchor hound's phrase from this new kid made the others really laugh.

The scent grew stronger, snaking toward the woods. Whoever left it was in no hurry.

Whoever left it happened to be dozing on a rock outcropping about a quarter of a mile into the woods. Uncle Yancy, a red fox and the husband of Aunt Netty, filled with blackberries, peaches, and grain from Sister's stable, needed a nap to aid his digestion. Uncle Yancy would frequently sit on the window ledge and watch TV at either Shaker's or Doug's cottage. Now that Doug had taken the horn at Shenandoah Valley Hunt, he wondered if anyone would be in there. He could see the picture better from Doug's window than from Shaker's. He liked to keep up with the world. Raleigh and Rooster never minded his curiosity, but that damned cat would torment him sometimes. She'd call out to the hounds, *"Look who's here, you lazy sots."* Then some offended creature would open his big mouth and Yancy'd push off.

He lifted his head from his delicate paws. *"Oh, bother."*

Bitsy, on her way home from a very successful night, screeched, *"They'll be fast, Uncle Yancy."*

"Ha! The foxhound isn't born that can keep up with me."

Bitsy landed on a low maple limb. *"Pride goeth before a fall."*

He stretched as the sound grew closer. *"Not pride. Simple fact. If you want a good time, fly with me as I send these young ones in the wrong direction. Might even unseat a few humans, too. Why any creature would want to totter around on two legs is beyond me."*

"That's why they ride horses. Then they have four," Bitsy sensibly concluded.

"I hadn't thought of that. Of course, some of them can't stay on those horses, now can they? A weak and vain species, the human, but a few are quite lovely. Oh well"—he shook himself—*"let's cause as much mayhem as possible."*

He left the rocks, walked down to Broad Creek, crossed it, then climbed out on the other side. He shook off the water.

"I'm telling you, Uncle Yancy, these young ones are fast."

"Bitsy, they aren't supposed to run in front of the pack. They're supposed to run as a pack."

"That's what cubbing is for, to teach them. And I wouldn't be so cocky if I were you. If St. Just is about, he'll make trouble."

St. Just, king of the crows, hated foxes, especially red foxes, because Target, Uncle Yancy's brother, had killed his mate. St. Just swore revenge on the whole fox nation and he had led one young red to his death last year.

Finally heeding the little owl, Uncle Yancy started trotting east.

"It's getting stronger!" Trudy yelped as she approached the rocks.

Sybil, up ahead, spied Uncle Yancy slipping through a thick stand of holly. "Tallyho!"

Yancy decided to run after that. He broke out of the holly, crossed an old rutted path, dove into a thick thorny underbrush, then slithered out of that and headed for the edge of the woods.

"Over here." Dasher, a second-year dog hound, littermate to Diana, reached the edge of the creek the same time as Cora. He splashed across the creek, then began whining because he couldn't pick up the scent.

"Don't be a nincompoop!" Cora chided him. *"Do you really think a fox is going to walk straight across a creek? You go left, I'll go right. And who's to say he didn't double back? Trudy,"* she called to the youngster, *"you and your idiot brother work that side of the creek."*

While hounds searched for the scent, Sister and the field quietly waited on the rutted wagon road.

Crawford had just unscrewed the top of his silver flask when Dasher hollered, *"Here."*

"Drat." Crawford knocked back a hasty gulp, motioned for Marty to have a sip, which she declined. As they trotted off he screwed on the cap, its little silver hinge ensuring it wouldn't fall off. Not a drop sloshed on him even though he'd filled it to the brim. He was quite proud of himself.

"Stronger!" Cora, again ahead, spoke in her light, pretty voice.

Bitsy flew back to watch the hounds, then took off again to give Yancy a progress report. *"They just ran into the thorns."*

"Damn," Yancy cursed. These hounds were faster than he thought.

He broke out of the woods and into the easternmost meadow of Roughneck Farm, which was filled with black-eyed Susans, Queen Anne's lace, and cornflowers; it hadn't been weeded or overseeded in years. Sister thought of it as her wildflower experiment and was loath to return it to timothy, alfalfa, or orchard grass.

A hog's-back jump loomed in the fence line. Sister and Lafayette sailed over it as the pace was picking up. She saw Betty, up ahead, already flying over the spanking-new coop that marked the westernmost border of After All Farm.

"This fox is a devil," she thought to herself.

The hounds, in full cry now, roared across the wildflower meadow. Even Trident was on, his concentration improving.

Walter Lungrun, riding Clemson, an older and wiser horse, steered clear of Crawford, whose horse, Czapaka, a big warm-blood, occasionally refused a jump when he'd had enough of Crawford sawing at the reins.

New coops, not having yet settled into the earth, looked bigger than normal. Fortunately, Tedi and Edward painted theirs black. Unpainted coops seemed to cause more trouble than painted ones. Sister never knew if the trouble was with the horses or with the people.

As she trusted Lafayette with her heart and soul, she didn't give this jump a second thought, landing just as she heard Shaker double the notes on the horn.

They were close, close to their fox, who must have tarried along the way.

Uncle Yancy, putting on the afterburners now, was shadowed by Bitsy, who was quite worried about him. She wished she hadn't said *"Pride goeth before a fall,"* as she had no desire to see Uncle Yancy, everybody's uncle, perish. Rarely did Sister's hounds kill, but if a fox was ancient or sick, the hounds might dispatch it swiftly. In three seconds the quarry was dead, its neck snapped by the lead hound.

Bitsy tried to remember the last time there was a kill. It had been three years ago; one of the red tribe at the edge of the territory came down with distemper. Either way he was going to die because he refused to eat the medicines put out for him; he refused to go into one of the Havahart traps that Sister and Shaker put out in an effort to save him. He knew other foxes had been taken to the vet, but he did not trust any human, not even Sister.

"At least he died fast," Bitsy thought to herself.

If she was worried, Uncle Yancy was not. Yes, the pack was faster. Sister had retired quite a few older hounds over the summer who now graced barns and hearths throughout the membership. These young ones had speed. Sister was breeding in more speed. He would have to tell the others.

In the meantime, he had to shake these damned hounds. He heard Cora's distinctive voice, then Asa's, both smart hounds.

"But not as smart as I am." He chuckled as he raced for the covered bridge and trotted across it, dragging his brush purposefully to leave a heavy, heavy scent. Then he started up the farm road, covered in brown pearock. The Bancrofts spared no expense on those items they considered aesthetically pleasing.

He whirled around, 180 degrees, backtracking in his own footprints, then launched himself at the edge of the covered bridge and down into the waters of Snake Creek, which were high, muddy, and fast from all the rain. Swimming to the opposite bank proved harder than he'd anticipated.

"Hurry!" Bitsy blinked from atop the covered bridge.

Uncle Yancy made it to the far side. The swim had cost him precious time and tired him. He heard the hounds not a third of a mile away, closing with blinding speed.

"Damn them," he cursed as he raced for the place where Nola and Peppermint were now buried.

The red fox with a little white tip on his tail leapt over the zigzag fence, crossed the twenty yards to the other side, and leapt over that. The earth, still soft from the digging and from the rains, showed distinct footprints marking his progress. Tedi had put up a zigzag fence until the stonemason, in high demand, could build stone walls around the graves.

A muddy trail followed him as he headed along the ridge, then turned in an arc back toward Roughneck Farm. He was more tired than he wanted to be. A groundhog hole, messy but under the circumstances better than nothing, had been dug right along the fence line between After All Farm and Sister's wildflower meadow. He wasn't going to be able to make the loop back to his den at this rate and he wished he'd paid more attention to Bitsy, faithfully flying overhead.

"*Ouch!*"

Uncle Yancy looked upward. St. Just had dive-bombed Bitsy, pecking her.

"*You little creep!*" St. Just pecked at Bitsy again, who was built for silent flight. She couldn't maneuver as handily as the blue-black bird, but she was smarter. She flew low to the ground, right over Uncle Yancy. If St. Just tried for her, Yancy could whirl around and possibly catch the hated bird in his jaws, or even with his front paws.

St. Just knew better than to get close to a fox. He cursed Bitsy for helping the fox and squawked loudly. If only he could turn the hounds before they reached the covered bridge, he could get them on Uncle Yancy fast. But his outburst and his bad language offended Athena, who had just stopped over between the two farms. A nest of baby copperheads, born late but with a good chance of survival thanks to the abundance of game, were close to the large rock where they lived. She thought one would make a tasty dessert, and St. Just spoiled everything by scaring them back under their rock.

He offended her in principle. He didn't know his place. Then, when she saw him go after Bitsy, her blood boiled. She lifted off the evergreen branch, her large wingspan impressive, and noiselessly, effortlessly came up behind the crow with four big flaps of her wings. She zoomed for him, talons down. He heard her a split second too late. As he turned to avoid the full impact of her blow, she caught him on the right wing. Enough to throw him off and enough to tear out feathers painfully.

"Out of my sight, peasant!"

Feathers flying, St. Just feared he might fall to earth with them. He pulled himself out of the dive, veering back toward the woods. Uncle Yancy, pursued though he was, would have made short work of this mortal enemy and then left the carcass to distract the hounds. Fresh blood was always distracting to a hound.

"Thank God you're here," Bitsy hollered, her high-pitched voice frightening four deer grazing below.

"Thank Athena." The large bird hooted low, mentioning her namesake, then with a few powerful blasts she was over the wildflower meadow, heading to her home high in a huge walnut by Sister's house.

Back at the creek, the hounds charged across the covered bridge in full cry.

Sister was about to lead the field across, knowing there'd be some fussing from the horses inside the bridge, when she heard a change in Diana's voice. Wisely, for she trusted her hounds, she paused.

People panted. Horses' ears pricked forward; they thought stopping pure folly, but they did as they were told.

Cora had overrun the line. Asa came up to Diana. He, too, changed his tune.

"What's happening? What's happening?" Trident thought he'd done something wrong.

"Pipe down and listen." Dasher put his nose to the ground.

In a situation like this, Dragon was invaluable, for he was highly intelligent and had an incredible nose. But he'd been left back in the kennel since Shaker felt he had enough good hounds out and Dragon could be a handful. He thought the young ones, especially this T litter, might do better without Dragon today.

Little by little, Dasher, not as brilliant as his brother but methodical, worked his way back to the bridge. *"I think he's doubled back."*

Hounds milled around, then Cora said, *"Well, there's only one way to be sure. Dasher, go through the bridge; be careful, because some fool human will say you are doubling back on the line, and then Sybil, who's new, re- member, will rate you. But if he has doubled back, his scent will be stronger on the other side. Which direction, I don't know. Take Diana with you."*

Both Dasher and Diana tore back across the bridge.

"Heel," Ronnie Haslip whispered to Crawford, who nodded knowingly.

Technically they were right, but Sister did not call out to her hounds to join the others. Diana and Dasher were terrific second-year entry.

Sybil, forward of the bridge, turned to head back. Shaker sat right on the far side of the bridge, close to his lead hounds.

Dasher said low to Diana, *"Here, I think this is fresher."*

She put her nose down and inhaled. *"Yes, but we'd best be sure before we call them all back to us."*

They ran top speed and then were quite certain that the fox had headed up the ridge. *"Yes! He's here. Come on."*

Shaker, thrilled with these two, blew three doubling notes, sending the others on to them, claws clicking on the wooden floor of the bridge.

They emerged, cut hard right, and flew up the ridge. They all jumped the newly installed zigzag fence, running hard over Nola's and Peppermint's graves, headstones not yet carved.

Sister hesitated one moment, waiting for her hunts- man to get ahead of her. She then rode up the ridge but wide of the new grave sites. Ken Fawkes, usually a strong rider, lost control of his horse, who wanted to follow the hounds directly. The big dark horse, almost black, catapulted over the first line of the zigzag fence, took one giant stride, and was over the second. Deep hoofprints now mingled with Uncle Yancy's prints and those of the hounds.

The woods reverberated with the song of the hounds. Within minutes they were back over the fence line dividing After All Farm from Roughneck Farm.

Sister, knowing she had to head back to the new coop, turned and pressed Lafayette on. She cursed because the underbrush was thick. The leaves were still on the trees, and she couldn't see her hounds in the thick woods. This was another reason cubbing was harder than formal hunting. If she didn't hurry up she'd get thrown out and be way behind. She reached the new coop, got well over, then headed right on a diagonal across the open field. She could see the flowers and hay swaying and sterns swaying, too, where hounds pushed through, their voices in unison.

"He's close! He's close!"

And he was. Uncle Yancy slid into the groundhog hole, rolling right on top of the groundhog.

"I beg your pardon."

The groundhog, large and unkempt, but jolly, said, *"Care for some sweet grass?"*

"Thank you, no." Yancy couldn't understand how any animal could be as sloppy as this fellow. *"You know within a second those hounds will start digging at your main entrance."*

"Good. That will save me work."

"I shall assume you have other exits should it come to that."

"One of them right under a hanging hornet's nest. Three feet long it is." The groundhog, lying on his back,

laughed just as Cora dove toward the hole and began digging frantically.

Uncle Yancy's scent was so strong, it drove her wild. Red, moist earth splattered up behind her paws. Diana joined her at the edges, as did Asa and Dasher.

Trident asked his sister, *"Are we supposed to do that?"*

"I think you have to be first. There isn't room for us to get in there, but I think we're supposed to sing really, really loud."

Trudy and Trident did just that and were joined by every hound there. Triumph!

Shaker arrived, hopped off Gunpowder, and blew the happy notes signifying that these wonderful hounds had denned their fox.

Sybil rode up, taking Gunpowder's reins.

"I know my job," the gray snapped, incensed that Sybil thought he might walk off.

Betty rode in from the opposite direction as the field pulled up not ten yards away.

Shaker took the horn from his lips. "He's in there. He's in there. What good hounds. Good hounds." He grabbed Cora's tail, pulling her out of there. She weighed seventy pounds of pure muscle. "You're quite the girl."

"I am!" Cora turned a circle of pure joy.

Then Shaker called each hound by name, praising their good work. He petted the puppies.

Sister rode up. "A fine beginning. Shall we call it a day?"

"Yes, ma'am." Shaker smiled. "And did you see how Dasher and Diana came back across the bridge? That's as nice a piece of work as I have ever seen in my life."

Sister looked down at the two tricolor hounds. "Diana and Dasher, you have made me very, very proud."

They wagged their whole bodies.

"Proud of you, proud of you." Shaker again blew the

notes of victory, then, without a grunt, lifted himself back into the saddle.

As they rode back toward the kennels, Ken, ashen-faced, came alongside his mother-in-law. "I am terribly sorry. I couldn't hold him. I—"

She held up her hand. "Ken, to have the fox and hounds run across your grave is a good thing. No apology necessary. Nola would be laughing with the excitement of it."

No one else said a word about it while the Bancrofts were around.

Uncle Yancy thanked his host and stuck his head up to make sure there were no stragglers.

Bitsy, in a pawpaw tree, giggled. *"A near thing. And running over Nola and Peppermint like that."*

"That's an unquiet grave," the red fox said. Mask to the west, he headed for home.

CHAPTER 15

Crawford and Marty Howard hosted a First Day of Cubbing breakfast. Upon reflection they decided to pass on having an evening gathering. Instead they hired a local caterer who set up outdoor stoves outside Sister's stable. Crawford considered setting them up on the long rolling lawn overlooking Sister's fall gardens, but then he'd have to tell her. He wanted the breakfast to be a surprise, as did Marty. Having it back at the stable where the trailers were parked wouldn't disturb her lawn. As people often brought homemade breads, sandwiches, or drinks, sharing same at the trailers, Crawford and Marty thought they wouldn't need to ask permission and the surprise would be complete.

It was. People untacked and wiped down their horses to the scent of bacon crackling on the grill, succulent blond and regular sausages, and omelettes.

One gave the two chefs their omelette order and within minutes it was ready. Breads, jellies, fruits, cold cereals, and fresh milk along with sweets covered the long table to the side of the stoves.

The riders were thrilled, as were the hounds, who could smell the enticing medley of aromas. Whatever might be left over would be mixed into their kibble later.

"What a wonderful idea," Betty Franklin said to Sybil as they stood in line.

"I never realize how famished I am while I'm hunting, but the second I get back to the trailers my stomach makes as much noise as *The 1812 Overture*." Sybil laughed at herself.

Marty Howard was whispering directions to the caterer's assistant, pouring coffee.

"Right away, madam." He handed her a large cup.

She carried the steaming coffee to Shaker, still in the kennels.

He looked up and smiled as she came through the door. "Mrs. Howard."

"Here. What a great day. Now come on over and get your piping hot omelette. The Boss said for me to tell you to come on, you can wash down the kennels on a full stomach better than on an empty one."

"Did she?" He smiled broadly. "What a good woman." He gratefully took a swallow. "Very good."

"Jamaican."

"High test."

"Ninety-three octane." Marty waited for him to toss a collar in the bucket hanging from the wall, a bucket used just for this purpose, as collars were removed from hounds when they returned from their labors.

As they walked back together to the festivities, Marty asked, "Did you always want to be a huntsman?"

"Yes, I did."

"How did you learn?"

"My parents allowed me to move up to Warrenton to live with my aunt. I was twelve and I begged because the huntsman at Warrenton, Fred Duncan, said he'd set me to work in the kennels. That's how I started. Fred was a fine huntsman. He'd whipped-in to Eddie Bywaters, the last huntsman of the great Bywaters clan. I learned so much from Fred, and I could go over and watch Melvin

Poe hunt the Orange County hounds. Fred would take me up to watch the Piedmont hounds."

Marty loved hearing these stories and knew there was so much to learn not just about foxhunting itself but about the incredible people who had carried it forward throughout the generations. "When did you get your first job?"

"Here." He put his hand under Marty's elbow as she was about to step into a small depression. "Jefferson Hunt needed a first whipper-in, and even though I was young, Fred vouched for me. Raymond put me on every screwball horse he could beg, borrow, or steal before he'd hire me. He finally said, 'Kid can stick on a horse.' That was that. And I never want to leave. I love it here."

"Do you ever worry about the money? I mean, huntsmen make so little, and what if something were to happen?"

"I don't worry. Maybe I should, but I knew as a little kid that my life wasn't about money. This is what I've always wanted to do, and you know, Mrs. Howard, there isn't enough money in the world to get me to give it up."

"But what if you're hurt?" Marty belonged to the worrying class.

"The Boss will take care of me just like I'd take care of her. We've been though a lot together."

Marty thought about this, an attitude so different from the way she was raised and from the milieu in which she lived. "You're a lucky man."

Betty called out to Shaker, "How about those young entry?"

He gave her the thumbs-up sign.

Crawford, hoping to ingratiate himself with a person he considered a servant, and technically, Shaker was a servant, said, "Thank you."

"The hounds did all the work." Shaker smiled.

Sister, in line, observed the exchange as well as the high spirits of the group.

Bobby, in front of her, was chatting with Tedi. He noticed his wife. "Hey, hey there. I see you flirting with my wife."

Ken Fawkes, who was holding a plate for Betty, replied, "Bobby, I'll give you credit. You knew a good thing when you saw it."

Everyone laughed.

As Shaker moved through the line, people complimented him. He was their star. They watched him ahead, taking the jumps first, without a lead. They saw him traverse territory they could loop around thanks to the wisdom of Sister, and they watched him work patiently with the hounds.

"Well done." Bobby beamed as he passed Shaker.

"Can you eat all that?" Shaker looked at Bobby's full plate.

"I can. That's the problem."

Once everyone had a full plate, the caterer's assistant walked about refilling coffee cups, fetching hot tea or a cold Co-Cola.

People sat on their portable mounting blocks, hay bales, upturned buckets.

Sister, sitting next to Shaker, said to Ronnie Haslip, "Do you remember the day two years ago when Shaker had the flu so I took the horn?"

"Indeed, I do," Ronnie replied.

"I asked him for advice and he said, 'Well, I'll tell you what Fred Duncan told me: Hunt your hounds and don't look behind you.' So I did."

The horses hung their heads over the fence, observing the delighted people. The caterer gave them apples from the fruit basket.

"I like this guy," Keepsake commented.

Golly had positioned herself in the middle of the seated humans. She lay on her side, her tail lazily swishing up and down. Then she casually rolled on her back, her glittering eyes scanning the group. *"I'm here."*

Sybil laughed. "Sister, Golly is speaking to us."

Everyone focused on the cat, which encouraged her behavior. Raleigh and Rooster, seated by Sister, ignored the calico.

"Golly, come over here. I'll give you bacon," Tedi offered.

That fast, the cat sprang to her feet, zoomed over, and snatched the bacon from Tedi's fingers.

"Shameless," Marty commented.

The conversation bounced between everyone at once and then small fragments of people.

Tedi was mentioning to Sister her memories of a safari her parents had taken her on when she was a teenager. ". . . no one thought much about conservation back then. You know, I look back and I regret those tigers and giraffes my parents bagged. But I can't bring himself to throw out the hides. It seems sacrilegious somehow. And you know, too, Janie, I have much more fun foxhunting than I ever did or could on a safari. 'O, the blood more stirs, / To rouse a lion than to start a hare!' Remember? Hotspur. He was wrong."

"Sir Henry Percy never hunted fox, he was too busy hunting the Scots." Crawford joined the conversation.

"Never hunted behind Ashland Bassets, either," Edward commented, mentioning a pack of bassets whose quarry was rabbit. Following them on foot could be very exciting.

"Hey, where's Ralph today?" Betty asked.

"Moline," Ken answered. "Conference."

Moline was the headquarters of John Deere.

"Poor Ralph. Had to miss the first day of cubbing because of business. Work interferes with the really important things in life," Bobby said, and laughed.

As the gathering broke up, Crawford was telling Ron why they chose a breakfast instead of a party. He kept his voice low. ". . . memories. Marty discreetly inquired around and found out that after Nola and Guy disappeared no one ever gave a First Day of Cubbing evening party again. We thought better of it, but then Marty suggested we do this. I think we'll make a tradition of it."

"I hope you do. Of course, that means next year you'll have one hundred people out on the first day."

Crawford shrugged. "Good. I'll just buy more eggs." He picked up his mounting block, placing it inside the tack room of his trailer. "As nothing else had turned up, comes as no surprise, I think we've heard the last of Nola and Guy. It's for the best."

Ron replied, voice even lower, "God, I hope so."

CHAPTER 16

A thin wisp of ground fog snaked over the pasture where Lafayette, Rickyroo, Keepsake, and Aztec munched and a family of raccoons crossed toward the garbage cans in the barn. Occasionally if Sister forgot to close the tack room door the raccoons would open the desk drawer and pull out bags of bite-sized Hershey's bars. They loved sweets, as did the possums who followed them at a discreet distance.

Lafayette lorded it over the Rickyroo and Aztec, both young horses at six and five respectively. He relayed the day's hunting, from the first moment the bit was in his mouth to his wash down with warm water in the wash stall, in colorful detail.

Keepsake, eight years old and a thoroughbred/quarter horse cross, thought Lafayette was laying it on a little thick. He nibbled twenty feet away from the three thoroughbreds. He liked them well enough but he felt he was more intelligent, or at least less gullible.

He noticed the downstairs lights in the house going off, the upstairs bedroom light switching on. The blue light of the television shone from Shaker's window. He noticed Showboat, Gunpowder, and Hojo, three former steeplechasers, dozing in the adjoining pasture. Each of them had been donated to the hunt for the huntsmen's use. Sometimes that meant the horses were orangutans;

no one else could handle them, so this was the last stop unless the owner shipped them off to the killers. Few fox-hunters wanted to put a horse in the knacker's trailer no matter how badly the animal behaved. But the Jefferson Hunt membership had a wide sweep of contacts. Gunpowder had even spent time competing on the flat track. Having run over timber in steeplechase meets, these three disdained the jumps in the hunt field and thought any equine who even glanced sideways at such a puny obstacle, the largest being three feet six inches, was a wimp.

Keepsake could and would jump anything, so he shrugged off their air of superiority.

The night was thankfully cool and pleasant, the breeze still easterly. Sister turned off the air-conditioning and opened the bedroom windows.

The horses and hounds could faintly hear Mozart's *A Little Night Music* floating from her bedroom. Then her phone rang.

She groaned, wondering what the problem was. A night call usually meant a problem. A master's work is endless, whether physical or political, putting out the brush fires flaring up within the hunt club, any hunt club. Some fool left a gate open, another printed up the trail riding schedule and one date was wrong. Someone else hated that cubbing started so early in the morning and they were sure this was a conspiracy to keep them home.

Any group of humans swirls about in a fog of gossip, misunderstanding, and good intentions. Political maneuvering makes for strange bedfellows—and in many an instance the bedfellows really are in bed together. Fox-hunting seems to foster even more of that than other activities. The people, by nature, are hot-blooded just like their horses.

By the end of any given day, Sister's reserves of emotional restraint ebbed.

Not all humans depleted her. The ones she loved energized her: Betty Franklin, Shaker Crown, Tedi and Edward Bancroft, and she thought she could learn to love Dr. Walter Lungrun. Maybe it was because he rented Peter Wheeler's old place and she'd loved Peter, had even been his lover for years. In some ways, Walter reminded her of her husband, a curious resemblance, although socially Walter was more reserved than Raymond. Raymond had come to life in a group, his natural element.

Because of that, Raymond had made a fantastic field master. He'd understood the hounds, but he'd loved the people.

Sister felt her husband had been a better field master than she. She would occasionally forget about the people, so intense was her focus on the hounds. But she put her field in the right place time after time, which they greatly appreciated.

Ray Junior had taken after his father. She'd assumed he'd follow her as field master and then master someday.

She often thought of her husband and son at nighttime. The house, quiet, yielded up memories. Even Golly, a naturally mouthy cat, rested her voice at night.

Melancholy and Sister were never on good terms. She wasn't one to dwell on her losses, on the sorrows that come to us all if we live long enough. They were part of life. If anything, she had learned to thank God for them. Her losses taught her about grace and true love. Her victories taught her to be generous and ultimately thankful.

Tonight as she listened to that most delicious of Mozart compositions, it occurred to her that the structure of music and literature were one and the same thing.

Then the damn phone rang just as this insight was unfolding.

"This better be good!" she growled into the receiver.

A muffled but queerly familiar voice said, "Master, look off the Norwood Bridge—the deep end."

"I beg your pardon." She sat bolt upright.

Both Raleigh and Rooster lifted their heads. Golly, on the pillow next to Sister, pricked forward her ears to better hear the voice on the other end of the line.

"A fifty-five-gallon drum."

"Who is this?"

"Hotspur." With a click, the call ended.

Her hand shaking, she called the sheriff. He'd once given her his cell phone and his home numbers, which she'd prudently placed by the kennel, stable, kitchen, and bedroom phones.

She reached Ben and related her bizarre phone call. Then she hung up, slipped on her moccasins, her white terry cloth robe with her initials, JOA, stitched on the left breast pocket, and hurried down the back stairs into the kitchen. She charged out the back door, running toward Shaker's.

All the horses trotted along with her in their paddocks.

Trident, gazing at the stars, still thrilled from his first hunt, saw her dash to the huntsman's cottage. *"What's Sister doing?"*

Asa, also outside for a walkabout, said, *"Go to sleep, son. You've had a big day."* But he knew something was coming down.

Sister knocked on Shaker's door knocker, a brass crown. "Shaker, Shaker, forgive me for disturbing you."

He opened the door, bare-chested, toothbrush in hand. "What's happened?"

"Oh, Shaker, I heard a voice from the dead."

CHAPTER 17

The Norwood Bridge curved out below a bluff above the Upper James River. Even this far from where its mouth poured into the Chesapeake Bay, the James proved a formidable river. Strong currents, sudden fluctuations in volume, and rough patches of rapids followed by successive small falls meant anyone navigating these waters best be wary.

At times the waters could become surprisingly clear; other times rains pulled down earth from the Blue Ridge Mountains, sending cascades of runoff flowing into the James, making it muddy for days, even weeks.

The village of Norwood, named for Norwood Plantation, still a working farm, clung to the bluff above the river, the source of transportation and commerce well into the 1840s when the bateaus were replaced by the railroads. A small redbrick former church, its steeple pleasingly proportionate to its base, served as the town's post office. While small homes perched along the river roads, larger dwellings sat grandly on the bluff itself, where they had been surveying the river and its passing traffic for three centuries.

Sheriff Ben Sidell watched divers, three of them, submerge then rise again. The Norwood Bridge connected Nelson County with Buckingham County. This was not the deepest part of the Upper James, but was, however, one of the most undisturbed parts of the river.

Few motorized vessels plied these waters. Tubers, rollicking along, would cascade by until they were stopped by the first set of rapids, if indeed they lasted that long. Canoers enjoyed this stretch as the river straightened out from its northern bend. They paddled past fishermen, quietly waiting in their rowboats.

Once a year the bateau festival filled the small town. Flatboats heading downriver and people in period costume drew droves of tourists to watch.

Although it was Sunday, August fourth, Ben acted immediately upon hearing about Sister Jane's mysterious phone call.

After a long talk with Shaker, she'd also called Walter, who agreed to spend the day with Ben Sidell. Sister wanted a hunt club person there and she felt Walter, both by training and temperament, was a good choice.

"If a body was tossed off this bridge, even if sufficiently weighted, it surely would have been carried downstream," Ben said, "be nothing left."

"Two hurricanes tore through here since 1981," Walter replied, "plus plenty of gully washers. But if you follow the direction of the current, a body would have eventually snagged on the shore, maybe there"—he pointed to an eddy on the Buckingham side—"or hung up farther down on the next big arc. Surely someone would have seen it."

"Well, there might only be old shoes to see. Nature's aquatic garbagemen work very efficiently." Ben sighed.

"The murder weapon might have been tossed off the bridge."

Ben pursed his lips. "Yes, but that would work its way downriver as well. Obviously, it's hard to say what killed

Nola—a rock or a hammer or even the butt end of a re-volver. The side of her skull was shattered. Almost like the murderer had snapped into a killing frenzy."

"The reptilian brain." Walter crossed his arms over his chest. "See it with animals. A few will go crazy with killing. That old part of our brain usually means violence."

The temperature was rising, the heavy river smell rising with it.

"I see a lot of strange things in my business," the sher-iff said. "As the social controls have eroded, it seems self-control has eroded with it. We're becoming more violent, not less."

"Rwanda."

"Yugoslavia. Attacks on our country." The sheriff, a pleasant-looking man about the same age as Walter, in the prime of life, squinted as the reflection of the sun off the water temporarily blinded him. "People can usually find a reason to harm someone else. Mix religion into it like the Islamic terrorists and you've glamorized hu-mankind's worst instincts."

Walter half smiled. "Whoever killed Nola didn't need an ideology or national cause."

"And given that she was buried with that huge sap-phire on her finger, it sure wasn't robbery. No, her death was about rage or lust."

"Let's go back to the murder weapon for a minute. As-suming that Sister's caller is telling the truth, if whatever was tossed over this bridge was heavy enough, like a sledgehammer, isn't it possible it sank headfirst into the silt, stuck there, and has been covered and uncovered and probably covered again over the last two decades?" Walter put on his sunglasses, blue elliptical lenses.

"I suppose." Ben leaned against the bridge rail, back to the sun. "Walter, you're a member of the hunt. Why do you think Sister Jane got this call?"

"Trust."

"Huh?"

"He trusts her."

"Hmm." Ben turned this over in his mind. "If it was Guy Ramy he would call her instead of his own mother?"

"You don't know that he hasn't been in contact with Alice. She'd never tell."

"True." Ben nodded.

"If he's guilty, he wants us to find whatever is in this river."

"But he doesn't want us to find him."

"Not yet, anyway."

"I wonder if he'd tell Sister where he is."

"I don't know. But Guy would be about forty-eight now. That's a long time to carry around guilt. He may have killed her, but he also loved her."

"You were in junior high, right?" Ben had talked to a lot of people and his memory was good.

"Seventh grade."

"You didn't really know these people?"

"We lived in Louisa County. I saw them at horse shows. My mother and father knew the hunt club crowd. Dad owned a small tire company in Charlottesville. My mother worked there, too. Sooner or later, everyone would need their tires replaced on trucks or trailers."

"Funny, when I go out to question people, whatever the crime, I sweep up a lot of dust."

"Guess you do."

"In your line of work, I'm sure you pick up a lot, too."

"People usually talk to their doctors." Walter jingled the keys in his pocket.

"There's jockeying for power in the hunt club. Hey, maybe it was a crank call. People are worried about Sister getting too old," Ben said.

Walter took his hand out of his pocket, waving away this thought. "She'll outlive us all."

Ben laughed. "She just might."

One of the divers surfaced, flipped up his face mask, and clung to the side of the boat.

Carl Walsh, sitting at the oars, cupped his hand to his mouth and hollered, "Sheriff, found the top of a fifty-five-gallon drum. Can't see the rest of it, it's sunk all the way in the mud."

Ben crossed the bridge to the northerly side. "Well, see if they can get chains around it."

"Bet there's a stove and a refrigerator down there, too." Walter crossed over with him.

"Just one?" Ben hid his anticipation behind humor.

An hour later, a black fifty-five-gallon drum rested on the shore directly under the bridge. The label had long since washed away, but it appeared to be an old oil drum, maybe a paint drum. A few holes, tiny, had been punched into the metal by rocks or fast-moving debris.

What was curious about it was that the top was welded into place. A rattle could be heard inside when the drum was jostled. And it was heavy, off balance.

"Must be someone in Norwood with an acetylene torch." Ben didn't want to move the drum any more if he could help it. "Carl, call in for a department photographer, too."

Another forty-five minutes passed before Frank Kinser, a distant relative of Doug's, was there with his torch. The photographer arrived, too.

Walter stood back as the blue sparks flew.

Within minutes the lid, cleanly cut, was lifted off.

"Jesus Christ!" Frank cut off his torch, his eyes wide.

A few scraps of cloth clung to a jumble of bones. In the bottom of the drum was a blacksmith's anvil.

The photographer clicked away. Ben carefully observed the remains but did not touch or remove them. Walter felt that there would be hell to pay.

CHAPTER 18

Technology makes a good servant but a bad master. When the Internet first got rolling, Sister Jane hopped on the bandwagon. Her phone bills soon reached stratospheric proportions. She continued using e-mail only to send out notes to the Hunt's Board of Governors and dear friends. The research possibilities pleased her, but more often than not she found she'd much rather pull out her old *Encyclopaedia Britannica*s. The writing could be quite good, and pausing to peruse subjects other than the searched-for subject always provided unexpected delights.

Keeping expenses down was a struggle she shared with millions of Americans who were no longer driven by hunger or need but were victims of advertising and their own acquisitive natures. Wonderful as the Internet might be, it cost money. Before you knew it you were paying for services and technology you didn't really need.

One of these nonnecessities Sister still indulged was Caller I.D. When her mysterious phone call came in, the number appeared on the small telephone screen: 555-7644. Naturally, she gave the number to Ben Sidell, but she already knew it was the outside pay phone at Roger's Corner.

The sheriff called Roger, who dutifully looked out the window, but by then no one was standing at the pay phone. The last hour before Roger's ten P.M. closing time often proved hectic as people came by for a last pack of cigarettes or muffins for breakfast.

Roger's Corner stayed open on Sundays, but Roger himself took the day off. That Sunday morning, Sister drove down there and parked by the blue eggshell that housed the phone. Gone was the tall glass phone booth with the folding door. The replacement was a cheap small plastic egg offering no protection from the elements. She knew what it looked like, but still for some reason she wanted to check out the phone.

People waved to her as they strolled in and out of the store. Why she wanted to pick up the phone, she didn't know.

Kyle Dawson, Ronnie Haslip, and Dr. Tandy Zachs came and went, all of them riding or social members of the hunt. Finally, she realized she couldn't stand there all day, as no new thoughts were coming to her. She climbed back into the truck and drove to After All Farm.

The sheriff's car and Walter's truck, parked in the driveway, made her question if she should go in. She decided she would when Tedi, who had heard her drive up, opened the front door and waved her in. "Come on. Kitchen."

Seated in the cavernous kitchen she found Edward, Sybil, Ken, Ben, and Walter. The men rose when Sister entered the room.

Edward pulled up a chair for her.

Ben smiled but gave her a look. She interpreted it to mean she should keep quiet. Walter sat beside her, draping his arm over the back of her chair. She liked that.

"I'm sorry to barge in."

"You could never barge in," Tedi replied.

"Mrs. Arnold, I was just informing the Bancrofts that I received a telephone tip, a voice that was unidentified, telling me to search off the Norwood Bridge." Ben kicked himself. He'd slipped up in his haste to gather together a team to rendezvous at the bridge at sunrise, and neglected to order Sister to keep her mouth shut.

Ben assumed gossip wasn't Sister's lifeblood, but she could have told a few friends. He'd talk to her afterward, but he was worried. He'd made a mistake. He didn't want Sister Jane to pay for it.

Sister understood Ben's intention when he said that he'd received the phone call.

"Sheriff, I take it you found something or you wouldn't be here," Edward surmised.

"Yes. I asked the Doc to be with me this morning." Again, Ben didn't round out the fact that Sister had called Walter's from Shaker's cottage. "A fifty-five-gallon drum mired in the silt and muck was discovered at seven-thirty this morning. Once we raised it, we cut off the top, as it was soldered shut." Everyone held their breath as Ben continued. "Upon opening it, we discovered it contained human remains. How long the body had been there I can't ascertain, but I would guess for years. We might have a positive I.D. later today."

"So soon?" Ken questioned.

"Larry Hund is meeting the coroner in about an hour." Larry was one of the area's best dentists, a man who had been practicing for twenty-five years.

Tedi folded her hands together on the table and it seemed to Sister that the sapphire burned brighter on her hand. "Ben, you think you know who that body is. That's why you're here. Who is it?"

"Like I said, Mrs. Bancroft, I think we'll have a positive I.D. in an hour or so."

"Was the body recognizable?" Sybil felt a rising panic.

"No flesh remained, a bit of clothing. We know it was a man," Ben replied.

"Oh God," Sybil whispered.

"Hotspur." Tedi Bancroft suddenly felt a wave of sympathy for Alice Ramy. "Does Alice know?"

"I have a deputy with her now and I'll be going over there after I leave here," Ben quietly answered. "Again, the I.D. isn't positive, but we are working from the standpoint that the body may be Guy Ramy because of circumstances."

"And you know that whoever killed Guy didn't dispose of the body alone. It would take a Hercules to stuff a man like Guy into a fifty-five-gallon drum, solder it, and then heave it over the bridge," Edward said with a grimace.

"Yes, we are working from that angle as well," Ben said. "Two or more people."

Ken, ashen-faced, simply said, "Horrible. This is horrible."

Ben had hurried to the Bancrofts' because bad news travels fast. He did not want them to receive a phone call from Mr. Kinser or an onlooker. He wished the I.D. could be 100 percent certain, but the feelings of the Bancrofts were important to him. Ben was a sensitive man in a rough line of work. And he knew the discovery of two bodies would have the killer or killers rattled. What they had thought was long buried had arisen from the dead. Feeling in danger, they might endanger others.

"Is there anything we can do to help you?" Edward inquired, his silver eyebrows raised, his face drawn in concern.

"Be alert," Ben replied simply. "And call me if anything occurs to you, no matter how trivial it might seem."

"Yes, of course," Tedi said.

"Let me be off to Mrs. Ramy's. Oh, Sister, walk out with me to the squad car, will you? Walter, too. Perhaps you two can give me an idea of how to handle Mrs. Ramy."

As Sister, Walter, and Ben walked outside, Sybil rubbed her eyes for a moment.

Tedi patted her daughter on the back. "It's sordid, isn't it?"

"You know, Mom, he was a beautiful thing, like some wild animal—just a beautiful thing."

"Not anymore," Ken said softly as he watched the three people outside.

Ben leaned against his brown squad car. "Sister, I apologize to you. I should have asked you last night not to tell anyone about the phone call. Did you talk to anyone else?"

"Walter"—she nodded at the handsome doctor—"and Shaker. Shaker won't tell anyone. He's not a talker unless it's about hounds."

"Nonetheless, remind him."

"I will."

"Walter?" Ben asked him.

Walter shrugged. "No one."

"Mrs. Arnold, do you have any idea why you were called?"

"No, Ben, I told you, I really don't and I wish I did." She made a straight line in the brown pearock with the toe of her boot. "And please call me Sister or Jane, won't you?"

"I'll try." Ben liked this woman. "Look, this is what I know. Whoever called knows you, trusts you, and lives here. Everyone stops at Roger's Corner in these parts."

"It's one of us," Sister said with no surprise.

"Yes."

"I wish I could tell you more about the voice. A man's voice. I sort of recognized it. He was disguising it, of course, muffling it and speaking in a higher tone, but—" She shrugged.

"You may get another call. Whoever called you knows you called me, and whoever called you may be the murderer."

"After all these years?" Walter hooked his thumb in his belt loop.

"Guilt. Often they want to get caught."

"And more often they don't," Sister sensibly said. "My hunch is whoever called me helped the killer toss that drum over the deep end of the bridge all those years ago."

"I think your hunch is right," Ben agreed.

CHAPTER 19

"There's no hope. I don't care if I live or die!" Alice Ramy cried, teetering on the brink of hysteria.

She'd held herself together when Ben Sidell visited her. Now Tedi, Edward, Sybil, and Ken had come by to express their sympathy. Sister Jane had also come with them after Tedi had asked her please to do so. Alice couldn't put a good face on it any longer.

Tedi, perched on the edge of the wing chair where Alice sat crumpled, said, "You do care. You must care."

"Why?"

"For Guy," Tedi responded.

"He's dead. Dead." She stared at Tedi with vacant eyes.

"You already knew that, didn't you?" Edward tried to be consoling, but this wasn't the path to take.

"No! I prayed he had run away. I didn't want him to be a murderer, but I didn't want him dead."

Sister, standing by the other side of the chair, said, "Alice, I believe Nola and Guy died together. If not at the same moment, then because of each other. I pray their souls rest in peace, but I know mine is in a state. I want to find their killer or killers."

"How?" A flash of life illuminated Alice's eyes; anger, too. "Especially now. Too much time, Sister, too much time."

Sybil, sitting across from Alice with Ken by her side,

spoke up. "Fate. It's fate that they died and now it's fate that they have reappeared. We're supposed to find the killers."

"Fate is just an excuse not to do your homework." Alice smiled ruefully, tears in her eyes now. "When Guy brought home a D in geometry he said it was fate. I said fate is just an excuse not to do your homework. It stuck. There is no such thing as fate."

Resting a strong hand on Alice's shoulder, Sister leaned down. "Then let's do our homework. Try to remember—"

Alice interrupted, "I have!"

"Things can pop into your head at strange times. Come to some hunt breakfasts. Talk to the gang. Something might click," Sister encouraged her.

"Nobody wants to talk to me."

"Of course they do," Tedi said warmly.

"Xavier keeps chickens," Edward said, smiling.

"Fighting chickens," Tedi sniffed.

"Not illegal to keep them. Just illegal to fight and bet on them," Ken responded, trying to humor her, calm her. He didn't really know what to say.

"Guy used to come home from those cockfights plucked cleaner than the chickens. I don't believe he ever won a red cent."

"He won sometimes," Ken said, trying surreptitiously to check the time. "I was there. You just never saw a penny, Alice, because he spent it on wine, women, and song."

"Guy could be very naughty." Alice couldn't conceal a note of pride. After all, how many women bear a son who is widely considered movie-star handsome?

Tedi, having a different take, said, "So could Nola, unfortunately."

"Oh, Tedi, she was high-spirited," Sister said.

"High-spirited with other women's husbands."

"Mother," Sybil exclaimed.

"You thought I didn't know. Nola was a bad girl. I loved her. I couldn't help but love her, but men were chess pieces to her. Every man a pawn and she the only queen."

A moment of embarrassing silence followed, broken when Alice surprisingly said, "She met her match in Guy. That's why they fell in love. Both of them wild as dogs in heat." She looked fleetingly at Edward, then Tedi. "Forgive me."

"It's the truth," Tedi agreed.

Edward, not knowing about all of Nola's amours, shifted uncomfortably in his chair. No father likes hearing these things about his daughter. Tedi certainly had never told him. Nola was the apple of his eye.

Ken, sensing Edward's pain, said, "Dad, she wasn't as bad as all that. Nola was a terrible flirt. She didn't, well, you know . . ."

Tedi knew that was a flat-out lie but decided to let it pass. No point going into the details in front of everyone. It wouldn't help Alice.

"Come to our hunt breakfasts. Reacquaint yourself with your neighbors and friends," Sister said, again extending the invitation. "We go out cubbing Tuesdays, Thursdays, and Saturdays. If weather's iffy, I change around the days, but call me up. Once formal hunting starts October twenty-sixth, I'll send you a fixture card."

"You're just trying to get me to let you hunt here. Guy used to beg me to let you do it, but I still won't. Poor little foxes."

"Those poor little foxes make fools of us all. But Alice, you know that's not why I'm here. I mean it. Come out and see us. You'll be surprised how friendly everyone is. All of Guy's friends are there. You know Ralph and

Xavier. Ronnie Haslip, of course. Ken will be there on Saturdays; sometimes he can squeeze in a weekday. Oh, the Franklins. The boys in their mid-forties—they're all Guy's old running buddies."

"Maybe."

"Alice, excuse me, but I have to go. Richmond business calls." Ken stood up.

"Haven't been to Richmond since 1986." Alice noticed her mantel clock had stopped running. She'd forgotten to wind it.

"Downtown is a little sad. No Miller and Rhoads, no Thalheimer's." Ken mentioned the great department stores that used to draw shoppers like a magnet in the old days. "But it's much the same. What's changed is the West End. The shops, the businesses, Alice, they're all the way out to Manakin Sabot on Broad Street. You just wouldn't believe it."

"Don't want to see it." Her obstinacy was returning, which meant she felt better.

"If you change your mind, I'd be happy to take you down. Be fun to find some fall clothes," Sybil suggested.

Ken smiled. "Sybil, we need to build a new wing on the house for all your clothes."

"She always looks so nice," Alice said. "Thank you, Sybil, but I think I'll pass on Richmond."

Ken walked over, took both of Alice's hands in his, leaned down, and kissed her on the cheek. Sybil also leaned over to kiss her good-bye. Alice hadn't been kissed since Paul died in 1986. She craved human touch but didn't realize it.

"You take care now. And you call me if you need anything," Ken said warmly.

After Sybil and Ken left, the four contemporaries remained quiet for a few minutes.

"You've kept the place up," Edward complimented her.

"Full-time job. Wouldn't be so much work if it weren't for the chickens. I change their water every day. I scrub out their coop every day, too. Doesn't stink like chickens can, you know."

"That's wonderful." Edward nodded pleasantly.

"Edward, Tedi, were you afraid Nola would run off with Guy?"

"Yes," Tedi forthrightly answered for both herself and her husband.

"I was, too. I always assumed you didn't think my boy was good enough for her." An edge sharpened Alice's voice, not the most melodious in any circumstances.

"No, Alice, that wasn't it." Edward approached this with his usual tact. "A fire that flames that blazingly hot can turn to ashes in a heartbeat."

Tedi's eyes searched out her husband's. She had underrated him. Like most women she felt she understood emotions far better than men. Edward might not choose to talk about emotions, but he understood them, a real victory.

"I thought of that, too." Alice glanced down at her crepe-soled shoes, then up again at Edward. "It scared me. For him, I mean. I don't think Guy had ever truly been in love until Nola."

"For what it's worth, I think she loved him," Sister said. She moved to sit opposite Alice.

"Did you?" Tedi genuinely inquired.

"I did. I didn't know what would come of it. They both had a history of being carefree, if you will, but there is something to be said about the changes that happen to you when you meet the right one. One does settle down eventually."

"I thought she'd throw him away." Alice didn't sound rancorous. If anything, she was grateful to finally be able to speak about this.

"I did, too," Tedi said. "It wasn't Guy. Don't get me wrong. It was money. Nola loved money. She might have married him, but it would have fizzled. And regardless of what you might think, we did not spoil either of our girls. Yes, they both went to the best schools, but they didn't get cars handed to them on their sixteenth birthdays. They had to earn the money. And every summer each one took a job. Oh, it might have been something fun like working on a ranch in Wyoming, but still, it was the beginning of responsibility. And, well, it's as clear as the nose on our faces, Sybil was by far the more prudent, the more sensible. Nola worked, but she spent it as fast as she made it. Then she'd run out and come begging. I certainly never made up her debts, but I think"—Tedi nodded at Edward—"her father may have."

"Once or twice, my dear, I didn't make it a habit."

"Oh, Edward." Tedi didn't believe a word of it.

"She wouldn't have had money with Guy," Alice argued. "Burned a hole in his pocket. He could have made money. He had the brains for it, but not the discipline. But he was only twenty-five when he died. Almost twenty-six. I'd like to think he would have found something to gainfully occupy him."

"I'm sure he would have," Sister said. She had seen Ralph, Ken, Ronnie, and Xavier each settle down and prosper. She thought Guy would have come 'round, too.

"Perhaps the fates are kind," Tedi said, smoothing her skirt. "Nola and Guy were killed at the height of love, the first blush. They never knew disillusionment."

"I told you I don't believe in fate," Alice stubbornly insisted. "And I don't see how dying at twenty-five can be considered kind. So they would have fought. Guy would have gotten drunk or picked up sticks and left for a while. He would have recovered. She would have, too. It's all stuff and nonsense, this love business."

"Not when you're young and maybe not when you're old. I might be seventy-one, but I tell you, let another woman go after Edward and I'll knock her sideways."

"You flatter me." Edward smiled. "I'm the one on guard here. I have a wife who looks thirty years younger than myself. It can be quite nerve-racking. Why, one of Ken's friends tried to woo her at a company gathering over the Fourth of July."

"Now who's the flatterer?" Tedi shook her head.

"Well, I'm the cynic. Year in and year out Paul Ramy brought me flowers on my birthday, chocolates on Valentine's Day, and usually a charm for my charm bracelet at Christmas. That was it. No variety and no spontaneity. I think Guy became romantic just because his father wasn't. Now, my son always brought me little presents, even as a child." She stopped herself and swallowed. "When Ben Sidell came here I thought it was more questions. I didn't think I'd find out what happened to Guy."

CHAPTER 20

Diminutive, intense, levelheaded, Gaston B. Marshall became a pathologist by default and county coroner by fiat. When Vee Jansen, the coroner since 1949, died of a heart attack in 1995, Gaston inherited the job.

In other counties, especially above the Mason-Dixon line, county commissioners might have grumbled at having such an ancient coroner as Vee Jansen performing autopsies. This would have been superseded by a new wave of grumbling as a much younger man assumed the duties. But in central Virginia, in this county, where everyone claimed everyone else as shirttail cousins, Gaston was readily accepted when he became coroner. He was a homeboy. Gaston B. Marshall, a professor of medicine at the university, now had two jobs. The extra stipend from the county was useful. Gaston was the father of three grade-school children. The university, for all its grandeur, paid poorly.

The other good thing about this job was Gaston was left to his own devices. If he wanted students to assist him, no one quibbled. If he wanted to utilize his findings in his lectures, names of the deceased changed, he could do it. Being county coroner proved a rich source of teaching material. His students could see things they might not see at the university hospital. During one autopsy of a drunken gentleman, well born but bone idle, when he attempted to lift out the liver it literally disintegrated in his hands. If nothing else, those students witnessing the diseased liver would think twice before drinking too much.

On the Sunday the body was recovered from the river, he had but one assistant, a female intern utterly enraptured by pathology, Mandy Collatos. Perhaps the appeal was you were always right but one day late. In the case of Guy Ramy their findings were twenty-one years late almost to the day.

Walter Lungrun stood in scrubs over the stainless-steel table, the channels on the side sloping downward for drainage.

Ben Sidell, a by-the-book man most times, wanted Gaston to see the drum, so he delivered that as well. It sat near the table. A large double sink, also stainless steel, ran along the wall.

All three physicians wore thin rubber gloves.

"You know if there hadn't been punctures in the drum I believe he would have been mummified." Mandy was proud that they had extracted the skeleton doing precious little damage to it, no easy task.

"Yes." Gaston finished placing the bones in their proper position. The major joint areas had come apart when the skeleton was removed, much as a joint pulls out of a chicken leg. Plus the anvil in the bottom of the drum had broken bones probably on the drop into the river. The drum had settled after that.

Walter watched intently.

"Dr. Marshall," Mandy said, pointing to two ribs, left side.

Gaston bent down, his upturned nose almost touching the graceful, thin rib bones. "Uh-huh. When a body has been out this long, you hope for the best. We were lucky Nola was buried in red clay. It preserved her longer."

"The methods of killing were different for these two," Walter said.

"Yes. Interesting . . ." Gaston noticed that Guy's right shinbone was shorter than the left and thicker. "Old break."

"Casanova Point-to-Point Races. Late seventies," Walter said. He marveled at the body's ability to knit itself back together.

"You were there?"

"Actually, I was. My mother took me. I was always crazy for horses. Guy crashed a timber fence. No fault of his own. The jockey in front of him bobbled in front of the jump, flew off, and Guy's horse braked hard." Walter smiled slightly. "He threw Guy straight into the timber. He was out foxhunting the next week in a cast. At least that's what I heard."

A knock on the door made Gaston pause in his examination. "Come in."

Larry Hund, the dentist, entered the room. He was carrying a folder. "Still has a jawbone."

"Larry, we see a lot of strange things in here—including one another." Gaston motioned for him to step up to the table.

Larry pulled out the dental charts and swiftly checked the teeth, most still in the jawbone. "Guy Ramy."

Gaston and Mandy, nothing if not thorough, finished up in another hour, obsessively checking and double-checking, measuring bones, making detailed notes.

Larry inspected the drum before leaving. "Boy, someone wanted him to stay put. Got an anvil in there."

"But he didn't stay put, did he?" Gaston yanked a paper towel off the dowel.

"I don't know how you can do your work." Larry smiled. "It's one thing when bare bones are on the table.

But when you have to cut into a corpse that's been out there for days or weeks . . ."

"You get used to it, but I don't think any of us look forward to working on a body exposed for a few days. When it's hot, one day will do it. I can smoke cigars, shove Vicks VapoRub up my nose or camphor oil, the damned stench still gets through. After they've been out a week, unless, of course, they're frozen, it actually begins to improve."

"What's the fascination?" Larry rarely had an opportunity to talk to Gaston like this.

"Answers. I can often get the answers and, in the case of wrongful death, clues to the killer."

"Well, I don't know about this one." Larry picked up his folder. "How will you ever find the killer?"

"I don't know." Gaston sighed.

Mandy put the body in a cooler drawer, slid it shut with a thunk, and inserted a paper card in the small slot in the front, with a number on it.

"Anyone else in here?" Larry was curious.

"No, it's been quiet." He finished toweling off. "You did a good job on Nola, by the way. I don't remember if I thanked you. So many teeth were missing. I don't know if her killer smashed her skull in first or hit her in the face first."

"Do you think it's weird—pathology?" Mandy asked Larry.

"In a sense," he honestly answered. "The typical response to death is aversion, even repulsion."

"True," Gaston agreed. "I had to overcome that myself in med school. But then, I remember it as clear as yesterday, we were in lab working on the circulatory system and I was lifting up the aorta, like rubber those cadavers, and I stepped back to look at the body. The arteries and the veins were a tracery of life. It was beautiful. I looked at bodies differently after that, and let's face it, I wasn't meant to be a plastic surgeon. No bedside manner."

"Yeah, you don't have to talk to your patients," Walter said, smiling. He regularly dealt with people in acute distress.

"Right," Larry laughed at Gaston and Mandy, "your patients don't talk back."

"Oh, but they do," Gaston countered, "they do."

CHAPTER 21

Aunt Netty, cross with Uncle Yancy, trotted over to Target's den. The last quarter of the moon, a thin melon slice in the Prussian blue sky, pulsated with feeble light.

Target, a hefty eight pounds if he was an ounce, sat near the main entrance. His mate, Charlene, was eating blackberries curling over the fence line near the edge of the woods about a quarter of a mile from the den. Just beyond that fence, rolling pastures swept up to the farm road and then on to the kennels.

Their three cubs this year, half grown, had left early to set up homes around Wheeler's Mill. Roughneck Farm, After All, and Foxglove, filled with reds and grays, were reaching the saturation point. Target and Charlene knew that the old, nasty red who had lived underneath the mill had succumbed to old age. The place needed foxes, and it was better to get their cubs established early before the reds farther south got the bright idea to move in.

Plentiful game meant the young ones would be fine for food. Also, Walter Lungrun occasionally put out dog food supplemented with liquid wormer as well as tasty bits of sweet feed. The molasses flavor was delicious.

"Netty, you've got on your mad face." Target laughed at his sister.

"Yancy's in one of his hoarding moods. He's burying

161

dead crickets, which is the dumbest thing. Chicken, rabbit pieces, yes. But crickets? That run on the first day of cubbing has affected his mind."

"*I thought it was being married to you,*" Target wryly said.

"*What a pathetic attempt at humor. I wouldn't be sitting here laughing. Tuesday, Sister will take out more puppies and she'll have Dragon in the pack. He wasn't with them Saturday or Yancy would be a goner for sure.*"

"*Sister ought to draft out that hound. He's too fast. He'll ruin the pack.*" Target knew for a pack of hounds to be good they should run together. Dragon pushed ahead too far.

"*It's his second year. She'll give him the year to see if he improves. And you know she loves his blood, lot of Piedmont blood in her D line.*" Piedmont Fox Hounds, founded in northern Virginia in 1840, was the oldest organized hunt in America.

Henry Hudson brought hounds with him when he discovered the river that now bears his name. American settlers hunted with hounds almost from the founding of the first surviving colony in 1607. But Piedmont was the first hunt organized in the modern sense, and those who wore its colors, old gold, could be forgiven a bit of swagger.

"*He's an arrogant hound,*" Netty said.

"*I got my revenge last year when I lured him into a copperhead.*"

"*He'll never forget it, which is why I'm here. To remind you that Tuesday, Sister will cast hounds this way and Dragon will be with them. I'd stay in my den if I were you.*"

"*Ha! I'll break his neck yet.*"

"*Unless he breaks yours. He's fast, Target, and he's seventy pounds of hard muscle to your eight. He can* snap your neck in a split second if he bumps you and rolls you. He has that kind of drive."

"Netty," Target said, incensed, standing up. "I'm almost as fast as you are."

She wanted to say, "but not as smart." Instead, she cajoled him. "True enough. I'm just giving you a heads-up. The whole pack is faster, and if Bitsy hadn't been around it really would have been a near thing for Yancy, the damned fool."

"Wonder why Sister is breeding for more speed? They're already fast enough and I must commend her and them for their nose. Boy, she has really improved the way they track a scent." Target mentioned the ability of a hound to scent.

"She has, and let's not forget, we've had more moisture this year. That's going to help them, too. We'd better be on our paws. I know neither Sister nor Shaker wants to kill any of us, but accidents happen."

"If I have to die I'd rather die that way than from mange." Target flicked his tail. Netty's infernal and constant advice irritated him.

"Wouldn't we all. Here's to old age! But take your medicine. Sister spends good money on that stuff and now she's putting it on dog kibble instead of stuffing it inside dead chickens. It's easier to get at."

"I do eat the damned stuff, Netty!"

Before he could cuss her out and tell her to stop mothering him, Athena, talons spread, swooped over them. "Hoo hoo hoo." She laughed as they both flattened. She turned and landed on the lowest limb of the slippery elm. "Good evening."

"Athena, you scared the wits out of me," Netty grumbled as she dusted herself off.

"Why, Netty, I don't think that's possible."

Netty, somewhat mollified, said, *"You're looking well."*

"Shrews, I've been eating shrews. Does wonders for me. Well, Target, cat got your tongue?"

"No, it's good to see you. I hear you helped out Uncle Yancy the other morning."

"St. Just was calling the hounds on after they'd lost scent."

"I'll kill him if it's the last thing I do."

"You know, Target, that's what he says about you," Aunt Netty said, adding her two cents.

"I'm here with the news. Guy Ramy's body, sealed in a fifty-five-gallon drum, was dredged out of the James this morning. A red-winged blackbird watched the whole thing."

"Blackbirds, crows, ravens," Target snarled, *"can't believe a word they say."*

"Don't let your hostility to the species blind you to the truth," Athena sagely counseled.

"You're quite right," Aunt Netty agreed, and wanted to kick her brother hard with her hind leg. One needed to pay court to Athena. She stared crossly at Target.

Although full of himself, he wasn't stupid. *"You are right, Athena. I hear the name, St. Just, and my blood boils. He killed my son."*

"And you killed his wife. You're even. Be done with it." She raised herself to her full height, as she'd been leaning down to speak to the foxes. Athena, at two feet tall, was undeniably regal.

Target weighed his next words. *"Yes, but I think it's gone beyond that. I don't think he'll stop. After all, he called the hounds on Uncle Yancy."*

"I know. My concern is that you don't endanger other animals with this blood feud. There's enough going on now. Finding Guy Ramy is not a good omen for any of us."

"The humans are already stirred up about Nola Bancroft." Aunt Netty moved over to sit beside her brother.

"The human who killed these two knew enough to put them where vultures couldn't get them or dogs dig them up. He or she knows a little something about animals. Right?"

"Yes." Aunt Netty nodded her head.

"And although none of us were born then, we know from the humans' incessant talking that Nola and Guy disappeared after the first day of cubbing in 1981. A full cycle. Cubbing has just begun." She leaned down toward them again. *"And if they turn up something or someone gets a notion, they'll start digging, literally. They'll disturb our dens and nests and flush game. They'll make a mess."*

"I'd better tell the cubs at Wheeler's Mill," Target thought out loud.

"I already did. And Bitsy is telling Butch, Mary Vey, Comet, and Inky." Athena mentioned the gray foxes.

"Do you really think it's that bad?" Target wondered, not wanting to challenge her, just wondering.

"Actually, I'm afraid one of them's going to snap." Athena's low voice dipped even lower. *"Bitsy, Inky, and I saw Ralph Assumptio, crying, parked by the side of the road."*

"That's it. He's the killer, then," Target declared.

"Maybe. Maybe not." The brown bird cast her golden eyes upward as a blue heron, late, headed for home. *"My point is they are all feeling the strain."*

"Do the hounds know?" Aunt Netty asked.

"Yes. Bitsy is telling them."

"Who cares if they know?" Target didn't dislike the hounds, but he felt them an inferior member of the canine family because they allowed themselves to be domesticated.

"*Are you argumentative tonight or thickheaded?*" Netty nudged him on his shoulder. "*The hounds are closer to the humans than we are.*"

"*And the killer is a foxhunter as surely as I am the Queen of the Night.*"

A little while after Athena had left, Charlene returned. Target and Netty filled her in, then they all discussed what Athena meant about the killer being a foxhunter. They weren't sure.

Athena had been figuring. There had been no reports of struggle. If there'd been a fight in a car or truck, someone would have noticed the blood and the damage to the vehicle. If someone had sold their vehicle immediately after the disappearance, someone would have noticed that, too. Both Nola and Guy willingly followed or climbed into the vehicle of their murderer. Nola's car was left at the Burusses'. Guy's was parked downtown on the street. Athena had gathered all this with Bitsy's help by listening to the humans talk on their porches or on the phone, windows open.

She had just been sharing all this with Bitsy, sitting on a crossbeam in Sister's barn. Bitsy nodded. "*Guy and Nola knew their killer.*"

Athena added, "*And trusted him.*"

CHAPTER 22

The humidity, suddenly oppressive, pressed down on the green pastures, the blazing white and deep pink crepe myrtle, the orange daylilies. Even the green metallic dragonflies, surprised by the rapid climb in temperatures and the dew point, sat motionless on lily pads in ponds. Rockfish dozed in deep creek eddies, frogs burrowed in cooling mud.

Lafayette, Rickyroo, Keepsake, and Aztec stood nose to tail under the enormous pin oak in their pasture. Showboat, Gunpowder, and Hojo did the same under a fiddle oak in their neighboring separate pasture.

Golliwog reposed on the library sofa. Raleigh and Rooster stretched out at Sister's feet beneath her desk.

The Louis XV desk, a wedding gift from Raymond's mother, was not an idle antique. Despite its great value, Sister worked at the desk much as the royal court secretary who had scribbled at it centuries ago.

The library, not a large room, housed Sister's most beloved books, especially her sporting library. Some of those volumes, precious to her as well as collectors, had been written and printed in the eighteenth century. She loved the pages themselves, crisp paper of such high quality, one would have to search the great libraries of Europe for its equivalent today. The type, velvet black, had been cut into the paper by metal, each letter set by hand. The typefaces, elegant yet simple, had been carefully selected by the bookmaker or possibly even the author.

Sister had observed that modern books, printed on cheap paper, thermographed print, disintegrated in decades. The author not only had nothing to do with the process but was actively kept from it.

Sister inhaled the special tang of her library as she worked. Old fires, leather bindings, a scented candle on the mantelpiece added to the allure of the room along with the Heather St. Claire Davis painting of herself on Lafayette leaping down an embankment over a creek bed, hounds in the near distance, the huntsman right up with them.

The twenty-first century, mass production having vulgarized just about every single human activity, still could not cheapen foxhunting. For this, the older woman was profoundly grateful. This pastime could never become a vehicle for mass merchandisers. Whippers-in would not be embroidering advertisements for tires, cars, or deodorant on their coat sleeves. Saddle pads would not bear a pharmaceutical logo. Velvet hunt caps, black derbies, glistening silk top hats would be spared a dotcom address.

Sister wasn't a snob, far from it. Nor was she especially rich. Raymond, to his eternal credit, had done well as a stockbroker, leaving her with a portfolio large enough to provide for her needs. Raymond figured life would never get cheaper, only more and more expensive, as Americans demanded ever more services, which meant ever more taxes. He knew the cities would always vote themselves more money. Country people would have to fight not only for their way of life but simply to have a life. He had invested wisely and died knowing that whatever his failings as a husband, he had been a good provider.

Sister was of that generation who expected men to provide for women and children. Indeed, it was a disgrace if a man's wife worked. Poor women had to work, so if a woman took a job it meant a man had failed. Through supporting a host of charitable organizations, well-to-do women did work. They just weren't paid for it. That was fine. It made the men feel better and perhaps some of the women, too.

She didn't think of herself as a rebel, but she'd taught geology at Mary Baldwin College even after marrying Raymond. He'd fussed, but she'd loved it so much. She stopped working when Ray Junior was born in 1960. When Ray was killed in 1974 she probably should have picked up teaching again, but somehow she couldn't seem to put one foot in front of the other for a year. The second year after her son died she functioned perfectly well but felt numb. The third year she came back to herself. Had it not been for her husband, foxhunting, her friends, and Peter Wheeler, she thought she might have disappeared into the hole the White Rabbit had vanished into. Maybe life was *Alice in Wonderland*.

There wasn't a day when she didn't think of Ray Junior and miss him. She missed her husband, too, who died in 1991, although missing a husband stirs emotions of a darker shade than missing a son. A husband left one with transgressions to forgive. A son left blasted promise. Then again, she'd transgressed enough herself to forgive Raymond his exuberance for life, which spilled over into an excessive appreciation for beautiful women. We were all human. Sister could forgive. It might take her time, but she could. She could never figure out if she was a good Christian or if exhaustion finally won out.

A photograph in a silver frame lit up the left corner of

the desk. Raymond, herself, and a twelve-year-old Ray Junior, all in formal hunting attire, rode as a hunt team at the Washington International Horse Show. Raymond, resplendent in his scarlet weaselbelly and his white vest, grinned, his teeth sparkling white against his tanned face. Sister wore a black shadbelly, Continental blue colors on the collar, patent leather tops on her Spanish-cut boots so polished, they reflected the photographer's flashbulb. Ray wore a hunt cap, black melton, fawn-colored breeches, and butcher boots. He was properly dressed for a junior, the unspoken rule of thumb being that even if a child has earned his colors, he doesn't wear tails, called weaselbelly for a man, or a frock coat or tops on his boots until his voice changes and he shaves. For girls, whose voices change but not as dramatically, the rule was harder to interpret but by sixteen few masters would look amiss if a young lady rode out in a frock as opposed to a simple melton. A frock coat has two buttons on the back and a double vent, whereas the melton has a single vent on the back.

Sister, having grown up foxhunting, knew the sartorial rules, but sometimes even she had to consult the authorities from prior centuries in her library. If stymied she'd call Cindy Chandler at Foxglove Farm or Dr. Chuck Beegle at Brookhill Farm. Among the three of them they could usually find the definitive answer.

Nola had often caused feuds in the hunt field. For whatever reason, Nola appointed herself the fashion police, which did not go down with older members. The fight over Frances's veil was but one of many such eruptions. She pitched a fit when Gordie Tomlinson rode out in dark brown gloves. One should wear mustard-colored gloves or white knit gloves, depending on the weather and the formality of the occasion. Even a British tan deerskin pair would pass muster, but Gordie wore dark brown, which sent Nola into orbit.

Sister had to chastise Nola for her behavior and tell Gordie that while dark brown wasn't perfect, she was only too happy to accept it except for High Holy Days. Nola fumed for weeks after that, declaring that Sister was letting standards go to hell.

The most recent fuss had occurred the previous March when Ralph Assumptio carried a blackthorn knob end whip on a Saturday, a formal day. Ronnie Haslip snapped at Ralph over this lapse in taste.

Ralph should have properly carried his staghorn crop, thong attached. However, the broad fat loop at the end of the crop to which the thong attaches had torn clear through on a hard, long hunt two days before. Ralph left his crop with Betty Franklin to repair. Betty enjoyed doing leather repair, she said it was kind of like needlepoint only harder. So, he grabbed his blackthorn knob end.

Sister rode back, heard the explanation, then told Ralph naturally he could carry his knob end until repairs were completed. This had to be declared in front of the whole field to satisfy all parties. If Ralph had thought about it, he would have obtained Sister's permission for this variance before the hunt.

Knob ends, technically, can be carried during cubbing and during informal days after Opening Hunt. Most every hunt granted its members at least one informal day during the formal season. This allowed members time to repair torn jackets, dry out boots if they'd crossed high water, bleach stock ties, or do whatever needed to be done to restore their formal kit.

She glanced again at the photograph of the three of them. She used to grumble to big Raymond about the cost of outfitting a child. She wished she had shut up. He had been worth every penny. Many's the time she'd dragged that poor kid through the shops in Marshall and Middleburg where good used hunting attire was sold. He was an angel about it, especially since he'd really wanted to go to Horse Country in Warrenton.

He would have been forty-one in December.

Where does the time go? Where does the soul go?

Would she see him again when her time came?

She banished these ruminations from her mind. They served no purpose and would make her cry. She had a draw list to compose for Tuesday's hunt. She looked down at the sheet of paper, organized into bitches, dog hounds, second-year entry, first-year entry. Each hunt she kept a list of who participated. Then she'd take the sheet back to her desk and make a notation of who did what. A sharp pencil is worth more than a good memory.

Dragon had to go this time. Trident and Trudy had gone, so she'd take their littermates, Tinsel, Trinkle, and Trinity. Rassle and Ruthie, also first year, should go. She hated to leave Cora in the kennel because Dragon would then be the strike hound, but Cora had gone Saturday and she had a tendency to run weight right off herself. Sister wanted to start the season with her hounds a few pounds over their fighting weight so by Opening Hunt they'd be perfect. Then she and Shaker needed to watch them like hawks. A hound can easily run thirty or forty miles in one day, and on a screaming day, even sixty. They run much farther than the riders, for the hounds are running into coverts, coming back, going out again. The riders, confined to ground horses can navigate, cover fewer miles. Still, after a hard day many an experienced hunter would dismount only to find his legs like jelly.

If a hound was starting to get light, Shaker would feed her or him separately or leave the animal in the kennel until back up to sufficient weight. Sister would not hunt a hound whose weight had fallen too low for her liking.

Her kennel practices bordered on the obsessive, but no one could ever say this woman did not love her hounds or her horses.

Her fierce concentration prevented her from hearing a car roll up the driveway.

Raleigh lifted his head. *"Visitor."*

"Maybe it's an intruder." Rooster sprang up and raced for the back door.

"Yoo-hoo, Janie," Tedi called out.

"In the library."

Rooster greeted Tedi, then escorted her to the library, where Raleigh met her, too. Golliwog opened one eye; that was the extent of her greeting.

"Bills?" Tedi asked.

"Tuesday's draw list. I need to mix my steady Eddies with the youngsters. Can I get you anything?"

"No. Ken just left for Richmond much too late. Edward and Sybil went to the club. She had a bad spell, floods of tears, which is why Ken got off so late. I just had to get out of the house, which I suppose makes me some sort of chicken. I can't bear to see all those pictures of Nola right now. And I feel guilty because I should feel more compassion for Alice than I do."

"Join the club."

"She doesn't make it easy, does she?"

"You were kind to go to her."

"Who better to understand both the shock and the relief?" Tedi sat in the overstuffed club chair, tucking a needlepoint pillow behind her in the small of her back.

"It's been a grisly time, hasn't it?" agreed Sister, now sitting comfortably on the sofa.

"Don't jiggle the sofa," Golly complained.

Sister reached back to pet her.

"You ought to smack her," Rooster advised.

"I'd smack back. In fact, why don't you stick your wet nose here? I'll smack you, too," Golly threatened.

"Chatty, isn't she?" Tedi thought the long-haired calico an exceptionally beautiful cat. "Do you know I have had the most curious experience. These last three days I've noticed a little screech owl, she's no bigger than a minute, either in the barn or in the tree. She winks at me. I swear it. And I see her around. I feel as if this owl is following me. Sybil says, 'Mom, you're out there.' "

"She probably likes you. Just because an animal is undomesticated doesn't mean it can't take an interest in you."

"Do you really think so?"

"Sure, look at Inky or Aunt Netty." The two foxes were both well-known to hunt club members.

"I hope we don't hop Aunt Netty until it cools down. She'll run the legs right off of the hounds and us."

"That she will. You know, Inky will sit at a distance when I'm in the hound graveyard or when I'm gardening up here around the house. She'll sit and stare. She's a dear little thing."

"The black fox legend doesn't scare you?" Tedi brought up the legend that the appearance of a black fox presages upheaval.

"No, not really. It's not that uncommon a color variation. On the other end of it, look at that cub over at Wheeler's Mill. So blond, he looks like a golden retriever and just as leggy. He's going to be an odd-looking creation."

"Let's go out to dinner, my treat." Tedi smiled. "In fact, let's take Shaker. Come on, you can finish your draw list later." She checked her watch. "You call Shaker. I'll call Keswick Hall."

"Oh, we'll have to get all dressed up."

"I mean the Sport Club. We can go in Bermuda shorts and sit at the little table by the bar. I don't want to get dressed up, either."

Within forty-five minutes all three of them were awaiting their appetizers. Sister sipped hot tea, Shaker drank iced tea, while Tedi indulged in a martini, the tiny corkscrew of lemon peel dancing around in the gin and vermouth. She said she wanted a twist instead of an olive because olives were for cool weather, lemons were for hot.

The three had also made a pact to not discuss Nola or Guy. One, it was too depressing. Two, they felt they were going around in circles about it. Three, Tedi especially needed to be distracted, which is exactly why she had left her daughter and husband at Farmington Country Club while she repaired to Keswick. Both country clubs also had hunt clubs bearing their names.

By the time the main courses arrived, all were in much more relaxed moods. Sister ordered sesame-crusted salmon; Tedi tried the pan-seared tuna, which she found delicious. Shaker stuck to chicken.

By the time they'd ordered their desserts they were telling old hunting stories and laughing.

Nancy Holt, the club tennis pro, came in and was hailed over to the table. She hunted with Keswick Hunt Club during the season on her day off, Wednesday.

"And what are you doing at work?" Tedi asked the tall, attractive woman.

"Just finished a kids' tournament. Hey, I didn't know Crawford Howard paid an extra five thousand dollars so Doug would come over to Shenandoah."

"What?" All three stopped, forks filled with rich dessert poised in midair.

"Yes. Doakie Sproul was in the tournament. His mother

told me they were surprised but grateful." Mrs. Georgianna Sproul, wife of the master of the Shenandoah Hunt, was Doakie's mother.

"That son of a bitch." Shaker put his fork down.

"Uh-oh. Did I say something wrong?" Nancy put her hand to her mouth.

"No, you did not. Sit here. Would you like dinner?" Tedi patted the seat.

"No, thank you, but I'll take a drink."

As the drink was ordered, Shaker's face grew redder. "That asshole. That total shit." He drank a sip of tea. "I'm sorry, ladies."

"I guess you didn't know." Nancy had no great love for Crawford since he kept running into her during joint meets. He'd use her for a bumper when he couldn't hold Czapaka.

"Who did?" Tedi wondered. "And how come Wyatt Sproul didn't tell you?" Wyatt was Shenandoah's master.

"Wy is a good man. He must have thought I already knew." Sister was putting two and two together.

"Doug would have told you. Means he doesn't know," Shaker said, his color returning to its normal ruddy shade. "Sister, do I have your permission to strangle Crawford?"

"No, dear, he's not worth going to jail over."

"We have to get even." Tedi, too, was disturbed at this underhanded ploy.

"Oh, Tedi, we will." Sister returned to her impossibly rich chocolate ice cream.

All four people realized Crawford had secretly paid to bump up Doug's salary. Not only would this make the huntsman's job more attractive but it would help Sister Jane accept that Doug should be at Shenandoah Hunt, not a particularly well-heeled club. Much as she wanted him to carry the horn, she didn't want him to starve doing it.

Sister realized Crawford wasn't motivated by a desire to help Doug, but rather one to weaken Jefferson Hunt. Doug was an inspired first whipper-in, and one reason for the club's success in the field. Crawford was betting on his substitute, like any rookie, making mistakes. If the season wasn't as good as it might be, if other clubs boasted better seasons, a certain amount of unrest would bubble up in the club. The hardened hunters knew better, but the fair-weather hunters and newcomers to the sport could be easily discouraged by a lackluster season. Especially if other clubs were having a good one.

Then he'd move in, and fan the unrest. As he was fanning, he would make certain everyone would become aware of the many fine things he could do if he were master, but you can't expect a man to spend his hard-earned cash in lavish amounts if he isn't going to carry the title of joint-master.

Tedi leaned back. "He'll stop at nothing."

"That idiot will be joint-master over my dead body." Shaker's eyes blazed.

"Don't say that—not under the circumstances," Sister gently corrected him.

CHAPTER 23

Spotty scent kept the hounds picking on the morning of September 10. They'd find a thread of enticement in the woods at Foxglove Farm, tease it toward the hayfields, then lose it in the middle of the hay, bent low under a steady wind slicing down off the Blue Ridge Mountains.

Days like this tested hounds, huntsman, and staff. During formal hunting, if the field was running and jumping, they usually paid little mind to the hard work of hounds, the conditions of soil and wind. But most of the souls who roused themselves to be at the fixture at seven-thirty in the morning knew hunting and were respectful of hound work. Cubbing brought out the best.

The tails, down, on Sister's old brown hunt cap flapped as she reined in one hundred yards from the huge chestnut in the middle of the hayfield. Two jumps beckoned enticingly in the fence line, but there was no telling if the hounds would head in that direction.

Walter took off work to hunt Thursday mornings, but as this was Tuesday, she found she missed him. Most wise employers in Virginia Horse Country will allow their employees one morning off, especially if the employee will work late another day. Beneficent as this sounds, it's a little bit like the schoolteacher who wishes everyone well on the first day of deer season and suspends classes. They're going to go, so you might as well make the best of it. City people frothed at the mouth over this when they moved to these parts to start a business. They often left declaring the eternal backwardness of Southerners.

Tuesdays and Thursdays, the numbers in the field remained low until Opening Hunt, perhaps ten to twenty depending on the weather. During formal hunting, Sister Jane averaged about twenty-five on weekdays and sixty on weekends.

Today, Tedi, Edward, Ralph, Xavier, Ronnie, Jennifer Franklin, Crawford, Marty, and Sari Rasmussen, a school friend of Jennifer's, waited with Sister in the hayfield.

The fox whose fading trail they'd been following, Grace, was a vixen from Target and Charlene's litter last year. Slender with a lot of black on her mask, she loved to fish in the ponds at Foxglove Farm. These two ponds on different levels had a waterwheel between them, moving water from one level to another, aerating the water. Grace's mother would shake her head and wonder why any child of hers preferred fishing to sauntering into the barn to eat grain and a few fat barn mice. Foxglove's house dog, a German shepherd, betrayed no interest in chasing foxes.

Once Grace heard Dragon's big mouth, she took off, running up the creek, over the rocks, and finally bursting into the hayfield. She knew hounds were far behind her and struggling with scent, so she doubled back on her track and slipped into her brother Reynard's old den. Reynard, killed last year by an act of human malice, had a roomy den that no other creature currently used. Grace's den was under one of the barns at Foxglove Farm. She could walk to work, as she put it.

She curled up for a well-earned snooze.

The field waited for ten minutes as the morning sun changed from scarlet to pink to gold.

Betty Franklin, on the left side today, stood at the edge of the hayfield. Sister figured Sybil was still in the woods to the right. Every now and then she heard Shaker's "Whoop."

He could blow a beautiful hunting horn but preferred to use his voice until hounds found scent, then he'd call other hounds to the line. When hounds burst out of the covert he'd blow "Gone Away."

The riders watched the hounds fan out over the field. Sister was very proud of her members, even Crawford, as they didn't automatically chatter and gossip at checks like this. Since he so desperately wanted to be joint-master, Crawford was now listening intently and making certain his behavior was unimpeachable in the field.

Target heard the hounds as he was heading home from the south side of Hangman's Ridge. He trotted across the sunken fields, crossed Soldier Road, then loped across the floodplain fields until the earth rose in front of him. He crossed under a three-board fence and entered the swaying hayfields directly across the farm road from where Sister waited.

Every now and then he'd catch a word or two in the distance from Dragon. He laughed to himself.

He walked through the hay, jumped on top of a coop, and sat, waiting for someone in the hayfield opposite to notice him. He was, at most, four football fields distant.

To add insult to injury, he groomed himself.

Edward had kicked his feet out of the stirrups to let his long legs dangle. When he picked up his stirrups again he looked across the field.

"Tallyho," he whispered.

Tedi passed it up to Sister. "Tallyho."

Sister's eyes followed the direction of Edward's cap. He'd taken off his hunt cap, pointed his arm straight toward the fox, and also pointed his horse's nose toward Target.

Crawford saw and foolishly bellowed, "Tallyho!"

He should have remained silent. Since hounds diligently kept their noses to the ground, he didn't spoil anything except he again demonstrated how slender his grasp was of both the necessities and proprieties of hunting.

"*Tallyho, yourselves,*" Target murmured, and continued grooming.

On ascertaining that Target, whom she recognized, was in no hurry to depart, Sister cupped her hands to her mouth, being certain to holler in the direction of her huntsman. She let out the rebel yell, "Yip yip yo-o-o-o."

That particular cry alerted Shaker that it was the master viewing and the master was unlikely to "tallyho" a groundhog, house cat, or fawn, each of which had been tallyho'd at one time or another by a member of the field.

He raised his voice to a high pitch. "Come to me. Whoop. Whoop."

Trinity, although on her very first hunt, knew she was being called back to the huntsman, so she obediently turned, as did her sister, Tinsel. Delia, the mother of Dragon, Diana, and Dasher, called out to the others. Delia, moving a step slow these days, proved invaluable in steadying young ones. If she ran at the back of the pack she didn't much mind. She'd had her day up front and she didn't straggle, she stayed with the pack. A hound like Delia is a godsend to a huntsman.

Even Dragon, who resented interference, as he saw it, from Shaker, wanted to chase a fox. If Shaker was calling them, something must be up.

As the hounds returned to the huntsman, Sybil, who had been shadowing the pack on the right side, swung back with them.

Shaker wished to speak to his hounds, not humans.

Sybil knew enough to stay on the right, so he merely waved her forward a bit. He was sure she'd learn the ropes quickly, but he hadn't realized how much he had relied on Doug Kinser, who would have been across the farm road by now.

"Let's find a fox." Shaker smiled down at the upturned faces, then squeezed Hojo, a loud paint, his Tuesday horse, into an easy gallop. They moved smartly through the hayfield where the happy sight of the entire field, caps off, pointing to Target, poised on the far coop, greeted him.

Shaker slowed to a trot, let his hounds get up front of him, then urged them toward the farm road. The point was to give Target a chance to run; it would have been unsporting to do otherwise.

He let out a loud "whoop" to wake up the fox.

"What an ugly sound." Target looked brightly at the huntsman.

Wind swept the golden hay where hounds were working toward him; he could see sterns aloft. Target knew his scent was being blown away from the hounds but, as they closed in, they'd pick up his scent when he moved off. His pads would leave a scentprint for hound noses.

Betty quietly moved forward on the left, at a walk, no need to make a show of it.

Sister held her breath. "What is Target doing?"

"Dragon?"

Dragon lifted his head at the sound of Target's voice.

Tinsel and Trinity lifted their heads, too. No one had told them about this part.

"You couldn't find a fox with radar," Target taunted Dragon, then lifted off the far coop, swirled in midair, and ran flat out through the hay toward the sunken meadows. He figured he'd make a burst straight for his

den, only zigging and zagging when he had to throw them off.

"*I'll break your neck!*" Dragon roared back, his deep voice sending shivers down the spines of the humans. "*Follow me,*" he called over his shoulder.

Target had vanished into the hay, but Dragon relied on his nose to find him. He knew he could be fooled by sight and his eyes weren't as good as a fox's or a cat's. But his nose—his nose was superb.

He leapt over the first coop. Why go under the fence line? Give everyone a show! He reached the second, cleared the coop without even touching it, put his nose right to ground on the other side, and let out a soul-stirring note in his rich baritone.

"*I'm on!*"

Shaker cheered the other hounds toward him. Delia double-checked Dragon's findings. Dragon was now about fifty yards ahead. "*Scorching!*"

The young ones got a nose full of burning scent and became so excited that they tumbled over themselves. They picked themselves back up, hoping no one noticed.

All voices lifted to celebrate the thrill of the chase.

Shaker and Hojo smartly sailed over the first coop, raced across the farm road, sunken perhaps a foot below the hayfields, then went up and over the second.

Sister, heart racing, a grin from ear to ear, rode Keepsake over both coops and was thankful they'd just rebuilt them. Behind her she heard the rap of hooves as someone got in too close. Mostly she heard the "oomph," "oomph," "oomph," of humans exhaling as they landed safely.

She kept about forty yards behind Shaker, fighting the urge to go right up with him.

"Squeeze him over," she heard Marty Howard calling

behind her. Sister glanced back to see that Crawford had gotten stuck on the farm road between the two jumps.

Under these circumstances, a rider is supposed to circle and go to the rear or wait, if he can't circle, and let everyone else by. Crawford, however, bottled up the rest of the field. No one wanted to thunder past him for fear of spooking Czapaka or, worse, crashing into him. He didn't have sense to go down the road and get out of everyone's way.

Finally, with a terrific squeeze and smack of his crop, he lurched over the second coop. Ronnie Haslip, not deigning even to look at Crawford, effortlessly sailed over both coops, flying by Crawford perched on his big, beautiful warmblood. Ronnie was followed by the two high school seniors, Jennifer and Sari, who didn't want to get stuck behind Crawford again, just in case.

There was an old stone fence line on the south side of the hayfield. After that pretty jump it was open country, Soldier Road, more open country, and up Hangman's Ridge or the long way around it at the bottom.

Betty, thinking ahead, was already over the stone wall on Magellan, a horse who had a tendency to stand back and leave a half step earlier than her trusted and true Outlaw. She and Magellan were still getting accustomed to each other, but she was thrilled at having two horses to hunt.

The day was turning out to be so good, she felt half guilty about leaving Bobby at work—but not so guilty she wouldn't do it again.

Sybil didn't move fast enough, and Shaker preceded her over the stone wall at a low point where a few gray stones had fallen down. She swung in behind him, then tore out to his right side. He didn't criticize her since he knew she already understood she was not in the right position.

Keepsake, a handy fellow, thought the stone wall a lark. He liked taking different types of fences and he really liked having Sister on his back. She was much lighter than his former owner. Sister felt like a feather on his back.

This time Crawford took the jump last and cleared without incident.

Hounds streamed across the sunken meadow filled with the last of the black-eyed Susans and the first of the Jerusalem artichokes. Pendulous blackberries marked its eastern boundary.

Sister paused a moment at Soldier Road. She couldn't hear or see any motor traffic. She trotted over, jumped the old sagging coop—it needed replacing—and rode into the sunken meadow on the north side of the road. She galloped past more black-eyed Susans, Jerusalem artichokes, cornflowers, Queen Anne's lace, and white morning glories, their magenta throats pointing to the sun. Purple morning glories tangled through the grasses.

Hounds screamed. Their music gave her goose bumps.

Target, putting on the afterburners just to prove a point, shot straight up Hangman's Ridge, which at its summit was seven hundred feet above the watershed meadows below.

"Force those damned hounds to climb—and the people, too, if they're dumb enough," he thought.

Sister, however, wasn't going to push anyone that hard quite this early in the season. If it had been December, the air cool, the horses 100 percent fit instead of 85 percent fit, she would have climbed up. Today she circled around to the old rutted wagon path. It cost her precious minutes and she'd have to hustle once she reached the ridge to make them up. This she did.

Target, for effect, had raced to the hanging tree, left a mark at its base, then charged straight down the other side. He could now hear Dragon behind him. The hound was fast. Target had indulged in too much chicken the previous evening. A straight shot to his den might not be the best plan after all.

So he hatched a diabolical new one. Once at the base of the ridge he crossed the farm road there and dashed through Sister's old apple orchard.

Sister, now on the ridge, saw the last of her hounds go by the hanging tree, then straight down the ridge. The wagon path on the other side of the ridge connected to her farm road. If she pushed Keepsake toward it, they'd have to cover a quarter mile to reach it.

The wind, always stronger on the ridge, whipped at her face. As she passed the ancient oak, its heavy branches moaned in the wind, as if the souls punished there were crying for release.

She banished that thought, slowed to account for the steeper grade down. The footing was slick in spots. At the bottom she pressed on into the apple orchard.

Target ran right up to the kennel. *"Wake up!"*

Diana lifted her head, as did Cora, Trinkle, Trudy, Trident, Asa, Dasher, and all the others.

"Target! Fox! Fox!" everyone screamed at once.

Golliwog, on her way to the kennel to remind the benighted canines there that they were lower life-forms, saw Target scurry around to the front of the kennel. She was between the stable and the kennel, and the big red ran straight for her.

Golly puffed up and jumped in the air as high as she could go. She looked like she'd sucked on an air hose, she was so big.

Target flew right under her, laughing.

As she came down she cursed, *"You stupid ass!"* As the hounds weren't far behind she considered it wiser to get out of their way than to continue to upbraid Target,

who was never properly deferential to her. She did not
like the attitude of the reds. She hurried to the bending
hickory near the barn, unleashed her claws, and reached
the lowest limb just as Dragon appeared by the kennel
yards.

"Target! In the stable!" All the kenneled hounds ran
back and forth, the hackles on their necks up, their sterns
fluffed.

Dragon sped toward the stable. Target was already
through it and could hear the hounds getting a little
closer than he preferred. Well, he had other tricks up his
sleeve.

The whole pack roared through the stable, knocking
over buckets in the aisle, even slamming into the hay
bales stacked at the aisle's end to be distributed for the
evening's feedings.

Target reached Sister's colorful fall gardens, ran smack
through them, then into the gardening shed, and leapt
out the open window on the back wall.

No chance of turning back toward his den now. But
there was a good hole with lots of entrances and exits
just behind the hound cemetery. He sped through the
cemetery.

Zinnias were squashed, red and yellow petals sprin-
kling the ground as the pack chased Target. Shaker trotted Hojo between the flower beds, cursing as he rode.

"Damn that sly son of a bitch!" Then he heard the
crash of breaking glass and moved faster over the manicured lawn only to see the pack jammed into the gardening shed, howling their frustration.

Sister came up behind just in time to see Dragon jump
through the window, followed by the others. They tore
the window clear out of the jamb, the sound of tinkling
glass a counterpoint to their cries.

Across more beautiful lawn, through an allée of locusts and hollies, curving through another allée of still-green scarlet maples into the usually peaceful hound cemetery bounded by a wrought-iron fence.

The gate, open as always, let hounds in. The line of the scent went out the other side, which had no such gate. Dragon in his fury turned and literally ran through and over the pack, out the gate again, and around the other side. With some confusion and cussing, the rest followed, running around the sculpture of a hound in the middle. It was as though the stone hound was running with them. Sister pulled up hard behind Shaker by the iron fence.

"Oh, thank God!" Marty exclaimed.

No one else said a word, they just panted for breath.

Hounds found the den, digging and claiming victory for all they were worth.

Target, safe inside, made a mental note that Dragon, in his second year, had learned a great deal from his first year's experiences. He wasn't going to be easy to fool anymore. The ferocious drive that misled him last year had become more disciplined. Target would need to take this fellow more seriously. He would have to be more clever and he would have to teach him a lesson. Today would only build the handsome hound's confidence. Dragon needed to be knocked down a peg or two. Aunt Netty had been right.

Target also thought he'd better tell his offspring, especially the youngest over at Mill Ruins.

Hojo stood quietly while Shaker walked to the den, stood, and blew the notes of triumph. He praised each hound, then led them away with Betty's and Sybil's help.

"Another excellent day," he said, reaching for the reins.

"I didn't think we'd do much today." Sister smiled and

turned. The faces behind her, flushed with heat and excitement, radiated happiness as well as relief. Ralph breathed hard, laughing at himself for being a bit out of shape. Xavier huffed and puffed.

"Well, what do you think?" Shaker, back in the saddle, asked the master.

"I think we call it a day." She turned to Marty and asked, "And what were you thanking God for?"

"That you didn't jump the wrought-iron fence into the graveyard."

Tedi and Edward flanked Sister as they rode back across her lawn, the pathetic remains of her garden testifying to the fervor of the chase.

"Janie, winter is coming. You'll just prepare the new beds early." Tedi made light of it.

"You're right."

"You'll need a new window." Edward nodded toward the gardening shed. "I've got an extra. I'll have Jimmy bring it over and put it in for you."

"Thank you, Edward. You are the most generous soul."

"Well, he is, but don't be too impressed. You know we have the top of the old bank barn filled with Edward's treasures. Old windows, mantels, heart pine flooring. You name it, Edward's got it."

Edward smiled. He was a pack rat by nature, but he had compromised early in their marriage by storing his finds outside the house. When he'd swear these items, such as cartons of old *Esquire* magazines, the large kind from the forties and fifties, would be worth something someday, Tedi would always reply, "Yes, dear."

Sybil had inherited the pack rat gene. Nola, on the other hand, never saved anything.

As people dismounted at the trailers, talking about the terrific run, sharing a thermos of coffee, a cold beer or a ham sandwich, Sister rode with Shaker, Sybil, and Betty to the kennels. Once the hounds were inside she turned toward her own stable. Shaker would be busy with the hounds, washing out cuts and scratches from the gardening shed episode.

Jennifer and Sari, with no prompting from Betty, met her as she dismounted. "Sister, we'll clean up your horses for you."

"Why, girls, thank you so much."

"And Mom says I can work here on weekends if that's okay with you." Jennifer wanted desperately to work with Sister. She wanted to learn everything about hunting.

"Jennifer, you'll be a big help to me." Sister could never refuse a young person in love with hunting.

Sari, her dark eyes almost black, timidly spoke up. "Master, I could work, too, if you need an extra hand."

"Why, yes. You can start right now. I'll pay you for the day."

"No, we'll clean the stable because we want to," Jennifer said just as her mother joined her. Magellan was now tied to the trailer.

"Tell you what, I'll accept your generous offer for today. And you can ride Rickyroo, Lafayette, and Aztec. Ask Shaker about Showboat and Gunpowder. At least a half hour of trotting for those guys."

"Okay." The two girls were thrilled.

"Ten dollars an hour."

"Sister, that's too much," Betty protested.

"Good help is hard to find. Ten dollars an hour." Sister, feeling fabulous, winked at them all.

Jennifer took Keepsake into the stable as Sister joined the gang at the trailers for an impromptu breakfast. She liked these tailgates better than the big affairs.

She complimented Sybil on her second day as first whipper-in.

"I got behind at the stone wall."

"You made up for it. Whipping-in is a lot different from riding in the field. You can never stop thinking, reaching." Sister popped a deviled egg into her mouth.

When she walked back to the barn later, the two girls were cleaning away. Tack was hanging from hooks. Keepsake, washed, was content in his stall, telling the other horses just what a fine day it was.

Sister loved having young people around. She walked outside, listening to the girls talking, laughing. She heard the big diesel engines of the vans fire up, detected the throaty roar of the pickup trucks for those pulling goose-necks. People called good-bye to one another, called "good night" to her, which was proper. One said "good night" to the master at the end of a hunt even if it was ten in the morning—which it was.

She walked across her desecrated lawn thinking the destruction was worth the fun. Golliwog, Raleigh, and Rooster sashayed alongside her. They had been very up-set at the goings-on. Golly, of course, bragged about how she faced down Target just spitting at him, her claws unleashed.

They followed Sister under the hickories and hollies, past the scarlet maples that would turn flaming red in an-other month. They could smell the apples on the trees in the far orchard. Sister walked through the wrought-iron gate. Under the walnut tree in the middle of the grave-yard was a graceful stone statue of a hound running. On the front was inscribed: REST, DEAR FRIENDS, WE'LL HUNT AGAIN SOMEDAY.

Bronze plaques, each bearing a hound's name, were at-tached to the base, representing forty years of Jefferson Hunt hounds. Although the hunt was founded at the end of the nineteenth century, the graveyard was only forty years old. Newer plaques were affixed to the wrought-iron fence. A special tombstone had been erected for Archie, her great anchor hound, a hound she had loved as no other.

"Archie, you missed quite a day. And that pup whom you hated, Dragon, actually did very well, very well indeed."

As they left, Rooster asked why Archie had his name on a plaque and a tombstone, too.

"Her fave," Raleigh answered.

"Will we be buried here?" Rooster asked.

"No, we'll be buried up under the pear trees behind the house." Raleigh liked the idea of being by the house close to Sister.

"Not me," Golly bragged. *"I'm going to be cremated and when Sister dies she'll be cremated, too. We'll go in the ground together."*

"You are so full of it." Raleigh laid his ears back.

Sister walked on over to the den. "Target, quite a show."

He stuck his nose out of the largest opening. *"I am the greatest."*

Raleigh and Rooster knew not to do anything or Sister would tell them, "Leave it." She always told them what to do, and since she didn't give a "whoop" they looked down at the fox, even larger than he was last year.

Golliwog huffed up and spit, and as they walked away she bragged, *"He's afraid of me."*

The two house dogs thought it better not to answer or a nasty fight would explode.

Sister stopped again at the hound graveyard. Leaning on the iron fence, she remembered something about the first day of cubbing in 1981. She just now recalled a check at a remote part of After All Farm. They'd had a good hard run and finally lost scent at the estate's easternmost border where an old, well-tended slave graveyard reposed, small, smooth worn tombstones standing out against deep green grass, the whole bounded by a low stone wall. Most old graveyards were marked off by stone walls or wrought-iron fences. This graveyard belonged to the Lorillards, an old central Virginia family, both black and white. These were the original black Lorillards.

She'd stepped a bit away from the field, listening for Shaker or a hound. The hounds were casting back into the covert by a narrow creek bed. She'd turned to look back at Nola, Sybil, Guy, Ken, Ralph, and Xavier, off from the others, a small group of the younger set. Now she remembered seeing Nola, radiant from the run, at the center, the object of all male eyes, while Sybil cast her gaze down, then looked back into the Lorillard graveyard.

She remembered thinking to herself at the time that that tableau moment said it all.

CHAPTER 24

A cool jet stream of Canadian air dipped over Virginia in the middle of the night, bringing with it a breath of fall.

At five-thirty in the morning, heavy fog like gray cotton candy wrapped the earth. Sister rose and felt the chill, for she had forgotten to turn on the heat in the upstairs section before going to bed. She threw on her heavy robe, slipped on her sheepskin slippers, and clicked the thermostat to seventy degrees.

The house was divided into zones, each with a separate thermostat. The intention, to save money, never panned out and the need to check all four thermostats irritated Sister.

By the time she reached the kitchen she was wide awake—which could not be said for Golly. Nestled deep in the pillow, she still snored lightly. Both Raleigh and Rooster dutifully followed their master downstairs.

Sister put down kibble for "the boys," as she called them, then ground coffee beans and soon had a pot percolating. She couldn't see a thing from the kitchen window. The outdoor thermometer in the window read forty-nine degrees.

She poured coffee into a big mug, then hurried upstairs by the back stairway. She put on two pairs of socks, one thin, one heavier, jeans, and her work shoes with rust and yellow around the laces. Layers worked

best in changing weather. She slipped on a thin under-
shirt, a T-shirt over that, and topped it off with an old
navy pullover. Then she was down the stairs and out
the back door with Raleigh and Rooster scampering to
keep up.

The hounds would fuss if they heard her, so she gave
the kennel a wide berth, moving slower than usual because of the fog. Blurry shapes would suddenly appear,
then, as she neared, transform into the hay barn or an or-
namental pear. She reached the farm road and headed
without hesitation toward Hangman's Ridge, as though
drawn there.

Inky, returning to her den at the edge of the cornfield,
smelled the approaching human and two dogs, then heard
their footfalls on the dirt road. She shadowed them, curious, keeping downwind.

Raleigh wouldn't chase her, but every now and then
Rooster wanted to prove a harrier could hunt a fox as
well as a foxhound. Sister would walk out with Rooster
and let him hunt rabbits, making a big fuss over him.
She'd call him back if he picked up fox scent, which was
easy to tell since the fox covered more territory than the
rabbit, but if the line was good and he was slow to obey
she didn't get angry at him. Can't punish a hound for
hunting.

Inky enjoyed being a few yards behind everyone. She
could turn on a dime and give you a nickel's change. Even
if the wind shifted and Rooster got a whiff of her, she
could literally spin and run right under his belly. Hounds
were agile as far as dogs go, but the only creature as
quick and nimble as the fox was the cat. As they both
hunted the same game this made sense. They had developed the same strategies for killing mice, moles, rabbits,
and the occasional lazy bird.

A soft whoosh alerted Inky to Athena's presence. Another swoosh meant Bitsy. They passed low overhead.

Sister looked up but saw nothing through the fog. Rooster opened his mouth, but she swiftly put her hand around his muzzle, putting her finger to her own lips. All her pets knew the sign. Rooster said nothing.

The dampness of the fog made Sister wish she'd put on yet another layer. Rooster lifted his nose, then put it down on the farm road. Comet had passed that way, the dampness holding down scent. But he said nothing, keeping close to Sister.

They reached the base of Hangman's Ridge in twenty minutes. Mimosa trees near the farm road would appear and disappear in the fog, their beautiful pink-gold blossoms adding color to the gray mist.

The climb to the top, not as steep on this side of the ridge, proved steep enough to make them breathe heavily.

A soft light in the eastern sky, gunmetal gray underlined with dove gray, announced the sun would rise in another thirty to thirty-five minutes, but Sister knew fog this thick would not lift for hours after that. Only when the sun had sufficiently warmed the thick blanket wrapping the meadows, ridges, and mountains would it evaporate, leaving slivers lingering just above the creeks and rivers, tongues of silver gray.

Once on the ridge, Sister paused to catch her breath. Inky ducked off the dirt road, slinking under a clutch of mountain laurel, slick with dew.

The mild breeze on the ridge tousled Sister's hair. Ahead, the huge outline of the hanging tree took shape, its massive silhouette mute testimony to its centuries of life. What a pity such a magnificent oak had been used to kill.

Hanging, not a pleasant way to die, could at least be quick if the length of rope was correct and the drop proper. But those criminals executed here were strung up to dangle and choke to death, which could take four or five minutes. Occasionally the convict's windpipe would be broken by the violence of the initial jerk and lift as the horse on which he sat was slapped out from underneath him. Death came with merciful swiftness then.

Lawrence Pollard, the first man ever to be hanged from the tree, had so enraged his enemies, they hauled him up without benefit of a horse in 1702. His executioners believed he had swindled them in land speculation—which he had. By all accounts a dark-haired, handsome man, a smooth talker, an elegant dresser, he seduced the few hardy families who had settled this far west, the Wild West at that time, into putting up money to purchase tens of thousands of acres in what is now Lewisburg, West Virginia.

He did buy thousands of acres in that area, but he also kept a portion of the money for dissolute living in Philadelphia, the largest city in the colonies. Word of his profligacy filtered back to the Tidewater and even there leached out to the farthest borders of civilization, this particular county at the base of the Blue Ridge Mountains. Through guile, the irate investors lured Lawrence back to his death.

The last man hanged in this spot was Gilliam Norris, a Confederate veteran, a brave and well-respected man who lost his mind, killing his mother, father, two sisters, and brother with his service revolver.

In between 1702 and 1875, eighteen men were hanged, all murderers with the exception of Lawrence.

Two shapes in the tree startled Sister until she drew closer and recognized Athena and Bitsy. Neither flew away as she approached them.

The sound of a moan stopped her in her tracks. Both Raleigh and Rooster swept their ears forward.

Inky, behind them, stepped out of the fog.

Sister saw her and said to Rooster, "Leave it."

But Rooster paid no attention to Inky, as something by the trunk of the tree had his full attention.

"I'm here to find something. I don't know what it is," she said as if to reassure the animals, but mainly to calm her own fears.

When the swirling fog momentarily parted in front of her, she thought she saw the form of a man by the tree, disfigured, wearing silk breeches and silk stockings, his neck horribly twisted.

She tried to blink the apparition away. This spot could arouse even the most phlegmatic person's imagination.

But then she heard a hoarse whisper and recognized a verse from Psalm 42:

"My tears have been my meat day and night, while they continually say unto me, Where is thy God? . . . all thy waves and thy billows are gone over me. My soul is bereft of peace."

Raleigh growled, putting himself right in front of Sister.

Shaking, she backed away. She might be crazy as that hoot owl in the tree, but whatever she was seeing looked real enough to her.

As the fog swallowed the form back up, it let out a howl of pure anguish. Wind swept over the ridge with a slashing gust.

Sister turned and ran through the fog, only able to see three feet in front of her in a good patch. She was glad she lived a physically active life. She might be seventy-one years old, but she could run like the devil.

Skidding, slipping, sliding down the ridge, she didn't stop until she reached the base.

"Goddamn, I swear that really was Lawrence Pollard's ghost!"

"*It was,*" Inky said. "*I've seen him before. There are a couple up there. They can't go to ground.*" She meant they couldn't go to their den, her concept of home.

Sweat rolled down Sister's forehead, between her breasts, down the small of her back. She hadn't been so scared in years.

"*His tongue was hanging out.*" Rooster, too, was a little shaken by the apparition.

Then Athena and Bitsy swooped by in the fog, and that startled Sister.

"Dammit!"

"*Don't swear at me!*" Athena laughed because she'd scared Sister.

To Sister it sounded like "hoo, hoo-hoo, hoo-hoo."

Of course, Bitsy had to let out one of her blood-curdling shrieks, which nearly caused all of them to have heart attacks.

Bitsy thought she was singing "The Ride of the Valkyries."

Even Inky's ruff stood up on end.

"*God, that's awful.*" Raleigh blinked.

Sister got hold of herself and started back toward home.

Inky headed for her own den. "*Sister, those spirits up there got what they deserved. They can't hurt you.*"

"Why don't they leave?" Rooster asked.

Athena, her voice ghostly and deep in the fog, answered him. "*They can't let go. They can't find absolution or redemption. You know there's a stag like that. It's not just humans. He leads deer hunters to their death. He sets them up so they shoot each other. Kills two or three a year.*"

"*They'd better not hurt Sister. Human or stag, I don't care. I'll kill them,*" Raleigh growled.

"*Can't,*" Bitsy shrieked. "*They're already dead.*"

Sister jumped at the sound of Bitsy's voice. "Good God, that bird could wake the dead." Then she realized what she'd said and she had to laugh.

By the time Sister reached her kitchen, she needed that second cup of coffee. She wondered if she also needed prayer, psychiatry, or a good knock on the head.

Instead, there was a knock on the back door.

She opened the door and was happy to see Shaker's familiar, placid face.

"Morning, Boss," he said as he walked in.

At seven in the morning, it was not too early to call.

"Thick as pea soup out there," she said. She wanted so badly to tell him what she thought she saw.

"Yes it is. Patty's ready. I called Tony over at Keswick and he said I could bring her by." Patty was a gyp who was at the right time in her cycle for breeding. The huntsman at Keswick Hunt had a hound, Mischief, whose pedigree and conformation, hopefully, would match up well with Patty.

"Mmm, fine. Here, have a cup of coffee. I make better coffee than you do."

"You look a little peaked. You all right?"

"Well, I had a scare."

"I have them every month when my bills come due."

She smiled. "I have those, too. Next board meeting, I'll bring up the subject of a raise once again. And you know, if they don't vote it through I'm going to Crawford."

"I don't want his money!"

"If he wants to throw it around, I say we take it. I can handle him."

"I can't."

"You won't have to—but don't worry. I'll get this past the board. It's been four years since you've had a raise, and it's not right. I'm tired of it. He offered to buy a Dually for the club. Much as we need the truck, this is more important."

Sister Jane was in charge of hunting and everything to do with the hunting, but the board of governors was in charge of the purse strings and the social direction of the club. It could make for friction.

"That's not why I came over. Really it was about Patty." He sipped the delicious coffee, a perfect mixture of blends to start the day.

"Now that we don't have Doug's salary to pay, I know I have the ammunition to get this through." She paused. "Do you believe in ghosts?"

"I'm Irish. Of course I believe in ghosts." He laughed. "I remember the time you thought you saw the Grim Reaper. And he held someone's claim ticket, didn't he?"

"But you didn't believe me at the time, Shaker. You accused me of drinking."

Sheepishly he put his mug down. "I did." He glanced out the window. "Too bad we aren't hunting this morning."

"We'd need fog lights on our bridles."

He laughed again. "That we would, but I love casting on a foggy morning."

"Shaker, I walked up to Hangman's Ridge this morning. Before sunup. I don't know why. I felt like something was calling me up there. And I thought I saw a ghost. Actually, I won't be wishy-washy about it. I did see a ghost. He quoted from Psalms. All about misery. Scared me half to death. Then that damned little screech owl flew by and let out a hoot. I don't know why my heart is still beating."

He roared at this. "She's scarier than the ghost."

"Ah, so you do think there's a ghost up there?"

"More'n one. Earth's full of spirits, I think. Don't know

why, although my mother would say we have to pray them into Purgatory and then up to Heaven."

"Even the murderers?"

"God's grace."

"Yes, I guess forgiveness *is* His trade. I'm not sure it's mine. I wish I knew why I felt drawn to that tree. I've lived here for forty-eight years, Shaker. I know that old pin oak very well. But until this morning I never felt a call to go there."

"Maybe it's a warning, something to prepare you. You know, sometimes I have dreams. I think we get, uh, premonitions."

"I suppose. Yesterday after hunting I remembered something about the day Nola and Guy disappeared. Nola hunted. We pulled up at the Lorillard graveyard."

"My second season carrying the horn. Still a little nervous. Not at all anymore." He winked. Like any good athlete, Shaker always felt a twinge of nerves before an event.

"We'd run hard. Horses were blowing, people, too, and I stepped away from the field to listen for you. Anyway, Nola, Guy, Ralph, Xavier, Ron, Ken, and Sybil formed a small group a bit away from the others. Nola was the center of attention. It's not that they were coffeehousing, it was just the men's eyes. Sybil was staring into the graveyard. She knew she was invisible then. Even her husband couldn't take his eyes off Nola at that moment.

"When Nola disappeared and Guy didn't show up, my mind was focused on finding them. I didn't think of what I *felt*. I certainly didn't think of that moment at the Lorillard graveyard."

"And what was it you felt?"

"That Sybil would always be overshadowed by Nola even though she was the better woman. At least I think so."

"Me too."

"That Nola had conquered each of those men there, except Ken, I suppose. Maybe she slept with Ralph and Xavier, I don't know, but she could have had them had she wanted them. Even Ron. If she'd put her mind to it."

"Could have had Ken, too, I'll reckon."

"You think?"

He nodded, then got up and opened the bread box. "I'll owe you one." He took out a package of chocolate-covered doughnuts.

"Or two or three."

"Nola could have had most any man. Maybe not for life, but for a night. She was, I don't know, I can't think of the word, like some potion."

"You, too?"

He smiled, breaking the doughnut in two. "I was a young huntsman. She wouldn't have looked at me twice."

"Plenty of other women have. Huntsmen can pretty well have their pick of the litter." Sister stated one of those hunting facts that everybody knows but few people say out loud. Huntsmen are like rock stars to many female members of the field. It doesn't seem to work so strongly in reverse. If the huntsman is a female, the male members don't automatically fawn over her.

He shook his head. "Not me."

"By the end of the season maybe," Sister said, teasing him. "But you knew even then, young as you were, twenty-five or so, that Nola could be . . ."

"Cruel. Nola was cruel to men."

"Well, I don't know as that's the right word, but if you knew that about her, you would still have gone to bed with her?"

He straightened his back. "No, ma'am, I would not, but I would have wanted to."

"I don't get it."

"It's a guy thing. You can know a woman is pure poison and still want her. For some men, they only want her more."

"Women, a lot of them, anyway, always want the man who will hurt them. The Bad Boy. Maybe it's the same."

"Maybe. All I know is when she'd fix me with those blue eyes and start smiling, I could feel the blood in my body burn."

"She affected women, too. That kind of beauty is erotically charged for both sexes, but to different degrees."

"Guy kind of had that quality, too. He could have most any woman he wanted. Probably why Fontaine Buruss hated him. Fontaine thought they all belonged to him."

"Did men dislike him?" Sister asked.

"I think most men didn't trust him around their women. Or maybe they didn't trust their women around Guy," Shaker astutely commented.

"Do you think Guy was sleeping with other women when he was going with Nola?"

"No. Funny, I don't think he was."

"What about her?"

"Yes."

"Who?"

"Ralph Assumptio, for one."

"Who else?"

"Fontaine."

"Jesus." She paused. "Raymond?"

"No." Shaker would have lied, but it was true. Sister's husband had not been sleeping with Nola. Raymond had slowed down a bit by then. Got caught too many times and made too many messes.

"That's a relief." Sister exhaled. "I would hate to think Raymond was mixed up in this. But he wasn't, I mean, he wouldn't."

"Raymond was a good man. He had a weakness."

"He did, God bless him." Sister had spent enough emotion on her deceased husband. She wasn't going to waste any time dwelling on the negative. "Do you think Ralph, Fontaine, or some jilted lover could have killed Nola?"

"I don't know. You think you know people, but they can surprise you."

She waited, lowered her voice. "Sybil?"

"Kill her own sister?" Shaker was genuinely shocked.

"She'd spent her life in Nola's shadow. And what if Nola decided to make a conquest of Ken?"

"Nola flirted with everyone. And Ken would have to be one of the dumbest men, dumber that snot, to kill the goose that laid the golden egg."

"Nola?"

"His marriage. He'd just married into the Bancroft family, and his people don't have doodly-squat."

"I thought that, too. Well, what about Xavier?"

"She was done with him before first day of cubbing."

"He held a grudge."

Shaker shrugged. "I don't know. Like I said, you think you know someone and then they fool you."

"You're a good huntsman. You trust your instincts. What's your instinct?"

"That the killer is going to break cover."

"And?"

He reached for his third doughnut. "I don't want to accuse a man of murder, but I remember that Ralph Assumptio was courting Frances that fall." She nodded that she remembered and he continued. "He married her at Christmas, and he wasn't especially happy at his own wedding."

"Everyone said he got loaded the night before."

"More. I think Ralph was still in love with Nola."

"Their marriage seems happy enough."

Shaker shrugged. "Who knows?"

"You're right. Who does know?"

"I'm not saying he killed her. I'm saying I think he was in love with her and I think her body being found has shaken him up."

"Did Guy know she was sleeping with other men?"

"It would have killed him. I don't think he knew, but time was coming when he would have found out. Too many of us knew her, I mean. Those of us in our twenties. It was bound to come out sooner or later."

"Would he have killed her?"

"I don't know."

Sister frowned. "Maybe he found out that last day."

Shaker refilled his and Sister's coffee cups, then sat back down. "Or maybe Nola really fell in love. It happens. Maybe she said good-bye to whoever else."

"I remember Guy bumped Ralph going over a jump that day. Caused a fuss."

"They were fixing to fight sooner or later."

She reached down to pat Raleigh's head. "Did you tell Paul Ramy what you thought about Ralph back then?"

Shaker shook his head. "No. First off, I couldn't prove it. Yes, I saw Nola kiss Ralph, oh, spring of '81, something like that. But that doesn't mean I could prove she slept with him. At the time I didn't think it served any purpose other than to upset Paul, who was already upset."

"Upset him because his son's girl wasn't faithful?"

"Uh-huh." He nodded in agreement.

"Well, have you told Ben Sidell?"

"I did. He's okay, Sidell."

"Yes, I think so, too. Why didn't you tell me?"

He put down his coffee mug. "When have we had time to talk? We've been working nonstop to get ready for cubbing, and now we're cubbing and," he paused, "I don't like saying things I can't prove, things that could hurt people, even to you, and I know you won't talk."

"I understand. Oh, before I forget, Jennifer Franklin and her friend Sari Rasmussen are going to work here on weekends, and I expect they'll show up after school sometimes, too, now that Jennifer's got her driver's license. Do you want them to work any of your horses?"

"No. Too hot for them. Especially Showboat."

"Okay." She looked out the window. "Fog hasn't lifted a bit. Well, let's clean the kennels." They stood up and took their cups to the sink.

"You know, when Nola first disappeared I figured she was cutting a shine," Shaker said. "Either she ran off with Guy or she dumped him and ran off with the Prince of Wales. I didn't worry until a week passed."

"I did. I figured she'd at least call her mother or sister to laugh about what she'd done," Sister replied.

"Women like Nola provoke people."

"This sounds suspiciously like blaming the victim."

His melodic tenor voice rose. "No. Anyone who lives above the rules gets pulled down eventually. Might take a long time, but people will take their revenge."

"You're right." She washed the cups while he leaned on the counter. "Oh, to change subjects, you know Sari's mother, Lorraine, is a very attractive woman. She's been divorced for two years."

"And?"

"Just some information," she said, smiling.

"Cupid."

CHAPTER 25

The Board of Governors of the Jefferson Hunt met the third Wednesday of each month except for July. This month's meeting would be September 18, which gave Sister a little time to gather the votes for Shaker's pay raise. She hoped the discussion about when and where to locate the Hunter Trials would wear them out so the raise would slide through.

As Thursday's hunt and Saturday's hunt both produced bracing runs, the buzz around town was that this was going to be a good season. Sister knew the numbers in the cubbing field would swell and she could expect a sizable field on Saturday, the twenty-first. She was already wondering which young entry to subject to the increased numbers of people and had an evil moment where she thought about pushing up the first cast to six-thirty in the morning. They'd revolt. No, she'd keep it at seven-thirty but deliver a little lecture about cubbing's purpose being for young entry, hounds first, last, and always.

Monday was her town day, meaning errands, including the most hated shopping for groceries. Well, she'd combine politicking with shopping. Her first stop was Ken Fawkes's office, in a discreet modern building that blended into the landscape. Unlike most of her contemporaries, Sister liked modern architecture so long as it was good. Perhaps she preferred Palladian architecture, but something as beautiful as the Seagram Building in New York City deserved to be praised.

This was Ken Fawkes's first year on the board. She'd called ahead and was instantly ushered into his office, decorated in a minimalist style that was a total contrast to the way in which Sybil had decorated their home. She realized she'd never been in Ken's office and this reflected something new about him, an aesthetic sensibility all his own.

"How good of you to stop by," he greeted her, his white broadcloth shirt offset by a simple royal blue tie.

"Well, you're kind to let me barge in. I won't take much of your time."

They sat down facing each other over a coffee table of highly polished black marble with thin green veins snaking throughout.

"Coffee? Anything to drink?"

"No, thank you. Ken, I'll get right to the point. As you know, thanks to Doug leaving to take the horn at Shenandoah Valley, we have his salary in the till." He nodded and she continued. "Shaker hasn't had a raise in four years, and that one was negligible, another thousand a year. We've just got to give this man more money."

"I agree." He folded his hands together, his elbows on his knees, and leaned toward her with a grin. "Means you want to keep my wife as a whipper-in, does it? She's free."

"She has talent." Sister smiled. "Where would we be without your contributions, the contributions of the Bancrofts? I am grateful."

He demurred. "That's foxhunting. If you have it, you give. Like church."

"I find I'm closer to the Good Lord out there than with my butt parked in a pew."

"Me too."

"You know, I have this terrible confession." She leaned toward him, their heads closer over the exquisite marble. "I can tell you this because you're an Episcopalian, too. I've always thought of Episcopalians as junior varsity Catholics," she said, grinning mischievously.

He laughed, leaning back into his seat. "Wait until I tell that to Sybil."

"Ken, I may not get to Heaven with thoughts like that."

"You know, they say foxhunters don't go to Heaven because they have their Heaven on earth." He paused. "Of course, you have my full support for a raise. Would five thousand dollars be acceptable?"

"Yes, I think that would be." She beamed at him. "Now, one more thing. Ralph Assumptio has been a true-blue hunting member and I value him, but he is obsessed with money matters. I actually think that helps us on the board because he goes over every single thing with a fine-tooth comb." She cleared her throat. "I expect resistance from Ralph. He'll be swayed by you before he'll be swayed by me."

"Oh, I don't know about that, but I will talk to him."

What neither acknowledged was that Ken had sent Ralph a lot of business over the years. Ralph could just keep quiet and come through on this one thing.

Sister thanked him and as she reached the door she asked one more question. "You know, I recalled a lovely picture of you and Sybil. Funny how things come into your mind. I was remembering that first day of cubbing back in 1981 for the obvious reason—well, we'd such a good run and we pulled up at Lorillard graveyard. Do you remember?"

"Vaguely."

"You, Sybil, Ralph, Nola, Xavier, Guy, all together,

all so young, flushed from the run. It was a pleasant memory. Being up front, I can't see what goes on behind me on a run. Did you see Guy bump Ralph?"

"Oh, that long coop. Ralph was touchy. It wasn't that bad."

"Not bad enough to induce murder?"

His eyes widened. "Ralph never really liked Guy. He just hated that we called him Hotspur. Said it glamorized the bastard. Pardon my language." Ken cleared his throat. He'd been taught not to swear in front of a lady. "But kill Guy? No."

She left, stopped by Franklin Printing. Betty and Bobby offered their full support for the raise.

By noon she'd called on every board member except for Ralph. She'd give Ken the day to reach him and then she'd have a word with Ralph at tomorrow's cubbing.

She pulled up to the feed store. Given all the stops she needed to make, she'd left Raleigh and Rooster home. She missed having them in the truck with her. She enjoyed their "conversation," as she told friends. She'd chatter away to her dogs, who always seemed so interested in everything she had to say.

She bumped into Alice Ramy emerging with a dolly loaded with chicken feed.

"Alice, let me help you." Sister unloaded the fifty-pound sacks onto the back of Alice's pickup. Alice, although a few years younger than Sister, was frail with tiny, light bones.

"Thank you." Alice shut the tailgate. "Sister, I'm told I can have Guy back. I don't know what to do."

"Would you like me to make arrangements? It might be easier." Alice nodded as Sister put her arm around Alice's waist. "Tell you what. I'll follow you home and unload the feed. You make a cup of tea, or even better, a gin rickey. It's still warm enough for a gin rickey. I'll call Carl from your house." Carl Haslip, Ronnie's cousin, owned the best funeral home in the county.

An hour later, the feed safely stacked in the chicken coop, Sister called Carl, who lifted this burden off her shoulders.

Alice wanted Guy placed next to his father. She didn't want a service. Enough time had passed was how she put it.

The two women sat on Alice's back porch, where a canopy of wisteria draped over the crossbeams, for the back porch was under a huge pergola. Alice had taste in some things, plus she made a wickedly delicious gin rickey.

"Thank you, Jane."

"I was glad to help."

"I haven't been a good neighbor. Wasn't much of a neighbor to Peter, either." She mentioned Peter Wheeler, whose farm adjoined hers to the south. "I miss him. I don't know why. All I ever did was complain to him or about him."

"He was a good man. I miss his sense of humor."

"Guy adored him."

"Mutual, I think."

"You know that fellow who is in there now? Walter, the doctor? He puts me to mind of Raymond."

"Oh?"

"Different coloring, but same size and build, and even the bone structure of his face." She sipped a deep draft. "A quieter man than Raymond."

"My husband liked being the center of attention."

"And how. Guy was like that, too. Don't know where he got it. Both Paul and I were quiet-living people even when we were young."

"He was beautiful. Beauty generates its own energy."

Alice watched her cat, Malarky, climb up the wisteria

to nestle in a branch and gaze down at them. "Yes, he was beautiful. He took after my grandmother. Same eyes, same black curly hair. I always wished I looked like her. She was beautiful even in old age."

"Now, Alice, you're an attractive woman."

"Liar"—she stretched her legs out—"but I thank you all the same." Malarky shifted his weight, sending wisteria leaves twirling downward. "Fatty," she called up to him.

He ignored her.

"Won't be long before the leaves turn, even though it's seventy-four degrees today. The other morning I walked out in the fog and it was chilly."

"Lot of fog now. Earth's warmer than the air." She turned to face Sister. "Since they found Guy I've thought about things. I guess I knew he was gone. He would have found some way to reach me even if he had killed Nola. He wouldn't have killed her, but even if he had. I just don't know who killed him, but I think we'll find out."

"Yes, I think we will, too. Alice, did Paul ever tell you anything he'd discovered?"

"No. He said he could account for people's movements. I guess you'd say everyone had an alibi. He didn't really have suspects."

"Did Guy ever talk about someone he hated or who might have hated him?"

"Mmm, sometimes Ronnie Haslip would get on his nerves. Guy thought Ronnie was flirting with him. I just laughed at him. And he and Ralph started bickering. They'd got on well as children and all through high school. But those last months of Guy's life they were at odds."

"Did you know why?"

"No. You know, the night before he died, he stopped off home. I was watching an old movie, *Dark Victory*, with Bette Davis. He sat next to me on the sofa and said he was getting bored with everyone. He needed a change."

"Do you think he meant Nola?"

"I don't know. He wasn't very specific. But he said the time had come for him to do something with his life. He wasn't upset, just kind of sober. I can't think of a better word."

"Did Paul find out anything that upset you?"

"No. I knew Guy partied too much with all those rich people. I knew he had some growing up to do."

"Ronnie Haslip, Xavier, and Ralph weren't rich then."

"No. But the Bancrofts, the Taylors, the Jansens. Too much too soon. All of them."

"Yes."

"Did you ever worry that Ray would fall in with that crowd, or their younger sisters and brothers, when he became a little older?" Alice sipped her drink, held one of the ice cubes in her mouth, then released it on the next swallow of gin rickey.

"I did."

"Well, you and Raymond weren't poor. I suppose Little Ray could have kept up with the Joneses."

"That was Big Ray's department. But Alice, I don't think Raymond or I would have tolerated that behavior in our son even if we could have afforded it. This county is full of people who just suck off their trust funds."

"Most don't amount to a hill of beans."

"I don't begrudge them the money. What I can't stand is that they don't do anything for anybody else. They party, golf, hunt, travel, ricochet from one thing to another. They marry, have children, divorce, marry again, and think the world belongs to them. I have to tolerate the ones in the hunt club, but I sure don't have to socialize with them."

Alice smiled. "I've never heard you talk like that."

"Alice, you've never heard me talk," Sister bluntly replied.

A silence followed, then Alice spoke. "I haven't liked myself much since Guy disappeared. I lived for my family, and when they were gone I didn't have any friends. Well, you are right. I haven't heard you talk, really talk. I haven't heard anyone talk. And how much life do I have left? I don't want to live it like this. My son has come back to me. Not as I wished, but he's come back and, you know, he reproaches me. Guy wouldn't want me as his mother now."

Surprised by this outburst, Sister softly said, "Love never dies. His love is as real today as the day he died. He would want you as his mother. He wants you to be happy."

"Do you think so?"

"I do. I draw on Raymond's love every day. He wasn't perfect. Neither am I. But he loved me and so did my son. I live with that love."

Alice finished her drink. "I never thought of it that way. I only thought of what I'd lost. Well, I've cried through many a night. I cried when Ben Sidell told me they'd found Guy. The more I cried, the more I knew I had to do something. I can become someone my son would like to know."

"What are you going to do?"

"The first thing I'm going to do is take some classes at Virginia Tech. I'll have to commute, but I checked out the classes on the computer. I can take classes on Mondays and Wednesdays. I'm going to get a little apartment in Blacksburg, go down Sunday nights and return Wednesday afternoons. I heard that Lorraine Rasmussen wanted to get out in the country, money's tight for her, and I've rented her rooms upstairs. We'll share the kitchen, the living room. She'll take care of Malarky and my chickens."

"Well, Alice, that's wonderful."

"Do you want to know what I'm going to study?"

"Of course."

"Poultry science and cattle breeding. I've always wanted to breed high-quality cattle, but Paul wouldn't let me do it. He said the market was like a roller coaster. Well, he's gone. I'm going to do what I want to do."

"Good for you."

"And one other thing. You were always nice to me even when I wasn't nice to you. So if you want to go through here when you hunt, you go right ahead."

"Alice!" Sister leapt out of her chair and gave Alice a hug.

"See, I knew all this time you just wanted to hunt my land." Alice, her face red, laughed.

It wasn't until she was halfway up her own driveway that Sister realized she never did buy her groceries.

CHAPTER 26

Each board meeting rotated to a different board member's home. Ralph and Frances Assumptio hosted this one. Frances spent her time and energy cleaning and decorating. The place, farther west from Sister's down Soldier Road, had a warm feel to it full of handsomely worn oriental rugs, old silver, and overstuffed club chairs.

One of the rules of the Jefferson Hunt was that no food or liquor could be served until after the board meeting. Past experience proved the necessity of this rule.

As usual, the entire board showed up. Shaker's raise passed unanimously. When Ralph wasn't looking, Ken winked at Sister, who winked back.

They had checked off everything on the agenda when Bobby Franklin, as president, asked pro forma, "Are there any new items not on the agenda?"

Crawford, wearing a flattering turquoise shirt, spoke. "I'd like us to consider building a clubhouse and showgrounds. We lack a central meeting place—neutral territory, if you will—and showgrounds would help our horse show committee immeasurably. We'd have a permanent home for our activities."

"Wait a minute. This club has no debt. You're talking about running up mountains of debt," Ralph piped up, his eyebrows knit together in concern.

"One of the reasons we have no debt is because Raymond and Sister built the 'new' kennels on their farm at their own expense," Bobby said, quickly giving credit where credit was due. He knew perfectly well what Crawford was up to.

"What happens when Sister leaves us?" Crawford blurted out.

"I'm not leaving," Sister said, enjoying watching him squirm. "I would never willingly leave the Jefferson Hunt. You might vote me out, but I won't leave on my own."

"Never!" Betty vehemently spoke.

The rest rumbled their agreement.

"Well, what I meant to say is, what if you have to leave us, what if it's not your idea?" Crawford recognized his blunder and wished these damned Virginians weren't so subtle. And how they prized it, too. Made him sick. Everything took twice as long because of their damned subtlety.

"You mean if I died?" Her gray eyebrows raised quizzically.

"Well—yes," Crawford sheepishly replied.

"The kennels will still belong to the Jefferson Hunt Club, as will the rest of Roughneck Farm." She had dropped a bombshell.

No one knew what to say.

Betty started to cry.

Bobby also wiped away tears. "Now, we don't have to go into this. It's not our business."

"You know, I wasn't withholding it to be obstructionist." Sister folded her hands on the table. "It's just no one likes to think of their own demise. When Peter died, it shook me." Murmurs echoed this sentence, as it had upset all of them. "He'd had good, long innings. I never thought Peter would die. He was made of iron, but the

last year when he didn't ride anymore, I guess deep
down, I knew. When a foxhunter stops riding, well?" She
shrugged, and the others knew what she meant.

"You aren't going anytime soon. Only the good die
young." Bobby recovered himself.

Everyone laughed.

"I should live forever, in that case. But I had to think
about how I had arranged my effects. And I'd pretty
much left everything as Raymond and I had once decided. But that time is past. I have no true physical heirs,
but I have plenty of hound children and horse children—
and your children." She smiled warmly. "The Jefferson
Hunt will always have a home. I wish I could leave you
more money. Who knows what the future will bring. But
you have the physical plant."

"Hear! Hear!" Ken applauded.

The others followed his lead.

"So we don't need to go into debt." Ralph Assumptio's long face lit up.

"I rather wanted this to be a surprise, but Crawford,
your concern, which is quite legitimate, forced my hand."

"I certainly had no idea. I didn't mean to." He truly
meant it.

"And I agree with you, Crawford, that a showgrounds
would help us," Sister said. "We might even be able to
rent it out to other groups and make a bit of money.
Imagine that, a hunt club more in the black than in
the red."

Everyone laughed again.

"You have an idea about the showgrounds?" Crawford ran his forefinger and middle finger over his lips, an
unconscious gesture of thoughtfulness.

"I think it's a good idea, but I really don't want it at
Roughneck Farm while I'm alive. I couldn't stand the
commotion."

"What if I bought a piece of property near your place?" Crawford suggested.

"I don't think that will be necessary," Ken said. His voice carried authority, an authority he didn't have in his youth. "Naturally, I'll need to discuss this with Tedi, Edward, and Sybil, but there is a triangle of land, those acres on our western border. The old logging road goes into it. Perhaps we could donate that to the club and start on the showgrounds next spring, if all goes well."

"Still taking on debt," Ralph grumbled, lowering his head like a bull. He'd been sullen lately. "Bulldozers, grading—why, just the preparation for a ring can easily cost thirty thousand dollars. It's the drainage that gets you. Now, I don't want to discourage your gift, Ken, assuming your wife, mother-in-law, and father-in-law agree, but a building program would still mean debt—a grandstand, fencing, fencing around the show ring, that cash register starts ringing up. And you need a sprinkler system, otherwise you've got a dust bowl in the summer. You need a tractor and harrow to drag the ring. You need night lights. You need P.A. equipment, otherwise no one will know what's going on, and I can tell you right now a bullhorn isn't going to cut it. That's for starters, folks. And how big do you want the ring? Big. Doesn't do you a bit of good to build a small one."

"Now, Ralph, we can figure these things out." At that moment Crawford wanted more than anything to strangle Ralph.

"He's right, though," Betty chimed in. "It's a long-term project, but if the land is donated, with effort and a lot of bake sales, hunter trials, and hunter paces, we could raise the money over the years and then build it." Betty feared debt, too. She and Bobby struggled to pay their mortgage sometimes.

The last thing Betty, Bobby, or Sister wanted to do was

wear out the members by always trying to squeeze money or work out of them.

Ronnie Haslip, uncharacteristically silent for most of the meeting, said, "If you build a ring, you should build it three hundred feet by one hundred and fifty feet and board it solid so you can also play arena polo there. Could bring in a little more revenue. And you might want to think about stables, the kind that used to be at the Warrenton Fairgrounds. Then you've expanded your versatility." He held up his hand as Ralph opened his mouth. "And your budget, I know."

Bobby twiddled with his pencil, then spoke, a rather high voice from such a large body. "How can we do this without exhausting our members? This is a huge project. If we add more obligations like more shows, hunter trials, bake sales, you name it, we are going to plain wear out our people. Today, just about everybody works a real job and they don't have time."

"Well, what if I headed up an exploratory committee?" Crawford suggested. "Maybe we could float a bond so people aren't going crazy with these nickel-and-dime projects."

"My nickel-and-dime project brought in fourteen thousand dollars last year," Ralph reminded them. He was justifiably proud of his horse shows, one of which was A rated.

"No disrespect, Ralph, but those shows are a lot of work," Ronnie said. "If Claiborne and Tom Bishop didn't give us the use of the Barracks," Ronnie named their large indoor arena, "gratis, we'd be lucky to make a thousand dollars. And it takes just about everyone in the club to work that big show you do, the A one."

Shows were rated by the American Horse Shows Association. Tempting though it was to think of it as a report card, it usually reflected the level of competition, the courses, etc. A show rated B wasn't necessarily a bad show, it was just somewhat simpler and didn't attract many professional riders who wanted to gain points, rather like professional tennis players trying to keep their rankings on the computer.

Sister kept out of most board discussions unless they related to hounds, hunt staff, hunt territory. She kept out of this one but was listening intently.

"Crawford, do you have dollar figures in mind?" Ken short-circuited Ralph's indignation. "These horse shows are a godsend to us even if they are a lot of work. How much more could we bring in if we had this facility?"

"You could charge the polo club, homeless since the old fairgrounds were torn down, at least five thousand a summer. Other groups would be charged on a day rate. I can get figures from Expoland, Commonwealth Park, and the Virginia Horse Center."

"Those are big operations." Bobby tried not to let his personal animosity for Crawford cloud his judgment.

Crawford was struggling with the same problem in reverse. "I also thought I could see what the Albemarle County Fair brings in. And I will get a variety of construction figures based on different types of footing, ring sizes, stuff like that. I expect the exploratory process will take four to five months."

"The fair suffered the last two years, rained out," Betty flatly stated. "It's a huge problem."

"Which is why we also need an indoor arena if we're going to do this right," Ronnie said, gathering steam. "And I don't want to do this if we aren't going to do it right. Have any of you ever seen the Mercer County Fairgrounds in Kentucky or the Shelbyville Fairgrounds? They're beautiful. Right out of the 1890s. If we're going to do this, then we must do it properly and it should be a thing of beauty."

"And a joy forever." Ken laughed partly because Ronnie had turned so serious.

"He's right, though," Bobby said. "And I don't want to go into debt. Crawford, I am underlining that thought three times. But I agree with Ron. If we do it, we do it right."

"Well, would any of you care to serve on my exploratory committee?" Crawford threw down the gauntlet.

"I will," Ralph said. "To keep an eye on you!"

Everyone laughed.

"Me too," Ken agreed.

Betty nudged Bobby. He ignored her as she spoke up herself. "I'd be happy to do some research on this. It's exciting."

Sister said, "Might I suggest you ask Walter. He'd be invaluable in dealing with details like handicap access, sanitary facilities. And he's got a wealth of common sense, too."

"Good idea," Betty said. She liked Walter.

"All right, if there's no further discussion, will someone make a motion that we adjourn?"

"Wait. One more piece of hunting news," Sister said, and rolled her eyes heavenward as if announcing a miracle from Heaven. "Alice Ramy will let us hunt through her land." Just then an enormous thunderclap startled all of them. "Perfect timing." Sister laughed. The power wavered, then went out.

"I've got candles. Don't worry." Frances bustled in from the kitchen as Ralph lit the graceful hurricane lamps on the mantelpiece.

"How did you do it?" Betty was agape.

"You know, I didn't do a thing. If we give credit to anyone, let's give it to our former member, Guy Ramy. His memory changed his mother's mind."

A silence followed this.

Ken finally said, "Well, that's wonderful. I think each of us board members should make the effort to call on Alice and personally thank her."

"Hear. Hear!" Bobby lightly rapped the table with his gavel. "Excellent development. Excellent idea."

A flash of lightning, another thunderclap, and a torrent of rain dropped out of the sky.

"I don't ever remember this many thunderstorms. This year's been peculiar," Ralph said. He struck a safety match, lighting more candles.

Everyone talked about the weather, Alice, and local events while Betty and Sister helped Frances bring out the food. Ralph opened the bar.

After everyone had a drink in hand, Ralph pulled out a flask holder from behind the bar. "Would you look at what my lovely wife bought me?"

Bobby Franklin reached for it; the British tan leather was cool to his touch. He put his thumb under the small metal button knob, popping up the leather flap that secured the top. Carefully he lifted out the silver-topped flask. Holding the glass to the candlelight, he whistled and said, "Handblown."

"Let me see that." Ken took the flask. "Even got your initial on it."

"Frances thinks of everything," Ralph boasted.

"Wonderful woman," Ronnie agreed. "Only ever made one mistake."

"What's that?" Ralph's eyebrows knitted together.

"Married you," Ronnie said, and laughed.

As they ate, talked, joked with one another, Betty said to Sister, "Bet we don't hunt tomorrow."

"It will clear up."

"You always say that." Betty dabbed her mouth with a linen napkin. "That Frances makes the best deviled eggs. Guards the recipe with her life."

"Hounds are going out unless it's a monsoon."

And that's what it was. So hounds stayed in the kennels and Sister finally knocked off her overdue grocery shopping. She knew, given the moisture, that Saturday's hunt would be slick but that scent ought to hold. She couldn't wait.

CHAPTER 27

Aztec's ears swept forward and back. Although possessed of 360-degree vision, give or take a degree, Aztec couldn't see more than three feet in front of his well-shaped nostrils thanks to persistent fog. Relying on his hearing, he could tell hounds, on a light line in front of him, were working hard to stay with scent. He knew scent should have been glorious, but it wasn't. Foxhunting is a humbling sport, and Nature makes a volatile partner.

Sister listened for hounds, Shaker's voice, the horn, and for the horses behind her. She couldn't move out too quickly because the field, twenty-four strong this early morning, would be scattered like ninepins in the blanket of fog. Mostly they walked and trotted. If hounds hit a hot line, she'd need to use her knowledge of the territory to try to keep up without losing people or running into a barn.

The fog hung over them, refusing to lift. Foxes, knowing the night would bring a full moon, stayed in their dens resting up for what they hoped would be a party night. Lunacy didn't just apply to people.

Fortunately for the hunters, the trails of scent from the night before still lingered. Those late coming home, around sunup, left even fresher scent, but as yet the pack hadn't hit it.

Betty Franklin, on the left side, crept along Snake

Creek's bank. The ground was soggy, but she knew where she was. If hounds really moved off she thought she could stay with them until they entered either the hayfield about four hundred yards to her right, or ran straight through the woods and came out into the cornfield bottom. Once in an open field, Betty knew she'd become disoriented. All she could do was ride to cry, but ultimately that's all any whipper-in can do under harsh conditions.

Sybil, feeling jittery, hoped she wouldn't get in the hounds' way. Hounds met at her parents' big house at After All. Under normal circumstances, Shaker and Sister together with Betty and Sybil would have met at the kennels and roaded them over. This would give hounds time to settle, horses and humans time to limber up, but the fog prevented that. Instead, they loaded everyone on the hound trailer and drove to After All, parking down at the barns.

Even though Sybil was born and raised on this land, the fog transformed the most ordinary things into the extraordinary.

She jumped, startled, as the covered bridge appeared before her like the gaping mouth of the mask of tragedy. Her fear made Marquise, her horse, leap sideways.

"Sorry, Sweetie."

They clip-clopped over the bridge. She thought Betty was up ahead. In a situation like this, Betty would go forward on the left side and Sybil would come behind on the right side. Sybil could hear hounds ahead of her moving along the creek bed. She had no idea where the field was but reminded herself that Sister knew the land even better than she did. Sister had had twenty-five more years to study it.

She climbed the low ridge, sending small stones rolling down the slick mud behind her. She pulled up by her sister's and Peppermint's graves.

"Nola, you'd enjoy today."

Never having spoken to a grave or a dead person before, she felt slightly foolish, but there persisted deep within her the idea that Nola was near. Not just her remains, but her spirit. And that spirit loved her. Yes, when small they fought like banty roosters. As they became teenagers, Sybil swallowed her resentment of her sister's beauty, her extroverted personality. Alone upstairs at night, one or the other would slide down the polished hall floor, socks barely making a squeak. Then they'd sit together on the bed, compare their days, make fun of everyone else, study the models in *Seventeen* or *Vogue* magazine, and talk endlessly about horses.

When Ken Fawkes courted Sybil, Nola fought with Tedi and Edward right alongside her. She even told her father he was a snob. Ken might be poor, but he wasn't stupid and he made Sybil happy. She loved Nola for that. Somehow she hadn't even minded that at her wedding the maid of honor unintentionally outshone the bride.

A ripple of anguish washed over her as she wondered, yet again, what Nola's last moments were like. Was she terrified? Perhaps. Defiant? Most likely. Did she know she was about to die? Sybil prayed that she did not. Perhaps her murderer was merciful in that he didn't torture her. Maybe he killed swiftly and Nola never knew what was happening.

Ken told her not to dwell on it. They couldn't change the past. Focus on the present, on their life together and their sons.

He was right, but she couldn't keep her mind from playing Nola's last day over and over again. Nothing unusual ever stuck out like a red flag. The day's cubbing had put everyone in high spirits. The party that evening at the Burusses' filled them up with food and spirits of a different, more liquid sort. Nola didn't lean over and confess any "sins" to her. Actually, Nola confided in Sybil less once Sybil was married. She'd tease her by saying she didn't want to upset a proper matron.

She shook herself. Concentrate on today. Listen for the hounds.

She wondered where the field was. Ken was with them.

At that moment they were moving, creeping, really, up the right side of the creek, heading upstream. Even Athena and Bitsy, who often enjoyed shadowing them, stayed in the rafters of the stable. Why fly around in the fog when mice scampered right under your talons?

Ralph Assumptio and Ronnie Haslip rode side by side. Everyone out that day wanted to ride next to a buddy and in view of the riders in front, if possible. No one spoke.

Sari and Jennifer rode together; Walter and Ken, Crawford and Marty hung right behind Sister, which irritated Ken, who thought Crawford had no business being up front. Bobby and Xavier brought up the rear, doing their best to keep the twenty-four riders from fading into the fog. That's all they'd need today, someone out there riding around, turning foxes, getting in the way of hounds and finally hollering their damned head off because they were lost and scared.

Tedi and Edward, also furious at Crawford for his pushiness, stuck with Ken and Walter until the path narrowed as the creek forked sharply left, northwest. They scooted in front of the two men, who graciously nodded, "Go ahead."

"Whoop. Whoop." Shaker's cry faded away up front.

Sister knew they'd be in the cornfield soon enough. The corn was planted north to south because of the lay of the land. If she hugged the end row, which she'd have

done even if she could see, she'd come out on the farm
road leading up to Hangman's Ridge.

Cora and Dragon, brimming with drive, wanted to
find a better line than the tattered trail they currently
followed.

"*If we could bolt Charlie, we'd have a run,*" Dragon
said. Charlie was Target's son from last year's litter who
had a den close by.

"*You might be able to bait him,*" Cora said. She was
glad that Asa, Diana, Dasher, and the others were close
behind. The fog didn't bother her as much as the humans
and the horses, because she relied on her nose even in the
brightest of weather. Still, it's always reassuring to see
one's surroundings.

Charlie's den had fresh earth scattered outside as he'd
been housecleaning. It emitted the sweetish, skunky odor
of fox. Charlie, an ego as big as his luxurious brush,
wanted every male animal in the universe to respect his
territory. He even intruded on Uncle Yancy's territory
and marked that. A loud lecture followed this insult.

Not only did he hear Dragon coming, he smelled the
sleek hound.

Dragon crawled halfway into the entranceway before
his shoulders proved too broad for further movement. "*I
know you're in there.*"

"*So does everyone else in this kingdom.*" Charlie
thought of his territory as a kingdom. His mentality was
truly feudal.

"*Give us a run. I'll give you a head start. How about if
I let you get to the other side of the cornfield?*"

"*I wouldn't trust you any farther than I could throw a
dead mouse.*"

Charlie, who was full of himself and eager to make
Dragon eat his words, slipped out his back exit. Dragon,
butt still in the air, continued hollering down the front

entrance. It took Dragon about five minutes before he
realized he'd been had. Then he put his nose to the ground.
"Hot! Hot! I'm right." His rich baritone reverberated
throughout the woods, echoing deeper as the hound was
engulfed in the thickening fog.

The rest of the hounds sped over to Charlie's den.
Dasher could see Dragon's pawprints. He followed the
prints as well as his nose to the exit hole.

His sister was right behind him. He spoke low, then
she spoke louder. *"It's good!"*

Cora called to the others moving through the fog.
"Burning scent! Burning scent!"

"Hurry hounds, hurry," Asa encouraged them. *"All
on. We want to be all on."* Then under his breath he
whispered to Diana, *"Especially in this pea soup."*

Within seconds the hounds converged on Charlie's
den, picked up the escape route line, and flew on it. All
could hear Dragon up ahead by perhaps a quarter of a
mile, too far ahead.

Charlie, flying fast and low, wanted to put as much
distance as possible between himself and Dragon.

Shaker couldn't see anything, but he blew "Gone
Away" as he recognized Dragon's voice, then Cora's, Diana's, Asa's, and the young entry who yelped as much as
sang. Sounded like the whole pack, to him. He heard no
stragglers.

The first problem was to get through the woods, over
the coop in the fence line, through the corn to get up with
his hounds. Like most huntsmen, bravery came naturally
to him, but he was old enough not to be stupid. This was
a day to let Gunpowder pick his way. He trusted his
horse more than he trusted himself.

Betty, already in the cornfield, as she'd had the presence of mind to move forward while hounds were picking at the old line, cantered through a line of corn, the

long green leaves swishing. She knew she couldn't get into too much trouble if she stayed in a row. Once out of the field, the old zigzag fence between the corn and the farm road was easy enough to jump even in the fog.

That couldn't be said of the coop between the woods and the cornfield. Shaker and Gunpowder found it and got over because Gunpowder, long-strided and with the élan of a thoroughbred, trotted two steps and arched over effortlessly.

Sister heard her hounds, then the horn. She'd fallen farther behind than she realized.

Sybil, too, was jolted out of her reverie. She pushed along the low ridge, leaving Nola's grave behind her, but she knew she'd gotten thrown out. Right now she was utterly useless to the huntsman. She cursed herself, then the fog as she tried to make up the ground without breaking her neck.

Sister hugged the creek bed and crossed where the smooth rocks led down into the creek and where Snake Creek fed into Broad Creek. The footing, still slick and deep, was better here. Aztec, his light bay coat oddly translucent in the strange muted light, reached the other side of this part of Broad Creek with no problem. When Sister looked back to see if the person behind her, now Tedi Bancroft, had made it across, she couldn't see anyone. And she could only hear her when Tedi appeared by her side.

"We've got to kick on, Tedi."

Edward charged out of the fog, then held hard, pulling sharply back on the reins. "Sorry, Master."

"Can't see the hand in front of your face. I was telling Tedi, we've got to kick on and hope for the best." She cupped her hands. Normally she wouldn't speak much during a run, but the hounds were well ahead. She wasn't going to cause any hound heads to come up and she wasn't going to turn a fox, either. "If you can hear me, listen for hoofbeats. We've got to move out. If you can't hear the hoofbeats, ride to cry."

"All right," Walter called back.

Bobby, bringing up the rear, had visions of picking up people like scattered croquet balls. But he was a fox-hunter, and foxhunters stay with hounds.

Sister trotted along, spied a rock outcropping, its red streak glistening like blood in the moisture-laden air. Curious. A narrow path forked off from the left of this rock, which would bring her near the coop much more quickly than if she stayed on the wider path. She decided to chance it.

She squeezed her legs, Aztec extending his trot; he had a lovely floating trot, easy on an old back. The club hadn't brushed back this trail, one of those jobs waiting to be knocked out before Opening Hunt. She crouched low, her face alongside Aztec's muscled neck.

"Take care of me, honey."

"Piece of cake," he snorted.

Ralph, Xavier, Walter, and Ronnie cut left by the rock, hoofbeats fading away in front of them. Wordlessly they moved out. Behind them came Ken, Jennifer, and Sari, excited at hounds in full cry and the wildness of the morning.

Bobby kept pushing up stragglers.

Enough people had slid by Crawford when they had the chance that he and Marty rode in the middle of the group, which he didn't like. He so wanted to be in the master's pocket on this day, but he couldn't hang in there. He wasn't quite enough of a rider. Czapaka, a big warmblood and not as nimble as some of the other smaller horses, bulled through the narrow path; a low-hanging pine bough smacked Crawford in the face, disturbing a squirrel up above.

"Watch it," the squirrel chattered.

"You're nothing but a rat with more fur," Czapaka called over his shoulder, which caused the squirrel to throw pinecones on following riders and scream at the top of his lungs. Squirrels aren't known for their emotional self-control.

Sister emerged from the overgrown path knowing the three-board fence should be twenty yards in front of her; Jimmy kept all the fence lines clear. This fence line was the dividing line between After All Farm and Roughneck Farm, with Broad Creek cutting through both properties as it flowed in a southerly direction. The old boundary had been set with squared-off stones back in 1791, when the original land grant was subdivided. The stones stood to this day.

Sister slowed. She didn't want to run into the fence, plus she knew Aztec, bursting with talent, would just lift off and clear the fence. She thought it unwise to ask some of the riders behind her to follow suit. The coop, once she found it, would be more prudent.

Off in the distance she heard Diana's voice, and Cora's bel canto. *"Fly! Fly! Fly!"* The other hounds in chorus, *"Yes."*

"Where is that damned coop?" she whispered, eager to be with her hounds.

A blackened shape interrupted the fence line.

"That's it." Aztec curved to the right, then swung to the left with long, fluid strides to hit the spot perfectly in front of the coop, the rain-soaked earth squishing underneath his hooves. He gave an extra surge of power because of the footing, clearing the coop with a foot to spare, which made Sister laugh as she hadn't expected Aztec to jump so big. He was still young, inclined to overjump.

"Good boy." She patted his neck.

Behind her she heard Tedi land, then Edward, both superbly mounted, as always. She headed left again, following the face of the corn.

Shaker was in the cornfield, behind his hounds. Betty sat now on the farm road, waiting for the hounds to emerge like small ghosts from between the straight-planted rows.

She heard Shaker's high-pitched "Whoop." If he was going to turn or call them back, she'd hear the horn, the three or four long, piercing notes of equal length.

Betty hoped Sybil was on the far side of the cornfield. She couldn't see a thing, contenting herself with the knowledge that no one else could, either.

The bulk of the pack now ran thirty paces behind Dragon. Delia, bringing up the rear, was fifty paces behind.

Charlie scampered over the zigzag fence, ran between Outlaw's legs for effect.

"*Gotcha!*" he shouted over his shoulder.

Both Betty and Outlaw, hearts in their mouths, had to settle themselves for a second, then Betty laughed. The gall of that fox.

"Outlaw," she whispered. "Steady yourself. The whole pack is going to run right through us."

He twitched his ears forward and back. "*Okay.*"

Within two minutes they did just that, then Betty jumped over the fence on the opposite side of the farm road and was swallowed by the fog. She was heading for the orchard. Had she been able to see she would have spurred on Outlaw the minute Charlie ran between her legs, but she couldn't. She thought the wiser course was to let the hounds blow through her; she wouldn't hurt anyone that way and she could ride hard through the orchard, a kind of shortcut.

Sister, face wet from corn leaves, heard the flap, flap,

flap behind her as other riders were getting it full in the face. There was no ducking the corn, the silken red tassels loaded with the moisture.

She felt clammy. The dew point was soggy to the max. Then Sister felt the first drops of a drizzle. She blasted out of the corn row, lifted over the zigzag fence, hooves sunk into the farm road, the red clay now viscous. She hooked left.

Shaker, ahead, blew them on.

Before she knew it, she'd jumped over the zigzag fence on the opposite side of the road and headed straight into the apple orchard. The scent of the apples, almost ready to be picked, filled the air.

The voices of the hounds suddenly stopped.

Trident whispered, *"What happened?"*

Diana said, *"We've lost the scent."*

Dragon, furious, growled, *"I was right behind him! He's got to be here!"*

Shaker rode up to his hounds. "Try on. Eee-lou."

Dutifully, all hounds put their noses to the ground, but nothing. A youngster wanted to run heel, but Cora put her right.

"But it's good here," Rassle whined.

"I know, but you're heading backwards. Must stay forward." Diana confirmed Cora's correction.

The field finally caught up. Betty stayed on the other side of the apple orchard since Shaker didn't blow her in.

Sybil was at the foot of Hangman's Ridge; having gotten herself turned around, she finally found her way out by following first the creek bed, then emerging into the north side of the cornfield. She followed a row in the fog and drizzle to the farm road at the base of the ridge.

Sister rode up to Shaker. "You know, we'd better call it a day."

"Damn, how could he give us the slip like that!"

"I don't know. He's got some kind of mojo, but the fog isn't lifting. If anything, Shaker, it's thickening and my built-in weather station"—she tapped her collarbone broken in the seventies—"tells me this drizzle will be a downpour soon enough."

"Okay." He put his horn to his lips, blowing in his whippers-in.

"Thank God," Betty thought to herself as she picked her way through the fog back down into the apple orchard.

Betty couldn't understand how Charlie could turn his scent off. If he'd ducked into a den, they'd know. But he'd vanished. Not a trace.

Sister turned to face the field, huddled together, exhilarated that they'd survived the fog hunt, as it would come to be known. "Folks, well done. This wasn't an easy task, but it was an exciting one." She turned to Edward. "Do you mind leading people home? Since I'm here I thought Aztec and I would road hounds back to the kennels. We'll come back to pick up the hound wagon."

"I'd be happy to take everyone back." Edward touched the brim of his cap with his crop.

"Shaker, ready?"

"You read my mind."

"Sybil," Sister addressed a bedraggled Sybil, who had just joined them, "Shaker, Betty, and I will put hounds up. You ride back with the others."

"Thank you."

After each field member said, "Good night, Master," and rode off, Sister turned to her hounds.

Edward took the riders back over the zigzag fences and followed the edge of the corn row. Tedi rode up front with him. Folks tried to stay within sight of one another.

The fog, pewter gray now, swirled droplets of moisture. People waited to jump the last coop into After All

Farm, although you could barely see it until one stride in front of it.

Ralph Assumptio, boot to boot with Xavier, passed his old friend his flask.

"You know what? Let's walk the fence line and find the gate. This is stupid. We have the whole rest of the hunt season in front of us, and I, for one, don't want to buy real estate during cubbing."

Xavier savored the marvelous port in Ralph's flask. "You got that right, buddy."

"I agree," Ken called from in front of them, although they couldn't see him.

"Me too," Sybil chimed in.

The sound played tricks on them in the fog.

"Ron, you still with us?" Xavier asked.

"To your right." Ron gently squeezed his horse, who walked forward, the two of them appearing spectral in the swirling mists.

He handed Ron his flask, then turned to Xavier. "What do you have in yours?"

"Schnapps."

Ralph wrinkled his nose. "You carry that stuff so the rest of us won't drink it."

"I like it."

Ken's voice floated toward them. "Xavier, admit it."

"Admit what? I like schnapps. I like sweet stuff. My waistline ought to prove that. Sybil, where the hell are you? Not with your husband, I hope. The entire point of foxhunting is to depart from one's spouse." He knocked back some of his schnapps. "Within limits, of course."

"I'm on your left," she called out.

Ken laughed. "Xavier, don't give my wife ideas."

They heard a rub up ahead at the jump. Someone's horse's hind hooves literally rubbed on the jump.

"If I recall, the hand gate is maybe two hundred yards

down the line, wrong direction from the house, but we can follow the fence line back once we're through the gate." Ron handed Ralph his flask.

Rolling his shoulders, Ralph replied, "Well, let's do it. It's too damned raw out here."

Ken's voice again reached them. "I'll go first. Why don't we fall in line and try to keep the horse in front of you in view."

Ron moved toward the fence, or what he thought was the fence. "I don't hear anyone up ahead."

"Must all be over." Xavier picked up his reins.

"Or unconscious from missing that jump." Ron laughed.

"We'd have heard the screams," Ken called out, his voice moving farther and farther away.

"Sybil, where are you?" Ron asked.

"I'm the rear guard."

"I'll take your word for it." Ralph raised his voice so she could hear, but the fog carried sounds strangely; little sounds were magnified.

"I'm here," she called back reassuringly.

They walked along, silent for a few moments. The squish, squish of their horses' hooves accentuated the increasingly dismal day.

A soft whisper in his ear made Ralph sit up straight in his saddle. It sounded like "I'm going to kill you."

"What'd you say?" Xavier, too, heard the whisper.

"Nothing," Sybil replied, soaked and cold.

Ralph, the fence line to his right, now heard, "I know it was you." He couldn't quite recognize the voice. A knife edge of fear ripped at his stomach.

Ron turned in his saddle. "Where the hell is the gate?"

Xavier grumbled, "I don't know."

Ken called, "Keep up."

"We're behind you," Ron called back. "Just moving slower."

"Gate, please." Ken uttered the traditional foxhunting command that directed the last person to close the gate.

Ralph thought he was between Ron and Xavier, but he could no longer see them.

Ron reached the opened gate, passing through. "Sybil, gate please," he bellowed.

"Okay," she responded, her voice fading away.

The voice whispered in Ralph's ear again. "Time to join Hotspur."

Ralph pressed with his right leg, and his horse swerved left. He didn't pass through the gate, but instead he tore off through the cornfield.

Ron heard him take off. "What the shit is going on?"

Xavier clucked to his horse and caught up to Ron. "What's going on?"

"That's just what I said." Ron frowned. "Ralph!" No response. "Sybil."

"Here I am." She appeared out of the silver.

"What's going on?" Ron again asked.

"I don't know." Sybil shrugged.

"Well, Ralph's not here." Ron yelled, "Ken!"

"Yo," Ken called back, from an indeterminate distance.

Xavier leaned forward. "Look, we're going to get lost out here. Let's trot. The sooner we get back the better."

"Yeah, but where's Ralph?" Ron, truly worried now, pointed his crop at Xavier.

"I don't know." Xavier knocked his crop away with his own crop. "What are you so worried about? For all we know, he's ahead of us. Maybe he's ahead of Ken."

"We can't leave him."

"You two go back. I know this country. I'll look for him," Sybil calmly replied.

"Sybil, we can't leave a lady out here. I'm telling you, there's a storm coming up," Ron said sternly.

"Don't think of me as a lady. Think of me as a whipper-in and there's a lost hound. I'd be out then. Just tell Ken when you see him that I'll be late getting in and not to worry. If the weather turns nasty I'll put my horse up at Sister's." She disappeared into the fog.

"Sybil! Sybil!" Ron shouted.

Then they both heard a light rap on the coop.

"She's going the wrong way," Xavier exhaled, thoroughly tired of the whole thing. "Come on, Ron."

"Something is really wrong. I don't think we should leave them."

"Leave Ralph? We don't know where he is, and Sybil's right, she does know the territory even if she is heading in the wrong direction," Xavier said.

Ron's eyes narrowed. "How do you know it was Sybil who just took that jump?"

"Look, old buddy, I'll grant you that things have been really crazy. But maybe Ralph got sick of crawling through the mist. Maybe he spurred on and he's halfway back to the trailers by now."

"He turned in the opposite direction. I heard him hit the corn."

"What do you mean?"

Ron shook his helmet as a raindrop hit the velvet top. "I heard the stalks, the leaves, you know, the long leaves. I heard them hitting him."

Xavier sat silent, then spoke. "Hear anything else?"

"Just that rub on the fence when Sybil jumped in. She should have headed back toward Sister's."

"We have to go in. We do. We can't do anything to help. It's going to rain. It's already raining." Xavier peered up into the deepening gray as the drizzle slicked his face. "If they aren't there, then we can worry. Come on."

With reluctance, Ron passed through the gate, waited for Xavier to walk through, then he leaned over from atop his kind, patient horse and closed the gate, dropping the metal kiwi latch, shaped like a comma, through the steel circle.

Ralph galloped through the corn. His face wet, broad flat corn leaves were hitting him. He thought he heard hoofbeats behind him. He reached the farm road as the first raindrop splattered. If he had been in better command of himself he would have prudently turned left, jumped into the orchard, and ridden to Sister's barn, perhaps a fifteen-minute trot. But panic had overtaken him, and he turned his horse right, pushing toward Hangman's Ridge.

Inky heard him pass as she snuggled in her den. Five minutes later she heard a second set of hoofbeats, only this horse wasn't running. This horse moved at a deliberate trot. As the weather was filthy, her curiosity was dimmed. She wasn't going out to see what was going on.

Ralph, breathing heavily, eyes wide, transmitted his terror to his horse as he urged the animal up to the right. They reached the flat plateau of Hangman's Ridge.

"Oh shit." Ralph shook his head. He hadn't wanted to come up here, but his mind was fuzzy. Hands shaking, he reached down for his flask, flipped open the leather case, now slippery, and pulled out the heavy, handblown flask. He unscrewed the top and emptied the entire contents. The fire wiggled down his throat, into his belly. He took a deep breath.

Clutching the flask, he moved toward the giant oak, ignoring the warning snorts of his horse, a far better judge of danger than Ralph.

"Trooper, get a grip," commanded Ralph, whose spirits were now stronger thanks to those he had imbibed.

The enormous glistening tree loomed out of the fog. A shrieking sound so unnerved Trooper that he shied, all four feet off the ground. Ralph hit with a thud, his flask rolling across the wet grass.

Trooper turned and fled back toward the farm road. The horse smelled another horse moving up through the narrow deer paths on the side of the ridge. He didn't bother to whinny. He lowered his head and ran as if his life depended on it, the stirrup irons banging at his sides.

Ralph, cursing, picked himself up. Only then did he see, or think he saw, the hanging corpse of Lawrence Pollard, the fine lace of his sleeves drooping in the wet.

"And being found in fashion as a man, he humbled himself and became obedient unto death, even the death of the cross," Lawrence quoted Philippians, chapter two, verse eight. Then he moaned, "Obedient unto death, even death on a hanging tree." The wind that always blew on the ridge carried his voice away.

Ralph, sweat running down his face, his hands wet with sweat, backed away from the tree. He turned to follow his horse in flight. Running, slipping, sliding, falling, picking himself up—only to run smack into another horror.

"Oh God," Ralph sobbed.

"You'll see Him before I do."

Down in the kennels, Sister and Shaker were removing collars from hounds who had hunted. The boys were then released to go to their side of the kennel, the girls to the other side. This allowed the master and huntsman to inspect each hound, making sure no one's pads had been cut, no ears sliced by deadly Virginia thorns.

A crack brought hound and human heads up.

"What was that?"

"No one's sighting a rifle today," Shaker said, hands fallen to his sides. He looked toward the north.

"Sound plays tricks in this weather. Could have been a backfire on Soldier Road," Sister said halfheartedly.

"Small caliber," Asa told them.

"Handgun," Diana added, her ears lifted, her nose in the air. Although there was nothing to smell inside the draw pen, she still trusted her nose above all other senses.

"All right, boys." Shaker led the boys to their door.

"Come on, girls." Sister did the same for the gyps.

Once the hounds were in their proper kennels, both humans, without speaking to each other, walked out the front door of the main kennel to listen.

Far away they heard hoofbeats, trotting. As the sound came closer, they walked through the intensifying rain to the stable.

The girls inside had finished cleaning the tack.

"Can't see a bloody thing." Shaker felt uneasy.

"We came in in the nick of time." As Sister reached for a towel hanging on a tack hook, Sybil materialized out of the fog, leading Trooper.

"Sybil?"

"Sister, I found him wandering through the orchard. Guess he jumped the fence by himself."

A shaking Trooper stared wild-eyed at the people. The other horses, munching hay in their stalls, stopped.

"Girls, gently, gently, put him in the end stall, take his tack off, and wipe him down."

As Trooper passed the others, he rolled his eyes. *"I saw the ghost. Ralph wouldn't listen,"* he kept babbling.

Keepsake, hoping to calm him, said, *"There are a couple up there."*

Sybil dismounted as Jennifer took her reins. "Somehow Ralph became separated from the group, so I went out to look for him. Can't find anything in this."

Sister, worried, said, "He could be walking back here or to your farm. No telling."

"Or he could be hurt." Shaker said what she was thinking.

"Girls, take care of Sybil's horse, too, please."

"Yes, ma'am. Then can we help you look?" Sari asked.

She waited a moment, her mind racing. "Yes. Take care of Trooper and Marquise first." Then, voice lower, as if speaking to herself, she murmured, "Trooper is a sensible horse."

Shaker, his shirt soggy against his skin, touched Sybil's elbow. "When did you last see Ralph?"

"At the gate between the cornfield and our line. The hand gate. Of course, couldn't see anything, but that's where I heard him last. Ken, Xavier, Ron, Ralph, and I decided to go through the gate to get back home. You couldn't even see the coop anymore until you were right up on it. No sense getting hurt. But we got strung out."

"The first thing to do is call your mother. It could be that everyone is back safe and sound."

Sister hurried into the tack room, knowing in her bones that all was most emphatically not safe and sound.

CHAPTER 28

"And why weren't you out hunting today?" Tedi, steaming cup of hot chocolate in hand, asked Cindy Chandler, the owner of Foxglove Farm.

The pretty blonde smiled. "I was going to go."

"Sure, Weenie," Betty Franklin, nursing roped coffee, teased. She'd roaded hounds back to the kennel and left her horse there. As a whipper-in, her concern was the hounds. And Sister never minded Betty putting her horse up in Sister's barn. She'd driven Jennifer's car to After All since Sister asked her to go on ahead and be her stand-in while she and Shaker removed collars.

"I really was. Cat Dancing and I are ready," she mentioned her beloved mare, "but Clytemnestra and her calf, Orestes, broke down the back side of the fencing and escaped. Still haven't found them."

"Cindy, can't you call that damned cow Bessie? Does it have to be Clytemnestra?" Betty checked her watch. "God, it's terrible to have to work for a living. I'd better roll on."

Tedi scanned her living room. "Sybil's still not back."

Betty frowned a moment. "Maybe she's at the barn."

Members had carried cakes, biscuits, and sandwiches they'd packed for a small tailgate into Tedi's dining room. As with most spontaneous gatherings, it proved much more fun than the arduously planned variety.

Edward had shepherded the field back to his barns. Not often acting as field master, he had neglected to make a head count.

"Have any idea where the cow headed? Tracks?" Betty returned to the case of the missing cow and calf.

"I tracked her across Soldier Road but lost her trail in the wildflower meadows. This fog is unbelievable. Don't know how you all were out there without getting lost."

"Well, that's another story." Betty laughed.

"We were never lost. No, not the trusty Jefferson Hunt Club." Ken sipped his coffee, a shot of Irish Mist adding immeasurably to his pleasure since he was wet and chilled.

"Rain dropped buckets on me, like the heavens had unzipped, so I went back home, took a hot shower, and then came over to ask Tedi and Edward to keep an eye out for Cly and Orestes. I'd better alert Sister, too," Cindy thought out loud.

"Once this fog lifts, we'll find her. She's hard to miss," Tedi said.

Clytemnestra, the black and white Holstein cow, was quite flashy. Her pastures, rich in redbud clover and alfalfa, should give the cow no reason for complaint, but Cly liked the excitement of escape. Also, she was nosy and wanted to see what was happening on other farms. She was teaching her offspring her tricks. Although still a little fellow, he eagerly absorbed his mother's lessons. Their jailbreak over the summer when Sister, Walter, Shaker, and Doug built the new in and out jumps only inflamed them to further adventures.

People slowly began to head home. They checked on their horses in their trailers, then drove away.

"Hey," Betty said, poking her head back inside the living room. She had left, gone to Jennifer's car, then returned.

"Ralph Assumptio's trailer is down at the barn, but he wasn't at the breakfast."

"Edward," Tedi called, and her husband came in from the library.

"What, dear?"

"Did you see Ralph at breakfast?"

"No, don't think so."

"Ken?" Tedi asked her son-in-law, who wanted to change clothes and head for the office.

He shook his head. "No."

"Good God, he must still be out there." Tedi blanched.

"Bobby brought up the rear," Betty said. "We might reach him in the truck." She walked into the kitchen to use the phone. Tedi followed. "Oh, Bobby, glad I got you. I'm still at the Bancrofts'. We can't find Ralph."

"What?"

"His trailer is here but he's not, and no one remembers seeing him at breakfast." Betty's eyes met Tedi's.

"The last time I saw Ralph was at the coop between the cornfields and the woods. A couple of guys were back there," Bobby recalled.

"Let me talk to him." Ken took the phone from Betty. "Hey, Bobby. Ronnie, Xavier, Ralph, and I had a drink while everyone was negotiating the coop. Sybil was back there with us, too. That's the last time I saw him. You're sure he didn't come in and go home with someone else? Maybe put his horse on their trailer?"

"No." Bobby felt terrible. His job was to bring up the rear.

Edward felt responsible, too.

"Ralph wouldn't leave his trailer here without asking," Tedi said, truly worried now.

As Ken talked to Bobby, the other line rang. Ken put Bobby on hold and heard Sister's voice.

"Is Ralph there?" she inquired.

"No. We just noticed. I'm on the other line with Bobby."

"We need to look for him. I'm sending Sybil to where Snake Creek feeds into Broad. She'll follow the creek back to your covered bridge. Ralph's smart enough to use the creek. Put Betty on."

"Let me say good-bye to Bobby."

"Tell him to stay at work. We have enough people to find Ralph. Okay?"

Ken relayed her message to Bobby, pressed the flashing button, and handed the phone to Betty.

"Boss?" Betty's voice rose.

"Take Edward. Go to the Bleeding Rock. Retrace our steps that way. You'll come out at the coop. Maybe he came a cropper at the coop."

"Okay."

"Ask Ken and Tedi to drive along Soldier Road. He might be walking on the road."

"Where are you going?"

"Cornfield and all around the base of Hangman's Ridge. If we don't find him in an hour I'm calling Ben Sidell. In fact, tell the others to take their cell phones. If no one finds Ralph, call me on my cell in one hour."

"Roger."

"Oh. Jennifer and Sari want to help. Do you mind?"

"No."

"Good. I'll put them in the orchard and tell them to follow hound tracks backward to the cornfield in case Ralph tracked hounds." She hoped the tracks hadn't completely washed away.

"Okay."

"One hour."

"Right." Betty hung up and gave the others Sister's orders.

They threw on Barbour coats or Gore-Tex jackets and hurried out of the house.

Sister scribbled her cell phone number on a pad and handed it to Jennifer. "Call us. We'll be in the cornfields and then around the bottom of Hangman's Ridge. If you don't find anything when you finally reach the cornfield, come straight back to the barn. Don't leave the barn until you hear from me."

"Yes, ma'am," Jennifer said.

With that, Sister and Shaker hopped into the truck. They parked and combed the cornfields, rain pouring down, fog as dense as ever, but found nothing unusual.

Then they climbed back into the truck, mud caked on their boots, every new step seemingly heavier than the last, and they checked the base of the ridge. The rain had washed away any tracks.

"We might as well go to the top of the ridge. At least we can drive up," Sister said, water running off her coat and onto the floor.

"Why would he go up there? Even in the fog he'd know Hangman's Ridge. He'd have to have climbed up," Shaker sensibly said.

"That's true, but maybe he rode up to get his bearings and try to find the farm road. We don't know where he parted company with Trooper. He could have covered a lot of ground and he could have suffered a concussion and been disoriented."

"We've tried everything else," Shaker agreed. He kept the headlights on low since high beams would only reflect back off the fog, making vision even worse. "Can't see a bloody thing!"

"Drive along the flat part. At least to the tree."

"Christ, in this stuff we'll probably run into it." He crept ahead.

The great gnarled shape hove into view, silvery fog sliding over branches.

Not until they were almost right up to the tree did they see Ralph flat on his back.

Shaker braked. Both he and Sister bolted out of the truck.

"Oh no." Sister covered her face for a second. Ralph had been shot right between the eyes.

Shaker knelt down to feel for a pulse. Sister knelt on the other side of Ralph's body. She, too, touched his neck.

"Warm. He can't have been dead long," she said.

"We heard the shot."

"Oh, Shaker, if only we knew what he knew."

"If we knew what he knew, we'd be dead, too."

Sister, a surge of fury running through her, cried, "Why didn't he tell us!"

"Because he knew he'd be killed." Shaker held up his hands in a gesture of defeat.

She stood up. "Goddamn whoever killed him!"

CHAPTER 29

The horses calling over the pastures told the hounds what had happened. The news passed from animal to animal. Domesticated animals wished to protect their humans.

The wild animals, with the exception of the foxes, generally didn't care what humans did to one another. Sister took care of the foxes, and they wished no harm to come to her.

Athena, Bitsy, and Inky sat protected under a heavy canopy of oak leaves.

"The killer's come out of his lair," Bitsy said. She had grown fond of some of the humans.

"Bad enough Nola was killed. Bad enough," Inky repeated to herself.

Athena turned her head upside down, then right side up. *"Cold-blooded. If we hadn't sheltered in the Bancrofts' barn we'd know who shot Ralph."*

"The humans won't figure it out, will they?" Bitsy worried.

Athena breathed in, her huge chest expanding outward, parting her feathers enough to show the beautiful shaded variations underneath. *"This is bad. Very bad. When a killer breaks cover like this he's both ruthless and now reckless."*

"What about Sister? Is she safe?"

252

"Who knows?" Bitsy shrugged. "Any human who gets in the way is in danger, I would guess."

"Pity you foxes can't lead the killer to his death. It would be a fitting end," Athena said.

"A lot of things happen during a hunt. Maybe we will get our chance," Inky said, "if we can find out who it is."

"Well, this is certainly a hunt. If a mouse sits stock-still, I might miss him. But if he moves, then I've got a chance. This human is moving." Athena blinked. "He really has broken cover."

"But he's foiling his scent," Inky said.

"He'll make a mistake. He'll come into view. I just hope the next human who flushes him out is ready."

CHAPTER 30

For some people, Ralph's end came as a relief. Eager for tidy answers, they assumed he had killed Nola and Guy and had finally, undone by the unearthing of the dead, shot himself. The fact that no gun had been found did not disturb their desire for an easy answer. Then, too, most suicides don't shoot themselves between the eyes.

Others, no less eager for answers but less inclined to take the easy way out, wondered what Ralph could have done to provoke such a violent end.

Sister felt a sense of foreboding; an evil had been unleashed. Then she realized the evil had always been with them, they'd just chosen not to notice.

She and Shaker sat on that ridge for two full hours. First came the sheriff and his crew, then the Rescue Squad to remove the body once it had been photographed, examined, and finally released.

The kids waited back at the stable as they were told. Sister informed them they'd found Ralph. She spared them the details. When she and Shaker finally returned to the farm, they discovered the girls had done all their chores.

Raleigh and Rooster stuck to Sister's side likes burrs.

The rain continued, but the fog started thinning out. An oppressive mugginess made it hard to breathe, and even though the temperature remained tolerable, the closeness of the air felt like a shroud.

As they lacked a kennelman, Sister and Shaker were responsible for the job of cleaning the kennels after a hunt. Tired but usually happy from the day's hunt, they tackled this with the help of a couple of cups of black coffee. Today the girls had given them an unexpected respite. When Betty returned to pick up Jennifer and Sari, Sister insisted on giving the girls each a fifty-dollar bonus. Betty didn't protest. She was too shaken up by Ralph's murder.

The outdoor runs glistened in the downpour. The indoor runs and pens had been powerwashed. Each of the raised sleeping beds was filled with fresh, soft sawdust chips.

The hounds were snuggled down in their cozy beds, sleeping after a good hunt. They had enjoyed having the two young women fuss over them.

After the girls left, Sister and Shaker sat down in the kennel office. They'd told everything they could think of to Ben Sidell, but they hadn't had a chance to talk to each other. Given the swift shock of it, they found they hadn't much to say to each other immediately.

"Hell of a note." Shaker wiped his face with a towel.

"It's not a sight I'll soon forget." She took the towel from him and wiped her own face and hands. "If only I'd led the field back to the Bancrofts'."

"Sister, you couldn't have seen any more than Edward did. Fog was thick. Cut it with a knife."

"My ears are more educated."

"True, but you'd have been up ahead. Ralph was in the back. Once it stops raining we can go back to the coop. Maybe we'll find something on the ground, but it would appear he left the coop and rode to the ridge."

"I've been thinking. He didn't go alone. And someone

who really knew the territory, despite the fog or maybe even because of it, could have taken him up there, shot him, flown down the back side of the ridge, and been at the trailers not long after everyone else came in."

"True."

They sat there on the beat-up wooden chairs that had been donated to the kennel office almost thirty years ago.

He drummed his fingers on the metal desktop. "Why would Ralph willingly ride with his killer?"

"Maybe he didn't know he was going to be killed. Maybe the killer said he needed help or he knew a shortcut—"

"Ralph knew Hangman's Ridge. He had to know he was going wrong."

"He still could have been bamboozled in some fashion."

"Killer could have forced him up there." Shaker wiped his hands on his thighs. "And somewhere along the way he made Ralph dismount."

"Sybil was out there." Sister shifted uneasily in her chair.

"Easy to slip away in the fog." He poured himself more coffee. "I'm drinking too much of this stuff. So are you."

"What if whatever the killer knew about Ralph was enough to ensure his cooperation?" Sister ignored his coffee comment.

"I wonder if we'll ever know."

She said with weariness, "Shaker, I believe it was Ralph who called me about looking in the river off Norwood Bridge."

"Jesus." Shaker sat up straight because some pieces were falling into place.

"Just hear me out. I don't think Ralph killed Nola. He might have killed Guy; he couldn't stand him because of Nola. But I don't think he killed her. I think he accepted that he'd lost her. That romance was busted, and he was already courting Frances. On the rebound maybe, but people are like that."

"They are."

"But somehow he was connected with those murders. There is no doubt in my mind he helped the killer lift that fifty-five-gallon drum and toss it into the James."

"But over all these years you'd think he'd have told, or the guilt would have gotten to him."

"Well, I couldn't live with it. You couldn't live with it. But obviously he could. And maybe, just maybe, he stood to gain by his actions."

"I suppose he gained his life." Shaker shrugged.

"Why?"

"Well, he knew the killer might kill him if he didn't help."

"Possibly. I think, though, that he came out ahead in some other way."

"Was Ralph a vengeful enough man to want to see Nola dead?"

Sister turned this over in her mind. "No, but he might have wanted to see her suffer. You know, to see her finally get dumped by someone. But you're right, I don't think Ralph could have helped her killer. Which leads us to—what?"

Shaker's thick auburn eyebrows jerked upward. "The killer might have told him Guy killed Nola. Ralph exploded and killed Guy. Or Nola's killer had already done the deed and needed help disposing of Guy's body. He'd be plenty tired from digging Nola's grave, not that Ralph would know that."

She shook her head. "If Ralph had known Nola was killed or thought she was killed by Guy, then he would have told Tedi and Edward."

"I don't think so. Look, we can never know what goes

through someone's head, but maybe Ralph thought, 'done is done.' He can't bring her back. Maybe he had a special sympathy for the murderer. Or maybe the killer could somehow pin it on him? How could Ralph prove he was innocent?"

"That's a good point." She didn't know if too much coffee was making her jittery or if she was jittery anyway. "Either way, he was vulnerable."

Shaker slapped the table. "And who stood to gain more than Sybil? She'd get Nola's part of the Bancroft fortune. Millions upon millions upon millions. Right?"

"We know one thing for certain we'd only suspected before."

"What?"

"The killer really is in our hunt field."

CHAPTER 31

The rain stopped Sunday morning, revealing skies of robin's egg blue and temperatures in the middle sixties.

Sister, Shaker, and Walter met Ben Sidell at the mailbox for Roughneck Farm. They drove in two four-wheel-drive trucks to the cornfield, then parked off the farm road to walk to the coop between the cornfield and the Bancroft woods.

Impressed by Walter's attention to detail at Norwood Bridge, the sheriff was glad the doctor accompanied them. Sister just felt better when Walter was around, although she didn't really know why. The same was true for Shaker. He grounded her.

The mud sucked on their work boots. The ends of their pants' legs were sopping wet from the grass.

Raleigh and Rooster bounded along with them. At first Ben resisted, but Sister convinced him their superior senses might turn up something helpful.

A half-moon puddle glistened before the coop, the depression the result of many hooves digging in before the jump.

Ben crouched down. The rains had washed away hoofprints. He stood up, leaning his hands on the top kickboard as he studied what had been the landing side of the coop on the way home from Saturday's hunt. All he had found near the body was Ralph's new flask. He'd hoped he'd find more here.

"And this was the last place anyone saw Ralph?"

"Yes," Walter answered. "It was the last any of us saw him, those of us who stayed with Edward."

"Shaker, Betty, and I left him at the apple orchard," Sister reminded Ben.

"Right." He cupped his chin in his right hand. "And you couldn't see the hand in front of your face."

"Right," Walter again replied.

"Well, how'd you get over the coop?"

"Trusted my horse," Walter said.

"And you still jumped it?" Ben thought these fox-hunters were crazy.

"Sheriff, you do things in the hunt field you'd never do anywhere else." Walter heard a caw as St. Just flew overhead.

"Over here," Raleigh barked at Sister.

Sister walked to where both the Doberman and the harrier stood. A sodden handkerchief lay in the cleared path between the cornfield and the fence line. "Sheriff, I don't want to touch this."

They hurried over, and Ben knelt down and peered at the handkerchief. He pulled on a thin latex glove, picked up the wet, muddy handkerchief, and dropped it in a plastic bag.

"Keep coming," Rooster, farther down the fence line, called out.

Shaker walked up to the hound. "Sheriff. A string glove."

The white woven glove lay in a puddle.

A few minutes later the other glove was found where the cornfield curled right toward a small tributary feeding into Broad Creek.

The four humans and two dogs, wet to the knees,

ankle deep in mud, sloshed to the base of Hangman's Ridge.

"Hansel and Gretel," Sister sorrowfully said. "Maybe Ralph dropped or threw away his gloves and handkerchief on the way."

Shaker exhaled. "Anyone could have dropped gloves or a handkerchief. I just don't know why Ralph would have left the other people. It makes no sense to me even if he was nervous. Wouldn't there be protection in numbers?"

"Guilt—or he snapped. People do," Walter said. He jammed his hands into his jeans pockets, then asked Ben, "What do you think?"

"I try not to jump to conclusions."

"What can we do?" Walter asked.

"Wait for a crack in the armor," Ben evenly replied. "The morning newspaper, which I'm sure you read, reported he was shot, the weapon hadn't been found, and the sheriff is investigating." He smiled ruefully, folding his arms across his chest. "That's a nice way of saying we don't know a damned thing."

"You're a doctor, Walter. Do you think our killer is rational?" Sister asked as she knocked one shoe on the other. Mud fell off in red clumps.

"I'm a neurosurgeon, not a psychiatrist."

"For which we're all grateful." Sister half smiled at him. "But you see people in crisis daily. Surely you get a feeling about the real person. Do you have a sense of this person?"

"Well, yes, I think our killer is rational and opportunistic. The fog gave him—or her—a chance to do what he or she was ultimately planning to do. Sister, I think it was Ralph who called you," Walter said.

"Me too. Shaker and I thought of that. And I told the sheriff, too."

"Shock. It's a hell of a shock to see someone you know like that." Shaker wanted to get his hands on the killer. "Poor bastard, flat out in the rain."

"Which brings me back to why?" Sister said. "Why make a spectacle of Ralph? Why not kill him away from everyone? Why not dispose of his body and be done with it just like he thought he had done with Nola and Guy? I wonder if this isn't a warning."

"The hanging tree, a warning to all, the place of punishment." Shaker nodded up toward the ridge.

"Shaker's right. This was so dramatic. He's arrogant. He thinks he's invincible. He must have some incredible sense that he'd never be suspected."

"No one would think Sybil killed her sister," Shaker said quietly. He didn't want to think Sybil capable of such a deed, but she had the best motive that he could discern.

"Paul Ramy certainly fingered her for a suspect. But he couldn't make anything stick," Ben confided to them. "He thought if she killed her sister that her family would protect her."

"Tedi? Never!" Sister quickly responded.

"Sister's right. But Edward might cover for her," Shaker added. "He'd lost one daughter. What good would it do to have the other in jail? I assume that's what a father would think."

"I don't believe it. I know Edward is protective of his girls, well, fathers always are, aren't they?" Sister's voice rose quizzically. "But he's a man of principle. I don't know that he would provide an alibi for her. Even if he thought the original murders were an isolated incident, you know, if he was sure she'd never kill again, he wouldn't help her."

"Paul's reports say she stayed at the party, then went

to the C&O with Ken. Other witnesses confirm seeing her there."

"The Bancrofts could pay off the entire county," Shaker said.

"Oh, come now, someone would talk. Keep a secret for two decades? Not here." Sister interlocked her fingers. "I agree that Sybil had a financial and perhaps even an emotional incentive, but I don't think she did it. Had Nola lived, Sybil's inheritance would still be beyond most people's wildest dreams."

"Never underestimate the greed of the rich," Ben Sidell said. "But you're right, Sister, that our killer feels we can't touch him. He's fooled everybody for twenty-one years. I doubt he's even that scared now."

"Pride goeth before a fall," Sister said quickly. Then she whirled around, as did Shaker, their senses sharper than either Ben's or Walter's.

A brush, brush in the cornfield alerted them.

Raleigh and Rooster charged down a row, the stalks bending deeply.

"*It's Clytemnestra and Orestes,*" Raleigh informed them.

Encouraged by the canine companionship and hearing the human voices, the large Holstein cow and her calf walked out of the corn, making a squishy sound with each step.

"You two!" Sister was disgusted with them. "Raleigh, Rooster, let's herd them home with us. We'll get them over to Cindy's later."

"*You bet.*" The dogs paced themselves behind the two bovines, keeping just out of reach of a cow kick.

"Guess we might as well walk you home, too," Ben said. "I'll take down the yellow tape tonight." He indicated the police tape used to cordon off Hangman's Ridge. "Nothing else to find here."

CHAPTER 32

A Titleist golf ball, white, rolled to a stop next to a small grooming brush, bristles full of flaming red fur.

"You thought that golf ball was an egg when you brought it home, didn't you?" Inky mischievously batted the golf ball.

Charlie, a natural collector of all sorts of objects, replied, *"It's fun to play with, but I don't think the humans that play with them have much fun. They curse and throw their sticks. Why do they do it if they hate it so much?"*

"Human psychology." Inky observed the flat-faced species with great interest. For one thing, their curious locomotion intrigued her. She thought of human walking as a form of falling. They'd catch themselves just in time. It must be awful to totter around on two legs.

"They do like to suffer," Charlie noted. *"I believe they are the only species who willingly deny themselves food, sex, pleasure."*

"And they're so happy when they finally give in and enjoy themselves." Inky laughed.

Charlie's den used to belong to Aunt Netty, but she'd wanted to be closer to the orchard, so she had moved last year. Netty was like a perfectionist lady forever in search of the ideal apartment.

Charlie had enlarged the den. Given his penchant for toys, he needed more space.

"*Look at this.*" He swept his face against the dandy brush. "*Feels really good.*"

"*Where'd you get that?*"

"*Cindy Chandler. She left it on the top of her tack trunk. When she forgets potato chips or crackers, that's the greatest. Not only does the stuff taste good, the bags crinkle!*"

"*Some sounds are so enticing. Sister's big wind chimes— I like to sit in the garden and listen to them ringing at night.*"

Inky and Charlie, the same age, belonged to two different species of fox. Inky, a gray, was slightly smaller. She could climb trees with dexterity, and in many ways she was more modest than the red fox, who had to live in a grand place, making a conspicuous mound so everyone would know how important he was.

The reds found this lack of show on the part of the grays proof that they were beneath the salt. Nice, yes, but not truly first class. And their conversational abilities missed the mark most times, as well. The reds enjoyed chattering, barking, even yodeling when the mood struck. Grays were more taciturn.

Both types of fox, raised in loving homes, went out into the world at about seven or eight months. The annual diaspora usually started in mid-September in central Virginia.

And both types of fox believed themselves the most intelligent of the land creatures. They allowed that cats could be rather smart, dogs less so. Humans, made foolish by their own delusions of superiority, delighted the foxes because they could outwit them with such ease. Nothing like a small battalion of humans on horseback and forty to sixty hounds, all bent on chasing a fox, to reaffirm the fox's sense of his own cleverness.

"*Charlie, how* did *you disappear in the apple orchard?*" Inky had heard from Diana how the red fox evaporated as if by magic, leaving not an atom of scent.

He puffed out his silky chest. "*Inky, there I was in the middle of the apple orchard, fog like blinders, I tell you, the heavy scent of ripe apples aiding me immeasurably. I'd intended to duck into that abandoned den at the edge of the orchard. You know the one?*" She nodded that she did, so he continued. "*But along came Clytemnestra and Orestes. And I thought to myself that those hounds, young entry, mind you, have denned a fox each time they've been cubbing. Getting too sure of themselves. If I simply vanish, they'll be bumping into one another running in circles, whimpering, 'Where'd he go?' I jumped on a big rock and up on Orestes's back. Up and away.*" He flashed his devilish grin.

"*You shook their confidence,*" she admiringly complimented him, "*for which every fox is grateful.*"

"*The T's and R's are going to be very good, I think. Trinity, Tinsel, Trudy, and Trident, Rassle, and Ruthie. Good. And now that the D's are in their second season, well, we may have to pick up the pace. Aunt Netty was right.*"

"*Usually is,*" Inky agreed.

Outside, the arrival of soft twilight announced the approaching night.

"*Would you like a golf ball?*"

"*That would be fun.*" Inky liked to play.

"*I know where she keeps them at Foxglove. It's a piece of cake to reach into the golf bag and filch one. And her house dog sleeps right through it.*"

"*Charlie,*" Inky said and blinked, "*did you notice anything unusual in that fog when you were riding Orestes?*"

"I smelled Ralph. He sent off a strong, strong odor of fear. And I heard two other riders moving in different directions. They weren't together. I know one was Sybil, because I could smell. I couldn't get a whiff of the other rider. Too far away." He rolled upright. "Don't you find it odd that humans kill one another? To kill for food, well, we must all survive, but to kill members of your own species? Very nasty."

"You know, sometimes a vixen will go into a killing frenzy to teach her cubs how to kill," Inky soberly said. "I think humans can go into killing frenzies, too, but for a different reason. I worry that this person might do that."

"Possibly." Charlie swept forward his whiskers. "You know that Cly and Orestes didn't see the killer or they would have blabbed to everyone. Cly can't keep a secret. Cows are dumb as posts." He laughed.

As the two left the den, Inky wondered if murder was a pleasure for humans the way catching a mouse was a pleasure for her. If so, how could a killer ever stop killing?

CHAPTER 33

Plain pews of rich walnut accented the severe yet uplifting architecture of the local Episcopal church. When its first stone was laid in 1702 it was a rough affair. Few Christian people lived this far west, and those who did had little money. The native tribes of Virginia, divided into Iroquois-speaking peoples and Sioux-speaking peoples, warred against one another sporadically. The handful of whites found themselves in the middle, an uneasy place to be.

The small church proved a refuge from the unrelenting hostilities of the New World, a land devoid of familiar English nightingales yet filled with scarlet tanagers. For every animal left behind on England's shores, there appeared here some new, beautiful creature.

Stone or brick was necessary for buildings of any permanence since the Indians used fire when raiding settlers. The large church bell could be used to sound an alarm. Every farm also had a bell. Upon hearing it, people set free their livestock, hopped on their horses, and galloped to the church.

While it may not have been its most Christian feature, the church, like their homes, was built with a small room with gun slits in the walls. The settlers took aim at attackers through those narrow openings in the stone. A slate roof provided protection from fire.

Over time, truces were made, later broken by both sides. But as the Thirty Years War raged, followed by the English Civil War, the trickle of colonists swelled to a stream, then a river. The hardships of America were more alluring than the hatreds of Europe. A few adventurous souls pushed west toward the fall line.

The fall line was a series of rapids dividing the upland freshwaters from the saltier waters below. Above the fall line rolled the undulating, fertile hills of the Piedmont, which lapped to the very feet of the Blue Ridge Mountains.

Very few whites had reached the Blue Ridge. Those who did hung on for dear life. Building churches with rifle slits did not seem a Christian contradiction to them.

The early American experience was one of intense loneliness and backbreaking labor relieved by bouts of paralyzing danger. Church on Sundays meant seeing other people as much as prayer.

Once the Thirty Years War ended, the worst destruction that would befall Europe until the Great War, there was less reason for Europeans to flee. And after Charles II was restored to the English throne, he had the sense not to kill most of those who had overthrown his father, with a few exceptions. Even more Englishmen decided to stay home.

Hands were needed to work in Virginia, South Carolina, New York, and Massachusetts. So as the seventeenth century became the eighteenth, Africans were forcibly hauled onto the shores of the New World in increasing numbers.

The parishioners of this isolated church had argued among themselves over slavery. Many noted that the Bible not only has numerous stories about slaves, it never actually says that one human being should not own another. Reason enough, many said, reason enough. And so an economic monstrosity found theological dress clothes to hide in.

If the Native tribes thought the slaves would turn on their masters during attacks, they discovered these new people fought against them as ferociously as the Europeans.

Slave and master, back to back in the fortress room, would shoot at the raiders, then emerge to clean up the mess, the vertical hierarchy again restored. If anyone perceived the irony in this arrangement, they tactfully kept it to themselves.

By the time of the Revolutionary War, the fortress room attached to the church was no longer needed but, as is the wont of Virginians, they kept it out of tradition.

Ralph Assumptio's body lay in this room, his casket on a kind of gurney that would be pushed into the sanctuary at the appropriate moment by two burly employees of the funeral parlor, flanked by two honorary pallbearers. The other pallbearers acted as ushers.

Frances sat in the first pew with her two daughters and two sons, grown now with families of their own.

The entire membership of the Jefferson Hunt attended, all 135 people. Sister Jane sat to the right of the Assumptios, three pews behind. The Bancrofts and Sybil Fawkes sat in front of her. Ken, being a pallbearer, remained in the fortress room.

Shaker escorted Sister while Walter sat with Alice Ramy, who had driven all the way back from Blacksburg the minute she'd heard the news. This surprised some people, but Alice really had turned over a new leaf.

The closed casket was brought out. The service for the dead had begun.

For Sari Rasmussen, this was the first time she heard the priest read, "Out of the depths have I cried unto thee, O Lord."

Sister had heard Psalm 130 more times than she could count, but the profoundness of The Order for the Burial of the Dead never failed to move her. Some people hated funerals and wouldn't go. Sister called that selfishness. If ever there was a time when a person needed the sight of friends, words of sympathy, this was that time.

What always struck her about the service was the abiding sense of love. Love for the deceased, love for the survivors, love for God. At such a moment, there were those whose faith was shaken. Hers never was, not even when Ray Junior died. She'd heard her own heart crack, but she hadn't lost her faith. Had not women lost sons since the beginning of time? One bore one's losses with fortitude. Anything less was an insult to the dead.

Frances and her children may or may not have believed this way, but they held themselves with dignity.

As Sister sat there, she found it sad that Ralph himself could not hear the words intoned by the Episcopal priest, "Depart in peace, thou ransomed soul. May God the Father Almighty, Who created thee; and Jesus Christ, the Son of the Living God, Who redeemed thee; and the Holy Ghost, Who sanctified thee, preserve thy going out and thy coming in, from this time forth, even for evermore. Amen."

She recalled Raymond, at the end, sitting up on a hospital bed that they'd put in the living room so he could receive visitors and see the hounds and horses go by. The large windows afforded him a good view. She remembered every word they'd said to each other.

"I'm dying like an old man," he rasped.

"Well, dear, you are an old man," Sister teased him, hoping to keep his spirits up.

"You, of course, are still a nubile lovely." He coughed as he winked at her. "I don't mind being old, Janie, I mind dying like a candyass."

"You haven't lived like one."

He coughed again; the muscles in his chest and back ached from the continual spasms. "No. Didn't live like a saint, either. But I thought I'd die on my feet."

"Heart attack?"

"War. Or misjudging a fence. That sort of thing."

"I'm glad you stuck around as long as you have." She reached for his hand, cool and elegant. "We've had a good, long run. We took our fences in style. Maybe we crashed a few, but we were always game, Raymond. You most of all."

He leaned back on the plumped-up pillow. "Fox-hunting is the closest we'll come to a cavalry charge."

"Without the bullets and cannonballs."

"Wouldn't have minded that as much as this. It's not fitting for a man to die like this, you know." He sat up again. "What I've always longed for is a release from safety. We're ruined by uniformity and tameness." His eyes blazed.

"I know," she simply said.

He tried to take a breath but couldn't. "You've done a good job breeding the hounds. I forget to tell you the good things you do."

"I inherited a good pack."

"We've both seen good packs go to ruin in the hands of an idiot, of which there are many. Christ, put MFH behind a man's name and he thinks he's God."

"The fox has a way of humbling us all. Raymond, for what it's worth, I have been an imperfect wife, but I love you. I have always loved you."

He smiled. "It all does come down to love, doesn't it? And even if you've only loved for one day, then you've lived. Well, I love you. And as we both know, my feet are made of clay. But my love for you has always been true. Like the hunt, it takes me beyond safety, beyond tame-

ness." He smiled more broadly. "Apart from this igno-
minious end, I am a most lucky fellow."

"Sounds like a Broadway play." She squeezed his hand.

He brought her hand to his lips and kissed it. "Oh, for
a straight-necked fox and a curvaceous woman." He
kissed her hand again. "Has to be hunting in heaven. I'll
look up Tom Firr, Thomas Assheton Smith, the other
Thomas Smith, Ikey Bell, oh, the list could go on." He
cited famous masters and huntsmen from the past. "And
I shall look for Ray, mounted on a small thoroughbred,
and we'll ride together." He stopped talking because he
couldn't fight back the tears.

Nor could Sister. And as she snapped out of her reverie
she discovered her cheeks were wet but her heart was
oddly full. As Raymond had said, it's all about love. And
love remembered washed over her with a power beyond
reason.

Poor Ralph had no such comfort at his death. As Father Banks continued the service, a still, white-hot anger
began to fill Sister.

Did he beg for his life? Knowing Ralph, she thought he
probably did not, even if he were terrified.

Did Nola? Or Guy? Sister prayed and prayed mightily
for them all.

Three people snatched from life, not one of them feeling a tender hand on their brow, a kind voice offering all
the love there was to offer.

Nola, Guy, and Ralph had not walked on water. Each
could be foolish and, as Nola and Guy were so young
when they died, they had never had the chance to learn
wisdom. They never outgrew the behavior that must
have infuriated their killer. It's possible both Nola and
Guy would have remained wild, but unlikely. The duties
and pains of this life fundamentally change all but the

most dedicated to immaturity. And those duties are actually wonderful. It's duty that makes you who you are. Duty and honor.

Sister never thought of this as bending to the yoke; for her, it was rising to the occasion. Nola and Guy never had the time to recognize their duties, much less fulfill them. At least Ralph did. He made something of himself, proved a good husband and father.

The stupidity of these deaths, the casual evil of them, overwhelmed her.

She sat there, boiling, knowing the killer had to be in the church.

"Whoever he or she is, they're a consummate actor," she thought to herself.

As the service ended, the pallbearers, Ken, Ronnie, Xavier, Bobby, Roger, and Kevin McKenna, Ralph's college roommate, took their places around the polished mahogany casket. In one practiced motion they lifted Ralph on their shoulders and, in step, arms swinging in unison, carried him down the center aisle, then out into the glowing late-September light.

The congregation followed the family at a respectful distance and filed into the cemetery, home to three centuries of the departed.

The service ended with Shaker, standing at the head of the casket as it was lowered into the ground, blowing "Going Home." This mournful cry, the traditional signal of the end of the hunt, brought everyone to tears.

Afterward, Sybil walked alongside Sister. "Are you going to cancel Tuesday's hunt?" she asked.

"No. Ralph would be appalled if I did such a thing."

Shaker, on Sister's other side, added, "If the fox runs across his grave it will be a good omen."

"We sure need one," Sybil said, her eyes doleful.

CHAPTER 34

Tuesday and Thursday's hunts, sparsely attended, did little to lift Sister's spirits. Although hounds worked well together, two young ones rioted on deer. Betty pushed the two back, but the miniriot upset Sister even though she knew the youngsters might stray on a deer during cubbing. Diana was settling in as anchor hound with Asa's help, and that made up for the miniriot.

Saturday's hunt, on September twenty-eighth, started at seven-thirty in the morning from Mill Ruins, Peter Wheeler's old place. Walter lived there under a long lease arrangement of the sort usually seen in England. In essence, he owned the property even though Peter had willed it to the hunt club.

During the year he'd lived there, Walter had already made significant improvements. He'd fertilized all the pastures and replaced the collapsed fences with white three-board fencing. White paint, now lead-free, lasted two years if you were lucky. Walter said he didn't care, he'd paint the damn boards every two years. He loved white fences. Most folks switched to black, since that paint lasted five to seven years depending on the brand. Board fencing itself lasted fifteen years, give or take.

The horrendous expense of stone fencing was actually practical if you considered its life span. A stone fence might need a tap or two of repair over sixty or seventy years, but if properly built by a master stonesmason, stone fences ought to last for centuries.

One of Walter's secret dreams was, some fine day, to have the drive to the house lined with two-and-a-half-foot stone fences.

Today, Walter was living another of his dreams. This was the first hunt from Mill Ruins since Peter had lived there. It turned into a crackerjack.

Shaker cast down by the old mill, which was redolent of scent. So many generations of foxes had lived near or under the mill, great blocks of natural stone, wheel still intact, that the address among foxes had a certain cachet, say like Dumbarton Oaks in Washington, D.C., or East Sixty-eighth Street in New York.

Considered too tony for grays, the place was inhabited by reds.

Naturally, the hounds found scent at the mill, but they didn't get far with it since that particular fox had no desire for aerobic exercise.

The day, crystal clear, temperature in the middle fifties and climbing, wasn't the best day for scent. No frost had been on the ground, and the rains of last week were soaking in, although a deep puddle glistened here or there. The high-pressure system that produced those electric blue skies also sucked away moisture, hence scent.

Had Shaker been a lesser huntsman he might have returned to the mill to find another line. Shaker and Sister thought once you drew a cover, move on, don't dawdle. Occasionally they could blow over a fox clever enough to lie low as hounds moved through perhaps a trifle too quickly. But more often than not, moving along, especially if your pack had good noses, flushed more foxes than inching through every twig, holly bush, and scrap of moss.

He sat on Gunpowder and thought for a moment as

hounds moved along the millrace and back to the strong running stream that fed it.

Gunpowder, wise in the ways of the sport, snorted, *"Draw an S. Move up higher and snake down. If you catch him high, he'll probably come back low. If you catch him low, unless he belongs on the other side of this fixture, I bet you he stays low."*

An English huntsman from the Shires will often draw a triangle just like Tom Firr, the great huntsman who perfected this maneuver back in the nineteenth century. And such a cast or draw worked beautifully if your country was neatly divided into squares and rectangles.

America, having been cultivated according to European methods only since the early seventeenth century, wasn't that neat, that geometric. Plus, the sheer boastful size of the country forced American foxhunters to devise their own methods for seducing foxes out to play.

Whole European nations could fit into one midsized state like Missouri. American foxes took full advantage of their land's scale as well as the rich woodlands blanketing the East Coast.

Virginia, enriched by the alluvial deposits of the Potomac, the Rappahannock, and the James, as well as their many feeders and tributaries, offered wondrous means of escape. A fox could dash over Davis loam, a kind of rich, sandy soil, scramble up on hard rock, a real scent killer, plunge into a forest carpeted with pine needles and pinecones, more scent killer, and then clop down a baked red clay farm road.

Huntsmen and hounds needed to be quick, to be problem solvers, and to respect those venerable English texts while finding their own way. The American way, like Americans themselves, was a little wilder.

Shaker was going to need that wildness.

Sister patiently waited forty yards behind him. Keepsake, very proud to be used instead of Lafayette, Sister's usual choice for Saturday, pranced. He desperately wanted to show how perfectly he jumped.

Sister liked a horse that knew how to use his or her body. Good conformation, good early training usually gave a horse confidence. A horse in this way is no different from a professional golfer. The golfer perfects the various strokes; the horse perfects the various gaits and also learns to jump with a human on his back. Any horse can jump without a human up there, but the two-legged riders shift their weight, fall up on one's ears, flop back behind the saddle, slip to the side, jerk the reins, and, worst of all, they yelp and blame the horse.

The horse needs more patience than the human.

Horses liked Sister. She rode lightly. She might make mistakes, but she always apologized. Mostly she stayed out of the horse's way, for which it was grateful.

And proud as Keepsake was of his form over fences, Sister mostly liked that he didn't hang a jump. He gathered himself back on his haunches and sailed over, forelegs tucked up under his chin, neat as a pin.

As they hadn't yet jumped even a cigarette pack, Keepsake fretted.

The field behind her kept quiet. The Hilltoppers also remained silent. Bobby Franklin, that most genial man, ran a tight group. His Hilltoppers didn't jump fences, but they kept right up behind first flight, led by Sister. It would never do to let these two fields become strung out. No coffeehousing. No skylarking. No using the horse in front of you as a bumper. Bobby moved out, kept it fun, and the Hilltoppers often ran harder than the field because they needed to find ways around the jumps.

Immediately behind Sister rode Ken, Xavier, Tedi, Ron, Edward, and Walter. Thirty-two others filled out the first flight, with Jennifer and Sari riding tail. Being juniors, they pulled hard tasks, and riding tail was one of them. It was also a fabulous way to learn what to do and what not to do in the hunt field. Whoever rode tail usually picked up the pieces—loose horses, dismounted humans. In most hunts those in the rear were grooms, juniors, and riders on green horses. Often the riders on green horses were the first ones picked up.

Sister, unlike many masters, liked juniors up front, but they had to earn their stripes first. You earned them in the back.

Bobby used his juniors to go forward and open the gates. He figured he'd lose between three and five minutes on every gate, and this time had to be made up, otherwise he'd lose sight of Sister and the hounds. Not good.

There they all sat quiet as mice.

The noise came from St. Just, cawing overhead. *"I know where there's a fox with an infected paw. You could kill him."*

"Don't listen to him," Dasher warned the young entry. *"He'll lead you to a fox, but he'll lead you to Hell, too."*

The hounds heard a long, rising blast followed by two short toots.

Trident, still trying to memorize the calls, whispered to his sister, Trudy, *"What's that one?"*

"Uh, he's not calling us back, he's kind of telling us to go right." Trudy watched as Asa walked toward the right and crossed the stream.

"I don't know if I'll ever remember all the notes," Trident worried.

"You will," Delia reassured him. *"Watch Asa and Diana. Don't worry about the strike hounds just yet. You keep your eye on the steady hounds."*

"Why is he moving us out of the streambed? Isn't

scent better down here?" Trinity asked, the white Y on his head distinctive.

"Because the wind has shifted. He's pushing us into the wind," Delia answered.

"Why don't we just go right down here by the water?" Tinsel asked, a good question.

"The trees, the underbrush are cutting the wind. But up there"—Delia cocked her head toward higher ground—*"it's a little stiffer. And if we pick it up there, we'll follow it wherever it goes, and if we can't get anything heading into the wind we can always come back here where it will be cooler longer. Trust Shaker."*

"Do the other humans know this stuff?" Trident asked.

Delia laughed. *"No, dear, they're just trying to stay on their horses."*

"Do the whippers-in know?" Trudy crossed the stream, the clear water chilly.

"Some understand. Others just ride hard," Delia said.

Asa, now with them, spoke, his voice deep. *"It's an article of faith that every whipper-in believes he or she can hunt hounds—until they have the horn to their lips."*

"Why?" Trinity gracefully leapt an old log.

"Kind of like the difference between a strike hound and an anchor hound. The anchor hound has to know where everyone is and what the fox and humans might do. Remember, they're always behind us. The strike hound pushes out to get the line. That's all that hound has to do, have a great nose and great drive. Doesn't have to have a brain in its head, which I am here to tell you Dragon does not. So don't imitate that ass."

The young ones giggled.

Delia added, *"But Cora is smart. She's got brains and athletic ability. What a nose that girl has."*

Just then Cora found. *"Got one!"*

Dragon skidded up to her. *"Yo yo yo. It's good."*

"God, I just hate him," Asa grumbled as the young-sters flew up ahead, all excited.

Delia laughed as she ran with Asa.

Diana, nose down, figured the scent was about an hour old but holding. They'd better make the most of it. She didn't know who it was. Often she did.

They clambered up the banks, leaving the stream be-hind, and came into a huge hayfield, sixty acres of cut hay rolled up in huge round bales. This was galloping country.

Sister popped over the tiger trap jump that Walter had built in the fence line. The logs, upright, created a coop, but it looked formidable. In this case it was because Wal-ter was overzealous when he built it. The trap was three feet six inches but looked like four feet. A few people de-cided to join the Hilltoppers then and there. The rest squeezed hard, grabbed mane, and over they soared.

St. Just swooped overhead one more time, screaming about the fox with the sore paw, but no one was listen-ing. Furious, he pooped on a brand-new velvet cap, then flew away.

Keepsake stretched out, head low, covering ground ef-fortlessly. How he loved open fields, as did Sister. They moved so fast, she had tears in her eyes.

One of Ronnie Haslip's contact lenses blew out. He cursed but kept right up. He'd jump with that eye closed.

Betty, wisely using the territory, cleared a jump, three large logs lashed together with heavy rope, at the end of the big field. She listened intently. Shaker had blown "Gone Away" when the hounds all broke out of the covert on the line.

Now and then Shaker shouted encouragement. Why ruin the beautiful music of the hounds by blowing all the time?

The riders thundered across the field, took the three-log jump into another pasture, smaller, maybe twenty-five acres.

Hounds ran right out of it, crawling under the fence on the far side or just taking the triple-wide coop in the fence line. The jump, about three feet tall, was a glorious twenty-four feet long.

Shaker and Gunpowder glided over, as did Sister and Keepsake. Behind her, Sister could hear the sound of hooves hitting the earth, the slight jingle of curb chains on bits, the occasional sharp exhalation of breath. She never looked back. Her job was to stay behind the huntsman.

Ron and Xavier took the wide jump in tandem. Neither could resist a little warble of victory. A few people cheered behind them.

The fox, Prescott, one of Target and Charlene's new litter, hit top speed and hooked sharply left in the woods on the other side of the triple-wide jump.

He dashed over moss, rocks, then ducked into a den carefully placed under the roots of a massive walnut. Earth thrown out everywhere announced his abode.

Hounds marked him.

The T youngsters pushed right up front and Trident even dug in the den.

Shaker dismounted, blowing the triumphant notes of victory as the field rode up.

Within five minutes, after much praise, he was back up on Gunpowder.

"Thought I'd go back to the big meadow, hit the south side where Walter planted corn."

"Good enough," Sister answered, smiling.

They jumped back over the three logs, trotted over the smaller pasture, jumped the triple-wide coop. Others thought this a good opportunity to try jumping in tandem or even in threes, like a hunt team.

Since hounds weren't casting, Sister had pulled up to the side to watch the fun. As masters go, she was strict but not a killjoy. The attempts of the makeshift teams to hit the jump stride for stride was fun to watch. Ron and Xavier got their timing just right.

Ken, Tedi, and Edward almost managed it, and they received big smiles for their efforts.

Sister could hear the light chatter behind her. She knew they'd stop once hounds were cast.

"Remember when Nola and Guy took that jump holding hands?" Ron recalled, laughing.

"I think that was one of the few times I was really jealous," Ken said. "Sybil and I tried but couldn't do it."

Xavier handed his flask around. "Funny. You know what made me jealous? That Guy's nickname was Hotspur. Ralph and I hated that name. Ever notice how people have to live up or down to their names? Hotspur, impetuous valor. Went right to his head."

"Who first called him that?" Ken tried to remember.

"I think Nola started it." Ron licked his lips. Xavier put good stuff in his flask.

"She always had nicknames for everyone," Xavier said. "Mustache. That was mine. Shaved it off once we knew she wasn't coming home."

A beat followed this.

"Mine was Zorro," Ron said with a slightly embarrassed grin.

"The Gay Blade?" Ken couldn't resist.

"I could die laughing." Ron, sarcastic, handed Xavier back his flask. "No. Because I got into a fistfight at the Phi Delt house and got two black eyes. She said it looked like I wore a mask. Zorro was okay by me."

"She called Sister 'Artemis,'" Ken remembered.

"And she called you Di Maggio," Xavier reminded him.

"Oh, she did not." Ken's face reddened.

"Big stick." Ron laughed.

"Like she would know." Ken really was embarrassed.

"Oh, those tight breeches." Ron rolled his eyes. "And I've only got one contact in, but Ken, the bulge is noticeable."

"See, I was right, Zorro, the Gay Blade." Ken laughed.

"Let's see, she called Sybil 'Puffin' when they were little, but I don't remember any nickname when they were older," Xavier recalled.

"Big Sis," Ken replied. "Not original, but it fit. You know, I've only glimpsed her once today. Hope she remembers the territory."

"Sybil? You kidding?" Ron adored Sybil.

"What do you know, Cyclops?" Ken teased him.

"Hey, I can jump better with one eye closed than you can with two open." Ron winked as he said it.

"Well, you'd better start squinting, buddy, because Sister just took off." Ken clapped his leg on his horse and shot off after her.

"Damn, that's what we get for talking!" Ron knew he should have paid more attention to what was going on.

Hounds, now in the cornfield, pushed another fox. This run was brief but invigorating. Hounds, master, and huntsman were well pleased.

They gathered themselves up, riding back to the mill ruins and their trailers.

Sister chatted with Bobby as they walked back. He rode up to her and the Hilltoppers mingled in with the field, always a treat.

"Bobby, as I recall, your childhood nickname was Bruiser. Did it scar you for life?"

He laughed. "No. What made you think of that?"

"Nicknames. I overheard the Three Musketeers back

there talking about nicknames. Ron said he thought Guy had to live up to the name Hotspur after Nola gave it to him. Do you really think it was inspired by Shakespeare?"

"I don't know."

"He was impulsive."

"Quick with his fists."

"Wonder if we're missing something?"

"Like premature ejaculation?"

"Bobby, that thought never crossed my mind!"

What did cross her mind was Shakespeare's Hotspur saying, "Why, what a candy deal of courtesy this fawning greyhound then did proffer me!" She felt the killer was handing her and everyone else a candy deal of courtesy.

CHAPTER 35

"Amputate. It's the only way to save her," Dr. Middleton gravely said.

Walter and Sister bent over the stainless-steel table where the anesthetized vixen lay. Using Sister's instructions and a Havahart trap, Walter had caught the red fox with the infected paw.

He'd watched her limping about down by the ruins. When she went off her feed he knew the infection was worsening.

"How much of her paw do you think you'll need to remove?" Walter stroked the animal's beautiful head.

"I won't really know until I get in there and see how far the infection has spread. It's in the bone, and that worries me. Her white cell count is hitting the stratosphere. I've got to do this now."

"Of course, we must save her. I'll pay all expenses," Sister said. She loved all foxes, and this perfect young vixen with her spotless white tip had to be one of Target's daughters.

"My concern is she won't be able to survive in the wild." Dr. Middleton removed his glasses.

A compassionate veterinarian and also a foxhunter, Chris Middleton was a trusted figure in the community.

"She'll have to live in a kennel, then," Walter replied.

"I can build her a wonderful home with a doghouse, plus I'll dig a big den for her, too."

"You'll have to dig two feet down, lay in the chain-link fence. Even with one paw she's going to try to dig out."

"By the time she's ready to come home, she'll have everything she needs." Walter rubbed her ears.

"All right, then. I'll get to work."

"Do you mind if I stay?" Walter asked.

"No. Be glad to have you." Chris was already scrubbing up.

"Gentlemen, I'll leave you to it, much as I'd like to watch." Sister reached over and patted the vixen's side. "You'll get through this, miss. You're in good hands." She looked at Walter and smiled. "Maybe I should say a pair of good hands."

"He's smarter than I am." Walter smiled back. "I only had to learn one animal inside out. He had to learn dozens."

"Bird bones. Now, that's something." Chris pulled on a pair of thin latex gloves. "Walter, scrub up. I might need you."

"Okay, boys. Walter, call and give me a report." Sister opened the large, heavy swinging doors, passed down the short hall and back into the waiting room.

Sybil Fawkes, trying to get out the front door with her arms full of a large bag of cat food, was surprised when Sister appeared to open the door for her. "Where'd you come from?"

"Operating room."

"Not a hound, I hope, or Raleigh?"

"No. Walter managed to trap that injured vixen at his place. Chris's working on her now." She flipped up the hatchback of Sybil's Mercedes wagon.

"Thank you. Usually the girl at the front desk will help

me, but today everybody's busy." She exhaled heavily.
The forty-pound bag of food seemed heavier than usual.
She closed the hatch. "Sister, I wanted to tell you that I
know I'm not Doug Kinser, but I'm learning a lot out
there."

"I'm grateful for your help and I think you're doing
very nicely."

"Thank you. I get nervous, you know."

"No one day is like any other. If you think about it,
this is a sport that has no time-outs, no manicured playing field, no time limits. And when I watch other sports,
you know how I love baseball and football, I watch man
pitted against man. At least, usually it's men." She smiled.
"But with us, it's man against fox. Guess who wins?"

"Humbling." Sybil noticed the dogwoods turning red.
"Won't be long till Opening Hunt."

"No. I'd guess the first frost is two weeks away, max."

"Sister, thanks for all you've done for Mom and Dad.
Me too."

"Your mother and father helped me get through Ray's
death, and then Big Raymond's. That's what friends do,
and I am so lucky to have you all for my friends. This is
an odd time. Or maybe it's me. I hope everyone at After
All is—"

"Coping?" Sybil filled in for her. "Horrible as it was to
find Nola, in a way it was also an ending of sorts. Do you
know what I mean?"

"Yes, I do."

"I called on Frances this morning. She's bearing up,
but she hates that there are people who think Ralph
brought this on himself somehow. Maybe it's easier to
think that."

"Why?"

"Blame the victim. It eases the threat. People are always looking for easy answers, aren't they?"

"Do *you* feel threatened?"

Sybil paused, then looked Sister straight in the eye. "Yes."

"Has anyone verbally threatened you?"

"No, but"—she fumbled around for a moment—"I feel watched. I can't put my finger on it, but I feel a tension building."

"Yes." Sister knew exactly the feeling.

"And Ken said to me after Ralph's service, that night, he said this all gets back to Nola and Guy. And then he really upset me because he said some people might think I killed Nola for the inheritance." Her creamy complexion darkened. "I nearly slapped him, even though he doesn't believe it. I don't know when I've been that upset. Never."

"I would be, too."

"Have you heard that, Sister?"

She didn't lie. "Yes."

"You don't believe it—do you?" Sybil's voice rose, plaintive.

"No. If you were going to kill Nola you would have done it when you two were teenagers. Like normal siblings." She smiled, hoping to relieve Sybil.

Tears filled her light blue eyes. "The times I told her I hated her. That I wished she were dead. The time I threw a bottle of Coke at her head. God."

"You were kids. She gave as good as she got. What about the time she sewed shut the legs on all your breeches just before Opening Hunt?"

"Oh that!" Sybil smiled.

"The time she put ginger under your horse's tail. That was a rodeo show."

"I still don't know how I hung on." Sybil brightened. "I look at my two boys and wonder how I'll live through their teens."

"You will. Everyone lived through your teens and my teens, and well, that's just how it goes." She put her hand on Sybil's forearm. "You said you felt watched. Is there anyone in particular?"

"It's kind of a general feeling. I guess some people really do think I killed her. Maybe others wonder if I'll crack under the strain. They don't think I'm a murderer, or should I say murderess, but you know. Hard times and all that. And maybe I'm supersensitive. I'm jumpy. I can't help it. I feel this . . . this . . . awful creepy something. Like there's a monster hiding under my bed."

"Honey, I'm going to ask you a very offensive question. Under the circumstances, I hope you will forgive me."

"Go ahead." Sybil wondered what this lady could ever do to offend her.

"Did you ever sleep with Guy Ramy?"

Sybil blinked. "No. That doesn't offend me, but no. Why?"

"Revenge for all the beaux Nola took, so to speak."

"Oh that." Sybil shrugged. "She was beautiful. Kissed by the gods. I knew before first grade that I could never compare with Nola."

"That must have been very difficult."

"It hurt like hell. What could I do? She was my sister. I loved her."

"If it's any consolation, she loved you, too, and you are also a beautiful woman. But we all paled standing next to Nola. She was like Ava Gardner or Vivien Leigh. Otherworldly beautiful." She smiled. "Showing my age by my points of reference."

"Not at all. You'll never get old." She changed the subject. "You can tell Mother's feeling better because she visited the Tarot reader, Madame Pacholi. You know her real name has got to be Smith or Schwartz or something like that. Anyway, Mother had her cards read and a card came up that supposedly represented justice. So Mother feels certain justice will be done. Oh, and you'll love this. She asked about you, so Madame Pacholi read your cards in your absence. Let's see, I think some kind of queen came up, but the long and short of it is that you will be foxhunting when you are one hundred. Nifty, huh?"

"Tell that to Crawford Howard."

They both laughed.

"You know, speaking of being watched, there's this little screech owl who hangs around our place now and she doesn't seem to care if we see her. She blinks and winks. And sometimes the big one, the horned owl, will be with her. Maybe we have more mice than we thought."

"Every now and then I'll see the little one." Sister thought the little owl adorable, as long as she kept quiet. "I guess she's taken a shine to you and Tedi."

"Oh, she winks at Dad, too."

"The hussy."

"Why did you ask if I'd slept with Guy? There's more to it than revenge."

"Ken."

"What do you mean?"

"If Ken found out, he'd have killed Guy."

A kind of secret pride shot through Sybil, the thought that her husband would kill a man out of jealousy. This rapidly dissipated. "He's not the type. Ken's just not that passionate." She shrugged.

"It's a funny thing about men. We want them passionate and out of control and then we don't. One of the great things about getting old is qualities like kindness, humor, reliability, compassion—oh, how sexy they become."

"Raymond had all those."

"Actually, he did. But he was a passionate man and

rarely met a beauty he didn't try to conquer, within reason."

"God, you don't think he slept with Nola, do you?"

"No." Sister laughed. "He'd always consider a woman ten years younger, and then when he reached his sixties, twenty years younger, but Nola was always safe. However, I expect your mother had to slap him once or twice and always had the supreme good manners never to tell me."

"How did you stand it?"

"I loved him. You don't really know someone until you live with him, and every day Raymond exploded with energy, love of life. That's why I fell in love with him, and he never lost that energy."

"He was the most fun. He'd let us kids ride up front sometimes when he led the field. He'd make us feel important."

"Charm. Irresistible charm."

"Funny thing, you said you don't know a man until you live with him. But I think you can live with a man and not know him. I think any two people, whether it's husband and wife, or lovers, or parents and children, can miss seeing things. And sometimes they're things everyone else knows. It's peculiar." She paused a moment. "You say Ken could have killed Guy out of jealousy. What about Nola? Could she have killed Guy?"

"It's possible that two different people killed them," Sister replied.

"One. I believe it was one."

"I do, too, but I'm letting my mind go anywhere and everywhere."

"You know I would have never gone to bed with Guy Ramy even if he'd been attracted to me before I got serious about Ken. He was too—flash."

"That he was."

"Like a red Corvette. Nola ate that up."

"When she was sexually done with a man was she really done? She had an affair with Ralph. When it was over, did she leave him alone or would she come back just to exert power over him?"

"Done," Sybil simply said. "Poor Ralph. I loved him."

"Childhood friends. The best." Sister exhaled through her nose.

"And you know what else? I keep thinking about Peppermint, that Pepper led us to Nola. There's some kind of poetry to that, something I don't understand, I can't put it into words, but"—she closed her eyes— "God, I want this to be over!"

"It will be."

"Do you know something I don't?"

"No, but the discovery of Nola's and Guy's bodies certainly can't have added to their killer's tranquillity. He's arrogant and opportunistic, but stupid, too. His arrogance has made him stupid. Killing Ralph like that."

"Maybe he thought it was kill or be killed." She scuffed at the bluestone in the parking lot. "I hope I get to see him caught and punished."

"I think every person in our hunt field feels that except one."

"Who?"

"The killer."

CHAPTER 36

"She's going to be fine," Walker enthusiastically reported to Sister on the vixen's surgery.

"What good news! We could use a little good news around here," Sister, on the kennel phone, said warmly.

After more details on the recovery of the vixen, whom Walter had named Bessie, Sister hung up the phone and she gave Shaker a full report. When she was done, she told Shaker something that had been running around, unarticulated, in the back of her mind for quite some time. "You know, it's the most curious thing, Walter reminds me of Raymond. He even moves like Raymond. Same jaw, square shoulders. He's a touch shorter and quieter than Raymond, but it's uncanny. It's one of those realizations that's grown on me." She looked brightly at Shaker. "Have you noticed it?"

"Uh, well, I suppose," Shaker fumbled.

Sister knew in an instant that her huntsman knew more than she did. "Ah." A long silence followed. "Does Walter know?"

"No." Deeply embarrassed, he gave a small shrug.

"Shaker, don't fret. I should have figured it out. It's as plain as the nose on my face."

"Things happen."

"With Raymond they certainly did." She spoke with conviction, breathed, then smiled. "How did you know?"

294

"He confessed in a weak moment."

"Aided by scotch?"

"Scotch and emphysema. He asked me to watch out for Walter."

"I see. She was pretty, as I recall, Walter's mother."

"They were all pretty, but Janie, not one of them was as good a woman as you." Shaker's voice rose and he looked her straight in the eye.

"Thank you. But I have my failings." She glanced down at her hands, the red clay ground within. "I can't believe I've been so stupid."

"You weren't stupid."

"Not about that." She smiled sadly. "Not about that. But I think I've been half in love with Walter. Now it makes sense." She dismissed the notion with a wave of her hand. "Younger men don't look at older women. I guess I just realized how drawn I am to him." She sighed. "Love never dies."

"I don't know. I'm not good at those things."

She paused a moment. "Well, I've had my revelation. Love never dies." She fell quiet again, then suddenly sat up and said with much animation, "Shaker, that's it!"

"What?"

"Love never dies! The killer is still in love with Nola or with Guy."

CHAPTER 37

For the remainder of the day, Sister felt as though she had a red-hot marble rolling around in her brain. The mental discomfort was excruciating.

When troubled, the stable provided solace.

She brushed down Rickyroo, Lafayette, Keepsake, and Aztec and then turned them out. The horses calmed her, helped her organize her thoughts.

She cleaned out the brushes, hung up the wipe-down towels, inhaled the bracing mix of liniment, hay, and *eau de cheval*.

Golliwog nestled on a cooler, gray and gold, folded on the huge tack trunk that originally belonged to Raymond's grandfather, John "Hap" Arnold. Raleigh and Rooster flopped on their sides in a stall and snored, each exhale sending tiny motes of hay dust upward. The large wall clock above the tack room door read three-thirty.

Sister firmly believed the more horses were allowed to be horses the better they behaved. The animal is meant to graze and walk, graze and walk. Being cooped up in a stall, fed all manner of hopped-up grains, makes for a lunatic. She brought them in each morning, and fed them sweet feed in their individual stalls, because each of her boys needed time alone. She also added crimped oats and as much high-quality hay as they would eat. Then she'd go to the kennels to help Shaker feed and clean. By the time she returned, usually after about two hours, each horse had cleaned his plate. Then she turned them back out.

People complimented her on the condition of her horses, their glistening coats, their good hooves. Their eyes were bright, their attitudes cheery.

She replied that her methods were common sense. Avoid fads. Listen to the feed salesmen respectfully, but remember they're there to sell you a lot of stuff you don't need. Take excellent care of your pastures and your pastures will take excellent care of your horses. Keep your horses on a routine. Animals, including humans, like a routine, and this includes regular exercise. Be sure you work with the best equine dentist, vet, and blacksmith in the area. While you're at it, take yourself to the best dentist and doctor, too. You may skip the blacksmith.

Newcomers often asked questions, and Sister was glad when they did. Better to ask than to be taken to the cleaners by the guy who wants to put automatic waterers in your barn or the dealer who wants to sell you a fortune in vitamin supplements. Not that automatic waterers might not be useful for some people and vitamins useful for others, but if you didn't know horses, thousands of dollars would fly out the window.

One thing never changed. Over the forty years of her mastership she had watched new person after new person buy exactly the wrong horse. The only way to become a foxhunter is to buy a made horse, a seasoned veteran who can teach the human. He's better than an insurance policy. He *is* your insurance policy. But in all her years, she had only known a handful of people to exhibit such sense. Walter was one. His gelding, Clemson, lacked in the looks department, was a little clunky, even bigheaded. He had age on him, but that horse knew his job. He was giving Walter tremendous confidence. Walter could hunt and listen for hounds instead of riding in terror.

The Clemsons of the world should be gold-plated. In their own way they are as much treasures as a Secretariat.

She watched Aztec, Lafayette, Rickyroo, and Keepsake play with one another in their pasture and thought of the people she had come to know through foxhunting. Any hunt club reflects the history of its region. She thought of the older people, her idols from her childhood, her own peers, and now the young ones coming up behind her. She had learned a lot from all those people; she was still learning.

Leaning over the fence, she sniffed the first tang of the odor of turning leaves. The fiery marble in her brain had stopped rolling. She had a plan.

She found Shaker walking puppies, a task requiring strong shoulders since they pulled and leapt about. He smiled as she fell in with him and took a leash from his hands.

"To what do I owe this unexpected pleasure?"

"Shaker, I have an idea. It's unorthodox, but I think I can bolt our killer from his den, flush him right out. We've been running over him, you know."

"Darby, boy, steady." Shaker's low voice quieted a yapping young fellow. "Well, he's been in the covert, that we know."

"It's going to take some work on our part and a little luck." She was nearly pulled off her feet by Doughboy.

"The luck part"—Shaker's bushy eyebrows rose— "that's interesting."

Before she could spin out her idea, Ben Sidell drove onto the farm. He cut the motor, stepped outside the squad car, and walked over to them. "Afternoon."

"Good afternoon, Ben. What can we do for you?" Sister set her feet wide so Doughboy couldn't yank her off balance again.

"Wanted you to know the gun that killed Ralph was a .38. Can't trace it, so it has to be an old gun sold before registrations or one sold on the black market."

"What about the used market?" Shaker knew you could buy a used side arm without going through the computer checks.

"Possible. Do you have people in your field who carry guns?"

"Yes. Both whippers-in carry a .22 filled with ratshot which, I am happy to say, they have not had occasion to use for years, and Bobby Franklin carries a .38 hidden in his jacket."

"Why?"

"We don't want to upset people," Sister forthrightly replied.

"No, I don't mean that." Ben stifled a smile as he folded his arms across his chest. "I mean, why would he carry that caliber? Why not a .22?"

"Should a horse break its neck, or a hound, we want to end its suffering as soon as possible. And again I'm happy to say the last time we had to do so was in 1984."

Shaker added, "And sometimes the deer hunters don't finish the job. They don't track their deer, or it gets away. We have to kill them."

"Very upsetting." Sister reached down to pat Doughboy, who sat quietly observing the sheriff. As he was only five months old, she was very proud of him.

"I see. Well, I would imagine that many of your members have old weapons."

"Probably." Sister's voice rose upward.

"You have members, older members, many of whom might have guns that they bought back in the fifties or sixties."

"I suppose. What would you like me to do?"

"Get them. I want to test them. I can go to each house and demand them, but I think the most efficient method is to have you ask for them."

"I'd be glad to do that. Did you drive the whole way out here to ask me that?"

"Uh, yes." He shifted his weight from one foot to the other. "And"—he paused a moment—"it's such a beautiful place here. I like visiting your farm. And I was wondering if you might advise me, which I will keep to myself because I realize the position you're in, I was kind of wondering if you could suggest someone I could ride with—take lessons, that is."

"Ah." She smiled, as did Shaker. "Lynne Beegle. Actually, I should ask what kind of riding."

"Foxhunting. The more I find out about this sport, the more it intrigues me. It's complicated."

"Oh, just keep the horse between your legs." Shaker laughed.

"There is that." Ben smiled.

"As I recall, Ben, you're from Ohio, and there are some good hunt clubs there. Rocky Fork Headley, Chagrin Valley, Miami Valley, Camargo, Grand River, and Gully Ridge. And they've been there for a long time. I think Chagrin Valley was founded in 1908."

"Camargo and Rocky Ford Headley were founded in 1925," Shaker added.

"How do you remember all that?"

"You tend to remember what you like. I just thought you might have seen hunting in Ohio."

"No. Not until I got here."

"Well, it's a way of life in Virginia."

"A way of death, too," Ben commented, a wry tone to his voice. "You don't need to hunt the fox, you're so busy hunting one another."

Sister exhaled, which brought Doughboy's ears up. He looked at her quizzically. "These truly are extraordinary circumstances."

Shaker murmured his agreement with that statement.

After Ben drove away, the two walked the puppies back to the puppy palace, as they called it.

"Want to hear my plan?"

"Can't wait."

CHAPTER 38

"Janie, are you sure?" Tedi's lovely blue eyes were sorrowful.

"Yes. But I can't prove a thing yet."

Tedi, Edward, Walter, Shaker, and Sister sat around Sister's kitchen table. She had thrown together a quick dinner for them. Each had come with the express instructions to tell no one where they were going that night. Not a soul.

Sister started the bowl of peas around to the left. "Tedi and Edward, I know this is most disquieting."

"We'll handle it." Edward spoke with authority.

"The killer has to be Sybil, Ken, Xavier, or Ron. If you think about each one, each has benefited since Nola's and Guy's deaths. When Ron first hung out his lawyer's shingle, you used him and you also switched insurance over to Xavier. Right?" Walter asked.

"Right." Edward nodded. "Ken encouraged us, and both men gave us very good service."

"They all ran around together," Tedi added. "Our support in the early stages of their business lives was beneficial."

"And would it be possible for Sybil to divert some of her monies to either Ron or Xavier without either of you knowing about it?" Sister added.

"Up to a point," Edward succinctly replied. "If the sums were excessive, I think I'd know."

302

"I've been thinking about Hotspur." Sister changed the subject. "The only way that Henry IV could defeat him was to divide and conquer. He picked Hotspur off before he could join up with his father. Had the two been united, Sir Henry Percy's father would have sat on the throne. They were much better soldiers than the king. I believe our killer separated Nola and Guy. She'd been unfaithful to Guy."

Edward interrupted, "But it's not like she was married to him!"

"No, but love isn't rational. It would seem to me that both Nola and the killer had something to lose. Nola would lose Guy, and she had finally fallen in love with Guy. What the killer would lose, I don't know. If we knew the answer to that I think we'd solve this." Sister looked at Walter; she couldn't stop staring at him, but she made sure he didn't see her doing it. "Well, perhaps I make too much of this Hotspur thing. My mind works in fits and starts. They don't all lead in the right direction, but they do fire me up."

"Me too." Shaker reached for the fried chicken, then handed the plate to Tedi on his left. "And I find the older I get the more wood I need to get fired up. Sister, let's get down to brass tacks here."

"Well, yes. I digress. I want Walter to grow a military mustache or paste one on and play a key part. And I want us to find two actors who can ride who resemble Guy and Nola."

"Have you lost your mind?" Edward sat up straight in his chair.

"Maybe there isn't much of it left to lose. Now hear me out before you become ruthlessly logical, Edward. I believe our killer is still in love with Nola or Guy. We've got to shake him or her out of the covert. Bolt our fox."

"Ah." Walter was getting it, as was Tedi.

"Perhaps you have noticed how much Walter resembles Raymond. With a mustache, the resemblance will be impossible to miss."

All eyes were on Walter, who blushed.

"Uncanny." Tedi blinked.

"Remember Raymond's big hunter, A. P. Hill? Found a horse who looks much like him and is very kind." She smiled at Walter. "We'll take care of you, Walter." She said to the others, "I want to place Walter far enough away so when he is glimpsed—and it will be just a glimpse—people won't really know if they've seen him or not. And I want Nola and Guy together down by Cindy's two ponds at Foxglove Farm. There's got to be someone we can use—call Central Casting, if we must. I want to blast this murderer into the open. Let us resurrect our dead. They'll beckon to the killer. However, we can't use a Ralph stand-in. We can't do that to Frances."

"It's lunacy."

"Edward, we have no hard evidence. I'd rather be a lunatic than do nothing," Tedi said, touching Nola's ring.

Sister softly said, a bit of humor in her voice as she hoped to defuse Edward's resistance, "I know, Edward, you won't overestimate my faculty for constructive thought. I've had to resort to imagination."

"Well, I'll do it," Walter said with determination.

"You lead the field. What are you going to do when people see these apparitions?" A note of sarcasm dripped into Edward's voice.

"Maybe I won't see these apparitions."

"Ah. You'll be up front. By the time someone tells you, they'll fade away." Tedi was catching on.

"Sybil will be whipping-in that day." Edward could not believe for one instant that his daughter was a killer.

"I'll put her in the field and let Jennifer whip. She doesn't know but so much, but she knows enough to keep the hounds between her and the huntsman. Can't ask for more than that. Will you all help me?" She touched Shaker's forearm as they had discussed it. She knew he would do it, and Walter had just agreed.

"I will. I'll do anything to get Nola's killer, and this will clear Sybil's name. I know people suspect her. The gossip eventually seeps under the door."

"Impossible! Sybil would never have killed Nola." Edward's face turned crimson. "I can't believe anyone would say something like that about Sybil."

"I'm willing to try anything." Tedi leaned toward Sister. "I'll help you find our Guy and Nola. I have all of Nola's clothes."

"And we can all pray," Sister breathed in. "A bit of mist. Just a bit."

CHAPTER 39

Sister and Tedi worked like demons.

Tedi, thanks to friends in the film business, found two physically appropriate actors who could ride a little. She flew them to Richmond. Her friend, senior master of the Deep Run Hunt, Mary Robertson, put them up so no one would see them back in Jefferson Hunt territory. She also, prudently, worked with them a bit on their riding.

Actors, eager for employment, regularly overstate their credentials. The young lady, Melissa Lords, had ridden once or twice in a Western saddle.

Mary had her work cut out for her. But she'd managed to get the beautiful Melissa somewhat comfortable at the trot.

When Tedi drove down to check on their progress, she burst into tears at the sight of Melissa.

The actor, Brandon Sullivan, had more riding experience. His fabulous looks kept the barn girls in a twitter.

Mary would deliver the horses, Melissa, and Brandon to Roughneck Farm early in the morning of the hunt. She'd ride as a guest that day. This would stir no suspicions, as Sister often drove down for a day's sport at Deep Run and Mary Robertson, Tom Mackell, Red Dog Covington, and Ginny Perrin, the joint-masters, returned the favor.

Walter would park in the hay shed to hide his truck that morning.

Sister chose the day by calling Robert Van Winkle, the weatherman, a local celebrity who had a genuine passion for studying weather.

He told her there might be a bit of ground cover October fourth or fifth. An edge of chilly air should be cutting into central Virginia then.

True to her word, she asked the membership to allow the sheriff to test their .38s. People complied with her request. Nothing came of it, which was no surprise.

She called Alice Ramy in Blacksburg and told her if any wild rumors reached her at Virginia Tech or back home, to dismiss them until they could talk.

By Thursday, October third, she felt they were as ready as they'd ever be. It was still warm with azure skies. She fretted over the weather.

That afternoon she and Shaker walked out puppies.

"Had a good look at Sari Rasmussen's mother yet?"

Shaker rolled his eyes. "A meddlesome woman."

"Me or Lorraine?"

"You." He laughed. "I've spoken to her a few times—when she comes by to pick up Sari. I'm starting to like the days when Jennifer's car breaks down."

"Good."

They walked along, praising the young ones. Clouds of butterflies whirled upward from the horse manure in the farm road. Small butterfly umbrellas of yellow, orange, milk white, and rust attracted the puppies' attention as they passed.

"Nervous?"

"Yes," Sister answered truthfully.

"I still think you should give Ben Sidell a heads-up."

"I don't know. He'd be wasting an entire morning. Nothing may happen."

"The problem is, if something does flare up, if we do rock the killer's world, it could get real ugly. You carry your gun."

"I will."

"Let's stroll through the orchard. Won't hurt these chillun' to smell apples."

The boughs of the old trees bent low, their bounty ready for picking. The Mexicans specializing in such small orchards were due next Monday. A young enterprising fellow, Concho, contracted with the small orchards, and his business was booming.

Puppies lifted their heads, nostrils wide open. The rich fragrance of apples greeted them as it did the humans. However, the hounds could also smell the different types of insects there as well as all the various types of bird droppings. Their experience of the orchard was richer than that of humans', whose senses were duller.

The hound pads pattered over the grass, creating a rhythm. Their light panting provided a counterpoint. The heavier tread of Sister and Shaker sounded like a backbeat.

Once out of the orchard they headed back toward the kennels.

"Occurs to me we are putting down a T cross." Shaker finally spoke.

"Uh-huh." Sister felt the warm sun on her back like a friend's hand, reassuring.

Sometimes, especially if the summer or fall lacked rainfall, the earth packed hard like brick. Getting a line of scent proved damnably difficult. Older hounds, having endured bad scenting conditions, stuck it out, kept trying. Younger hounds became frustrated more easily. Cubbing season coincided with rutting season for deer, so their odor was intensified and tempted young ones. If they couldn't find fox scent why not try this other heavy, powerful aroma, so powerful even humans could smell it.

Whippers-in would crack their whips, pushing back the "bad kids" if they could reach them. The thick coverts of Virginia sometimes delayed a whipper-in and hounds skedaddled.

Staff could forgive a hound breaking once and needing to be corrected. Touching a deer twice, the proper word being touching not chasing, called for other measures.

Sister and Shaker would get the whippers-in or two trusty members to lay a T cross of scent.

Early in the morning, the dew heavy on the meadows, one person would put down fox scent. The line ended up in a glorious pile of dog cookies.

Crossing this just like a T bar would be a line of deer scent. This line led directly to a thick covert. One or two persons hid in there with noisemakers and ratshot.

Deer scent and fox scent can be purchased at hunting stores. Whoever handled the potent little bottles needed to be careful or they'd reek for days.

If hounds broke at the cross of the T and headed to the covert, an unpleasant surprise awaited them. The humans hollered at them, fired ratshot in the air. If a hound occasioned to be particularly thickheaded, persisting in pushing the deer scent, a little peppering of ratshot on the nether regions cured him.

Usually, the cacophony startled the hounds and they turned tail quickly, joining their comrades who stuck to fox scent.

By the time the group reached the cookies they knew they had made the right decision.

The foxhound is a problem solver, a most intelligent creature. It remained the province of the human to make sure that the hound solved the problem correctly and was properly rewarded for it.

"If this works and the killer goes on the false scent, you'll be in high cotton." He opened the chain-link gate to the puppy run. " 'Course if that doesn't work you are going to have a lot of people spring-loaded in the pissed-off position."

"I know." She shut the gate as the last young one scooted in.

"Even if you don't see anything, by the time you get back to the trailers there will be questions. For all I know, these two actors will be back there waiting for their Oscars."

"Well, they're supposed to come back here."

"Boss, Murphy's Law."

"Oh, shut up. Don't you think I've gone over this until I'm dizzy? I don't know what's going to happen." She said this in a good-natured way.

He sighed. "Maybe it's a blessing we don't know the future."

CHAPTER 40

Hounds' voices pleased hounds and humans, but Golly thought them cacophonous. Her oh-so-sensitive ears could listen to Bach or to the sound of a can of cat food being opened but not to hounds. She avoided the kennels on hunt mornings. The hounds in the draw pen exuded a state of rare excitement. The ones left behind howled piteously.

Only after everyone settled down would she venture forth, pushing open her cat door, next to the much larger doggie door. She'd sit just outside looking left, right, up, and down with an air of studied superiority. Then, every move considered, she would daintily walk to her destination.

This morning, Saturday, October fifth, she sat outside despite the noise at the kennels. This was the day the Jefferson Hunt would hunt Foxglove Farm.

Walter, Melissa Lords, and Brandon Sullivan had arrived at the barn at six-thirty A.M. Each person so resembled the deceased that the effect was startling even without a mist. And Robert Van Winkle's forecast had been on the money. A cold front nudged through, and thin fog hugged the creeks and swales. Walter, knowing the territory, led Melissa and Brandon to their places.

Raleigh and Rooster sat with Golly, watching the activity.

"Why don't you jump in the back of the pickup?"
Rooster suggested to Raleigh, who could jump much
higher than he could.

"She'd see me and make me get out." Raleigh sneezed
as a whiff of goldenrod tickled his nose.

*"Dirty pool. We get stuck here and hounds get to go—
and on such an important morning,"* Rooster grumbled.

Golly knew her human. *"She'll put you in the tack
room if you don't behave and you won't go anywhere.
You sit tight. Once they move off you'll have to circle in
the woods, but you can do it if you want to follow."*

Rooster looked at Raleigh, who lay down, putting
his elegant head on his paws. *"I don't like one thing
about this."*

Rooster grumbled, *"I bet those good-for-nothing red
foxes won't run. On top of everything else, a blank day."*
He closed his eyes on "blank."

Golly replied, *"You never know what a fox will do.
But Sister needs you."*

"Thought you could take or leave humans," Raleigh
wryly said.

Golly puffed out her chest, showing off her long, silky
fur. She was vain about her coat, but then she was vain
about everything. *"This is hardly the time to mock me,
Raleigh. You know perfectly well that I love Sister. I just
don't see the reason to fawn and slobber over her as you
do."* Her ears twitched forward. *"There they go. Hurry!"*

The meet was at eight. It was now seven. As the light
changed and the temperature dropped, the first cast time
would be pushed from seven-thirty to eight and then finally to nine in the morning, except for the High Holy
Days. People needed more time on those days since
everyone and their horses had to be perfectly turned out.
Braiding manes and tails took a long time on a frosty
morning. Fingers ached.

Not that the members of the Jefferson Hunt didn't sparkle and shine even during cubbing, but braids were not called for, nor silk top hats. And even though it was probably a trick of the mind, brown boots always seemed to clean up faster than black ones.

As soon as the "party wagon" filled with hounds pulled out, followed by the horse trailer, Raleigh and Rooster took off for Foxglove Farm.

Sixty-three people gathered at Foxglove. As hounds were decanted from their trailer, the whippers-in, Betty and Jennifer, stood with them. Members and guests hurried to tighten girths, find hairnets, knock the dust off jackets.

By the time the hounds walked to Cindy Chandler's graceful stable—with its whiskey barrels filled with mums and baskets of hanging flowers outside, her turquoise and black stable colors painted on each outside beam—everyone was mounted.

Some hunts insisted that staff wear scarlet even during cubbing. At other hunts, staff wore red shirts. And there were those hunts whose staff turned out in tweeds. The Jefferson Hunt staff wore informal kit. After Opening Hunt they would ride exclusively in scarlet even on informal, also called ratcatcher, days.

Although many people erroneously believe there is an absolute standard for hunt attire, in truth, the standard is set by each individual hunt. There was a hunt in Florida, before World War II, that rode in white. Considering the climate, a sensible choice.

As Sister trotted forward to greet the riders, the hounds looked up at her but dutifully stayed with Shaker.

Raleigh and Rooster, who had sped across the sunken meadows, lurked behind the hay barn. Both canines considered their early run just a romp. They were ready for more.

Sybil, curiously, wore an old jacket of Nola's, a dark blue fabric with rust windowpane woven through it. When her mother commented on it, Sybil said she'd left her lightweight cubbing jacket at her house so she'd grabbed one of her sister's. All extra coats, jackets, vests, and stock ties were kept in the stable closet at After All. Tedi wondered if Sybil had noticed a missing jacket and derby. Her darker question, of course, was just what did Sybil know?

Ken, too, commented on her attire. Both her mother's and her husband's questions irritated her. Half the field was too young to remember Nola's clothing and the other half had seen her in her sister's jackets before. She dismissed them and said everyone was too jittery. Ken soothed her by saying how happy he was to be riding in the field with his wife for a change.

"Good morning. Welcome, visitors. I see some friends from other hunts." Sister smiled. "I'm thrilled to have the senior master of Deep Run with us today, Mary Robertson."

Mary smiled. "Glad to be here." She, too, had butterflies.

"I see some friends from Rockbridge Hunt and Glenmore Hunt, Keswick and Farmington. Welcome." She turned to her hounds. "You children better find Mr. Fox and show everyone good sport."

"No problem," Dragon shot off his big mouth.

"God, I hate him!" Asa repeated his leitmotiv, voice low.

"I'd be remiss if I did not thank our hostess today. Cindy Chandler, thank you for allowing us to hunt Foxglove."

Cindy, immaculately turned out, replied, "My pleasure. Don't forget the breakfast afterward. There's fried okra."

Crawford involuntarily grimaced, which made Sister

laugh. Most Northerners couldn't abide this particular southern specialty.

Tendrils of mist curled through the lowlands. The long rays of the rising sun painted the buildings with scarlet and gold. The temperature was a cool forty-five degrees. It was beginning to feel like hunt season!

Traditionally, the master decides on the first cast. In many hunts, the master isn't a true hound person and so agrees with whatever the huntsman suggests. Sister, loving her hounds beyond all measure, would sit down with Shaker the night before a hunt and plan the day's hunt.

Plan your hunt; hunt your plan.

The advantage of this over the years was that each person developed an appreciation for the other's mind. Sister might suggest going low on a windy day, and Shaker might remind her the muck on that particular bottom would be rough sledding. Try high first even with the wind. They'd bat ideas back and forth, they'd check the humidity, the wind, the temperature. They'd obsessively watch The Weather Channel, then sit down, grumbling that those people knew nothing about the weather hard by the mountains, which could change in the bat of an eye.

They'd devise their plan, rise early in the morning, open their window, or hurry out the front door to check the weather. Had there been a light frost? It would occur up here before it would in town. Did the wind change? What was the speed and direction? If Nature decided to change her clothes overnight, the two of them could alter their plan to suit. Both people were flexible and both were true hunters. They worked with Nature as their partner. People who slaved in air-conditioned offices, drove home in cars with air-conditioning or heated seats, had mostly forgotten that humans don't control Nature. If she shifts, you shift with her.

Today's plan was to cast eastward, over the rolling hayfields, past the huge old chestnut. If scent held on the pastures it ought to be a hell of a day. If not, they'd comb through the woods, good trails throughout, and surely hit a line.

They'd go east to the one-room schoolhouse at the edge of Cindy's property. By then, people and horses would be relaxed. Walter would appear then disappear in the swale before the schoolhouse. Then they would turn northward, making a semicircle until reaching the waterwheel at the twin ponds, one above the other. Mist ought to be thickest there. Melissa and Brandon would be the wraiths of the ponds.

The cast they'd devised kept the wind glancing at them at about a ninety-degree angle up to the schoolhouse. Turning there, hounds would be heading full into the breeze.

"Think they'll hit?" Raleigh deferred to Rooster, who as a harrier possessed more knowledge of hunting.

"Shouldn't take long. This place is crawling with foxes." Rooster lifted his head. *"Crawling."*

Inky, sitting in the hayloft, the top door open to keep the hay fresh, looked down. *"Didn't crawl. I climbed."*

"Inky, what are you doing here?" Raleigh liked the small black vixen.

"Well, it's not like I live that far away. Curiosity got the better of me."

"Who will give them the first run?" Raleigh asked.

"Yancy. If he poops out, Grace is fishing down by the waterwheel ponds."

The waterwheel ponds, built by Cindy for practicality and beauty, had a small waterwheel that kept the water moving between the two levels of the ponds. Grace, Charlie's sister, would fish there for hours.

Cindy would watch through her binoculars. Grace's

Christmas present was a juicy salmon placed outside her den.

"*Rooster, come on.*" Raleigh loped toward the sound of the horn. "*See you later, Inky.*"

The two house dogs hurried past the stable, past the freshly painted outbuildings, down the fenced paddocks, and out into the larger pasture. They need not have hurried, for the hounds were drawing northward in a thin line of trees lining the creek, twenty yards at the widest point.

A heavy gray cloud cover began to creep over the Blue Ridge Mountains. This would help hold scent down—and the temperature.

Uncle Yancy heard them coming. He waited by the fence line at the chestnut tree pasture. He'd give them another five minutes, then he'd walk across the pasture, mark the chestnut tree, trot to the in and out jumps on the road, go over them, and then run all the way to the old schoolhouse. He'd dive into the den under the schoolhouse. That ought to get everyone's blood up.

Back in the covert, Ruthie wrinkled her nose. "*What's this?*" Tears filled her eyes.

Delia touched her nose to the spot. "*Skunk. Don't go there, dear.*"

Her brother took a whiff and his eyes watered, too.

"*Mmm.*" Cora inhaled the musky fox odor of Yancy.

Dasher ran past his brother, irritating him, put his nose down, then bellowed, "*Dog fox! Yippee.*"

"*Just wants to show off for the Saturday crowd,*" grumbled the king of show-offs, Dragon.

"*You poor baby.*" Asa bumped him as he ran by, which only irritated Dragon more.

Seeing the handsome young hound snarl, Betty, on the left bank of the narrow creek, said quietly, "Dragon."

"I know. I know." He put his nose down and hollered in his pleasing voice, *"Good. Good. Good."*

Shaker blew three sharp "rat-ta-tats," which brought together the other hounds that had been fanning away from that spot. They all ran in, put their noses to the ground, then opened, honoring Dasher and Cora.

Dasher, now in the front, was quite proud. He usually deferred to his brother, a bully, but today the glory was his, and Cora let him have it. Even if she picked the line first, it was okay that he opened, it would build his confidence.

Shaker now blew "Gone Away," one of the happiest series of notes a human can blow on a horn. Each longish one-note blast is topped by doubled or tripled notes. Usually three such bars suffice, but in his excitement, a huntsman who is a true windbag can go on and on and on. You'd think they'd pass out from light-headedness.

The members of the field squared their shoulders. The Hilltoppers, right behind them, also put their heels down and lifted their chins.

Sister waited until the last hound, Tinsel, cleared the covert. Having somehow gotten turned around in the excitement, Tinsel finally went right and Sister then squeezed Lafayette. Off they flew.

Lafayette, her usual Saturday horse, earned that honor by virtue of his brains, his beauty, and his smooth gait. Aztec and Rickyroo were still young and learning their trade. Keepsake, at eight, was a wonderful horse who did whatever Sister asked of him. She took Keepsake to other hunts because he would ride in the field without fussing. Lafayette had to be first. He believed deep in his heart that everyone was there to see him.

Over the cut hay pasture, over the coop in the fence line, over the still uncut hayfield with the chestnut tree, over the in and out with the usual rubs and tumps and oomphs. Over the next field and over its jump and down into the thin, parked out woods, the underbrush cleared away, with another trickly creek. Splashing through the creek, cantering alongside the fence, then over the sliprail jump, a little airy, and down a steep incline to another jump at the bottom. This one usually scared the bejesus out of people since you approached at a slight drop and you landed on a bigger drop. It wasn't perfect, but it was the only way. Down and over Sister and Lafayette went. Oh, how Lafayette loved drop jumps, because they let him stay airborne longer. And on to another hayfield cut so trim, it looked like a front lawn. The three-board fence around it had a freshly painted black coop.

Sister could see Jennifer way at the other side of this field on her right. There was a coop there, and the girl took it in good form as she moved along with hounds but far out of their way. Jennifer was having the time of her life.

Shaker, in his element, screamed encouragement to the hounds, his horn tucked between the first and second button of his brown tweed jacket, his forest green tie a little bunched up behind the horn.

After Sister and Lafayette cleared the coop, she turned to glance behind. Mary Robertson was right behind her. She thought to herself how good her field was. They put the visitors before themselves, and no one had to be told to do it.

As she approached the swale, frothing with mist, she slowed to trot along the edge before heading down into it.

As they had planned, Walter rode up out of the mist onto the far side of this low pasture.

She saw him out of the corner of her eye. On a horse like A. P. Hill, a stout handsome hunter, Walter looked so much like Raymond, she couldn't hold back a tear.

She pressed on. A murmur behind her swelled and she heard a gasp.

Xavier's voice came out of the mist. "Did you see that?"

Tedi simply replied, "I'm not sure. It's too strange."

By the time the field came up out of the swale, the schoolhouse now in view, a few riders were bug-eyed. Sybil came up alongside her mother; they were still cantering.

"Mother, did you—"

"Yes."

As the pace again increased, conversation decreased.

Uncle Yancy paused at the door to the schoolhouse long enough for everyone to admire him, then he ducked under the stone steps into the den.

"*Yo ho ho and a bottle of rum,*" he sang in his reedy voice.

Dragon, there first, started digging. "*Yancy, you push your luck.*"

"*Three blind hounds, three blind hounds, see how they run, see how they run—*" Yancy threw in vibrato for effect.

"*Come on out!*" Diana called in as she dug next to her brother.

"*When the deep purple falls over sleepy garden walls.*" Yancy loved the sound of his own voice.

"Good hounds, Good hounds." Shaker praised them, then blew "Gone to Ground."

Jennifer held Hojo's reins. Usually Shaker took Gunpowder on Saturdays, but he wanted to see how his younger horse would handle the crowd. Handled it just fine. Shaker scanned the field, saw a few of them whispering excitedly. A few wondering whether to speak to Sister about what they thought they'd seen.

"Dragon, come on, boy."

"*Yancy! Yancy, you're a coward. Show your face.*"

"When I'm calling you-oo-oo-oo," Yancy imitated Nelson Eddy. It was not a success.

Dragon blinked as he heard the *"oo-oo-oo."*

Shaker pulled his tail. "Dragon, come on, fella. You're a good hound."

"Some of us don't agree," Asa barked.

Out came Dragon, dirt all over his face, to the cheers of the humans. He looked around at the other hounds, then at the humans. *"I am the greatest!"*

Shaker patted each head, sure to let the young entry know they could not have accomplished this victory without them. Then he nimbly vaulted up into the saddle, winked at Sister, called his charges, and headed northwest into the breeze, exactly as planned. By now, the cloud cover was overhead, but the eastern sky was still clear. The effect was dramatic.

As they rode across the beautiful pasture, rambling roses clambering over some of the fence, Bobby Franklin spied Raleigh and Rooster. Hearing the excitement, they'd come out into the pasture instead of staying in the woods. Bobby hadn't seen "Raymond," but the buzz reached him. He figured it was some type of illusion, but he did note that Walter was absent. Being an instinctual creature, he shut up. He sensed something was afoot. He became very alert.

As hounds weren't cast yet, Bobby gave the field over to Kitty English, a reliable person, and rode up to Sister.

"Sister, Raleigh and Rooster are here." He turned in the saddle and pointed to where the two house dogs, in their excitement, had revealed themselves.

The two culprits hurried back toward the woods, but too late.

"Those devils!" Sister fumed. "Well, there's nothing to do for it now. Thanks for telling me."

"And Sister," he whispered, "a few people think they saw, in the mists, Raymond on A. P. Hill."

"Trust me, Bobby. It's going to be a strange day."

"Okay." He touched his cap with his crop and rode back to the Hilltoppers.

Hounds moved on, a little scent here and there but picking.

Grace, down at the waterwheel ponds, heard them. She'd been fishing when Melissa and Brandon, led by Walter, took up their position on the far lip of the upper pond. The soft lap of the waterwheel had covered the sounds of their arrival, but Grace moved away before they reached the pond. She crept back because they didn't speak. Her experience with humans was they just had to yak.

As she silently circled them, Melissa's horse swept his ears forward and back. He snorted, stamping his foot. She made a little sound.

Brandon whispered, "Pat his neck."

They sat there in the swirling silver mists while the air danced over the ponds. Grace was astonished.

She stayed behind them until she heard hounds coming. Then she trotted over by the waterwheel and dipped down into the meadow heading back toward the stables, which were one mile away. Fishing was good and she wanted to get back to it, so she thought she'd run to the first den between the ponds and the stable, which was a large entrance on the creek embankment.

Grace usually didn't mind giving the foxhunters some fun, but today she preferred fishing. She tracked across the ponds pasture, swallowed in ground fog, rubbed against a fence post, and walked along the top of a fallen log. She put down so much scent that if one of the humans got down on all fours, he'd smell it, too.

Cora had reached the waterwheel, gently turning,

each large cup of water spilling to the pond below. The sound alone was better than any tranquilizer. She smelled the two horses and riders, then saw them. They frightened her for a second. She let out a gruff little yelp.

Diana came right to her. *"Why aren't they riding?"*

"Don't know. But they rode past the kennels at seven. The lady is very nervous. Let's take the pack up ahead. I'm pretty sure we can pick up scent there. It's fresh." Cora put her nose down.

Melissa's horse had quieted, but she was so frightened, he began to worry and jig a little.

Brandon whispered, "Remember, smile. Pick up your reins a little. Our horses might want to join the others."

A smile froze on Melissa's gorgeous face, moist with mist.

Cora and Diana loped along the pond embankment, then tore down the side of it.

Shaker flanked the embankment. He said, as much for Melissa and Brandon as for his pack, "You'll get 'em!" He dipped deep into the cauldron of mist rising over the twin ponds, then he, too, dropped into the pasture, rivers of mist snaking through it, silver stripes next to green.

Within thirty seconds, horn blowing, hounds baying, the field reached the waterwheel ponds.

Edward, even though he knew Melissa and Brandon stood in the mists, was shocked when he caught a glimpse of them. Melissa, the spitting image of Nola, stopped his heart. He sucked in his breath.

Tedi, all steely resolve, refused to cry.

Ron Haslip, overwhelmed, blurted out loud, "Guy! Guy and Nola!"

Xavier pitched forward on his horse.

Sybil screamed.

Ken stopped, so all the horses behind him had to stop, too.

Walter, hiding in the woods near the pond, imitated a mourning dove. That was the signal for Melissa and Brandon to evaporate into the shroud of silver.

Raleigh and Rooster stuck with Walter.

Just like remembering blocking on a stage, Melissa and Brandon turned their horses' heads. They disappeared as St. Just cawed overhead.

Chills ran down people's spines.

Although hounds were running, people couldn't help it. They started talking.

Sister, pretending not to see or know, said quite firmly, "Hark!"

The field shut up and followed her, but she and they could feel a force building, a long hidden emotion.

Hounds flew to the creek, which meandered into the pasture closest to the stables, finally feeding into Broad Creek not far from where Broad Creek crossed Soldier Road. Grace ducked into the den.

Clytemnestra and Orestes in the back pasture heard hounds moving closer.

"*I'll crash this fence!*" Clytemnestra loved any act of destruction.

With a moo of rapture, Clytemnestra lowered her head, crashing through the three-board fence as though it were matchsticks. Then she frolicked past the stables, hind end higher than her front end; she even turned a circle. Orestes followed suit.

As the hounds and Shaker appeared out of the mists streaking toward the creek, Clytemnestra put on a tremendous show, mooing, bucking, prancing, a mockery of ballet.

"Bloody cow," Shaker said.

"*Happy one.*" Delia, at the rear, giggled.

The field, close behind Shaker and the hounds, didn't

laugh at Clytemnestra's antics. They'd seen too many strange sights.

As the field began to emerge from the mists, a commotion occurred at the rear.

Ken bumped Sybil hard as he turned his horse.

"Ken, what are you doing?" Sybil sharply reprimanded him. "Where are you going?"

Tedi cupped her hands to her mouth. "Sister! Ken, turning back to the waterwheel."

Sister whirled around in the saddle. "That son of a bitch!" She plunged back in the fog.

Mary Robertson, field master at Deep Run Hunt as well as MFH, calmly addressed the people riding up. "We're going back to the trailers. Please follow me."

Ken, hearing someone chasing him, clapped the spurs to his horse and flew south, toward the sunken meadows. He'd find Nola later.

Raleigh and Rooster, hearing Ken ride off, followed him.

"Mother! Mother, what's going on?" Sybil cried.

Edward grabbed Sybil's horse's bridle. "Honey, we've got to go in. Your mother and I must talk to you."

Tedi sandwiched her in by riding along her other side. "Just do as we say, honey. Please."

Betty Franklin trotted in from the left and saw Sister charge into the mist, then come out behind her, heading south. She pulled up, then obeyed the call of the horn. Jennifer, coming in from the right, saw nothing but came to the horn.

The field, in shock, watched as first Ken flew out of the ground fog and then Sister.

Clytemnestra, oblivious, kept bucking along, throwing her massive head to the right and the left. Orestes imitated his mother.

Cindy Chandler sat there knowing there'd be more

fence to repair, as well as wondering what the hell was going on.

Sister pushed Lafayette. The wonderful older thoroughbred had no bottom, he'd not wear out. He'd catch that horse in front of him. He'd show him who was the best of the best.

Ken, on a good horse, jumped out of the pasture, heading for the sunken acres. He knew the territory. Knew if he crossed Soldier Road, he could get into the brush at the bottom if Sister pushed too hard. If he could keep his lead he could ride straight to Roughneck Farm, get in her truck, and get away. Just where he'd go wasn't in his mind at that moment.

A vision of twenty-one years ago was going through his mind. He wanted Nola.

Sister reached around and pulled out the .38 tucked in the small of her back. She fired a warning shot over her head.

Ken spurred on his horse.

Shaker, hearing the shot, knew it wasn't ratshot. "Jesus," he thought to himself. He told Betty and Jennifer to load up the hounds. He knew hounds would follow him, so he had to wait while they were hastily loaded. Then he was off.

Ken thought he could outride Sister, thought that because he was forty-eight and she was seventy-one he had the advantage. He should have known better. He'd ridden behind her for thirty years. She was tough as nails and always on fast horses.

He jumped into the sunken meadows and raced across, traces of rising mist all around him. He heard the two dogs behind him. Raleigh couldn't have been more than twenty yards behind. Rooster was only a few paces behind the Doberman.

He crossed Soldier Road, got across the wildflower meadows just as Sister and Lafayette crossed Soldier Road.

Shaker and Hojo cleared the fence into the sunken meadows. He looked up ahead in the distance and saw Sister leveling her gun on Ken. She fired and missed.

"Christ," he thought. "If she kills him she'll go to jail even though he deserves it." He laid his body low over Hojo, and the gelding knew just what to do. He put on the afterburners. They were over Soldier Road in no time.

Ken plunged into the wooded base of Hangman's Ridge. There was enough cover that Sister couldn't hit him. Raleigh and Rooster, however, were right behind him, giving tongue for all they were worth.

Ken cursed the fact that he didn't have a gun. He'd shoot them and he'd shoot that goddamned old woman riding hard on his tail. The bitch. If she'd come to him quietly he would have paid her off generously. And killed her later, of course.

Sister and Lafayette pulled up at the base of Hangman's Ridge for a moment, and she saw Shaker heading for her. She heard Raleigh and Rooster. She followed their voices. Like any good hunter she trusted her partners—in this case, one harrier, one Doberman, and one thoroughbred.

Warily she rode into the brush. She heard her dogs making a huge fuss and Ken cursing them. He was climbing. Well, it was faster than going around the ridge.

She pushed up the ridge. Shaker was now a third of a mile behind her.

While leading Melissa and Brandon home, Walter had heard Ken, then Sister, riding away. Now, hearing gunfire and a third set of hoofbeats, he urged the two actors to do their best and trot.

He nudged them toward Hangman's Ridge.

Ken finally reached the top of the ridge, his horse

blowing hard. He pushed on, heading to the hanging tree. The mists from below, rising, dissipating, wove in and out of the branches like silvery silk ribbons. He looked up. There sat Athena and Bitsy, an unnerving sight, especially since Athena held her wings fully outstretched, spooking his horse, who jumped sideways as Ken kicked him on.

Sister was over the ridge now, and Lafayette was gaining on Ken's horse. Sister leveled her arm and fired. She hit Ken in the right shoulder. He didn't make a sound but he bobbled in the saddle.

Lafayette drew even closer. She fired again, and this time hit him in the left shoulder. Blood seeped out of the back of his coat.

He had no grip left in his hands. Ken fell off the horse, his spurs digging up the earth as he hit hard.

His horse, grateful, stopped, sides heaving, covered in lather.

Athena kept her wings spread. She looked spectral.

Sister pulled up Lafayette to stand over Ken. "I have three bullets left. I will put one through your head."

"I'll tear his throat out." Raleigh leapt on Ken.

"Off, Raleigh."

The Doberman obeyed but sat by the bleeding man, ready to strike.

Shaker came up alongside. He dismounted, whipped off his belt, and tied Ken's hands behind his back.

"Well done," Shaker said. "Jesus, I thought you were going to kill him."

"Day's not over. I just might." She stared down at Ken. "Why?"

He didn't answer, so Shaker kicked him in the kidney. "Speak when a lady speaks to you."

"I was going to lose everything."

"But you already had lost everything." Her face darkened.

He looked up at her through watery eyes.

"You lost your soul." She slipped the gun back into her belt as Athena folded her wings.

Just then Walter, with an exhausted Melissa and Brandon, rode up by the wagon road.

Ken saw Melissa. His head fell to his chest as he sobbed.

CHAPTER 41

"The sordidness of it." Alice Ramy stared at a tendril of poison ivy, flaming red, twining around a walnut tree.

Sister, Alice, and Tedi Bancroft sat on the bench in the hound graveyard. The three women had gravitated there as they walked together Sunday afternoon. They found themselves bound by time, by losses and loves, and finally by the profound shock of Ken Fawkes's perfidy.

"You risked your life, Janie. I don't know how to thank you. Edward and I can never truly thank you."

"He didn't have a gun. I was safe." She grinned raffishly.

"He'd killed three people. He would have killed you if he could." Alice noticed the long rays of the sun, the changing light from summer's harshness to the soft, sweet light of winter.

"I don't know if Sybil will ever thank me."

"She will. Edward and I will get her through this. And the boys, she has to live for the boys now."

"Poor girl . . ." Alice's voice trailed off.

Alice put her arm around Tedi's shoulders. "At least we know. That's something."

Tedi's left hand fluttered to her face, the blue from Nola's sapphire pulsating. "I loved her. She was like the light on my face, but"—she struggled against her emotions—"she was wrong. Nola's capriciousness cost her life, Guy's life, Ralph's life, and her sister's happiness.

She didn't deserve to die, but she was wrong, so very wrong."

Sister quietly said, "Tedi, when you're young and you have that kind of power, that power Nola had over men, maybe you just have to use it."

"I feel so guilty." Tedi choked up.

"Oh don't, Tedi. Don't." Alice hugged her. "I don't blame you. Those babies come out of the womb as who they are. We might help them or hurt them, but they're formed. You didn't make Nola the way she was. And maybe Sister's right—when you have that kind of power, you use it."

Tedi put her face in her hands. "If only I'd known!"

"Nobody knew except Ralph. And even he didn't know all of it." Sister leaned back on the bench. "I suppose we can be grateful that Ken confessed. We'd still be trying to put all the pieces together."

"To think that he'd been having an affair with Nola for six months and none of us knew. I guess they were better actors than we realized." Sister watched a small branch dip as a red-tailed hawk landed on it.

"What a fool." Tedi spat out the words.

"Well, that was it, wasn't it? She made fools of men? I don't know why Nola did it. It's one thing to exert your power, it's another thing to hurt men." Alice dropped her arm off Tedi's shoulder and held her hand. "We'll never really know what went on inside. I think at the end Guy knew. Maybe he sensed he'd never really have her. He was twenty-five. He was thinking about the future in a way he never had before. He wanted her to be part of it."

"You warned him." Tedi remembered Alice trying to steer Guy away from Nola.

"Children don't listen."

"Amen." Tedi sighed, wiping away her tears with her free hand.

Ken's confession stated that he had been sleeping with
his sister-in-law. She'd grown bored, as Nola was wont
to do with any man. She toyed with him while flaming
around with Guy. But Ken wouldn't give up. He said
he'd tell Guy. Then he said he'd kill Guy. Nola finally
threatened to tell her sister, to tell her parents, if he
wouldn't leave her alone.

Ken knew Sybil would divorce him. He loved being
married to all that money. He couldn't expect to receive a
settlement since he was the one having the affair. The
Bancrofts would cast him out without a penny. He'd also
grown fond of his new social position.

But Nola, being Nola, couldn't resist tantalizing him.
She surreptitiously flirted with him during the first day of
cubbing, even while she hung all over Guy. She brushed
by Ken at Sorrell Buruss's party, pressing against his body.
And she made sure he saw her every move with Guy, running her hands through Guy's black curly hair, kissing
his cheek, leaning seductively against him at the bar.

Guy left the party early. He told Nola to meet him at
the office. There was some paperwork he had to do, but
then they could really party once he was done.

The party was wild. Ken lured Nola outside with the
promise of great cocaine. They all did drugs back then,
and Nola was never one to pass up a free toot.

He dangled his little vial in front of her, leading her
ever farther away from the house. When he was sure no
one could observe them, he tried to kiss her. She kissed
him lightly, then wanted the coke. When she opened the
vial to find only a few grains, she told him he was pathetic. She also told him Guy was a better lover. He lost
it, grabbed her by the neck, and strangled the life right
out of her. Just to make sure she was dead, he smashed
her skull in with a rock, then dragged her body to the

compost pile and covered her up. This took perhaps ten minutes.

He returned to the party, danced a few dances, then told his wife he would drive Ralph home in Ralph's car since their good friend was blotto. He'd be home by seven so they could go to the C&O.

Ralph, tipsy, didn't complain when Ken took him by the elbow and hustled him out. In the car, Ken spun a tale that Ralph was only too willing to believe: Guy had killed Nola because she was still in love with Ralph and that her affair with Guy was over. They drove to Guy's office and called to him. When he came outside, Ken surprised him and hit him over the head, stuffed him in Ralph's car, and drove toward After All, not five miles away. Ken pulled off the road and shot Guy before going to the house. They stuffed Guy into a big paint drum—the farm always had drums around because the fence painting never stopped. Ken dropped in the blacksmith's anvil and soldered shut the lid.

Ken promised Ralph he'd make this all worth his while. He'd give him business for the rest of his life. He'd help him buy the tractor dealership as a silent partner. Besides, he insisted Nola was dead in part because of her feelings for Ralph. He was already implicated. In his slightly intoxicated state, it all made a strange sort of sense to Ralph.

Ken, Sybil, Ralph, and Frances met at the C&O. Later, back home when Sybil was asleep, he crawled out of bed, got a shovel, and dug a grave where the excavation work was finished for the covered bridge. Then he pushed his truck down the driveway, started it at the end so Sybil wouldn't hear, and drove back near Sorrell's. He parked off the road, walked back to the body, old canvas over his shoulder. He picked up Nola, who was cold and starting to go into rigor. She was twice as heavy. He drove back, dumped her in the grave, and filled it in. The final landscaping around the new bridge did the rest.

The next night, he prevailed upon Ralph again. They loaded the drum onto the truck in the middle of the night, drove to Norwood Bridge, and heaved Guy over the side, secure in the knowledge he would never surface.

Ralph, distressed over Nola's death and people's reaction to her disappearance, asked Ken to tell about her demise, but Ken said he'd go to jail for killing Guy. This way, cruel though it was that Tedi, Edward, and Sybil didn't know the truth of Nola's disappearance, at least Ken would be safe and Sybil would have a husband. Surely Ralph understood why Ken had to kill Guy. Nor would he tell Ralph where Guy had buried Nola's body. Ralph wanted to know, bursting into tears at the thought. Ken told him to get a grip, to get over it.

Ralph, if he figured out the truth, kept it to himself. He had a lot to lose. Ken was as good as his word about giving Ralph money for the business.

And so they prospered for twenty-one years until Nola returned. Ralph, consumed with guilt long kept at bay, called Sister. Ralph took his first step toward redemption, but he didn't have the opportunity to take any more.

Ken knew Ralph had tipped off somebody about the location of Guy's body. It was a matter of time until he killed him. The thick fog gave him an opportunity to strike before Ralph cracked, told the story.

He whispered to Ralph. No one could see him. He didn't expect Ralph to bolt. Ken had planned a more conventional end for Ralph, poison, but when Ralph ran off in the fog, Ken, who had been on the other side of the fence line, jumped the coop. He had no trouble hearing the terrified man crash through the cornfield. He tracked him up to Hangman's Ridge, shot him, hurried down the steep back way, risked all by galloping in the fog, slowing only as he neared the stables at After All. He put up his horse and reached the house shortly after the other returned riders.

Not only was he not upset by this murder, he was exhilarated by it.

Ken made his confession in great physical pain but with a clear mind and no appreciable awakening of conscience.

The only glimmer that there was something salvageable inside was when he told Ben Sidell he regretted the pain he would be causing his wife and children. Sybil had been a good wife and a good mother. He opened his mouth to say something more, but nothing came out.

As for Nola, when he spoke of her, all his suppressed rage, lust, and love boiled over with each word. Nor had twenty-one years dimmed his blind jealousy of Guy Ramy. Ken still believed they both got what they deserved.

As the three women sat there discussing what had transpired, it occurred to Sister that Tedi had seen more of the world than either she or Alice ever would. However, when you reached a certain age, even if you never left the county into which you were born, you'd usually seen most of what the human animal can do for good or evil. And you also realized that most humans were so busy defending themselves and their version of reality that they missed the nose on their own faces. They hadn't the energy to change or grow, diverting it into a lonely self-centeredness. Truly intelligent people learned from others and from history.

"It's so peaceful here," Alice said.

"Yes, I come here often. Sometimes Inky, the black fox, visits here. She sits and looks at me. I sit and look at her."

"Foxes," Tedi mused, then touched Sister's hand.

"What went through your mind when you were chasing Ken?"

"I don't know exactly." She studied the hound sculpture. "Well, maybe in a way I do." Sister stopped, then smiled at Raleigh, Rooster, and Golly snoozing in the shade of the statue.

"Janie?" Tedi raised her eyebrows. "What were you thinking?"

"Just that I needed to catch him. But then once he was down I thought of Hotspur. You might remember his lines: 'And I can teach thee, coz, to shame the devil, / By telling truth: tell truth and shame the devil.' "

"Shakespeare and I aren't well acquainted." Alice smiled.

"Henry IV, Part I, Act III, Scene I," said Tedi, who recognized Sister's source. "I have to show off my expensive education from time to time."

"Well, it's over and we have to get on with our lives. I'd give anything to have Guy back, but what I do have is memories, and maybe a new way of looking at things. I intend to honor my son, not mourn him."

"Well said." Tedi felt the same way about her daughter.

"You know what I think? I've probably known it in the back of my mind, but not so I could say it." Sister gazed in wonder at tiny dancing particles suspended in a ray of light. "To wantonly destroy life is a sin, a stain, an affront to every one of us. I believe, with my heart and soul, that all life is sacred. That, it seems to me, is a truth that would shame any devil."

SOME USEFUL TERMS

AWAY—A fox has "gone away" when he has left the covert. Hounds are "away" when they have left the covert on the line of the fox.

BRUSH—The fox's tail.

BURNING SCENT—Scent so strong or hot that hounds pursue the line without hesitation.

BYE DAY—A day not regularly on the fixture card.

CAP—The fee nonmembers pay to a hunt for that day's sport.

CARRY A GOOD HEAD—When hounds run well together to a good scent, a scent spread wide enough for the whole pack to feel it.

CARRY A LINE—When hounds follow the scent. This is also called "working a line."

CAST—Hounds spread out in search of scent. They may cast themselves or be cast by the huntsman.

CHARLIE—A term for a fox. A fox may also be called Reynard.

CHECK—When hounds lose the scent and stop. The field must wait quietly while the hounds search for scent.

COLORS—A distinguishing color—usually worn on the collar but sometimes on the facings of a coat—that identifies a hunt. Colors can be awarded only by the master and can be won only in the field.

COUPLE STRAPS—Two-strap hound collars connected by a swivel link. Some members of staff will carry these on the right rear of the saddle. Since the Middle Ages hounds had been brought to the meets coupled. Hounds are always spoken of, counted, in couples. Today hounds walk or are driven to the meets. Rarely, if ever, are they coupled, but a whipper-in still carries couple straps should a hound need assistance.

COVERT—A patch of woods or bushes where a fox might hide. Pronounced *cover*.

CRY—How one hound tells another what is happening. The sound will differ according to the various stages of the chase. It's also called "giving tongue" and should occur when a hound is working a line.

CUB HUNTING—The informal hunting of young foxes in the late summer and early fall, before formal hunting. The main purpose is to enter young hounds into the pack. Until recently only the most knowledgeable members were invited to cub hunt since they would not interfere with young hounds.

DOG FOX—The male fox.

DOG HOUND—The male hound.

DOUBLE—A series of short, sharp notes blown on the horn to alert all that a fox is afoot. The "gone away" series of notes are a form of doubling the horn.

DRAFT—To acquire hounds from another hunt is to draft them.

DRAW—The plan by which a fox is hunted or searched for in a certain area, like a covert.

DRIVE—The desire to push the fox, to get up with the line. It's a very desirable trait in a hound, so long as they remain obedient.

DWELL—To hunt without getting forward. A hound that dwells is a bit of a putterer.

ENTER—Hounds are entered into the pack when they first hunt, usually during cubbing season.

FIELD—The group of people riding to hounds, exclusive of the master and hunt staff.

FIELD MASTER—The person appointed by the master to control the field. Often it is the master him- or herself.

FIXTURE—A card sent to all dues-paying members, stating when and where the hounds will meet. A fixture card properly received is an invitation to hunt. This means the card would be mailed or handed to you by the master.

GONE AWAY—The call on the horn when the fox leaves the covert.

GONE TO GROUND—A fox who has ducked into his den or some other refuge has gone to ground.

GOOD NIGHT—The traditional farewell to the master after the hunt, regardless of the time of day.

HILLTOPPER—A rider who follows the hunt but who does not jump. Hilltoppers are also called the "second field." The jumpers are called the "first flight."

HOICK—The huntsman's cheer to the hounds. It is derived from the Latin *hic haec hoc*, which means "here."

HOLD HARD—To stop immediately.

HUNTSMAN—The person in charge of the hounds in the field and in the kennel.

KENNELMAN—A hunt staff member who feeds the hounds and cleans the kennels. In wealthy hunts there may be a number of kennelmen. In hunts with a modest budget, the huntsman or even the master cleans the kennels and feeds hounds.

LARK—To jump fences unnecessarily when hounds aren't running. Masters frown on this since it is often an invitation to an accident.

LIFT—To take the hounds from a lost scent in the hopes of finding a better scent farther on.

LINE—The scent trail of the fox.

LIVERY—The uniform worn by the professional members of the hunt staff. Usually it is scarlet, but blue, yellow, brown, or gray are also used. The recent dominance of scarlet has to do with people buying coats off the rack as opposed to having tailors cut them. (When anything is mass-produced the choices usually dwindle, and such is the case with livery.)

MASK—The fox's head.

MEET—The site where the day's hunting begins.

MFH—The master of foxhounds; the individual in charge of the hunt: hiring, firing, landowner relations, opening territory (in large hunts this is the job of the hunt secretary), developing the pack of hounds, determining the first cast of each meet. As in any leadership position, the master is also the lightning rod for criticism. The master may hunt the hounds, although this is usually done by a professional huntsman, who is also responsible for the hounds in the field, at the kennels. A long relationship between a master and a huntsman allows the hunt to develop and grow.

NOSE—The scenting ability of a hound.

OVERRIDE—To press hounds too closely.

OVERRUN—When hounds shoot past the line of scent. Often the scent has been diverted or foiled by a clever fox.

RATCATCHER—The informal dress worn during cubbing season and bye days.

STERN—A hound's tail.

STIFF-NECKED FOX—One that runs in a straight line.

STRIKE HOUNDS—Those hounds who through keenness, nose, and often higher intelligence find the scent first and who press it.

TAIL HOUNDS—Those hounds running at the rear of the pack. This is not necessarily because they aren't keen; they may be older hounds.

TALLYHO—The cheer when the fox is viewed. Derived from the Norman *ty a hillaut*, thus coming into our language in 1066.

TONGUE—To vocally pursue the fox.

VIEW HALLOO (HALLOA)—The cry given by a staff member who views a fox. Staff may also say tallyho or tally back should the fox turn back. One reason a different cry may be used by staff, especially in territory where the huntsman can't see the staff, is that the field in their enthusiasm may cheer something other than a fox.

VIXEN—The female fox.

WALK—Puppies are "walked out" in the summer and fall of their first year. It's part of their education and a delight for puppies and staff.

WHIPPERS-IN—Also called whips, these are the staff members who assist the huntsman, who make sure the hounds "do right."

Read on for a sneak peek of
Full Cry
the wonderful new novel from Rita Mae Brown

A bloodred cardinal sparkled against the snow-covered ground. He'd dropped from his perch to snatch a few bits of millet still visible by the red chokeberry shrubs scattered at the edge of the field. The six-inch snow base obscured most of the seeds that the flaming bird liked to eat, but light winds kept a few delicacies dropping, including some still succulent choke berry seeds.

Low gunmetal gray clouds, dense as fog in some spots, hung low over the fresh white snow. In the center of this lovely thirty acre hay field on Orchard Hill Farm stood a lone sentinel, a one hundred-thirty-foot sugar maple. Surrounding the hay field were forests of hardwoods and pine.

Two whitetail deer bolted over the three-board fence. Deer season ran from mid-November to January 2 in this part of Virginia. Those benighted humans who had yet to reach their legal bag limit might be found squatting in the snow on this December 27, a cold Saturday.

Bolting across the field in the direction opposite the deer came two sleek foxhounds. At first the cardinal, now joined by his mate, did not notice the hounds. The millet was too tasty.

But when the birds heard the ruckus, they raised their crests and fluttered up to the oak branches as the hounds sped by.

Before the birds could drop back to their feast, four more hounds raced past, snow whirling up behind their paws like iri descent confetti.

In the distance, a hunting horn blew three long blasts, the sig nal for the hounds to return.

"Sister" Jane Arnold, master of foxhounds for the Jefferson Hunt Club, checked her advance just inside the forest at the westernmost border of the hay field. The snowfall increased huge flakes sticking to the horse's coat for a moment, to her eyelashes. She felt the cool, moist pat of flakes on her re cheeks. As she exhaled, a stream of breath also came from her mount, a lovely bold Thoroughbred, Rickyroo.

Behind her, steam rising from their mounts' hindquarters and flanks, were fifty-four riders. Ahead was the huntsman, Shaker Crown, a wiry man in his midforties, again lifting the hunting horn to his lips. The bulk of the pack, twenty couple—hounds are always counted in twos, or couple—obediently awaited their next order.

Sister cast her bright eyes over the treetops. Chickadees, wrens, and one woodpecker peered down at her. No foxes had just charged through here. Different birds had different responses to a predator like a fox. These creatures would have been disturbed, moved about. Crows, ravens, and starlings, on the other hand, would have lifted up in a flock and screamed bloody murder. They loathed being disturbed and despised foxes to the marrow of their light bones.

On Sister's left, a lone figure remained poised at the fence line. If Shaker moved forward, then the whipper-in, Betty Franklin, would take the old tiger trap jump and keep well to the left. Betty, a wise hunter, knew not to press on too far ahead. The splinter from the pack that had broken away now veered to the right, and the second whipper-in, Sybil Hawkes, was already in pursuit well away across the hay field.

Whether Sybil could turn the three couple of hounds troubled Sister. A pack should stay together—which was easier said than done. Sister blamed herself for this incident. It takes years and years, decades really, to build a level pack of hounds. She had included too many first-year entry—the hound equivalent of a first grader—in today's hunt.

First-year entry sat in the kennels for the Christmas Hunt, which had been last Saturday. Christmas Hunt, the third of the High Holy Days of hunting, overflows with people and excitement. Both Sister and her huntsman, whom she adored, felt the Christmas Hunt would have been too much for the youngsters. Today she should have taken only one couple, not the four included in this pack. Shaker had mentioned this to her, but she had waved him off, saying that the field wouldn't be that large today, as many riders would still be recuperating from the rigors of Christmas. There had been over one hundred people for Christmas Hunt, but she had half that today, still a good number of folks.

The hounds loved hunting in the snow. For the young entry this was their first big snow, and they just couldn't contain themselves.

Sister sat on Rickyroo, who sensed her irritation. She felt like a perfect ass. She'd hunted all her life and, at seventy-two, it was a full life. How could she now be so damned stupid?

Luckily, most people behind her knew little about the art of foxhunting—and it was an art, not a science. They loved the pageantry, the danger, the running and jumping, its music. A few even loved the hounds themselves. Out of that field of fifty-four people, perhaps eight or nine really understood foxhunting. And that was fine by Sister. As long as people respected nature, protected the environment, and paid homage to the fox—a genius wrapped in fur—she was happy. Foxhunting was like baseball: A person needn't know the difference between a sinker and a slider when it crossed home plate in order to enjoy the game. As long as people knew the basics and behaved themselves on horseback, she was pleased. She knew better than to expect anyone to behave when off a horse.

She observed Shaker. Every sense that man possessed was working overtime, just like her. She drew in a cold draught of air, hoping for a hint of information. She listened intently and could hear, a third of a mile off, the three couple of hounds speaking for all they were worth. Perhaps they hit a fresh line of scent. In this snow, the scent would have to be fresh, just laid from the fox's paws. The rest of the pack watched Shaker. If scent was burning, surely Cora or Diana, Dasher or Ardent would have told them. But then the youngsters had broken off back in the woods. Had the pack missed the line? With an anchor hound like the four-year-old Diana, who was now in her third season, this was unlikely. Young though she was, this particular hound was following in the paw prints of one of the greatest anchor hounds Sister had ever known: Archie, gone to his reward and remembered with love every single day.

Odd how talent appears in certain hounds, horses, and humans. Diana definitely had it. She now faced the sound of the splinter group, stern level, head lifted, nose in the air. Something was up.

Behind Sister, Dr. Walter Lungrun gratefully caught his breath. The run up to this point had been longer than he realized and he needed a break. Wealthy Crawford Howard, convivial as well as scheming, passed his flask around. It was accepted with broad smiles from friend and foe alike. Crawford subscribed to the policy that a man should keep his friends close and his enemies closer still. His wife, Marty, an attractive and intelligent woman, also passed around her flask. Crawford's potion was a mixture of blended scotch, Cointreau, and a dash of bitters with a few drops of fresh lemon juice. Liberally consumed, it hit like a sledgehammer.

Tedi and Edward Bancroft, impeccably turned out and true foxhunters, both in their seventh decade, listened keenly. Their daughter, Sybil, in her midforties, was the second whipper-in. She had her work cut out for her. They knew she was a bold rider so they had no worries there. But Sybil, in her second year as an honorary whipper-in (as opposed to a professional) fretted over every mistake. Sybil's parents and two sons would buoy her up after each hunt, since she was often terribly hard on herself.

Betty Franklin loved whipping-in, but she knew there were moments when Great God Almighty couldn't control a hound with a notion. She was considerably more relaxed about her duties than Sybil.

Also passing around hand-blown glass flasks, topped by silver caps engraved with their initials, were Henry Xavier (called Xavier or X), Clay Berry, and Ronnie Haslip, men in their midforties. These high-spirited fellows had been childhood friends of Ray Arnold, Jr., Sister's son, who had been born in 1960, and killed in a harvesting accident in 1974. The boys had been close, the Four Musketeers.

Sister watched her son's best friends grow up and graduate from college; two had married, and all were successful in business. They were very dear to her.

After about five minutes, Shaker tapped his hat with his horn, leaned down, and spoke encouragingly to Cora, his strike hound. She rose up on her hind legs to get closer to this man whom she worshiped. Then he said, "Come 'long," and his pack obediently followed as he rode out of the forest, taking the second tiger trap jump as Betty Franklin took the first. If the pack and the huntsman were a clock, the strike hound being at twelve, Betty stayed at ten o'clock, Sybil at two, and the huntsman at six.

Sister, thirty yards behind Shaker, sailed over the tiger trap. Most of the other riders followed easily, but a few horses balked at the sight of the upright logs, leaning together just like a trap. The snow didn't help the nervous; resting along the crevices, it created an obstacle that appeared new and different.

As riders passed the sugar maple, Cora began waving her stern. The other hounds became interested.

Dragon, a hotheaded but talented third-year hound and the brother to Diana, bellowed, *"It's her! It's her!"*

The thick odor of a vixen lifted off the snow.

Cora, older, and steady even though she was the strike hound, paused a moment. *"Yes, it's a vixen, but something's not quite right."*

Diana, her older brother Dasher, Asa, and Ardent also paused. At nine the oldest hound in the pack, Delia, mother of the "D" litters, usually brought up the rear. While her youthful speed had diminished, her knowledge was invaluable. Delia put her nose to the snow too.

The other hounds looked at her, even her brash son, Dragon. *"It's a vixen all right, but it's extremely peculiar,"* Delia advised.

"Well, maybe she ate something strange," Dragon impatiently spoke. *"Our job is to chase foxes, and it doesn't matter if they're peculiar or not. I say we give this field another run for the money."*

Cora lifted her head to look again at Shaker. *"Well, it is a vixen, and whatever is wrong with the line, I guess we'll find out."*

With the hounds opening, their vibrant voices filled the air with music as lush to the ear of a foxhunter as the Brandenburg Concertos are to a musician.